Becoming George Washington

Randy,

It has been a honor and privilege working with you and Prakash!

Carpe Diem

Steve

BECOMING GEORGE WASHINGTON

A Novel

STEPHEN YOCH

ISBN 13: 978-1-940014-52-4
eISBN 13: 978-1-940014-51-7

Library of Congress Catalog Number: 2015944124
Printed in the United States of America
First Printing: 2015
18   17   16   15   14   5   4   3   2   1

Cover design by Nupoor Gordon
Cover painting: Detail from *George Washington and Christopher Gist Crossing the Allegheny River* by Daniel Huntington, c. 1840. All rights to reproduction of the work of art identified herein is retained by the owners, Jonathan W. Warner and Susan G. A. Warner.
Interior design by Ryan Scheife / Mayfly Design and typeset in the Arno Pro and 1820 Modern typefaces
Maps by Danielle Melin

Wise Ink Creative Publishing
837 Glenwood Ave.
Minneapolis, MN, 55405
www.wiseinkpub.com

To order, visit www.itascabooks.com or call 1-800-901-3480. Reseller discounts available.

*For Andrea and our
awesome lads, Ryan and Ben.*

Table of Contents

Historical Note .... *ix*

Illustrations .... *x*

Washington-Fairfax Family Trees .... *xi*

Map: George Washington 1753-1758 .... *xii*

Prologue .... *xiii*

PART I: Surveyor and Loyal Brother *1–57*

PART II: Major Washington *59–109*

PART III: Necessity's Colonel *111–154*

PART IV: Monongahela *155–233*

PART V: Virginia Blues *235–262*

PART VI: Transformation *263–298*

PART VII: Forbes Campaign *299–339*

Epilogue *341*

Author's Note *343*

Acknowledgments *347*

Biographical Summaries *349*

Bibliography *355*

Extended Author's Note *359*

Reading Group Guide *377*

Historical Note

This is a work of historical fiction, with an emphasis on the word *"historical."* Every person in this book was a part of Washington's life. In some instances, I have combined or slightly adjusted the timing of events to assist the flow of the story.

Much of the dialogue is based on supposition. Where possible, I have used actual correspondence to track the content of conversations. When presenting historical quotations, I have purposely included the incorrect spelling and creative capitalization that characterized correspondence of the period. Letters presented accurately quote the original texts, subject only to minor modifications to improve readability.

I have also included terms such as *Indians, slaves,* and *Negroes,* all of which are clearly inappropriate in our time. Nevertheless, they were the words George Washington and his contemporaries used in daily speech. Eighteenth-century syntax and dialogue can also be awkward to the modern ear. I have attempted to maintain both the flavor of the speech of that time while keeping the book readable. Finally, the Extended Author's Notes identify and discuss controversial topics, or clarify when or interactions are invented.

Illustrations

Washington - Fairfax Family Trees .... *xi*

George Washington 1753-1758 .... *xii*

Map of Fort Necessity *136*

Map of Battle of the Monongahela *196*

Washington–Fairfax Family Trees

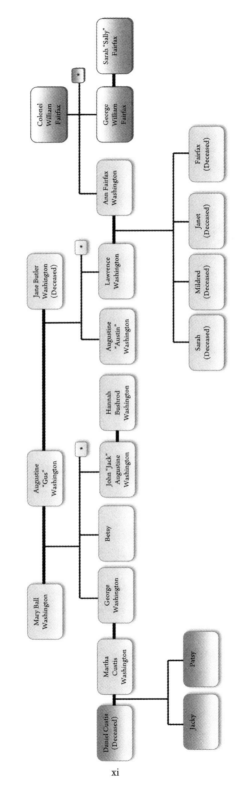

* Only Siblings Referenced in Book are Shown on Family Tree

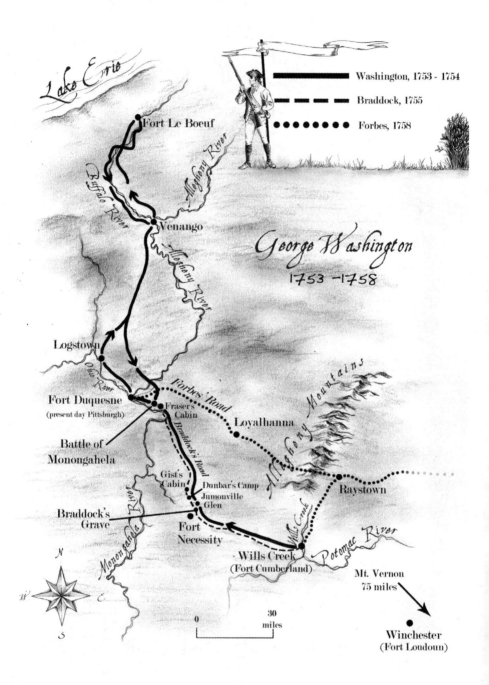

Washington, 1753 - 1754

Braddock, 1755

Forbes, 1758

George Washington
1753 - 1758

Lake Erie

Fort Le Boeuf

Buffalo River

Allegheny River

Venango

Allegheny River

Logstown

Ohio River

Forbes' Road

Fort Duquesne
(present day Pittsburgh)

Fraser's Cabin

Loyalhanna

Allegheny Mountains

Battle of
Monongahela

Braddock's Road

Gist's
Cabin

Dunbar's Camp

Jumonville
Glen

Raystown

Braddock's
Grave

Monongahela River

Fort
Necessity

Wills Creek

Potomac River

Wills Creek
(Fort Cumberland)

N
W   E
S

0   30
miles

Mt. Vernon
75 miles

Winchester
(Fort Loudoun)

Prologue

July 3, 1754 - Fort Necessity

Keep moving, keep them firing, George repeated to himself as he scanned the horror around him. From every direction, the screams and groans of his men pierced the pounding rain.

A swarm of musket balls followed George's progress. Fighting the impulse to flinch, he moved from man to man, encouraging them to return fire from the shallow trenches at a largely unseen enemy. The French and Indians were firing from protected positions in the surrounding woods at his four hundred tightly packed soldiers filling the ramshackle wooden stockade George had named "Fort Necessity."

I should've retreated when I had the chance, George thought. *What in God's name am I supposed to do?*

A light morning drizzle had grown to a drenching torrent, filling the trenches and transforming the trodden earthworks into a muddy morass, causing some wounded soldiers to drown facedown in the muck. The rain offered his soldiers little relief from the oppressive heat. The rising humidity only increased their misery as the men huddled side by side against the fort's pathetic ramparts.

Several times George caught himself involuntarily itching at his heavy wool uniform, which clawed at his skin. Whenever he stopped, he tried to appear calm, forcing his hands behind his back.

"Colonel Washington, I am out of dry ammunition! What should I do now?" cried a dirt-covered soldier.

George recognized the man at his feet as one of the original 159 men he had led from Virginia just over a month before. The crouching figure appeared to be about twenty-one years old, close to Washington's own age.

"Search the dead and wounded . . ." George hesitated, attempting to recall the man's name. ". . . McCannon." George strode along the line, yelling, "Return fire! If you need dry ammunition, get it from the dead and wounded!"

He saw John Boyd, one of his most dependable men, cowering behind the parapet. George had recently considered promoting Boyd to corporal. But now the man looked drunk, failed to return fire, and was providing a poor example to others. George grabbed him by the scruff of the neck and lifted him up, ready to berate him. At that instant, a musket ball plowed into the frightened man's face, spraying George with a mixture of blood and gore. Stunned for several seconds, he held the lifeless body, then released Boyd's largely decapitated corpse to the ground.

George stood frozen, unaware of the continuing barrage surrounding him as the rain began to wash the man's blood from his face. A ball passed so close to his ear that its hot breath startled him back to reality. Realizing he was in danger as the French and Indians adjusted their aim, he forced his shaking legs to stumble forward.

As he worked his way around the outside of the circular fort, he approached Major Adam Stephen, his adjutant. Over the din, a wide-eyed Stephen shouted in George's ear, "Colonel, are you injured?"

For a second, George didn't understand the question. Then he looked down at his uniform, which he had taken such pride in purchasing, was a torn, dirty, blood-covered mess.

"It's not me," George rasped, his mouth dry from exertion and the heat.

Major Stephen looked confused.

"It's not my blood."

Stephen nodded in understanding and said, "What are your orders? The men are trying to fire, but the powder is wet, and the damn French are hidden behind the trees."

At that moment, George noticed the French fire was slowing. Both inside and outside the fort, George could hear men yelling, "Parley!"

He felt his empty stomach collapse in on itself. They would demand his surrender.

Through the coming dusk, he surveyed his small fort. His position was indefensible. He turned, straightened to his full six-foot-two-inch height, and said formally, "Major Stephen, would you please order the men to cease fire and acknowledge the enemy's request for parley?"

Stephen snapped to attention. "Yes, sir." Then, in a softer voice, so as not to be heard by the surrounding men, "We really have no choice, Colonel."

He doesn't even dare use the word "surrender . . ."

George swallowed hard, knowing what had to be done.

Thank goodness my brother Lawrence did not live to see this day.

George gave a small nod to Stephen.

Defeat . . .

PART I

Surveyor and Loyal Brother

A brother's sufferings claim a brother's pity.

—JOSEPH ADDISON, *CATO: A TRAGEDY*, ACT I, SCENE I

Chapter 1

July 8, 1747 - Ferry Farm

"Don't turn your back on me!" Mary Washington said as she slammed the table with a wooden switch which she used liberally on child and slave alike. "Your Uncle Joseph says they will treat you worse than Negroes or even dogs." She waived the letter she had received from England. "The English Navy thinks we colonials are beneath contempt. It is not the place for you!"

Mary was a tall woman, with thick dark eyebrows and a strong, set jaw that allowed her to project her strict and inflexible temperament. George and his siblings rarely saw their mother's thin lips break into the radiant smile that had drawn their father to her. After the death of George's father, Mary Washington did not follow convention by finding a new husband. Instead, for the past three years, George's mother managed the Ferry Farm, demanding hard work from her five children, three dozen slaves, and herself. She gave few compliments but was free with criticism.

A gangly fifteen-year-old, George felt anger and frustration welling up. His mother, while always fierce and demanding, was rarely completely irrational. It seemed whatever she wanted conveniently benefited her and heaped more burdens on George, her eldest son. Despite his mother's menace, George would not and could not back down—not this time.

George spun to face her, eyes blazing. "Lawrence served the Crown and spent much time on His Majesty's ships. Colonel Fairfax has also looked into the issue. They both support allowing me to become a midshipman!" Lawrence, along with his powerful father-in-law, Colonel William Fairfax, had encouraged George's mother to allow George to join the British navy, even providing letters of introduction.

Shaking her head from across the kitchen table, Mary Washington replied, "Do not delude yourself. Your precious Lawrence and his high-hat relation care not for your well-being. They don't feed you, clothe you, or put a roof over your head. They think only of themselves and nothing of me or your real siblings, who depend upon you as the oldest."

You're wrong, George thought. He desired, above all, to regain the opportunities and station lost to him with his father's death. Lawrence and Austin, his older half brothers from his father's first marriage, had been educated in England. When his father passed away, George's chance to be an educated gentleman died with him. With the loss of his father's income, he was relegated to local schools and left to the mercy of his ill-educated and pedestrian mother.

Fighting back tears, George said, "Lawrence . . . Lawrence cares for me and he . . . he wants me to have a better life."

"There are no shortcuts." Mary pressed on with no softening, "Life requires hard work. Stop seeking military glory and licking the boots of the likes of the Fairfaxes. Do not cheapen yourself, George."

George said nothing, hoping it would help keep his rising emotions at bay.

"Now this matter is settled." Mary faced George with a hard and unblinking stare. "Go finish your chores and then you may visit Lawrence and inform him that his scheme has failed. Your duty is to remain here and assist this family."

George merely nodded and stumbled outside into the steamy morning. He began tending to the animals and ensuring the slaves had started their fieldwork. He looked hopelessly about the small shabby farm that had become his prison.

Later that day, George rode to his brother's home and spotted Lawrence atop his horse surveying his fields. Waving in George's direction, Lawrence trotted down to him. Lawrence's buoyant demeanor evaporated when he got close enough to see the crestfallen George. In one smooth motion, he deftly pivoted his horse to match George's pace.

"I can tell from the look on your face it did not go well, my dear brother," Lawrence said.

Still looking down at his horse's mane, George sputtered, "Damn her! Damn her all to hell!"

The rage, anger, and disappointment made him want to scream and shout at the unfairness of both his mother and his life. A boiling fury overwhelmed his ability to think or even talk as his brother rode beside him. After a moment of silence, George looked up at the accomplished man astride his magnificent sixteen-hand chestnut thoroughbred gelding.

I'll never be like him, George thought. *Father's death has prevented me from attending school in England, and now, because Mother has refused permission for me to join the navy as a midshipman, I will be barred from the military. I'll be . . . a nobody.*

Even before the death of their father, Lawrence had been George's mentor and the individual he most admired. Fourteen years older than George, Lawrence had served with distinction in the War of Jenkins' Ear in both the Caribbean and South America. The patronage of Virginia's governor had led directly to his promotion to major, selection as a justice of the peace, appointment as Adjutant General of the Militia of Virginia, and election to the House of Burgesses. Lawrence's position in the stratosphere of Virginia's elite had also been confirmed when he married the lovely and rich Ann Fairfax.

Lawrence pulled up on his horse, and George instinctively did likewise, "I believe she is wrong, but she is your mother. You can speak freely with me, but a gentleman does not speak ill of his mother. It is not only vulgar, but it violates the rules of civility to reprehend the imperfections of one's parents."

"I know, Lawrence," George said, fighting back tears. His horse shifted uncomfortably as George's anger boiled over. "But she is so selfish. All she wants to do is keep me on the farm to take care of her. I don't want to be a farmer! I want to be a soldier like you—I want to see the world!"

Since the death of his kind and gentle—but largely absent—father, George had felt a desire to escape the oppression of his increasingly harsh and unforgiving mother. The navy represented not only adventure, but a chance to avoid an unkind taskmaster who ruled his small world with an iron fist.

Reaching forward to pat and calm his horse, George sighed with resignation, "I don't know what to do."

As the two rode toward Lawrence's plantation, George lapsed into frustrated silence and let his thoughts drift to how his lot in life differed from Lawrence's. George had nominally inherited the Ferry Farm and slaves, however, they would not be transferred to him until his twenty-first birthday, and, in any event, his mother was granted a life tenancy. In contrast, Lawrence had inherited "Mount Vernon," a 2,500-acre plantation he named in honor of Admiral Edward Vernon, Lawrence's patron and commander.

After several minutes filled only with the sounds of their horses' hooves churning the soft ground, Lawrence spoke as the surrogate father he had become to George. "There are other avenues to success. We will continue your education and look for another opportunity. In all honesty, I had my doubts whether your mother would consent, although Colonel Fairfax was more hopeful. She relies heavily on you to take care of the farm and your siblings."

Turning in his saddle to face George, Lawrence continued. "I have been talking with the Colonel, and he has been lamenting the lack of decent surveyors. There will be superb business opportunities in identifying new land, and it is a valuable skill."

Still several yards away, George inched his horse forward as if he were approaching a cliff. "Lawrence . . . my schooling . . ."

"Nonsense," Lawrence said as he shook his head. "Reverend Marye and Schoolmaster Williams both indicated you were an excellent student, and we both know you are very adept at math. Surveying requires an understanding of mathematical principles, in particular Euclidian geometry. I am confident, with the proper tutor, you will quickly grasp these concepts.

"Father owned equipment manufactured by Jonathan Sisson in London. It is of the highest quality, was well maintained and stored, and should serve you well. Father also had a copy of Samuel Wyld's book on practical surveying and a sturdy surveying notebook with many empty pages for you to complete. You may take all of this with you when you leave tomorrow morning. I have discussed the matter with Colonel Fairfax, and we believe George Hume represents an excellent surveying tutor."

George could not hide his displeasure. Hume was a well-known surveyor of Orange, Frederick, and Spotsylvania Counties. He had performed work for the Fairfaxes on many occasions and was a force to be reckoned with in Fredericksburg. A pugnacious and fastidious Scot, Hume would be neither a gentle nor understanding teacher.

Noticing George's expression, Lawrence grinned. "I know, I know . . . he can be prickly. However, he is also the most precise surveyor in the Tidewater, and if you can survive training with him, you can survive anything."

George simply nodded. *Well . . . he can't be worse than Mother.*

As if reading George's thoughts, Lawrence continued patiently, "Remember, always control your countenance so as not to reveal your feelings. The silver lining here is you will be out of the house and eventually earning money, no longer dependent on anyone else." George knew Lawrence was too polite to say the "anyone else" was George's mother.

Speaking of money . . .

"How will Mr. Hume be compensated for teaching me to become a surveyor?" George asked, his curiosity getting the better of him.

"First of all, you will not have to pay him anything. I believe some arrangement has been made between Mr. Hume and the Colonel. In any event, he will have you as unpaid labor. That is, while under his tutelage, you will be volunteering your time. I suspect you will be able to work out some accommodation with Mr. Hume regarding your compensation; once you are sufficiently trained to be useful to him."

"Not likely," George said dryly.

Lawrence laughed. "Point well taken . . . I know, the Scots are not known for their generosity. I share your skepticism that Mr. Hume will be throwing money at your feet for your temporary indentured service."

George sighed then squared his shoulders.

Stop acting like a petulant child, he scolded himself. *He is giving you equipment, training, and a profession. While being a surveyor is not as exciting as serving in the Royal Navy, it is a highly respected occupation, putting me on par with the Old Dominion's doctors and lawyers.*

Straightening, he spoke deliberately. "Lawrence, I apologize if I have, in any way, appeared ungrateful. Thank you for Father's surveying equipment. I will take good care of it and use it well. I will also write an appropriate letter to the Colonel, thanking him for his kind assistance in this matter."

"Good!" Lawrence said loudly as he slapped his hands together, and the pair spurred their horses toward Mount Vernon. "You will be meeting Mr. Hume in a fortnight, when he returns from a surveying mission. I understand he'll be sending a note to you at Ferry Farm. You can use those intervening days to read the book I will give you and discuss the matter further with your mother."

Chapter 2

July 31, 1747 – Fredericksburg

O ver the next two weeks, George spent his limited free time studying the book on surveying and attempting to use his father's equipment. On the appointed day, he woke before dawn, completed all his chores, cleaned his clothes and horse, and began the relatively short ride to Fredericksburg. He had received a note in a precise script from Mr. Hume summoning him to arrive "punctually" at 9:00 a.m., along with all "accoutrements and materials appropriate to the profession."

The gray-haired, forty-nine-year-old Scotsman had dark, penetrating eyes and a large nose. He stood legs splayed and arms folded across his chest as George approached his neatly kept home. As George dismounted, he noticed he was a good foot taller than the stout Scotsman.

"Ye late!" Hume declared.

Scottish immigrants in Virginia were quite common. Most made an effort to moderate their Scottish accents, but George had heard men joke that Mr. Hume's Scottish brogue had become even more pronounced over the years due to a conscious desire to emphasize his heritage to everyone he met—whether they liked it or not.

George involuntarily looked back toward Fredericksburg. *The church bells in town chimed eight o'clock as I left. I know I am least one-half hour early. Yet . . . I don't want to get off on the wrong foot.*

"I sincerely apologize, Mr. Hume. I believe I heard the bells of Fredericksburg before I left to ensure that I would be early. Nevertheless, I regret any inconvenience." George tried to speak with a neutral voice, but some of his irritation must have shown through.

"I won't suffer that tone. I was fightin' wars and surveyin' these fine lands before ye were a sparkle in ye father's eye—may he rest in peace.

Now ye high and mighty relations want ye to learn the noble profession of surveying, eh?"

Thinking a question had been asked, George began to respond, "Yes . . ."

"Don't be interruptin' me! The fact you're a hulking boy does not give ye license to be speakin' out of turn and interruptin' ye elders."

George stood impassively.

"Do ye know what gives me the authority to be a surveyor in the king's lands?" Hume asked, keeping his feet planted but leaning forward at the waist as he spoke.

George tried to keep his face expressionless and said nothing, not wanting to appear to interrupt again.

"I asked ye a question! Do ye have a brain in that bulbous mass above ye shoulders?"

"Yes, Mr. Hume. I mean, no, Mr. Hume . . . I mean . . . I don't know, Mr. Hume."

"That's right, laddie, ye don't know, and that is why you're here. Ye will do what I bloody well say. While I have me doubts, I have promised the powers that be to evaluate whether ye are good for more than cannon fodder." As he spoke, he walked across the courtyard, picked up a saddlebag, and set it on the ground at his feet. After an extended silence and a long stare, he said, "Tell me what studies ye have of mathematics and geometry."

George described his limited education and his review of *The Practical Surveyor* by Wyld. Hume reached into his saddlebag and removed a large leather-bound book. "Have ye seen this book?" Hume handed George a book entitled *Geodaesia; or The Art of Surveying and Measuring of Land Made Easie* by John Love.

"No, Mr. Hume."

"Well, hold on to it. Ye may be needin' it, but take sweet care of it."

"Yes, Mr. Hume."

"So you read Wyld's book, eh? So you already know how to be a surveyor?"

George shrugged, not knowing how to respond to this intimidating little man.

"What a pile of rubbish. That book is clear to me because I already know how to survey. For a neophyte like yeself, it's as clear as mud. Am I right?"

Again George shrugged.

"Are ye daft? Speak up, laddie!" Hume ended his comment with a jab of his pudgy finger into the middle of George's chest.

This man is abusive. He's worse than Mother. This is a mistake. I must remain calm.

"In all honesty, I believe I still have very much to learn, which is why I am honored to be taught by Your Excellency."

"Don't be puttin' airs on me, boy. I've got more blue blood in the tip of me little finger than ye have in ye whole overgrown body."

George had no idea what Hume was referring to; all he knew was that Hume was the surveyor of three counties—an educated man who was widely respected and feared.

"Yes, sir."

"You're gettin' it, lad." Hume said, this time only puncturing the air with his finger. "The unvarnished truth—no muckin' about. That's what I require. So ye can't answer my question about authority? Well, I'll tell ye. On the twenty-third day of October, in the year of our Lord 1705, the Virginia General Assembly, under the auspices of the College of William and Mary, provided an act for the commissionin' of surveyors. We surveyors are required, under oath and penalties, to faithfully perform our duties. This is not a trivial responsibility, laddie. We must be nominated by the board of trustees of the college and approved by the governor and his council. We prescribe and divide land that goes to the king's servants, his men-at-arms, and his subjects. A biased surveyor is respected by none, and should not be. Ye fancy friends might be wantin' ye to be a surveyor for their unsavory ends. If that's the case, get on that mangy horse and go back to ye wee farm, and I'll have nothin' to do with ye."

Despite his fear of this menacing little man, George could not help but bristle at the personal attack. "I can assure you, sir, that I place my honor above all else and would not sell it for . . . for . . . all the tea in China."

"Not even for the exalted Colonel Fairfax? Or how about ye fine brother?"

George had struggled to remain impassive, but Hume's implied attack on him and his family was too much. George's normally placid features transformed, revealing his suppressed inner fire. With his arms straight and hard against his side, his fists clenched tight, George growled, "Respectfully, sir, you apparently do not know my brother or the Fairfaxes, if you believe they would expect me to behave dishonorably—I will not." George stared directly into Hume's eyes.

Should I leave? Surely the Colonel and Lawrence would not expect me to listen to these insults.

Seconds, then almost a minute, passed.

I am leaving. I know the Colonel and Lawrence may be disappointed, but I will not endure this horrible man.

The Scot stared back at George with hard and unblinking eyes. Just as George began to turn to leave, Hume clapped his hands together and announced in an almost friendly tone, "Good! We have that out of the way. If I ever sense otherwise, I'll throw ye out on ye ear and tell the truth to anyone who will listen. I knew ye father, and he was a good man, and I believe ye come from good stock. It remains to be seen whether ye got the brains to match. Ye certainly look to have the brawn. Regardless, I intend to put both to the test. Ye are going to be me assistant—I'm goin' to work ye hard. I'll countenance no excuses or laxity of mind or effort. Nor will I hear complaints to me or complaints by ye to anyone else. Ye have come to me to be educated like a man, and I expect ye to behave like one," the Scotsman declared as he once again took his accustomed stance of feet shoulder width apart and arms folded across his chest. "What say ye, laddie?"

Was that a test? Clearly I can't leave now.

With the disheartening realization that he was stuck, George answered, "I understand, Mr. Hume. I have come to learn and work hard, and I intend to do so."

"Well, ye will. Get on that ugly mare. We've got to meet me chainmen, and you've got work to do. I hope you've told ye family, you're in for a long day. I know ye have duties on the farm, so I will never keep ye for more than two full days at a time. I assume you're ready for two hard days of work?"

"Yes, Mr. Hume, your note was very clear. My mother and brothers will tend to the farm in my absence."

"Well, off we go."

With a profound sense of dread, George shuffled through the door of Ferry Farm after two days of hard work, knowing he faced both his mother's criticisms for leaving the farm and a backlog of work to make up for from his absence.

He was utterly exhausted, mentally and physically. Hume had him acting as a chainman, dragging heavy thirty-three-foot wrought-iron chains over rough terrain, through fields, hills, valleys, and streams. To make matters worse, Hume constantly questioned him about math, geometry, and compass readings and grilled him on the use of mathematical tables with a precision far beyond anything George had ever experienced.

The intricacies of modern surveying came as a shock to George. He believed he was probably up to the physical rigors; however, he genuinely doubted his mental ability to handle the calculations, careful plotting, and drawing the profession required. He used a circumferentor—a tripod mounted with a compass and sight—to determine boundary-line bearings, then he was required to carefully make readings and note the results in a logbook while also directing the chainmen to precisely measure the chain's length. He not only had to supervise his fellow laborers to ensure they moved the heavy chains and avoided obstacles, but also to diligently correct any errors in order to make an accurate survey.

As he lay in bed that night, exhausted but unable to sleep, George recalled one particular exchange that still bothered him.

"How's ye memory, lad? Can you rely on it?" Hume had asked.

Without hesitation, George had answered, "I believe so, yes."

"Jesus, Mary, and Joseph! Didn't ye learn a thing readin' Wyld's book? Never rely on ye memory! Always write down everything in ye field book. Fools rely on memory. Are ye a fool?"

"I should hope not, sir," George had said, looking up from his calculations.

"While I should hope not too, young Mr. Washington, that remains to be seen."

The constant testing and jibes of the irascible Mr. Hume provided George little comfort that he would ever attain his goal. Figures, charts, and the ever-pressing Hume filled young George's mind as he drifted into fitful sleep.

Chapter 3

October 5, 1747 – Spotsylvania County

"*O mihi praeteritos referat si Jupiter annos,*" Hume proclaimed as he climbed down from his horse, tired from another hard day of surveying.

George, who had been assisting Hume for more than two months, was coming to the realization that he would—eventually—master the art of surveying.

"I beg your pardon, Mr. Hume?"

"How's ye Latin, laddie?" Hume asked as they entered an inn.

Hume was aware of his lack of formal education, yet it irked George to respond truthfully, "Wanting, Mr. Hume."

"I am content in Virginia, but it does not provide its youth with the classical education of me Scottish homeland. It is from *The Aeneid*: 'Oh, would heaven my strength and youth recall.' Me father used to say it all the time, and I never understood it. I surely do now. I wish I had that youth and strength both Virgil and me father longed for."

In the months George had spent with Hume, he'd come to understand that the older man often made quips for his own amusement without necessarily being mean spirited. Having implicitly passed Hume's initial test, he became more relaxed working for the Scot. After calculations had been checked and rechecked, and they sat by the fire in an inn or tavern where they spent the night, Hume and George would often chat amicably once Hume removed what he described as his "tutor's hat."

"From whence did ye people hail, boy?"

"I believe from Sulgrave, Mr. Hume," George responded.

Hume leaned in with a conspiratorial smile. "I suspect that somewhere along the way, some good Scottish blood got mixed in, which is why ye can put in a hard day's work. No Englishman from the south is worth a pinch of tripe.

"A toast to the people of the north appears in order," Hume announced as he reached into a coat pocket and pulled out a sterling silver hip flask. Detaching a silver cup from the bottom of the flask, he poured himself a healthy swig of liquor. As he did so, George noticed a crest engraved on its side.

Leaning in, "If I may, what is the crest on the side of your flask?" George asked.

"This fine receptacle offers both the taste and last vestige of home." Suddenly, looking slightly downcast, Hume handed it over to George and stared into the fire.

Carved into the silver flask was a beautiful heraldic shield capped by a knighted helmet and crown further topped by a unicorn framed on either side by matching falcons and the motto "Remember" on the top of the shield. On the bottom of the shield were the words "True to the end."

"Me father was the tenth baronet of our lands and the one true Master of Wedderburn Castle. This is our family crest. It, along with a few other trifles, is all I have left of me inheritance."

With that, Hume pulled over an empty glass that was sitting on the table and cleaned its contents with his shirtsleeve. He took the flask from George's hands, poured a smaller amount into the glass, and handed it to George. "You've been workin' hard, and ye earned a taste of the finest spirit on God's green earth." Raising his cup, he said, "To the hard workin' people of the north."

George was unaware of any Scottish connection to his family, but he decided to say nothing and tentatively raised the glass to his lips. George had, of course, enjoyed beer and rum, and wine always flowed freely, especially at Mount Vernon, but he had never had Scottish whiskey. As he drank the liquor in one quick gulp, repeating Hume's own actions, he was engulfed by its warmth as it slid down his throat.

Hume rumbled with satisfaction, "That'll put hair on ye chest."

Desperately trying not to cough, George finally asked, "I sincerely apologize. I do not know the story of your family. I don't mean to pry but would be grateful to learn."

Hume shifted closer to George so as not to be heard by others. "Scotland has long sought relief from the yoke of English oppression. As a colonist, I am, of course, a loyal servant of the Crown," he said with a wink. "Me father believed that a foreign power—specifically George the First and his Hanoverian line—was wrongfully rulin' and that the rightful king was our Scottish lord, King James.

"Our army met the English king's hired mercenaries at the Battle of Sheriffmuir. We so-called Jacobites were ultimately captured in Preston. I was taken prisoner and sent to Marshalsea Prison in London to await me fate. The long and the short of it is me father kept his head but lost his title and lands. I, as his heir, was banished to these colonies.

"I arrived with not a farthing to me name. I was nevertheless blessed to receive the consideration of me kinsmen transplanted to this country. There were other good men who had suffered similar treatment at the hands of English justice. In fact, the governor of Virginia at the time was kind to me, as he remembered the execution of his grandfather. This land presents a man with an opportunity for a fresh start. I am deeply grateful to have found this happy port in me stormy life." Hume, who usually limited himself to one strong drink each evening, took a second one.

After a long pause, George asked, "I want you to know, Mr. Hume, that you can count on my discretion. But, if you will excuse my impertinence, how can you serve the Crown, as a surveyor and in other capacities, when they did so much to injure your family?"

Hume threw his head back with a hearty laugh. "Who are ye, laddie? You're surely not the blushin', stammerin' boy who showed up at me doorstep. It must be the whiskey comin' out. That is indeed both an impertinent and improper question."

"Excuse me, I'm sorry, I did not mean to—"

"A little impertinence and questionin' is a good thing," Hume interrupted. "To answer ye question: we lost. Bonnie Prince Charlie couldn't do it in '45 and neither could me father in '15. Maybe someday Scotland will be on its own, but the power of the English Crown prevailed: *Ad victorem spolias.* 'To the victor goes the spoils' . . . and I am the spoils."

Resealing his flask and sliding it back into his pocket, Hume continued. "Let me put it another way, lad. As the good Lord said, 'Render therefore unto Caesar the things which be Caesar's.' Me body and mind may belong to the king, but me soul belongs to Scotland."

"To lose so much must be hard," George murmured, almost to himself.

"Aye, laddie, but was no choice. *'Tu ne cede malis sed contra audentior ito'*: 'Do not give in to evil, but proceed more boldly against it.' If me father hadn't fought, we would have lost our honor. There are times in life where the loss of everything is God's will and inevitable. Me father only lived five years after the defeat, but his head was always held high— and so is mine. If I faced his choice between revolution and dishonor, I pray I would have done the same thing—or at least I would hope I would have the courage to do it. Mind ye, if anyone asks, me father was justly punished, God save the king and all that rot," Hume said, sarcasm dripping from a crooked smile. "'Tis enough treason for one night. Time for bed. Good night, young George."

"Good night, Mr. Hume. You may rely on me."

"I already do, laddie, I already do."

The next day, George found three pounds and two shillings on his saddle, along with a note in Mr. Hume's unmistakably exact handwriting confirming that George had completed the initial stage of surveying apprenticeship.

My first wages!

With the confidence that came from Mr. Hume's affirmation of his growing abilities as a surveyor, George took what money he could scrape together, and, with a referral from Colonel Fairfax, he met with a tailor in Fredericksburg known for making dependable wilderness clothes for gentlemen. He knew his attire was crucial in establishing his position as a respected surveyor. Given his lack of formal education, it was more important than ever that he "appear" to be the man he did not feel inside. While buckskin and hard wools might be more durable and comfortable in the bush, he decided to focus on a balance of functionality and appearance.

He purchased closely woven, fully lined pants with leather jerkins down to the shin, protecting his lower legs and the tops of his boots from the inevitable briars of Virginia's backcountry. Above the waist, he wore a gentleman's shirt made of fine broadcloth with collars, sleeves, and a cravat held in place by a serviceable silver buckle. Over his shirt, he wore a stout leather vest with good pockets to hold his writing instruments. Finally, he made his most expensive purchase: a large red coat with a fine felt collar and inlaid brass buttons—an item that provided both warmth and drew attention to himself as a working professional.

When the outfit was complete, he looked at himself in the mirror. He now stood almost six feet, two inches tall, with reddish-brown hair held in a clasp at the back of his neck, highlighting a strong face with wide-set, gray-blue eyes. George saw in his reflection a young man ready to face the world, if not one with the total confidence that comes from money and education, at least one with a determination to succeed.

Chapter 4

March 11, 1748 - Northern Neck

"What say you, Will, enthused for our grand adventure?" asked George as they followed James Genn and his surveying team.

With the encouragement of Will's father, Colonel Fairfax, sixteen-year-old George and twenty-three-year-old Will were permitted to join the expedition traveling to the South Branch of the Potomac, to survey the Fairfax family's more than five million acres of land in northern Virginia. Known as the Northern Neck, it was framed by the swath of land between the Potomac and Rappahannock Rivers. Will was to attend as the Fairfaxes' agent with a power of attorney to lease land, and George was to experience wilderness surveying.

Slightly built with dark, wide-set eyes, Will was rumored to be the product of a dalliance between his father and a Caribbean native. His dark complexion did not give him a look of vigor; instead he exuded an unhealthy softness. When not speaking, his face defaulted to a tight-lipped grimace that made him look as if he was trying to ignore an unpleasant smell. Even his classical education could not overcome the insecurity caused by his questionable lineage and distinctive appearance.

Will responded without looking up, "You shall learn to survey and I shall be shunted away by my family, forgotten in the backcountry."

"Well, it's hardly my first surveying trip," George said smiling and ignoring Will's usual pessimism. "Good Master Hume has worked me to the bone traipsing around Spotsylvania, Orange, and Westmoreland Counties these last eight months. However, I must confess, this is my first trip into the deep wilderness—as I know it is for you, my friend." Will merely shrugged in response.

As they left the well-traveled roads of the Tidewater, the challenge of the wilderness was even more than George had expected. The heavy woods, constant water hazards, and lack of farms were a far cry from the placid and controlled peninsula he considered home. This unexplored tract, while largely devoid of people, was abundant with animals and birds. Wherever they went, crows warned of their arrival, and the profusion of birdsong mixed with the hum of insects, providing constant background noise.

Cresting a high ridge, George turned to Will and exclaimed, "Dear God, Will, have you ever seen a more beautiful grove of sugar trees?" Without waiting for an answer, he continued, "And look at the valley! This river must overflow regularly. Such black and rich soil. We will be able to grow grain, hemp, and tobacco in abundance."

As if startled by George's enthusiastic comments, Will grumbled, "Indeed" and returned his attention to his horse's navigation of the narrow trail.

Undeterred, George cantered ahead to James Genn, the leader of the expedition, and said, "Mr. Genn, this valley is remarkable. This may be some of the finest land in Virginia. What do you think, sir?"

The axe-faced, laconic, and experienced Genn turned to George and slowly removed the hand-rolled cheroot that dangled from his lips. "I suspect you are right, Master Washington. I have seen much, and this is some of the most fertile and well-situated land for our growing country. I think His Lordship will be well pleased."

As they continued down the path, George maintained his giddy excitement at the beautiful country. George and Will, along with the rest of the party, eventually arrived at Pennington's Inn, one of the last "civilized" outposts, for supper and a room. Famished, they ate heartily and collapsed on primitive mattresses.

The next morning, as George awoke refreshed, an agitated Will stood outside the inn shaking and striking himself vigorously.

"What's the matter, my dear friend? Are you having a fit?" George joked.

"Dear God! Did you see where we slept last night?" Will exclaimed, sounding more like one of George's young sisters than a full-grown man. "I have never seen anything so disgusting in my life. Even my father's barns are cleaner. My legs and arms are covered with bites from these horrid pests."

George laughed. "I believe you are right. I suspect the vermin, lice, and fleas doubled the weight of my pathetic blanket. I'd take the open air over a disease-ridden inn any day."

"Eww! Eww! Eww!" Will said while he continued slapping his clothing. "Well, I'd take neither. Give me a feather mattress and clean sheets in a proper English home."

"What, my friend?" George spread his long arms expansively and gestured to the valley that opened below them. "And miss all this?"

"My friend, you may have this empty wilderness; I prefer Paris or London," sniped Will.

And of course you have to remind me that I have never been there, thought George.

In contrast to Will, George remained largely indifferent to the hardships of the trail. He continued to marvel at the landscape, as well as the skill and abilities of his fellow travelers. George's gun was well protected from the elements, and largely inaccessible, in an oilskin bag attached to his saddle. In contrast, the woodsmen carefully wrapped their musket locks in rags and stopped their muzzles with corks to guard against the rain. Thus, even in their protected state, their guns were always at the ready to meet beast or brave. The woodsmen were not only excellent shots, but were also keenly aware of the topography and weather, always anticipating how the trail conditions would change. George bombarded them with questions and received valuable insights—even at the risk of being irritating because of his persistence.

It rained virtually every day. The travelers were all eventually soaked to the bone. Although uncomfortable and waterlogged, George's excitement with his new environment overcame any discomfort. He reveled in the crash course on how to survive, and indeed thrive, on the frontier.

Twelve days into their journey, the group happened on an Indian war party. Mr. Genn quickly assured George and Will that these were "agreeable" savages. The thirty Indians were coming from a war with another tribe and had in their possession a scalp that was shown to George. As he held the surprisingly small and dry scalp, he turned to Will.

"Would you like to hold it?" George asked.

In disgust, Will recoiled and shook his head. George handed the light scalp back to its proud owner with a nod and bow.

After parting from the Indians, they continued to suffer challenging weather. A cold wind ripped down the rain-soaked valleys and pummeled the men as they pushed on into the wilderness. Mud became a constant companion, sticking to horses, men, clothing, and even food. No amount of clothing could keep them dry, as water eventually penetrated all their belongings. At night, George experienced the unforgettable smell of sweaty men under muddy tents. Night after night, he fell asleep to the roar of rain and giant trees groaning overhead under a relentless wind. The snoring of the tired men was broken only by the shattering crash of lightning followed by hard thunder. Nevertheless, a contented George drifted off to sleep next to a wide-eyed Will.

On April 4, Will announced he would separate from the survey party and attempt to negotiate leases with local landowners while he stayed in a comfortable farm home. Everyone knew this decision permitted him to conveniently avoid the hardships of the trail. After three miserable days, Genn, George, and the rest of the group circled back to the area where Will had been staying. For the first time in weeks, George enjoyed sleeping under a roof in a dry bed.

The next morning, the young men pondered their situation. Holding a warm cup of tea with both hands, Will scanned the inviting confines of the cozy cabin and then turned toward George. "It is time for us to head home." He made the pronouncement with the practiced tone of one used to being obeyed. "Genn and his men are now turning west. You and I have both accomplished our missions. Speaking for myself, I have had enough of the Northern Neck. I am sick of being mired in this sludge. Leases have been signed, and you have expanded your knowledge of surveying, but it is time to return. We are still some forty miles from Winchester, and mountains block our trail. Even leaving now, we are faced with a daunting task. Going on offers no allure for me."

"You are quite right, of course." George gave only a small nod while looking down into his cup. "Let's find Mr. Genn and obtain the necessary provisions for our long ride home."

Even as he said it, George's thoughts went in another direction: *I would dearly love to continue to see these western lands and learn from Genn and his experienced party. While the Colonel was not explicit, I know my duty is to stay with Will. If he returned without me, or heaven forbid something happened to him, the Fairfaxes would never forgive me . . .*

As the young men began their return to Will's home, Belvoir, they passed through a stunning pine forest. Most of the Northern Neck contained thick stands of hardwoods with heavy undergrowth tugged on clothing, leaving briars and bugs. In contrast, the towering pines covering the uplands of the rounded mountains of the Alleghenies offered a bed of needles that blocked undergrowth. Shafts of sunlight cut through the dense canopy above, reminding George of a painting of a great European cathedral he had seen in Williamsburg. This impression was enhanced by the comparative lack of sound in the pine forest. The lowland woods were always abuzz with birds, wildlife, and insects. In contrast, the open space in all directions, broken only by the pine columns, offered relief from the incessant bugs.

Even Will could not help but whisper, "I know no one wants to lease this top land, but if our travel through the backcountry had all been like this, we would not be heading back now."

"It is hard not to see the hand of the Almighty," George agreed, and the pair reluctantly left the forest to continue their return. "Your family truly has some of the finest land on God's green earth," George said as they rode out of the pine forest. "The future is here."

"And here it shall stay, while I shall remain with civilization," a tired Will proclaimed.

Chapter 5

November 29, 1748 – Belvoir

Six months later, Lawrence and George left Mount Vernon, a modest one-and-a-half-story home flanked by two chimneys, painted white, and well sited overlooking the Potomac. The pair rode to an engagement party at Belvoir, the Fairfax family estate. It was a beautiful, clear, crisp Friday evening in late fall in northern Virginia. Will's wedding was planned for late December, and the best of Virginia society were attending his engagement ball.

"I spoke with Will yesterday," Lawrence commented. "He can be a dour little fellow, but his pending nuptials seem to have lifted his spirits."

Lawrence was in an excellent mood and good health, George noted. His brother had been experiencing a persistent and violent cough that bloodletting and other treatments had not alleviated. However, Lawrence's condition appeared to improve in the cool evening air as they rode together.

"Will is as happy as I have ever seen him," George replied. "He showed me a miniature, and the girl looks comely. Certainly a union with the Cary family is a superb match. According to Will, she is not only pretty, but also pleasant and intelligent."

"With Will's marriage, I suspect your surveying trips with him will largely come to an end. What is your progress on becoming the surveyor of Culpeper County?"

George gave a small shrug as an amusing thought crossed his mind: *Wedding or not, I don't think I will be seeing Will in the wilderness anytime soon.* "I spoke to Colonel Fairfax about the possibility last week during a foxhunt. He told me he would be discussing the matter with some friends and thought a position would likely open after the first of the year."

"Good. We need to keep you on the road, earning money, and out of the clutches of your lovely mother," Lawrence said with a wry smile as they turned the corner and began to progress up the long tree-lined drive to Belvoir.

Standing on high ground overlooking the Potomac, the home commanded two thousand acres with stunning riverside views. Its formal gardens and outbuildings presented lavishness equal to any English country house.

The sunset was turning the sky a brilliant purple and red that only emphasized the festive night that lay ahead. The pleasant sound of strings and horns from Belvoir reached them a half mile away.

Every window in the lovely two-story Georgian brick mansion was lit, projecting warmth to arriving guests. While George was dressed in his best attire, he was suddenly aware of his trail-worn and poorly presented horse. The sight of the mansion's circular drive, the huge court-yard, and the spectacle of elegantly dressed men and women alighting from carriages only intensified his insecurity.

Shaking off his uneasiness, George turned to Lawrence and said with heartfelt sincerity, "I am so sorry Ann could not come tonight. Is my niece feeling any better?"

Lawrence's smile disappeared. "She is very weak and frail. Little Mildred, you know, is just shy of three months old." He spoke as if every word drove a knife deeper into his gentle heart. "With the passing of our other babies, we felt it prudent for Ann to remain. In any event, Ann has been feeling under the weather and was disinclined to attend.

"If your wife dies, you are a widower. If your parents die, you are an orphan. If all your children die, what do they call you?" The pace of Lawrence's horse slackened to match his rider's mood. Without looking up, Lawrence murmured, "Cursed?"

George let his horse drift back to ride even with Lawrence. He opened his mouth to speak, but no words came.

Seeing George's discomfort, Lawrence forced a grin and shook his head quickly, as if trying to shake off his worry and disappointment,

"So, dear brother, it is just us bachelors this evening. Shall we wear out the feet of the young women of Virginia on the dance floor?"

George readily agreed, happy to change the subject. In fact, he loved to dance. With kindness and patience, Lawrence and Ann had taught him the proper evolutions and etiquette of dance. In contrast to the oppressive silence of Ferry Farm, Ann and Lawrence immersed him in the music and happiness that pervaded Mount Vernon.

Once inside Belvoir, the brothers collected drinks and conversed with their neighbors about politics in Williamsburg, and the latest gossip. George spoke briefly with his friend William Chamberlayne about the progress in completing the fall harvest. Virginia's elite were in full force, including Lawrence's fellow members of the House of Burgesses. At one point, Lawrence glided up to one of his colleagues and joked, "I believe we have a quorum tonight."

George, meanwhile, considered the striking differences between Ferry Farm, with its six plain rooms, whitewashed walls, and lack of pictures or decorations; the comparative elegance of Mount Vernon; and the opulence of Belvoir. In its celebratory splendor, Belvoir was decorated with the finest French and English furnishings. The walls were covered with exquisite molding, rich paneling, gilded paintings, and ornate wall coverings. The floors were parquet and marble. Plush curtains of gold and white framed the large glass windows, and the many crystal chandeliers and lamps cast a dazzling light on the assembled guests.

After a time, Lawrence and George approached Colonel Wilson Cary—the bride's father, a member of the House of Burgesses, and a Cambridge-educated scion of the Tidewater aristocracy. The portly, red-faced, and slightly inebriated man exuded a contagious air of enthusiasm and friendliness.

"A pleasure, a genuine pleasure to see you again, Major Washington," Cary said as he bowed a little unsteadily toward Lawrence. "Military men all around in this family, eh? Colonel Fairfax and yourself just four miles upstream. I can be sure my young Sally will be well protected, eh?"

Lawrence, gracious as always, smiled and returned the bow.

"Colonel Carey, you can be assured that the Washingtons and Fairfaxes will always be at the ready to guard your lovely daughter."

George could not help but marvel at Lawrence's absolute self-confidence and enjoyment of the friendly banter. Lawrence always knew what to say and how to put people at ease.

"To that end, may I introduce you to my younger brother, George," Lawrence said as he smoothly tilted his head. "He is a great admirer and friend of Will."

George was grateful that Lawrence had not mentioned that they were half brothers, but rather accorded him the full kinship George deeply felt and desired.

Cary looked up at George as if noticing him for the first time and turned to Lawrence. "My goodness, your family makes them big, eh?" Then he looked up at George. "Nice to meet you, lad, a pleasure indeed." But before George could reply, Cary's eyes were already moving on.

"Lad?" I am taller than virtually every man in this room, but I am still a "lad." Damn his eyes! Am I ever—

At that moment, the doors at the end of the ballroom swung open, and Colonel Fairfax, Will's father, entered and announced in a booming voice, "Ladies and gentlemen, it is my honor to introduce the happy couple, my son and his intended bride, Sally . . . er . . . Miss Sarah Cary . . . er . . . soon to be Fairfax."

The room erupted with applause and happy laughter at the Colonel's rare gaffe.

As Sally entered the ballroom on Will's arm, all noise and conversation around George seemed to cease. Indeed, time itself stopped. His vision focused on the most beautiful and intriguing woman he had ever seen.

Everything about her drew his attention. She appeared only a couple years older than George but projected a lifetime's more sophistication. In a tasteful acknowledgment of the Christmas season, she wore a scarlet-and-white gown with green bows and delicate silk flowers around her bodice. A stunning pearl-and-silver necklace highlighted a long neck and shapely shoulders. Her hair was drawn back and held in place with flowers, emphasizing a thin yet beautiful face with striking and intelligent eyes.

Will had often described her as beautiful, bright, and elegant, but George had not given his words much thought. Such hyperbole was to be expected from a smitten bachelor, especially someone like Will, who constantly felt the need to remind everyone of his social superiority. The reality of Sally Cary's blinding beauty made George forget everyone, including Will.

Minutes went by, and George realized the crowd around him had moved toward the couple, and he had been left behind, transfixed. He knew he needed to regain his composure and return to Lawrence's side.

Lawrence and George were lower on the pecking order for introductions, and thus George had time to compose himself. As he walked across the room, he could hear snippets of comments: "Isn't she lovely?" ... "comes from a wonderful family" ... "speaks French" ... "a wonderful addition." These observations only increased his trepidation at the prospect of the upcoming introduction.

Lawrence, always the center of attention, had a group of people around him. All were confirming that Will had done well for both himself and the Fairfaxes. It took all of George's self-control not to stare at Sally as she and Will worked their way around the room. Fortunately no one seemed to notice his complete inability to participate in conversation.

Finally, the time came for Lawrence and George to meet the couple. To George's surprise, Lawrence was not, as was customary, the focus of the introduction. After a quick and polite exchange with Lawrence, they turned to George. Will's face lightened with an unexpected burst of warmth and enthusiasm. He grasped George's shoulder, forgoing the traditional stiff bow, and pivoted so he stood between Sally and George, saying, "Sally, may I present my friend, George Washington." It was apparent Will was so genuinely pleased to introduce them that he had inadvertently used Sally's first name.

Ignoring the mistake, Sally extended her hand. As George stared into her eyes, he froze, and for a brief moment, he forgot what to do. In the uncomfortable seconds that passed, Sally quipped, "Mr. Washington, I have heard so much about you, sir. Although I must confess, while I did expect a giant, I thought I would find you covered in buckskin and mud covered, as my fiancé always describes you in your exciting travels." And then her face lit up with the most kind and gentle smile.

Finally remembering to bend forward to kiss her hand, George regained his voice only enough to croak, "Pleased to meet you, Miss Cary. Your servant."

George knew that a more sophisticated man would have responded to her comment with a witty comeback. He had made a fool of himself and appeared the uneducated provincial that Will had no doubt described. He could feel blood rushing to his face and a sudden, desperate need to leave the room. As the couple moved on to meet other guests, he excused himself and walked out onto the veranda, grateful for the rush of crisp evening air.

Chapter 6

July 27, 1749 – Belvoir

Eight months later, George returned to Belvoir. The gentle July breeze coming off the Potomac provided little relief from the summer heat that rolled up the hill to the imposing mansion. Seventeen-year-old George was directed into the library. Colonel Fairfax sat before an open window. His face was utterly unreadable: the epitome of self-control and inscrutability. George both admired and feared this great man. The Colonel was responsible for the issuance of land grants, a member of the House of Burgesses, a justice, and a collector of customs for the south Potomac.

"Come in, come in, my boy," the Colonel said. "Pray, please have a seat. Do you require any refreshment?"

George sat on edge of a chair, his back stiff and straight. *His summons didn't say why he wanted to see me. I hope I've done nothing wrong. Wait . . . Did he ask a question? He asked if I wanted refreshment. I should accept, but not be demanding.*

"You . . . are very kind, Colonel. Whatever is convenient."

The Colonel's eye merely flickered. A moment later, a crystal wine glass was placed on the table in front of George by a servant, who as quickly retired into the corner.

Sensing he was supposed to speak, George inquired, "I appreciate your kind invitation to visit you. How may I be of service?"

George noticed that the table next to him was vibrating slightly, disrupting the serenity of the room. He realized his right leg had been bouncing with such nervous force that it was impacting the furniture. Placing his hand on his thigh, he willed his leg to be still and prayed the Colonel did not notice.

Without responding, the Colonel stood up and strode past him to a desk in the corner of the library, picking up a large official-looking document with a broken wax seal. As he walked back, he handed George the document and returned to his chair.

"Well?" the Colonel said, rolling his hand in encouragement. "Read it. I think you will find it interesting."

George saw, to his astonishment, that the College of William and Mary had appointed him the official surveyor of the newly created Culpeper County. He looked at the Colonel with a broad smile and spoke, louder than he intended, "This . . . This is . . . wonderful, Colonel. I don't know what to say. How can I begin to thank you?"

The Colonel allowed his face to soften into a satisfied grin. "It is your hard work and training with Master Hume and others that have impressed the powers that be."

"Colonel, I know it was your intercession that has made this possible. I am deeply grateful," George said trying to modulate his tone.

With a dismissive wave, the Colonel replied, "It was nothing. Although, I believe you now have the distinction of being the youngest surveyor in the Old Dominion. Your next step should be to meet with Master Hume to discern the appropriate dividing line between Culpeper and Orange Counties. With this task completed, you will be sufficiently qualified to perform surveys on my behalf in the Northern Neck, if that is of interest."

"Of course, Colonel, very much so. I love the country and would appreciate the opportunity to survey the area."

"Well, our timing is good. The best time to survey is the fall, and you should be fully ensconced in your new role by that time."

Two days later, George surveyed Flat Run in the eastern portion of Culpeper County, officially signing as the county surveyor for the first time. George took great care in completing the survey in a measured hand. He then signed his name with a flourish in the lower right-hand corner. The feeling was bittersweet, as he wanted desperately to show it to Lawrence before he provided it to his customer. Unfortunately, Lawrence had left two months earlier to seek treatment in London for his persistent and worsening cough.

Over the next several months and into the fall, George worked tremendously hard as surveyor. He focused his efforts on the Fairfax lands. He honed his backwoods skills in the spring and fall when the undergrowth was at its lowest and the temperature most moderate. He also grew increasingly comfortable directing a team of burly chainmen who assisted him with his surveys.

While George endured the hardships of a backcountry surveyor, he also enjoyed an extremely lucrative business in which he was able to perform several surveys a day while spending time in the wilderness and reveling in his autonomy. Although usually accompanied by chainmen or other assistants, George also spent large amounts of time utterly alone. The independence, confidence, and solitude that came from these excursions energized him.

I cannot understand those who hate or fear the backcountry. With a rifle on my shoulder, no beast will challenge me. I have come to know the Indians well enough to feel some confidence—to raise my hand and share a bit of rum, or stand aggressively, showing no fear to those less amiable. The rewards and challenges of frontier surveying, and the absolute responsibility that comes with leading a party, are what keep drawing me back.

While other young men of Virginia's Tidewater gentry immersed themselves in carousing, gambling, and chasing young ladies, George focused on making money surveying, far away from the parlors and drawing rooms of the planter elite. This hard work permitted him to avoid the excesses of his peers while accumulating funds. Indeed, George charged more than the typical fixed price of one pound and eleven shillings per thousand acres for frontier surveying. Colonel Fairfax had kindly agreed to pay George, despite his inexperience, two pounds and three shillings, the maximum permitted in rural Virginia counties.

George's growing prosperity allowed him to feed his obsession to acquire land. George's first investment was a piece of land on Bullskin Creek, a tributary of the Shenandoah Valley in Frederick County, which over the years would ultimately grow to 1,459 acres.

Chapter 7

November 16, 1749 - Mount Vernon

In the four months since he had been appointed Culpeper County surveyor, George had often been absent from both his mother's home and Mount Vernon. Now, as he walked through Mount Vernon's front door, Ann was standing in the dining room, handkerchief to her face. It was clear she had been crying and was trying to compose herself. George strode over and touched her shoulder.

"Ann, what in heaven's name? Are you all right?"

With a sudden flood of tears, Lawrence's wife collapsed into George's arms, sobbing. "Oh, George, he has been so sick. He keeps coughing and coughing. At times, there is blood coming from his mouth. He cannot hold down food. I so fear for him."

George felt a sudden pang of guilt, for he had been absent as Lawrence's condition worsened. "Have you sent for the doctors? What have they said?" He gently patted Ann's back as she rested her head on his shoulder.

"Yes, they have tried to bleed him and prescribe some medicines, but thus far, they have been to no avail. It's . . ." she paused without looking up; hesitating, as if naming the disease would somehow make it more real. "It's consumption, as we all feared."

Dear God . . .

"May I go see him?"

Pulling her head back from his shoulder, she cast her bloodshot eyes up at George. "Yes," she answered, "but please be quiet; he only recently fell asleep and has stopped coughing for now."

George silently walked down the hall and cracked open the door to Lawrence's room. His brother's skin was so pale it was almost gray. He rasped and heaved with every labored breath. Black spots of blood marred the pillow cradling his head. Retreating, George slowly closed the door.

Even before George's father died, Lawrence had always supported him. While Lawrence may have lacked their father's drive and business sense, he was also more approachable. Lawrence was willing to set aside what he was doing and take the time to inform, educate, and ultimately befriend his younger, wayward brother. As a result, George had made the thirty-five-mile trek from the Ferry Farm as often as his mother would permit.

Once Lawrence married Ann, she, too, never wavered in her support. She had welcomed George into their home, teaching him the graceful accomplishments of genteel Virginia society, including the importance of proper attire, dancing, and riding. Now the happiness of these two people he adored was being shattered by Lawrence's illness.

George returned to find a recomposed Ann sitting in the parlor. Bereft and exhausted, Ann reached out and grabbed his hand. "George, I am so sorry. I am . . . lost."

George offered a small nod.

Lawrence has already given up so much. He forfeited his seat in the House of Burgesses because of his sickness. I must do what honor requires. My brother Jack and my other siblings will be supportive. Mother will not, but it is Lawrence. How can I do otherwise?

George continued to hold Ann's trembling hand and said, "Lawrence is in no condition to run Mount Vernon, and you must take care of yourself and the baby. My mother and siblings can run the Ferry Farm. I may have to come and go between the farms, but with your permission, I will come here to help you and Lawrence."

"Oh, George, thank you," Ann replied as a tear ran down her pale cheek.

"I need to collect my things and make some arrangements, but rest assured, I will do everything I can to help you and Lawrence."

"I know you will, George. Lawrence and I are so grateful." George noticed that Ann's normally erect frame now appeared bent, no doubt under the stress of Lawrence's health.

"It is I who am indebted to you and Lawrence," George said, "but that is beside the point. We must get him on the road to recovery. I am hopeful my presence here will take some burden off the two of you."

With that, they embraced, and George returned to the Ferry Farm to make arrangements for his move to Mount Vernon.

Chapter 8

August 17, 1751 - Mount Vernon

During the year and a half George assisted Ann and Lawrence, his brother's health continued to worsen. When George wasn't surveying, he spent as much time as possible with Ann and Lawrence. Lawrence's increasingly downcast demeanor was further exacerbated by the successive deaths of his three young children, Janet, Fairfax, and Mildred, each succumbing to illness as an infant or young child. While the death of children was all too common, even among Virginia's elite, it struck the sensitive Lawrence especially hard.

Once a vital and healthy man, Lawrence had lost almost fifty pounds. He was now a gaunt skeleton who labored at virtually any exertion. He constantly held a handkerchief spotted with blood from his unremitting and painful coughs.

After a fine supper of duck and fresh summer vegetables, which George devoured and Lawrence largely ignored, the men retired to a patio overlooking the Potomac—a view George loved above all others. George could feel Lawrence's irritation, knowing his older brother longed to smoke a cheroot after his meal.

Yet another pleasure sacrificed on the altar of his disease . . .

The change in Lawrence was unnerving. Previously clear spoken and confident, he was now compelled to whisper gently for fear of triggering yet another painful coughing fit. With a snifter of brandy in hand, a pallid Lawrence took a careful breath and looked George in the eye. "I have come to a decision. The doctors in England did not improve my health, and this climate is injurious to my well-being. As you know, during my service in the late war, I had some experience in the Leeward Islands. I have spoken with physicians and knowledgeable friends. It is the belief of many that the temperature, fresh breezes, and healthy vapors will be most efficacious in treating my current condition. However, it is not a voyage I believe Ann should undertake given the recent birth of Sarah. Nevertheless, it seems appropriate that I should have a traveling companion. I have always regretted that you were not able to go to sea either as a midshipman or for education in England. While fate seems to have dealt me some poor cards, perhaps we can transform this unhappy voyage into an opportunity to further your education and hopefully improve my health."

George's brow knitted as he contemplated escaping the provincial life of Westmoreland and Culpeper Counties. Slowly excitement began to overcome the anxiety caused at the thought of disrupting his life. "When do you propose to take sail? Do you know the cost of the passage? How long do you propose to stay?"

Lawrence's drawn face cracked into a patient smile. "I have made initial inquiries but have not yet ascertained the cost. There are frequent ships traveling between the southern Potomac and Barbados. We should not have a problem arranging passage. I am also drafting letters to be sent in advance to Gedney Clarke. He is a prominent planter and relation of the Fairfaxes who owns land with the Colonel. Mr. Clarke is also a friend of the newly appointed governor of Virginia, Robert Dinwiddie. We will be provided with appropriate letters of introduction. With the help of the governor and Colonel Fairfax, I am assured that we will be pleasantly received. So . . . what do you say, George?"

Travel, the sea, and meeting men of prominence . . . besides, Lawrence needs me. George suddenly pictured his mother's inevitable scowl of disapproval. With conscious effort, he shook off the thought. *Honor requires me to go—the money and Mother be damned.*

"By all means," George replied with a broad smile.

Chapter 9

September 28, 1751 - Barbados

L awrence and George set sail over a month later on the *Success*. George could feel his time with Lawrence slipping away. He cherished every moment with Lawrence while hoping a cure could be found. Lawrence also seemed intent on using his dwindling energy reserves to discuss George's plans for the future.

When the ship docked, there was a note and card waiting for Lawrence from Gedney Clarke, welcoming them to Barbados. Clarke offered supper and provided rooms while they searched for an appropriate home. On November 4, they dined with Mr. Clarke and his niece. The meal included exotic fruits like "avagado pair" and "pine apple," which George devoured and Lawrence surveyed without appetite. It was a pleasant meal, although Mr. Clarke and his niece were clearly ill at ease; Clarke's wife was recovering from smallpox, and her health weighed heavily on both of them.

The next day, Lawrence and George appeared at the office of Dr. William Hillary, who examined Lawrence at length while George waited in the parlor. At the appointment's conclusion, the stooped and extremely thin Dutch-trained doctor walked out with Lawrence.

"We have reason for optimism," Dr. Hillary announced, "if Major Washington follows my treatment and the climate has its efficacious effect. I do not believe his malady is so deeply seated that it cannot be cured. I need to see the major every other day for treatment, and he must rest and receive plenty of fresh air. I believe the lodgings of Captain Croftan overlooking Carlyle Bay would be ideal. I bid you good day."

At the doctor's suggestion, the brothers surveyed Croftan's rental home. A pensive Lawrence commented, "The lodgings are adequate, if not somewhat exorbitant."

"But look, Lawrence!" George exclaimed, arms wide as they stood in the rear of the home overlooking the bay. "How could we possibly choose somewhere else?"

With a shrug, Lawrence's lips twisted upward, his good humor for once overcoming his suffering. "Go meet with the captain and make the arrangements. I leave it in your capable hands. I will take my repose."

While Lawrence rested, George took a minute to write an excited letter to Colonel Fairfax, describing their new lodgings: "The prospect is extensive by land and pleasant by sea, as we command the prospect of Carlyle Bay and all the shipping in such a manner that none can go in or out without being open to our view."

Almost every other day, the brothers met with the elite of Barbados while enjoying exotic and interesting meals. They dined with Surveyor General William Patterson, Thomas Finlay (the clerk of the general assembly of Barbados), and Captain Croftan (the commanding officer of James Fort).

When Lawrence was feeling indisposed, George took advantage of an invitation from Captain Crofton to see the fort. The captain took almost an entire morning introducing George to his officers, explaining the extent of the fortifications, the rationale behind their construction, and the careful placement of its thirty-six guns and two batteries. George was particularly impressed by the immense cannon, which was capable of firing a fifty-one-pound shot.

On November 15, George and Lawrence went to the theatre. George had attended amateur theatrical performances before, but he felt truly enthralled by his first professional presentation of George Lillo's *The London Merchant.*

At the beginning of their third week, George suffered a savage headache beyond anything he had ever experienced; it was as if spikes were being driven through his temples and into the front of his forehead. As the brothers headed home from another impressive supper, George noticed sores forming in his mouth, larger and more prominent than any canker sore he had ever had before.

When George woke on November 17, he knew he was very sick. Lawrence walked into his room and touched George's forehead with the back of his hand.

"I fear, dear brother, you may now be sicker than me," Lawrence announced.

George was seized with severe body aches, especially in his back and loins. His pain turned to dread when red spots appeared on his forehead that quickly turned to papules. These "herald spots" were well known to everyone in the colonies. They were the portent of a disease that killed almost half of those infected, and those lucky enough to survive were usually left grossly disfigured by the telltale pockmarks.

Lawrence sent for Dr. John Lanahan, who quickly confirmed George had contracted smallpox. The initial pustules that developed on his face quickly spread to his chest and arms. It felt as if the lesions themselves were digging furrows deep into him, stretching the skin upward while also etching painful cavities into his body and killing him from within. As the days passed, the pustules flattened and became hard, painful bumps that spread not only to his chest, but also to his backside. No matter which way he moved, it felt as if small lead balls under his skin were being driven deep into his flesh, grinding into bone and compressing his frayed nerves.

As George lay in bed, he pondered his situation: *Ironic that we came to Barbados for Lawrence's health, but it appears I will die before him. To die like this . . . to be buried on this rocky shoal in a forgotten grave. What a short and meaningless life . . .*

The Barbados heat, which had seemed so glorious when he arrived, was now an oppressive force boiling him alive. Despite the best efforts of his caregivers to keep him clean, George lay in sweat- and pus-covered sheets. Too feverish to read, his only pleasant distraction was birdsong through the windows and the fresh flowers brought in daily by his frail and loving brother.

Writhing in bed, day after day, alternately sweating and shivering, he thought—as young men inevitably do—of his appearance. *Please, dear God, I don't want to live grossly disfigured.* While he was never presented a mirror, he could see his reflection in the window, the ghastly red pustules erupting across his forehead, scalp, and nose.

Days turned into weeks as the disease worsened and then eventually stabilized and retreated. The steady and constant care of his brother and the servants, as well as daily visits by Dr. Lanahan, were the only breaks in the monotony. Finally, by the first week in December, George began to steadily improve, and the lesions receded.

On December 12, the doctor pronounced him fully recovered. After receiving the news, George asked the doctor, "Will my face be badly scarred?"

Clearly irritated by the young man's vanity, Lanahan snapped, "I've buried three people this week who would not have given a wit how they looked if it meant seeing another sunrise. Count your blessings, young Master Washington. I suspect you may have some small scars on your forehead, but you have survived and are immune. Good day, sir." As Lanahan left, George felt chagrined but also relieved by the doctor's conclusion.

A pale and exhausted Lawrence collapsed into a chair next to George. As George's strength returned, he had taken to reading in the afternoons on the veranda overlooking the bay. As the two sat together, it became increasingly apparent that Lawrence's condition was not improving.

"I am deeply gratified to see you are stronger and greatly relieved that you will now be immune from this scourge," Lawrence rasped.

"Only a little worse for wear," George said, pointing to his still scabbed nose.

With a pained smile, Lawrence joked without mirth, "You were never that good looking anyway. It will probably be an improvement."

George nodded as an extended silence settled over both of them, broken only by the sounds of the distant surf and the gentle breeze shaking the nearby palms.

"Now that the crisis with your health is over, we must, I'm afraid, return to the discussion of my unhappy fate. I think we both would acknowledge that my condition has worsened somewhat since our arrival. I confess that I feel like a condemned criminal without hope of reprieve. Nevertheless, I have been told there is another physician in Bermuda with knowledge on treating my condition. The slightly cooler fresh air may provide some relief."

George nodded in acknowledgment looking at his hands rather than Lawrence.

"I could go with you. Perhaps this new doctor and island will make the difference and stem the tide of your illness," George said with an eagerness he did not feel.

The energy that had always drawn people to Lawrence was a distant echo in his reply. "You have done enough, dear brother. It is time for you to go home. I need you to return to Mount Vernon and inform Ann of my decision to go to Bermuda. You have suffered on this forlorn island on my account. You have a life to live. Regardless of what happens to me, I will look to you to watch over Ann and my daughter."

While glad to be leaving the island and returning home, George also felt guilty that he was not staying with his brother and tending to his needs. At the same time, he knew he needed to return, not only for himself, but also, as Lawrence requested, to assist Ann. So, reluctantly, George agreed, and they began to arrange for his voyage home.

On December 19, 1751, almost two months after arriving in Barbados with Lawrence, George left Carlisle Bay on the *Industry*. He enjoyed Christmas at sea, dining on beef and "Irish goose." Once again, winter travel presented heavy seas and sickness, but by the end of January, the ship had cleared the Virginia Cape and made landfall on the lower York River.

George delivered letters from Clarke to Governor Dinwiddie. Because of George's connections to Colonel Fairfax, the governor invited George to stay, and a pleasant supper ensued. While Governor Dinwiddie had a reputation for being a stiff, gruff, and mercurial Scotsman, George found him otherwise. George's experiences in

Barbados, his curiosity, and the knowledge of Scotland he had gained from Mr. Hume, quickly put him in good stead with Governor Dinwiddie. George adeptly ingratiated himself by being appropriately deferential to the haughty governor, which allowed Dinwiddie to adopt the role of wise teacher addressing an earnest pupil.

Immediately following the meal, George went to Mount Vernon to inform Ann that Lawrence's condition was not improving and that he had decided to travel to Bermuda in the hope of more effective treatment. George did not linger at Mount Vernon. Instead he returned to the wilderness to regain some of the surveying income he had sacrificed while in Barbados. More importantly, George sought the independence and solace the wilderness always provided.

Chapter 10

July 24, 1752 - Mount Vernon

Not only did Bermuda fail to improve Lawrence's condition, but his health rapidly deteriorated, forcing him to return to Mount Vernon knowing his days were numbered. George arrived at Mount Vernon and was ushered into Lawrence's darkened bedroom, where he was met immediately by the pungent odor of disintegration. Awareness of the smell disappeared when Lawrence's head turned toward him. His brother was pale, blue lipped, and struggling for every breath. Only the shell of the strong man he admired above all others remained, as George moved swiftly and pulled up a chair next to the head of the bed.

Lawrence drew him closer. "George," he rasped, "don't mourn me. I had a good and eventful life. I received military laurels and position—" He began to cough, blood coming out with each painful expulsion.

After some minutes, and with great effort, he continued: "We Washington men do not live long. That is something you must never forget. My advice to you is . . . *carpe diem*. You must seize the day." George was familiar with Horace's admonition, as it was one of Lawrence's favorite sayings.

For a moment, George thought Lawrence was lapsing into sleep, but he regained himself and continued in a hoarse whisper, even as his body failed him, "You will not live long, so you must live to the fullest. As long as you remain in the clutches of your mother, you will never be able to grow and fulfill your destiny. While Ann and our brother Austin may be upset by my decision, I have decided if both Ann and our daughter Sarah do not survive, you will receive Mount Vernon and some other properties. It is consistent with Father's will. It should allow you to live your life independent of your mother. While she prevented us from getting you into the navy, if given another opportunity, you should serve the Crown in war. There are always fights over the West Indies, or one of the European powers will seek to gain control of this continent. Jump at any opportunity to serve."

With effort to control the blood boiling and bubbling in his lungs, Lawrence pressed on, risking yet another fit. "My commission and Ann's family will help you. Fate gave me no sons. My hopes and dreams rest with you, brother."

And with that, Lawrence slid back into a fitful sleep.

With tears freely flowing down his face, and enduring emotion far beyond that which he felt when his father died. All George could manage to say was, "Thank you, Lawrence . . . brother."

He was unsure whether Lawrence heard him as he got up and left the room. Embracing Ann in the parlor, he excused himself from the home. He stumbled outside and leaned against a sturdy ash, weeping with the anguish and pain that comes from the loss of someone irreplaceable, someone upon whom he utterly depended. He realized he had been unconsciously gripping the tree so hard that he had torn the bark and cut his hands. He felt a dreadful abyss open inside him that threatened to pull him under.

I have known for a long time that Lawrence was dying, but . . . I always had hope. Now we are told it is only a matter of days or even hours. This is . . . too much to bear.

And what of the gift of Mount Vernon? It is so contingent, as it depends upon the deaths of both Ann and young Sarah. I cannot even consider it, and it would be improper to include it in my thinking. I will support Ann and her family. It is kind of Lawrence, but it is irrelevant and not practical. To think otherwise would dishonor Lawrence's memory.

Then George's thoughts turned toward something else Lawrence had emphasized. *Of course, Lawrence is right. All the Washington men die young. Our great-grandfather, John, emigrated from England and struggled only to die at age forty-six. Our grandfather, Lawrence, was educated in England . . . a justice of the peace, burgess, sheriff, and attorney . . . yet he died at thirty-eight. And Father vastly increased his land holdings and developed a profitable iron business, but died at forty-nine. And now, my dear Lawrence is dying at a mere thirty-six.*

George clasped his hands, closed his eyes, and pressed his forehead against the rough bark. He whispered a vow to God and his dying brother: "Lawrence, I will not let you down. I pray for you and for an opportunity to serve the king."

Part of him wanted to give in to despair, but Lawrence's entreaties to make the most of his life made him suddenly feel guilty. He stopped, straightened himself, regained some control, and walked to the stables to collect his horse.

Two days later, on July 26, 1752, Lawrence's suffering finally ended. He was buried in a ceremony attended by the crème of Virginia gentry, including the Fairfax, Washington, Lee, Randolph, Carter, and Cary families.

Chapter 11

September 14, 1752 - Ferry Farm

George returned to Ferry Farm from a surveying expedition, tired, dirty, hungry, and still depressed from the loss of Lawrence a month and a half earlier. As George climbed down from his horse and handed the reins to a slave, leaving the animal to be unsaddled and his packs unloaded, he entered the plain, empty, and far from immaculate house. The minimal personal belongings were scattered helter-skelter about the room without thought and consideration, a far cry from the care Lawrence and Ann had taught him was so important. Its eleven leather-bottomed chairs were loosely arranged around two tables and a cupboard containing modest—though ample—china. George was aware that while minimally adequate, nothing gleamed with the quality or shine of Belvoir or, to a lesser extent, Mount Vernon before Lawrence's death.

As was typical, his mother was not in the house; she was likely in the fields, directing the slaves or field hands to squeeze every ounce of energy from those who labored for her. No doubt his younger brothers and sisters were also working somewhere on the farm under his mother's thumb. George was grateful for her absence and the silence.

On his small desk rested a couple of letters, most notably a fine envelope in flowing handwriting addressed to him and bearing the wax seal of the Fairfax family. Sally and Will had been extraordinarily kind to him since Lawrence's death. He was surprised and pleased to read:

> The honour of your presence is requested at Belvoir for a two-day theatrical performance of Joseph Addison's *Cato* commencing at tea time on the 30th day of September. This participatory event will be presented by unschooled thespians and aspiring

amateurs wishing to bring this important work to life in our fair Country.

We would be grateful for the honor of your attendance and participation. We are, with all due respect and regards, your obedient and humble servants.

The letter was formally signed in the same hand; however, below the signature, was an additional note: "George, my sisters will be coming from Ceelys on the James. We so hope you can attend and share in a couple of well-deserved days of enjoyment. SF."

George had read Joseph Addison's *Cato*, as had virtually every educated person in Virginia. He pondered the letter. *I've seen and enjoyed some theatrical performances in Williamsburg and Barbados, but what does this mean? I am being asked to* participate *in the play? I am not an orator or an actor, but of course I cannot refuse. Besides, I'm sure I will have some minor role.*

George quickly penned an acceptance, anxious for the new experience of a couple days at Belvoir in the presence of the beautiful and intelligent Sally Fairfax.

Chapter 12

September 30, 1752 - Belvoir

"Welcome, George," Will said as a servant directed George into the library.

George was a frequent visitor to Belvoir and this wonderful room in particular. Through the kindness of Colonel Fairfax, Will's father, George had been given the run of the extensive Fairfax family library, devouring not only its books, but also the constant influx of periodicals. Under Lawrence's tutelage and later Colonel Fairfax's, George had read Seneca's *Morals*, Cicero's *Orations*, Caesar's *Commentaries on the Gallic War*, and *The Odyssey*, as well as books on mathematics and agriculture and the latest newspapers, pamphlets, and magazines from London. He had even carefully copied the *Rules of Civility & Decent Behavior in Company and Conversation*, and committed the book to memory. While he was ostensibly a guest, he felt at home in the library, which had become his favorite spot in this amazing home.

Since Lawrence's death, Colonel Fairfax had provided George with constant career and personal advice. The Colonel had even taken the time to tour Belvoir with George, teaching him about art, etiquette, and the finer points of furnishing the mansion. The Colonel and George shared a passion for foxhunting, dogs, and horses. Will's lack of interest in these pursuits excluded the diminutive and nonathletic son from the Colonel's company. George sensed his growing closeness to the Colonel was the source of a widening gap between the two young men.

Will made a minimal effort to rise from his seat as George entered the library, simultaneously raising his drink and nodding George to a nearby chair. A cheroot smoldered on a nearby tray, its aroma filling the room.

"Sit down and have a drink," Will said. "You are going to need to save your energy. Sally and her sisters have been planning this event for over a month. *Cato* is all the rage. The fine families are putting the plays on themselves rather than waiting for professional performances. Obviously it is not my area of interest, but I cannot refuse to participate, or I'll never hear the end of it. Don't know about you, but I'd prefer to watch instead of having everyone watching me."

Over the years, George had come to understand and even sympathize with Will's insecurities. While he was one of the wealthiest men in Virginia, he was a small and relatively unattractive man who always had to fight unfair rumors that he was a mulatto. Despite Will's well-chosen marriage to Sally, and a brief period of happiness before and immediately after their marriage, he had returned to his pessimistic and introverted demeanor. While George and Will remained friends, they did not meet as often, and it was only the vivacious Sally who kept Will in the active social scene.

George didn't share Will's skepticism about the upcoming play. He was intrigued, although somewhat nervous about the prospect of a public performance. George recognized that he should probably respond in some way to Will's dour pronouncement, so he decided to change the subject: "Will the Colonel be joining us?"

Will chuckled. "Discretion is the better part of valor. My father has retreated to the Shenandoah, conveniently avoiding these festivities."

Before George could respond, he was startled to his feet as the serenity of the library was suddenly and loudly interrupted. Sally and her three sisters burst into the room, moving, conversing, and laughing like chattering songbirds. Their energy and excitement filling the air.

"Mr. Washington!" Sally exclaimed with obvious delight. "You are here."

George bowed. "And at your service, madam."

"Is he not perfect?" Sally said as she turned to her sisters. "He is tall and strong; he will play Juba."

Juba? He is one of the lead characters! They want me to play an African? What on earth have I gotten myself into?

George stammered, "Madam, I . . . I have no theatrical experience. I fear I would be a tremendous disappointment. If I am to participate at all, perhaps a more minor—"

"Nonsense." Sally interrupted. "We have more guests coming, but you must play Juba. We need a large and strong man, and I believe you will be the tallest here." Then, for the first time, speaking more slowly and looking directly into his eyes in a way that caused George to freeze and blush at the same time, she said, "Mr. Washington, you *will* be wonderful." And with that, she and her sisters fluttered out of the room, leaving the swinging door ajar.

The men watched as a servant began to silently close the library door. "No doubt they are on to their next victim," Will said as his mouth turned up at the corners.

A silence descended on the room. George felt uncomfortable about Sally's comments regarding his size and strength. Such direct statements by women were generally inappropriate, but given the exigencies of the play, they were probably permissible. Nevertheless, the foil between the two men hung over the room.

Will blew a long cloud of smoke that spread like a curtain, filling the space between them. After several long seconds, he smirked. "Well, George, welcome to Belvoir. I'm sure you're missing your little farm now."

Ignoring the jab, George forced his face to remain impassive.

Once George finished breakfast the next morning, he was amazed to see the work that had transformed one corner of Belvoir's ballroom. Under the supervision of Sally and her sisters, slaves and local craftsmen had constructed a stage with a background and props to reproduce ancient Rome and its countryside. Costumes had been made, and seamstresses were making modifications under the direction and with the assistance of the women. Their little theatre company had grown to the required eleven actors and actresses, along with others "volunteered" by Sally to assist in the production.

Sally announced they would be doing rehearsals and that more neighbors would be coming to see their theatrical debut. While ostensibly Will was the "director" as the host of the party, it was clear to everyone that Sally was the driving force. George marveled as she remembered every word of the play and constantly provided skillful direction.

George also learned that Sally would be playing opposite him in the romantic role of Marcia. While there would be no physical contact, he was nervous. George felt Will's general displeasure with the entire process. Whether Will's attitude was also attributable to George's role was unclear, but Will's general disdain was becoming increasingly evident.

George knew he did not have an orator's voice, and he was anxious about acting in front of others. A bout of pleurisy as a child had left him with a hollow chest and breathy voice. He wanted to perform well, and he did not want to let down Sally—or more importantly, himself; thus he dutifully recused himself and carefully memorized all his lines. He was keenly aware of his educational shortcomings and worked late into the night making sure he would acquit himself as well or better than any of his fellow performers.

As Sally was busy putting together costumes and providing direction to other performers, her sisters assisted George in practicing Juba's lines. Finally, without costumes, the performers ran through their first full rehearsal of the play.

There were a number of early scenes between Juba and Marcia, which George performed with Sally. While he felt very uncomfortable with the others watching, George was able to remember his lines and act better than any of the other male performers. As the play proceeded, George became increasingly confident and immersed in the play. At the same time, he felt some trepidation as he and Sally approached the climactic scene where Marcia (Sally) would find Sempronius (Juba's nemesis) lying dead and erroneously believe the prone figure was a murdered Juba (George). The power of the scene and Sally's beauty began to have its effect as she played Marcia.

Marcia [collapsing onto her knees next to the body on the floor]: "Ye dear remains of the most loved of men! Nor modesty nor virtue here forbid a last embrace, while thus!"

George realized Sally was not merely saying the lines as the other performers were doing; she was actually acting and playing the role of Marcia. She *believed* she had found Juba, her true love, on the ground. And now it was George's turn as Juba:

> Juba [drawing himself before her on his knees next to Semproius's body]: "See, Marcia, see! The happy Juba lives! He lives to catch that dear embrace, and to return it too with mutual warmth and eagerness of love."

George, on many occasions, had sat next to Sally. However, with their knees touching and both of them on the ground, they had never been in such an informal posture. Despite the presence of everyone looking at them, George felt both uncomfortable and exhilarated. He was drawn to her, and their faces moved closer as they spoke.

> Marcia: "With pleasure and amaze, I stand transported! Sure 'tis a dream! Dead and alive at once! If thou art Juba, who lies there?"
>
> Juba: "A wretch, disguised like Juba, on a cursed design. The tale is long, nor have I heard it out. Thy father knows it all. I could not bear to leave thee in the neighborhood of death, but flew, in all haste of love, to find thee. I found thee weeping, and I confessed this once, am rapt with joy to see my Marcia's tears."
>
> Marcia: "I've been surprised in an unguarded hour, but must not now go back. The love, that lay half smothered in my breast, has broke through all its weak restraints, and burns in its full luster; I cannot, if I would, conceal it from thee."
>
> Juba: "I'm lost in ecstasy! And dost thou love, thou charming maid?"
>
> Marcia: "And dost thou live to ask it?"

Juba: "This, this is life indeed! Life worth preserving, such life as Juba never felt till now!"

Marcia: "Believe me, prince, before I thought thee dead, I did not know myself how much I loved thee."

Juba: "Oh fortunate mistake!"

Marcia: "Oh happy Marcia!"

Sally was looking directly into George's eyes. In polite Virginia society, a woman would never be so bold as to make extended eye contact with a man—especially an unmarried man—while her husband looked on, but George forced himself to hold her gaze. Suddenly he felt a rush of panic and thought, *Dear God! What are my lines?*

After what seemed an interminable pause, he blurted:

"My joy! My best beloved! My only wish! How shall I speak the transport of my soul?"

Fortunately, no one seemed to notice his delay.

Marcia: "Lucia, thy arm! Oh let me rest upon it!" [Lucia comes from off stage to assist Marcia.] "The vital blood, that had forsook my heart, returns again in such tumultuous tide, it quite o'ercomes me. Lead me to my apartment. —Oh prince! I blush to think what I have said, but fate has wrested the confession from me; go on, and prosper in the paths of honour, thy virtue will excuse my passion for thee, and make the gods propitious to our love."

As Sally was led away, George stared openmouthed. Their faces had been inches apart as they delivered the scene flawlessly. Everyone in the room had stopped to watch them perform. At that moment, George had to summon all his will and self-control not to reveal his absolute

infatuation with Sally. Fortunately the moment was broken by the erup-
tion of applause.

In response to the adulation, Sally hopped into the air and clapped
with delight, springing back to George. She reached forward and
grasped his hands enthusiastically, pronouncing, "You were wonderful,
Mr. Washington!"

As she touched him, he felt an electric shock, and his face burned as
it turned crimson. While her public pronouncement seemed to diffuse
any perception that their performance had been anything more than
acting, she paused as she let go of his hand with a look that made him
think it was perhaps otherwise.

The play was practiced again, and George experienced the same
exhilaration performing opposite Sally. His performance anxiety
reached a fevered pitch as the members of the Tidewater elite, both
his peers and betters, filled the large ballroom to the point where virtually every inch was full of standing and sitting ladies and gentlemen.
Nevertheless, when it came time to deliver his lines, he did so without hesitation or mistake. While his performance with Sally lacked the
unbridled intensity of their practice sessions, it proved compelling to
the audience. When their second performance was over, George was
literally engulfed by the audience members, who heaped compliments
and kind words on him. His anxiety before the play had been so great
that he knew he would never want to experience it again, but he was
gratified—and profoundly relieved—by his success.

A head taller than everyone around him, he was easily able to see
Sally similarly surrounded by well-wishers. While trying to politely
respond to those addressing him, he couldn't help but look at Sally,
and when their eyes met, he once again found himself spellbound.
As his eyes locked on her sparkling gaze, the distance between them
disappeared, as did everyone else in the room. She inclined her head
in approval and with obvious affection. That gesture meant more to
him at that instant than anything his young heart could desire. It was
only when someone touched his sleeve to get his attention that he was
snapped back to those nearby, and the connection to Sally was broken.

However, the afterglow of that moment with Sally continued to dominate his thoughts.

In addition to the play, there were dances throughout the weekend where George remained the center of attention. Dancing came naturally to George. Like riding a horse, dance involved strong yet relaxed control of one's hips and legs. He also found it easy to remember the intricate steps of minuets and gavottes. His skill for dancing was not shared by most men. As a result, he reveled in the attention of lovely women, who otherwise might not have noticed him.

By apparent mutual consent, George and Sally did not sit near each other or converse much for the remainder of the weekend. George was uncomfortable under Will's brooding gaze and did not want to betray his own growing feelings for Sally.

As he rode back to Ferry Farm, he thought, *What an outstanding visit! My performance was a rousing success. Wonderful meals, dancing, games of whist and loo, and even a fox hunt.*

And acting . . . It is much more like dancing than I expected. It involves the same self-control and willingness to perform in front of others. And what an amazing play!

What an extraordinary woman!

He began to recall the curve of Sally's neck and her inviting full lips as they sat inches apart.

What in God's name is the matter with you, man? What are you thinking? She is a Fairfax. She is married to Will. While he may not be your closest friend, his father-in-law is your greatest benefactor. Forget her.

George then remembered the look in her eyes as they performed the play, and he recalled Portius's comments on Juba's inability to hide his love from Marcia: "His eyes, his looks, his actions all betray it: but still the smothered fondness burns within him."

By, Christ, I really am Juba.

No! Enough. I cannot think of this. I must block her from my mind and find other interests. I . . . need to be in the wilderness and away. Some separation will be good. Perhaps some distraction in Williamsburg.

PART II
Major Washington

Thy nobleness of soul obliges me.
But know, young prince, that valour soars above
What the world calls misfortune and affliction.
These are not ills; else would they never fall
On heaven's first favourites, and the best of men:
The gods, in bounty, work up storms about us,
That give mankind occasion to exert
Their hidden strength, and throw out into practice
Virtues, which shun the day, and lie concealed
In the smooth seasons and the calms of life.

—Joseph Addison, Cato: A Tragedy, Act II, Scene IV

Chapter 13

October 17, 1752 – Popes Creek Plantation

Before passing away, Lawrence had encouraged George to apply for his vacated commission as a major in the Virginia militia. Although he had been given Lawrence's blessing, George felt the title most rightly should go to Lawrence's closest relative, his brother Austin. Like Lawrence, Austin was educated in England, well read, and sophisticated. However, by disposition, Austin was far more like their father than the outgoing Lawrence. Two years younger than Lawrence, Austin was a quiet, gentle man who rarely spoke first in a conversation and never raised his voice. Austin lacked George's and Lawrence's erect military bearing; instead, he had his father's stooped shoulders, which, despite his size, projected an academic bent. Whether it was Austin's reserve or their differing interests, George had never felt as close to Austin as he had to Lawrence.

While Austin had not expressed any interest in Lawrence's commission, George wanted to raise the issue with him before pursuing the matter with Colonel Fairfax or Governor Dinwiddie. Almost three months had passed since Lawrence's death, and dining at Austin's home would be the best venue for addressing George's concerns. Austin had inherited Popes Creek Plantation from their father, and the sturdily constructed two-story home was clean, well maintained, and tastefully decorated, but not nearly as well sited as Lawrence's Mount Vernon.

After an excellent meal, George and Austin retired to the impressive library surrounding a large hearth with a crackling fire.

"Oh my goodness! You have acquired even more books since the last time I was here," George said as his fingers danced across the volumes filling the lovely mahogany bookshelves.

"I've added a few new treasures. Books, I'm afraid, are both my vice and passion." Austin's interests centered on esoteria, including political philosophy, theology, and new scientific developments at the forefront of the Enlightenment. "Obviously I have a long way to go until I approach the library at Belvoir, but as always, you are welcome to borrow whatever you would like."

George nodded vigorously, pushing one of the impressive volumes back onto the shelf. He eventually returned to the well-stuffed and comfortable leather chair positioned across from Austin. "There has been something weighing on me, and I want to make sure I do not engage in some activity that might undermine our friendship or be, in any way, dishonorable."

A concerned look spread across Austin's scholarly face as he gestured for George to proceed.

"There is . . . there is the issue of Lawrence's commission as major and his position as an adjunct in the Virginia militia." George paused, looked at his feet, and continued. "As he grew ill, Lawrence suggested I apply for the post, but I wanted to discuss this with you."

Austin's concerned look gave way to a wide smile. "Is that all, dear brother? For a moment, you had me gravely concerned. Let me guess: you would like to seek Lawrence's commission, but you don't want to offend or presume, as I, by age and relation, would have first claim. Is that it?"

George shifted in his chair as he spoke. "Well . . . yes. That is indeed . . . the issue."

"Let me put your mind at rest. We both heard Lawrence's stories of war but perceived different things. I heard suffering, sickness, and death. Your young ears heard glory, honor, and country."

George started to interrupt, but Austin raised his hand to silence George and continued. "No. Military life does not offer the same attraction for me as it did for Lawrence, and does for you. While I will suffer the wilderness as necessary, and I certainly enjoy a good foxhunt now and again, the idea of traipsing through the woods in the company of rough men presents no allure. Leave me to my books. I will save my battles for the House of Burgesses."

Relaxing back in his chair, George said, "Was it that obvious that I wanted Lawrence's commission?"

Setting down his drink, Austin chuckled. "Dear brother, it was obvious to everyone in the world except you. Rest assured, I will support your petition and all your endeavors. As family, we will all support each other. Since you were a lad wanting to join the navy, it has been clear to everyone that you wanted to follow in Lawrence's footsteps. I, on the other hand, tend toward our father's path of commerce and politics." Then, with his smile giving way to a more serious look, "I caution you not to limit your endeavors to military ones. You should also join the Masons and, in a few years, seek a seat at the House of Burgesses. Until you have finally and definitively found your way, you should continue to follow multiple paths so that you have options and opportunities."

"Thank you, Austin. As always, I am grateful for your kindness and advice."

Austin stood, signifying the end of the discussion, "Not at all. Now, we both have full days tomorrow, and you have a long ride back to Ferry Farm. I will see you off before you go in the morning, but wish you good night."

"Good night, and thank you again, Austin."

As Austin suggested, George joined the Masonic Lodge in Fredericksburg on November 4, 1752, as an apprentice. The composition of the organization's members meant more to George than its arcane rituals. The elite of Virginia's planter, military, and intellectual classes were represented at the lodge. George also embraced the Masons' enlightened ideals of universal brotherhood and equality and their focus on building better men in a better society. The twenty-year-old George felt growing confidence, having joined the Masons, realized success as a surveyor, and proceeded with seeking Lawrence's Virginia commission.

Chapter 14

December 20, 1752 - Belvoir

-

Two months later, George entered the familiar surroundings of the library at Belvoir in response to a summons from Colonel Fairfax.

"Come in." The Colonel rose as George entered the room. "It is so good to see you. How goes the surveying?"

George strode across the library to greet the Colonel. A drink in his hand, the Colonel looked the picture of a Virginia gentleman at his leisure. A man of contrasts, he preferred to wear buckskin frontier clothing when in the Shenandoah Valley or on a foxhunt, but when in Belvoir, he presented proper English deportment. In genteel attire, he could carry on erudite conversations on literature or politics, yet at the most basic level, it was the love of horseflesh and foxhunting—even more than familial connections—that drew George and the Colonel together.

Now far more comfortable in the great man's company, George replied confidently, "Happy Christmas to you and yours, Colonel. I am pleased to say I have conducted well over one hundred surveys since my appointment, in large part because of your kindness and assistance."

Directing George to a chair, the Colonel's rich and smoky voice filled the room. "Think nothing of it, my boy. It is your hard work and talent that made it possible. Now . . . have a drink."

Once George was comfortably seated with a glass in hand, the Colonel continued. "I must confess, I am privy to some happy tidings relating to you." He turned and picked up a sealed letter that sat on a long walnut table along with several books and a sword in its scabbard. "The contents of this letter, which I was asked to deliver to you, were disclosed separately to me by the governor."

George took the finely addressed and waxed sealed letter, which was addressed to "Major George Washington." He smiled with the recognition of the title's meaning. He broke the seal and confirmed that as of December 13, 1752, he had been appointed commander of a Virginia military district and been awarded Lawrence's colonial rank of major. While reading, George unconsciously stood.

When George finally looked up from the letter, he noticed Colonel Fairfax was standing in front of him. In his hand was the sword in its scabbard, which he had silently picked up from the table. "Let me be the first to congratulate you, *Major* Washington," he said. "I do not believe an officer and gentleman of your caliber should proceed without the benefit of good steel."

Momentarily speechless, George set down the letter and unsheathed the well-oiled blade to reveal shining metal with intricate inlay. He looked back at the grinning Colonel, who said, "Pray accept this as a gift."

Sliding the sword back into the scabbard, George replied, "You are too kind to me, sir. It is through your generosity that I hold this commission, and now this sword."

"We don't want you to proceed without the proper accoutrements," answered the Colonel with a dismissive wave.

"How can I thank you?"

"Think nothing of it, my boy. We are family . . ." He paused to look George squarely in the eye. "And Lawrence would have wanted this. This is only the beginning. I expect you to be a fine officer. As such, you must begin your education." The Colonel placed his hand on a stack of military manuals on the table. "I suggest you review these books, and we can begin your military training by discussing them after our next hunt."

"I will, Colonel. Thank you."

"The pleasure is truly mine, my dear . . . Major. Let us retire to supper. Afterward, will you be good enough to join me in a game of billiards? I know you will be polite enough to play poorly so I may believe I am competitive," said the beaming Colonel Fairfax.

"I suspect my appointment will distract me and unsteady my hand to your advantage," George said as the smiling men left the library and retired to the dining room.

George stood in front of the full mirror inspecting his new major's uniform. With a growing sense of confidence, George assessed his situation. He was now a major and the owner of almost two thousand acres in the Shenandoah Valley. On his twenty-first birthday, he would inherit ten slaves, Ferry Farm, and three lots in Fredericksburg. He'd established himself as a surveyor of Culpeper County and was earning a decent and growing income. With this in mind, George had decided to engage a Williamsburg tailor to create a major's military uniform. He looked at the cut of his fine red woolen coat with brass buttons on the lapels. George wore a white high-collared shirt and a curved gilded brass plate called a gorget under his neck, inscribed with the colony's coat of arms and the motto of Virginia, *"En Dat Virginia Quartum."* Translated, it meant, "Behold! Virginia Yields the Fourth," meaning Virginia considered itself the fourth kingdom of the British Empire.

He realized that the only person in the world with whom he really wanted to share this moment was Sally, the daughter-in-law of the Colonel and the wife of his friend Will. He knew he should go elsewhere; yet he returned to Belvoir, ostensibly to see the Colonel but with the main goal of seeing Sally. She did not disappoint, doting and fussing over George's new uniform, only worsening his hopeless crush.

Chapter 15

October 26, 1753 – Williamsburg

For ten months, George did little in his new military position to bolster Virginia's defense, other than collecting a stipend, filling out some minimal paperwork, and enjoying his new uniform. That changed when French troops moved south from Canada and began constructing forts on the western edge of the Virginia territory. The Ohio Country was an area of dispute between the British and French. French trappers had long ago entered the area, but lately, English colonists, with growing westward expansion, were intent on occupying the region. French troops appeared ready to fortify the crucial area at the confluence of the Allegheny and Monongahela Rivers, threatening land investments of the Virginia elite in the Ohio Company, including Colonel Fairfax, Governor Dinwiddie, and others.

George learned the governor needed an able and strong volunteer to endure a winter trek through the wilderness to deliver a message to the French, demanding they leave the area. At the urging of Colonel Fairfax, on a crisp autumn day George rode to Williamsburg to offer his services. Virginia's largest city consisted of about two hundred houses, a dozen of which were worthy of a gentleman's family. The wide streets and walkways were considered some of the most spacious in America, and its one thousand residents took pride in the city's handsome appearance.

George hoped that his prior meeting with Dinwiddie, his social and political connections, and his recent promotion to major in the militia would allow him to secure the appointment. George entered the elegant Governor's Palace and stepped into a side room to carefully inspect his uniform before walking to the governor's office. Lawrence and Ann had taught him the necessity of proper clothing and, taking the time to ensure no glaring imperfections undercut his efforts. Starting with his shoes, George worked his way up, carefully examining every aspect of his clothing, removing any lint and dust, and straightening himself, finishing with the hat he now held under his arm. Satisfied that he was the picture of an earnest and confident young officer, he walked down the hall to present himself to the imposing governor.

"Come in, Major Washington. A pleasure to see you again," the plump, bewigged, and formally dressed governor welcomed George as he was ushered into the well-appointed, wood-paneled office. "I received a kind letter from Colonel Fairfax indicating you would be coming to see me. He recommends you assist the Crown in addressing the French invasions in the Ohio Country."

A nervous George awkwardly bowed and then stood ramrod straight in front of the large desk as the governor sat down.

"Indeed, Governor, that is the reason for my visit." George then mechanically recited the speech he had memorized: "I submit for your consideration my petition to serve as an emissary on your behalf to the French. As you know, I have familiarity with the country due to my surveying missions, and your largess has permitted me to take up my family's commission." George fought a nervous tremor as he concluded. "I therefore believe I am well suited to perform my duties on behalf of Virginia and Your Excellency."

"Please be seated, my young friend," a slightly bemused Dinwiddie said, pointing to a chair. "Excuse me, I mean 'Major Washington.' My familiarity, I'm afraid, reveals my preference." As the governor settled into his chair, he interlaced his pudgy, ink-stained fingers, resting them on his prodigious and extending belly. "You are certainly being strongly considered to carry an important letter to the commandant of the French forces. We are demanding they abandon the Ohio Country to His Majesty. I must warn you, this will not be an easy duty. I received this," Dinwiddie said as he raised a letter and gestured, "from London. The king instructs that Virginia is to repel by force of arms any hostile attempt to occupy lands within the territorial limits of His Majesty's dominions. Rather than simply commencing hostilities, I intend to warn the French to cease their transgressions, demand they leave our land, and halt the construction of all forts on our lands. We also demand the return of some wayward Englishmen who have been held by the French. Obviously delivery of my letter involves a perilous winter journey through uncharted wilderness while enduring the constant threat of Indians. Indeed, you may be met with a hostile French force in response to your peaceful mission."

"I understand, Governor."

The governor's demeanor became stern. "I hope you do, Major. Your task will not only be to deliver my correspondence and wait for a reply, but to engage in important intelligence gathering. If, as I suspect, the French refuse to abandon their positions, a conflict may ensue. You are to ascertain the French positions, any forts, and the strengths of their troops. It is of paramount importance that you cement good relationships with the Indians of the area so that they may act as our allies in any dispute with the French. This mission will require not only physical strength and perseverance, but subtlety and keen observation."

George responded solemnly, "I appreciate your explanation, Governor. I am hopeful I can meet your expectations. I certainly have experience in the wilderness and have had many dealings with Indians in the course of my surveying. With the instruction of my late brother, I also have some ability in noting fortifications. I certainly do not presume your knowledge in diplomacy, but I am a careful observer and will dutifully report all my experiences and interactions . . . if, of course, I am appointed to this position."

George struggled to keep his face placid and expressionless. He knew he had exaggerated his experience, but he also desperately wanted the appointment and felt confident in his ability to succeed.

The governor stood, indicating the interview was over. "Thank you, Major. Please be kind enough to leave the address where you are residing with my secretary so I may contact you regarding the status of the appointment. I would be grateful if you would present my compliments to Colonel Fairfax when you next see him. Again, it is a pleasure, and I am hopeful that I will be positively contacting you shortly."

"I will be lodging at Wetherburn's Tavern and remain at your disposal." George bowed and left the governor's mansion, feeling optimistic and already thinking about the details of his intended trip.

Chapter 16

October 31, 1753 – Williamsburg

G eorge preferred to get up before sunrise. Wasting daylight was a sin his mother would not allow on the farm, and while they agreed on little, this maxim stuck. Thus, with satisfaction, George beheld the clear frosty morning with only wisps of clouds visible on the horizon stacked with reds, oranges, yellows, and purples transitioning from the dark predawn velvet that stretched overhead. Last night, within an hour of arriving back at the tavern, he received written notice that the governor had decided to appoint him to lead the mission.

As George rode out of Williamsburg with his charge from Governor Dinwiddie, he thought of the letter he had just written to his mother confirming his appointment as emissary of the Crown to meet the French. It was a great honor, but, at the same time, he knew his mother would only disapprove.

Yet another reason not to dally, thought George. *I'll deal with her dissatisfaction, if and when I return.*

George's thoughts then turned to the task at hand. *I'm certainly confident in the backwoods, but leading a group of men over the mountains into hostile territory is beyond my depth. Lawrence taught me the importance of retaining competent men and using their skills and understanding to my advantage. Colonel Fairfax said that smart officers should surround themselves with good sergeants to handle logistics and day-to-day operations. For this trip to succeed, I need experienced men who can help me execute a winter journey of more than five hundred miles round trip into hostile territory.* When George and the Colonel discussed the possibility of George's appointment as an envoy, the Colonel suggested George visit Fredericksburg and retain Jacob Van Braam to act as his French interpreter.

George knew Van Braam only as a fellow Mason and sometime fencing instructor.

I have no way of evaluating this Dutchman's skills, but I have limited choices, and the man has a good reputation, George admitted to himself. *His English is spotty. Hopefully his French is better.*

Having successfully retained Van Braam, the two men paused in Alexandria to purchase equipment and supplies for their long trip. The next stop was the result of clear and unequivocal instructions from *both* the Colonel and the governor. George was to travel to Wills Creek, near the Cumberland Gap, and hire Christopher Gist.

Although Gist was a civilian, George hoped he could play the role of the experienced "sergeant" on whom George could rely. Gist's intimate knowledge of the Indians, and his experience as a backwoodsman, made him a desirable member of the expedition. He was also extremely well read, and, depending on the audience, he had the ability to speak like a Virginia gentleman or a backwoods trapper. Having been previously hired by Virginia's elite to act as an agent in the Ohio, he was more an entrepreneur than a simple woodsman. As early as 1750, the Ohio Company had retained Gist to explore the Ohio territory and select sites for farming settlements. His knowledge made him the ideal individual to support George on the journey.

As George and Van Braam arrived at Gist's remote wilderness cabin, Gist was out front wielding a large axe with the practiced ease of a lumberjack, splitting hardwood logs as if he was cutting butter. Wood flew apart with each violent and practiced strike. Looking up at the approaching men, Gist set down his axe, wiped the sweat from his brow, and confidently strode toward George's horse.

Gist was striking in appearance, exuding vitality despite his forty-seven years. A mountain of a man, Gist stood approximately the same height as George but was far broader in the shoulders, with thick, strong arms and legs. Gist sported short salt-and-pepper hair, and his beard covered a swarthy, tanned, and heavily lined face.

"You must be Major Washington," Gist said as George's horse drew to a stop. Still several feet away and the horse stomped uncomfortably facing the goliath. "I've been expecting you. I received only yesterday letters from both the governor and Colonel Fairfax. You have mighty powerful friends." Gist's stone face transformed when he conversed to reveal a flexibility of features and expressiveness that made the man, despite his apparent hardness, both inviting and friendly.

George relaxed at Gist's welcome and replied in kind. "Indeed, Mr. Gist. However, it is not friendship that brings me to you today but rather an important mission on behalf of Virginia. I'm hopeful you will be able to join us. You come most highly recommended by both of those worthy gentlemen."

Now smiling broadly, Gist answered, "Well now, I could hardly say no to such fine folks, and it sounds like quite an adventure. The governor has also promised to pay me a pretty penny, so I am at your disposal, Major. I'm just finishing the last of my chores, I've got my saddlebags packed, and I've already said my good-byes. In fact, you'll be missing my wife and boys, as they are out. If you could give me a couple of minutes, I'll leave them a note."

As Gist was speaking, George dismounted and approached him. George noted that Gist, unlike most men, was at eye level and that he returned George's gaze with a relaxed confidence.

"I do not want to be responsible for you leaving your family prematurely," George said.

"Not at all, Major. You are very kind, but I've spent many years in the backcountry, and my comings and goings are part of my family's day-to-day. In our world, the 'comings' are more important than the 'goings.'"

"Well then, I am grateful you will join us, and we can proceed."

Gist stuck out his large, calloused hand. George was blessed with strong and large hands, yet when the men confirmed Gist's hiring with a handshake, Gist's grip was as formidable as that of any man George had ever met.

At Gist's suggestion, George also employed four other men to assist in carrying the baggage and providing support for the daunting journey. John Davison was also retained for his backwoods skills and ability to translate multiple Indian tongues.

While all the men he hired possessed greater age or experience, George had learned while leading survey parties not to undermine his control by showing uncertainty or trepidation. As Lawrence often explained to him, the difference between a "leader" and a "follower" was that a "leader pretends he knows what he is doing." Likewise, before he left on this expedition, the Colonel admonished George, "These men are not your friends. They are your subordinates. Respect must come first, and friendship *may* come later. Be fair, just, and decisive, but don't worry about hurting their 'feelings.'" George knew he must take both mentors' instructions to heart as he undertook the journey.

A harsh breeze rolled down the hills, slapping George's face and waking him to the heavy duty resting on his shoulders. A half dozen men left Wills Creek with twice as many horses, heavy packs, and an untested leader on a dangerous mission.

George was surprised by the rigor of the journey and his lack of preparation for winter travel. While he had spent an enormous amount of time in the backwoods since his first major surveying trip with Will years earlier, he worked primarily in the spring and fall—never in the winter months. Traveling through thick forests at high elevations, George was grateful for Gist and the experience of his men in navigating the difficult conditions.

Every night, the men had to select a campsite defensible from an Indian attack, sheltered from the wind, and located near water, yet not too close to risk flooding. The heavy—and often wet—tents had to be unloaded and erected. Wood had to be collected. Fires had to be started. Meanwhile the horses had to be unpacked, and these valuable animals needed to be inspected, fed, and carefully tethered. Soon after the men inhaled their meals after a long hard day, they collapsed under their blankets, too tired to do anything but sleep. The next morning, the laborious process of repacking started all over again. Wet and cold, day after day, the men slogged on for two hundred and fifty miles in snow, cold, and ice through the uninhabited wilderness.

By mid-November, they'd crossed the three-thousand-foot-high ridges of the Allegheny Mountains and passed through many thick forests and treacherous streams. Cold temperatures, freezing rain, and snow followed the men, soaking them to the skin in a way that could drive even the most seasoned woodsman to despair that he would never be warm again.

As they passed the confluence of the Ohio and Monongahela Rivers, George noted in his journal that the land was "extremely well situated" for building a fort that would provide "absolute Command of both Rivers." He could not know it at the time, but this future site of Fort Duquesne would be the focus of his life for the next five years.

Chapter 17

November 22, 1753 - Logstown

O ne important goal of the trip was to make contact with the Seneca chief known as "the Half King" and secure him as a British ally. George arrived at the isolated outpost of Logstown and waited while the Half King was summoned from a hunting trip.

After waiting a few days, on a cold, late autumn afternoon, George heard a commotion. He walked outside his tent to see the Half King approaching. George's attention was immediately drawn to the man's dark and intelligent eyes, which were already locked on George. In his early fifties, the Half King was nevertheless fit and whip-handle lean, with strands of muscles showing through his throat and arms. He wore a bizarre mixture of English and Indian attire, with his hair drawn back with feathers and inserted into clasps, securing a ponytail. Over a finely made Indian leather shirt, he wore a red English soldier's overcoat accented by a gorget, Indian leather leggings, and moccasins. He had a knife and tomahawk stuck under an English gentleman's belt, and in his right hand, he held an English officer's tricorn hat.

George raised an open right palm in greeting, and the chief reciprocated. Through George's interpreter, John Davison, the Half King said, "Welcome, one called Major Washington, but to us, your name was and is Conotocarius, meaning 'town taker' or 'devourer of villages.' This proud name was given to the one named John Washington. You come from a line of brave and noble warriors, and we welcome you as a brother."

George tried to hide his surprise that his great-grandfather, John Washington, was known to the Senecas. While one hundred years was a long time for British subjects, to the Senecas, a tribe that had ruled the area for centuries, it represented a lapse brief enough still to be part of the collective memory.

George suddenly realized his reaction was being gauged under the Half King's unblinking gaze. With a confident smile and nod, he responded, "I am on an important mission from your brother and our great King George, whose might stretches over great seas and mountains. We have come to deliver a message to the French commandant to tell him to leave these lands so that your brothers, the English, and your people may live in peace unmolested."

After the translation, the chief nodded in agreement. "It will be so. We will provide an escort for our brothers, the English, to carry this message to the French." Again with the help of Davison, the Half King explained that Fort Le Boeuf was four or five days' travel away; he also told them the best route and indicated that guides would be supplied.

Acknowledging the Half King's offered assistance, George asked, "Have you met the commandant of the fort?"

Gist had previously explained that Indians prided themselves on the ability to recall conversations verbatim. The Half King, who had been sitting on a log as they spoke, stood with a theatrical flourish. With a look and pause that compelled all nearby to fix on him, he proceeded to repeat his statement to the French commandant: "Both you and the English are white. We live in a country between. The land does not belong either to one or the other; but the Great Being above allows it as a place of residence for us. So, Fathers, I desire you to withdraw, as have our Brothers the English." Even before George was done hearing the translation, he had a sense of the Half King's statement for the exaggerated, yet expressive hand gestures. When completed, George gave an appreciative nod.

The Half King then repeated the response of the French commandant: "You need not put yourself to the trouble of speaking, for I will not hear you. The Indians are mere flies or mosquitoes." The Half King slapped his arm mimicking the killing of a mosquito. "I will go down that river and will build upon what I choose. If anyone tries to block the River, I have sufficient forces to burst it open and tread under my feet all that stand in opposition together with their allies." Again, with his hands, George could almost see the river and the French treading on their enemies as the Half King stomped on the ground. "My force is as numerous as sand upon the seashore; therefore here is your wampum, I fling it at you. Child, you talk foolish."

George nodded his head sympathetically in response to the Half King's explanation of the commandant's insults.

With a somber but earnest tone, George replied, "Brother, you may rest assured that your brother, the governor of Virginia, does not hold you in contempt as the French do. We respect you and will never cast you aside."

Following the translation, the Half King walked over and clasped George's forearms, nodding approval. The meeting ended with further exchanges of greetings, the sharing of wampum and tobacco, and promises to meet in the chief's longhouse with other leaders of the Six Nations, who would escort George's party to the French.

As George approached the bark longhouse the next day, it reminded him of the barns and outbuildings that dotted the Virginia countryside. However, as he got closer, the differences became apparent. The siding and roof were made of overlapping bark, with poles supporting a squared frame approximately twenty feet wide and eighty feet long. Strips of elm bark were lashed with rope to a sturdy wood frame.

As he entered the surprisingly airy interior, it was warm, dark, and smoky, with a central fire providing heat and light entering through vents in the sloped roofed ceiling. There appeared to be only two openings at either end of the long row house and smoke holes above two well-separated fires. The interior was full, as it appeared to accommodate multiple clans with two-tiered bunks lining the walls. At the top of the interior wood framework were storage areas for food and clothing.

A circle of elaborately dressed Indian chiefs sat around the central fire and bade George to join them. A man with long, powerful legs ideally built for the saddle, George was not accustomed to sitting "Indian style" and awkwardly joined the Indians on the ground. Friendly smiles were suppressed as he attempted to cross his large and thick legs.

Through Davison, George addressed the group: "Brothers, I have called you together in council, by order of your brother, the Governor of Virginia. I am sent to deliver a letter to the French Commandant of very great importance to your brothers, friends, and allies, the English. Your brother, the Governor, calls upon you, the Sachems of the Six Nations, for your advice and assistance in meeting the French." Pausing, George ensured he still had the leaders' attention and continued. "We ask for some of your young men to conduct and provide provisions for us on our way and to be protected against those French Indians, that have taken up the hatchet against us. Your brothers and our governor treats you as good friends and allies and holds you in great esteem. To confirm what I have said, I give you this string of wampum."

The Half King accepted the wampum, examined it appreciatively, then replied, "Now, my brothers. In regard to what my brother, the Governor, desires of me, I return you this answer: I rely upon you as a brother ought to do." Grabbing his heart with one hand, he reached toward George with the other and said, "As you say, we are brothers, and one people; we shall put heart in hand, and speak to our fathers, the French, concerning the offensive speech they made to me, and you may depend that we will endeavor to guard you on your travels."

With the meeting concluded, George ducked to exit the longhouse, winced, and covered his eyes from the bright autumn sun. *Well, that went as well as could be expected. They clearly don't like the French and are willing to cooperate with us, but they are holding back. At least they are willing to go with me to face the French at a nearby trading post. I must use our travel time to my advantage to further this alliance.*

George waved to his men in the distance, smelling meat on the fire and realizing, for the first time, that he was thirsty, hungry, and exhausted from the tension of his first diplomatic encounter.

Chapter 18

December 4, 1753 – Venango Trading Post

After a frustrating delay of several days waiting for other Indian representatives, the Half King, along with Chiefs White Thunder and Jeskakake, led George and his men to the abandoned trading post now occupied by the French. George wore his "Indian walking dress" of buckskins, leggings, thick moccasins, and a heavy match coat—a long cloak made of fur skins and leather—as he traveled through the backwoods. However, before meeting the French, he made a point of changing into his new and finely made officer's uniform. Fully appointed, the tall young Virginian looked the dashing soldier.

George reminded himself, as Lawrence had often admonished him: "Look a man directly in his eyes. Your height and strength of character are an advantage." George knew a stare from his penetrating blue-gray eyes caused others to blanch or become uncomfortable. Today was to be the ultimate test of Lawrence's lessons.

As George entered the clearing in front of the former trading post, the French fleur-de-lis was clearly visible on a pole prominently placed a dozen yards in front of the front door. A well-appointed French officer, in an unmistakable white uniform with blue trim, stepped through the doorway and stood at attention, flanked by two junior officers with swords in their scabbards. He appeared to be in his midforties. He had unusually dark skin but an unmistakable French visage, including a classically pointed aquiline nose framed by dark eyes. George's Indian escorts had informed him that French soldiers were deployed in the woods around the post with muskets at the ready. The apparently unflappable commanding French officer stood with his hands confidently clasped behind his back.

George mused, *At least they are not shooting at me . . . yet.*

In his consultations with the Indians, it was agreed that they would approach the French fully armed. To do otherwise would be viewed as a submission to the French, something the Indians would not endure— especially given the chiding the Half King had suffered from the French commandant. Thus George could feel the guns of the French on him as he stepped within ten feet of the French officer. George removed his hat and bowed to the French captain.

"My compliments. I am Major George Washington. I am at your disposal. I offer greetings from His Britannic Majesty, and I bear a letter from Governor Dinwiddie of Virginia, to be presented to the French commandant."

Jacob Van Braam, whom George had brought along as his French translator, began to speak, but the French Captain held up his hand to stop him. Then, with an exaggerated flourish as he removed his hat and bowed deeply, he responded in accented English, "The pleasure is entirely mine, Major. I am Captain Philippe Thomas de Joncaire, sieur de Chabert, and am pleased to make your acquaintance. Your letter is better directed to my commander located at Fort Le Boeuf, which remains some days' travel. I would be remiss if I did not offer you the hospitality of a meal, and, better yet, a fine French wine. In the morning, if you are so disposed, we may proceed to meet my commandant and deliver your communiqué."

Relief washed over George. "Yes . . . Yes indeed, Captain, that would be most agreeable."

Captain Joncaire gestured toward the ramshackle former trading post, which was little more than a drab log cabin. "Please, Major, would you be so kind as to join me inside for some refreshments while a meal is being prepared? I will instruct my men to take their ease, and I respectfully suggest you do likewise. You are welcome, as you are clearly on a mission of diplomacy."

Then, in rapid French, Joncaire spoke to his subordinate officers, signals were given, and smiling French soldiers began to appear from the surrounding woods with their rifles slung over their shoulders. George nodded to his men, who likewise became visibly relaxed. Gist leaned forward and asked for George's permission for his men and the Indians to set up camp in a nearby clearing. With those matters settled, George followed Joncaire into the meager cabin.

George's trepidation at the prospect of meeting the French was quickly replaced with the realization that the French captain, despite his bravado, had been nervous too. Once the tension evaporated, the captain took on a bemused and friendly expression.

As wine flowed freely, it became apparent the French officer was trying to solicit information from George regarding British intentions. George responded, "In all honesty, Captain, I know little. This is obviously valuable territory, but I am a mere messenger. You, however, at great expense, have been brought to this distant land by your king. It appears France has designs on this land. Am I correct?"

As the French officer continued to drink, his English became harder to understand, yet he spoke more openly. "My dear Major, I tell you that France will take possession of the Ohio, even though we know that England will raise two men for our one. By the time England finally acts, we will be so fortified that it will be a *fait accompli*—the Ohio will be ours. We will have forts along the rivers stretching from Quebec City to Fort Le Boeuf and along the great rivers of New France down to New Orleans, and all the while the Allegheny Mountains will guard our flank." Then, with an exaggerated nod of satisfaction and a knowing smile, he said, "You will see." Tapping George's arm, Joncaire continued, "But, Major, we are but pawns in a greater game. I bid you pleasant dreams, and tomorrow we are off to see my commandant." Joncaire stood somewhat unsteadily and bowed as George did likewise and exited the cabin.

As George's party and the Indians prepared to leave with the French to Fort Le Boeuf, Captain Joncaire appeared in their midst, carrying gifts. With exaggerated—and to George's eyes, clearly feigned—surprise, Joncaire exclaimed, "What! Major Washington, you did not tell me that you were traveling with the great chiefs of the Six Nations. If you had told me, I would have invited them to join us for supper last night!"

Unable to hide his irritation, George sputtered, "You . . . You knew the Indians were with us, Captain."

What? The French bastard is trying to undermine me with the Indians!

Without looking at George, Joncaire replied in English, "I would never have excluded my dear friends, had I known, Major." Then, without missing a beat, he spread his arms wide and switched to Iroquois. George frantically waved for Davison to translate as the Indians smiled, bowed, and accepted the gifts of wampum and liquor from Joncaire.

Grating at the one-upmanship, George whispered to Davison, "Well, man, what did they say?"

"I am sorry, Major. They are speaking extremely fast, and Captain Joncaire has his back to us. I can tell you one thing, sir: he speaks like he is one of the savages himself. He seems to be apologizing that you didn't tell Joncaire that the sachems were with you, and he seems to be extending an invitation for them to come to Fort Le Boeuf to meet the commandant with you . . . and him . . . or something along those lines."

"Well, let's get what's left of our sorry backsides over there and try to, albeit politely, set the record straight."

Over the next two hours, as more gifts, especially liquor, were heaped on the Indians by both parties, George began to understand Joncaire was sharper than he appeared at first blush.

Once they got under way, George gestured for Gist to ride beside him. In the course of the hardships of the trip, Gist's strength of will, judgment, and experience had profoundly impressed George. While not in uniform, Gist had proven to be precisely the type of able sergeant Colonel Fairfax had told George to rely on.

George knew Gist's backwoods humor was a contrived affectation. Gist was an educated man, born to a prosperous Baltimore family. Unfortunately, through mismanagement or happenstance, he had lost his fortune. As a result, he was now a down-on-his-luck woodsman scout, far removed from genteel Baltimore society. George suspected Gist's folksy demeanor was a conscious—or unconscious—way of avoiding discussions of his past business and personal failures.

Twisting in his saddle to face Gist, George asked, "Well, Mr. Gist, have you or any of the men had a chance to learn anything about the fort or the French?"

"A bit, Major," Gist said, gesturing with his head toward the other men riding behind them. "Some of the lads speak a bit of French, and some of the Frogs mangle English. The men have been doing a bit of friendly trading—the usual: French wine for Virginia tobacco. It sounds like there are about fifteen hundred Frenchies in the area on this side of Oswago Lake. When the old French general died, they dispersed about a hundred and fifty men to each of four garrisons, and they have a few other forts spread out along about a six-hundred-mile stretch of rivers and lakes. The Frogs think they're here to stay, and they're fixin' for a fight."

"Our host, Captain Joncaire, is devious," George growled, "as we all experienced this morning when he performed his little 'fantasy play' with the sachems regarding the 'invitations' to supper. The only good news is that he shared with me a bit more than he should had last night. Remind our boys to listen hard and say little."

Gist nodded in acknowledgment and allowed his horse to slow and drift back to pass the word to the other men.

Chapter 19

December 12, 1753 - Fort Le Bœuf

After a forty-mile trek through swamps, and after enduring almost constant rain and snow, the party arrived at Fort Le Boeuf on the west side of French Creek, close to the southeastern shore of Lake Erie. The fort, which was intended to house 150 men, was 180 foot square with four corner bastions. The walls were made of squared chestnut logs laid on top of each other instead of a typical vertical stockade. Portholes for cannon and loopholes for small arms were cut into the bastions, each of which mounted six-pounder cannon; one four-pounder cannon guarded the gate. Four buildings stood inside the enclosure, including a masonry powder magazine. The small buildings outside the fort, including log barracks and stables, provided support, although they could not benefit from the fort's protection.

As much as possible, George noted the fort's layout as he passed through the gate and was warmly welcomed by the French soldiers. Leaving Gist and Van Braam outside the commandant's house, George entered the most imposing of the small buildings inside the fort, which had windows and a porch.

He could feel his heart pounding in his chest as he stood ready to fulfill his duty. He was ushered into a sparsely appointed room with a table, candles, and two wooden chairs left askew near the small window in the corner. George took a deep breath and made an effort to calm himself before making the speech he had so long prepared. He could hear faint sounds from the outer rooms, but there was no indication anyone was approaching.

As the minutes rolled by, George tried to control his irritation that they were keeping an emissary from the king of England waiting. He could almost hear Lawrence whispering in his ear, "Calm down, George.

Controlled anger is a strength; uncontrolled anger is what you must guard against most." George nearly responded aloud, "I know, Lawrence."

After another deep breath, he arranged the chairs so that he might have his back to the window, illuminating his visitor's face. He then sat down in the chair, determined to remain relaxed.

After what seemed an interminable delay, the rumble of boots announced the commandant's approach. George snapped to his feet. Once again, he could feel his heart pounding as the door swung open. The candles on the table nearly flickered out under the press of air as the commandant and his entourage entered the small room. George stood transfixed, making no motion or statement. Regaining his composure, George bowed slightly.

"Monsieur," George said, "I present the compliments of His Britannic Majesty and His Excellency, the Governor of Virginia. I am Major George Washington, your servant." He then nervously bowed again.

The man appeared elderly to George, at least fifty. He wore an eye patch and was somewhat disheveled, not the imposing military figure George had anticipated. With a slight look of irritation, the commandant turned toward Joncaire and spoke in a flurry of French.

Captain Joncaire responded, "Major Washington, may I present His Excellency, Commandant Jacques Le Gardeur, sieur de Saint-Pierre, Knight of the Military Order of Saint Louis, commander of this fort."

George again gave a bow in response and was met with a slight, though discernible, nod and brief half smile from the commandant.

"On behalf of the Crown and the governor," George said, "I am charged with presenting you, sir, with this letter. I am instructed to await a response." George then handed over the letter, which still bore the unbroken wax seal of Governor Dinwiddie.

Without looking at the letter or breaking the seal, the commandant bowed and handed it to Captain Joncaire. Without taking his only visible eye off George, the commandant rattled off a couple of orders in rapid French and then left the room without further comment.

Captain Joncaire stood alone in the room with George, then said, "Well, my friend, I am instructed to have someone conduct you to a comfortable room and provide food and all courtesies to you and your men. Someone will be coming to get you shortly. *Adieu.*"

As the door closed, George realized he had stopped breathing. Feeling the weight of the world taken off his shoulders, he exhaled as he slumped into one of the empty chairs. He was startled when a moment later, there was a knock at the door, and a young officer conducted him to an adequate room with a bed, window, and washbasin. He was told in broken English that supper would be served at seven, and that he was free to walk about the fort.

Remembering his charge to not only deliver the letter but also ascertain French capabilities, George immediately commenced his reconnaissance. After his brief tour of the fort and surrounding area, George retired to his room. As he entered, he was surprised to see Captain Joncaire sitting on the bed, his feet up and his hands behind his head.

"Have you discovered all our secrets?" the smiling Joncaire asked as he hopped down from the bed with a flourish and a theatrical bow.

George, somewhat taken aback, sputtered, "Captain . . . I . . . I was only taking a stroll."

"Never mind, never mind. I should scold you for giving me unnecessary work. I have been charged with assisting in translating your damn letter. I understand you have a man in your party who speaks passable French. Is that correct?"

"Yes, Mr. Van Braam is Dutch, but he also speaks French."

"Well, my commandant is less than pleased with my translation, and we want to make sure we accurately understand your country's insolent demands," Joncaire said with a wink. "Could I trouble you to collect your man and have him assist me in the translation?"

"By all means, I will bring him to you directly."

"*Merci.* Please then be kind enough to join the commandant and me for our evening meal in the main dining room in two hours."

As Joncaire turned to leave, he stopped, paused, and then spoke with what George sensed was a forced attempt to be nonchalant, "My commandant has suggested that perhaps you should proceed to Quebec to present your communication directly to the governor of Canada. This would permit the clearest possible response on behalf of our emperor to your king's demands. What do you say, my friend? Quebec is beautiful and the women lovely. I can assure you that you would be received with all courtesy and respect."

George paused to consider Joncaire's offer. *This is a trap—and contrary to the governor's orders.* George recalled Dinwiddie's instructions. *I am supposed to get a prompt response. If I am sent off to Canada, heaven knows when I will get back. No. I will get what answer I can here and get back to Virginia as soon as possible to warn them of the French preparations.*

Resolved, George responded evenly, "Please extend my appreciation to the commandant for his kind offer. However, I have been instructed to return to Virginia with all dispatch. I believe to do otherwise would violate my superior's clear orders. I am sure you understand."

Joncaire smiled and nodded in a manner that made George realize he may have avoided yet another French scheme to thwart his efforts. "We cannot have that, *mon* Major," Joncaire said smoothly. "I will forward your response. In the meantime, I look forward to seeing you this evening."

At the appointed time and with some anxiety—and after carefully inspecting, cleaning, and brushing his uniform—George entered the dining room. As he did so, the French officers milling about turned and bowed. George reciprocated and awkwardly stood some distance away as a silence descended over the room.

Captain Joncaire strode in from around the corner and exclaimed, "Major Washington! I am so glad you are here. Let me introduce my brothers in arms."

With that, the tension was broken, and George was quickly presented to the half dozen officers present. No one sat at the table until the commandant entered. They all stood at attention and bowed in unison. George did likewise, in the interests of courtesy and diplomacy.

The table was well appointed, although not elaborately set. Serviceable silverware, china plates, and serving dishes were used, but crystal was absent. After a meal of well-cooked venison, fish, potatoes, and good French wine, the conversation shifted to George's task.

Through Captain Joncaire, the commandant asked in a friendly tone, "Did you face many exciting challenges in traversing the mountains in these difficult conditions, Major Washington?"

Not wanting to appear to be bragging or complaining, George answered in a measured tone, "Thank you for asking. The weather was sometimes unpleasant, but we were able to make a quick trip through these territories, as they have long been familiar and occupied by my people."

The commandant spoke with more edge in his voice as he responded. "When we entered these lands, they were devoid of any signs of an English presence. In 1749, we sailed down the Ohio, depositing a series of lead plates inscribed with our French sovereign's seal, settling any question of French sovereignty. We were the first to occupy these lands, and we shall continue going forward."

George realized everyone in the room was watching intently. He could feel his face redden, and he tried to remain calm. He had discussed these issues with the governor, and he replied as instructed. "Your Excellency, while I understand you may have recently deposited some plates along this river, the fact remains that the Virginia Company was chartered by our sovereign in 1606, and we claim the right to possession through and to the Mississippi and beyond."

The commandant's face darkened as the translation was relayed. "For such a young man, you claim much."

George could feel his back straightening at the slight. He forced himself to reply deliberately, but knew tensions were rising. "I claim nothing, Your Excellency. I am merely a messenger and servant of my colony and king."

After Joncaire translated for the commandant and waited for a response, he interjected with a grin, "Is it not our lot in life as soldiers to fight and die on the whims of our sovereigns? Our will is not our own—thank the Lord for good wine to keep us distracted from this troubled world." He then quickly translated his comment to his fellow officers and was met with uncomfortable nods of agreement as they awaited the commandant's response.

This is going badly, George thought. *I was being too haughty and aggressive. Think! You heard what Joncaire translated . . . do I remember enough French?* George had learned some French from the Reverend James Marye at St. George's Church in Fredericksburg. He'd never felt confident enough to claim any ability to speak French, but he could put together a few simple phrases.

I guess this is the time to let the cat out of the bag. Here goes . . .

With a broad forced smile, and before the commandant could respond to Joncaire's translation, George said loudly and with far more confidence than he felt, *"Pour vin bon et femmes du mauvaises"* and raised his glass in a toast.

After a moment of surprised silence, the commandant threw his head back and laughed, followed immediately by the room erupting in laughter. The table was pounded, and drinks were raised all around, including by the commandant.

Over the din, George leaned toward Joncaire. "Did I say it right? 'To good wine and bad women'?"

Laughing and slapping George on the back, Joncaire roared over the din, "Close enough, my friend! You speak French? What other secrets have you been keeping from me?"

"I only speak enough French to get my face slapped!" George exclaimed, laughing at his own joke.

Joncaire then turned to the group and translated George's quip. The room exploded again with laughter, and glasses were raised once more.

With that, the tension was broken, and a pleasant evening followed. George felt relieved he had survived the meal without serious incident and was grateful for the kindness of Captain Joncaire and divine inspiration in recalling a bit of French.

Chapter 20

December 13, 1753 – Fort Le Bœuf

The next morning, after breakfast, George walked out to meet Gist and his men.

"Good morning, Mr. Gist. How are you and the men faring?"

"Good morning to you, Major. Fine—except the frog-eating bastards are either snarling at the men or wanting to bugger them," answered a straight-faced Gist.

After the tension of the last twenty-four hours, George could not help but laugh. "Well, Mr. Gist, I guess if I had to choose, I'd rather have them fight, but at this point, let's have them do neither."

"As you wish, Major, but we have been on the trail for a long time."

"You'll have to keep the men in line for a while longer. I am told the commandant and his men are considering my letter. Captain Joncaire tells me to not expect an answer anytime soon. Nevertheless, make sure the men are ready to go on short notice; as soon as I have an answer, I want to start heading home."

"Fair enough, Major. I'll keep the boys busy and out of trouble."

"Thank you, Mr. Gist."

As casually as he could, George began to survey the entire fort—carefully stepping off dimensions, counting numbers of cannon, and engaging in the close observation Governor Dinwiddie required. Whenever he was sure no one was looking, he quickly pulled out his pocket notebook, recording what he saw. George and his men had already observed 220 birch-bark and pine canoes drawn up on shore and ready to reinforce the French downstream after the spring thaw. They also confirmed that the French were surveying and beginning construction of a large fort at the confluence of the Allegheny and Monongahela

Rivers—the head of the Ohio River. By the end of the day, George was confident he had thoroughly surveyed the fort and its surroundings.

George walked out to the tents where his men and the Indians had set up camp, and he soon found the Half King. As George approached, the chief stood, looking decidedly uncomfortable.

Through an interpreter, George asked, "Great Chief, I have noted that you have spent time speaking with the French. Would you be kind enough to tell me the subject of your discussions?"

"Brother Conotocarius, I have told them, as I have told you, of my people's desire to be left alone on the land. This commandant is kinder than the one who offended me before. Monsieur Joncaire is very different. His mother was one of my people, and he speaks my language well. He has offered us guns and liquor and other demonstrations of friendship," Davison, the translator, explained on the Half King's behalf.

By Christ! I have got to get him out of here before the French win him over, George thought. He tried to remain calm as he had the interpreter respond, "My friend and brother, the French do not speak the truth. They are not your brothers and partners as we are, and they seek to displace you from your land. You should leave this place now, and I will follow."

With an exaggerated shake of his head, the Half King disagreed. "This new Frenchman is generous and has encouraged us to stay and talk. He promises love and friendship and to live in peace with us. The Six Nations do not wish to fight with either the English or the French. The English have treated us well, but perhaps this new French man will be different."

He is a sly old fox. Is he playing us off each other?

"Brother, you cannot believe him," George responded. "The policy of the French is to control these lands and your peoples. We are your partners and brothers. They wish to rule over you and all your land and peoples. I beg you not to forget the last French commandant."

The Half King paused for a long time after receiving the translation.

Finally he said, "I must think on this and speak with the other chiefs. We do not leave today."

Damn! Damn! Damn! These French bastards are keeping me here and using the opportunity to play the Indians against me. I need to talk to the commandant.

George stormed across the field and into the fort, finding the affable Captain Joncaire sitting on a chair, leaning up against a building and joking with a group of young French officers. As George stomped into their midst, all conversation immediately ceased.

Joncaire smoothly and confidently got to his feet. "Major Washington, you look unhappy and—"

George, in no mood for friendly banter, interrupted, "I want to see the commandant . . . now, *please.*"

"My dear friend, as you know, he is a busy man, but . . . we shall see what we can do." The captain began strolling across the compound toward the commandant's office, with George at his heels.

"*Mon jeune ami*, I will find you if he is available. You need not follow me," Joncaire said, ignoring George's rudeness and agitation.

"I'll wait. I would like to talk to him *now*," George snapped as they entered the main building.

As George paced, waiting for the commandant, here could hear a smattering of heated French coming from the inner office. Joncaire reappeared after a few minutes. "The commandant is indisposed. Perhaps later—"

George held his ground and interrupted again. "I would like to talk to the commandant *now*. If necessary, I will wait . . . but I am confident the commandant will not be discourteous."

For the first time, Joncaire looked disappointed. He stared at George in exasperation. After a pause, he said formally, "Please sit down, Major Washington. I will inform the commandant again, and he will see you at his earliest convenience."

George sat, waited, and seethed. After a time, he began to calm down and thought, *Anger, George . . . You must control your anger. What have you accomplished today? You have managed to alienate the only Frenchman with whom you have developed any relationship. And what do you intend to do? Complain that they are plotting to win over the Indians? You're trying to do the same bloody thing. Joncaire is just better at it! You idiot. What are you going to say when you get in the room with the commandant? "Leave the Indians alone?" He will laugh in your face.*

Fine. So mentioning the Indians would be a mistake. It would only emphasize our anxiety and weakness. Shall I complain about the delay? It has only been a day and a half. He may be waiting for instructions from others. A gentle reminder would seem in order. What else? The English prisoners? Yes! I can raise the issue of them. I should have done it already. I can make a protest on that issue. Their incarceration would justify my attitude.

Deep breath and relax. Face placid and controlled. They have treated you with courtesy and you must do likewise. It was fortunate they made me wait. I will not lose control again.

After about an hour, a cool Captain Joncaire appeared and George stood.

"The commandant will see you now." With that, Joncaire opened the door and followed George into the commandant's office. Le Gardeur sat behind the desk and did not stand when George entered. Looking up from a sheath of papers, he simply said, "*Oui?*"

"Commandant Le Gardeur, thank you for seeing me. I obviously continue to await a response to my governor and king's letter. However, I have been told that numerous British subjects are being held by French forces. Let me protest such actions in the strongest terms. We do not believe you have any authority to hold the king's subjects on these lands."

George was somewhat unnerved as the commandant looked directly at him with his one good eye as Joncaire translated the reply: "We will answer the letter when we answer. You will wait. As to these alleged English subjects, they are individuals residing in country belonging to His Majesty the Emperor of France, and as such, they are either subjects of the French Crown and its justice, or they are trespassing Englishmen who have no right to tread upon French lands or waters. I will make a prisoner of every man who trespasses on the Ohio or its waters. Thank you, Major. That is all."

George was taken aback by the abruptness of the statement. The man's body language made it clear that it was not simply a matter of the translation. Feeling the need to say something answering the rebuke, George said tartly, "I will inform my government of your unsatisfactory response."

The translation came back quickly: "I hope you do. Good day."

With that, George was ushered out of the room.

The following morning, a knock came at the door. Captain Joncaire sauntered in, tapping an envelope in his hand and apparently having forgotten—or forgiven—the unpleasantness of the previous day.

"*Bonjour*, Major. I hope this morning finds you rested and well?"

George stood, his eyes on the letter. "Quite so, Captain."

"Good, because I believe you will be leaving us shortly. In this awful weather, you will need all your strength to get home. My commandant has charged me with providing you with this." Joncaire handed George the sealed envelope.

"Can you tell me what it says?"

"No," replied a somber Joncaire.

"I understand," George said, looking downcast.

A mischievous grin spread across Joncaire's face. "A little joke. The answer is 'no.'"

With dawning understanding, George replied, "France has rejected the demand to leave."

"But of course, *mon ami*. How could we do otherwise?" Then Joncaire walked over and sat on the only chair in the room, putting his feet up on the windowsill. His shrewd eyes sparkled. "We are soldiers, are we not? I suspect this will mean war. This is the chosen vocation for me and my father. It is always good to have a friend on the other side, if there is a war. Don't you think so?"

George looked at the man sitting at the window and realized that they had become friends of a sort. George decided for the first time to use Joncaire's Christian name. "Honestly, Philippe, I don't know."

With a broad smile, Joncaire said, "Well, I do, George. I must leave now and make sure you have provisions for your trip. No doubt you will want to talk to your men. The commandant, in his wisdom, is sending me back with you to the trading post. I will reoccupy my little prison of tediousness from which you rescued me. *Bon suit, bon ami.*" Before George could respond further, Joncaire was out the door and down the hall. George was close behind him, heading to the tents to inform Gist and the Indians of their impending departure.

George spent the rest of the day on two important tasks. First, he had to arrange the loading of the generous supplies the French had provided for his trip home. Second, he had to "battle" Joncaire over the Indians. Joncaire and the French were using every strategy at their disposal, including promises of even more gifts and liquor, to convince the Indians to remain and not travel with George and his party. The Half King initially refused to go, indicating he'd promised the commandant he would stay. Meanwhile, George's anxiety grew as daily snowfall and worsening weather made the prospect of his return to Virginia ever more daunting. Finally, on the morning of December 16, the Half King reversed himself again. The Indians, George, and his men—escorted by Joncaire—set off downriver back to the Venango trading post to collect their horses.

During their return trip, George and his men were often required to exit their canoes and pull their supplies over portages and obstacles, or to wade through ice-cold streams. Their French "escorts" remained hot on their heels in an overcrowded boat laden with liquor and weapons intended as gifts for the Indians. To the delight of George's party, and the French's embarrassment, the French twice overturned their canoes and lost supplies, prompting roars of laughter from George, his men, and the Indians. After a frigid, tedious, and exhausting trip, they arrived at the Venango trading post.

Chapter 21

December 25, 1753 - Venango Trading Post

George pulled the Half King out of Joncaire's earshot. "Good brother, will you and your party travel with me over the mountains to my native lands, or at least share part of the journey with me?" George implored through an interpreter.

Grabbing his own chest, the Half King responded, "Brother Conotocarius, it pains my heart, but we cannot travel with you, as Chief White Thunder has hurt himself and is unwell. We must go by canoe to our home and cannot suffer an overland walk. You will go in peace without us, but carry our friendship to your great Governor Dinwiddie."

"Good Chief, it saddens me that we cannot travel together and that the honorable White Thunder is unwell. I caution you that Monsieur Joncaire will attempt to trick you to his favor."

The Half King smiled patiently as he received the translation and responded, "Friend and brother, you do not need to worry. I know the French well—my real friends are the English. I am more concerned about you. I worry that you do not have food and provisions for the difficult journey home."

After assuring the Half King he and his men would be fine, George waved to the Chief and his party as they headed downriver. At some level, George was relieved to see them go, because it meant an end to the battle with Joncaire for the Indians' loyalty.

Despite his growing frustration with Captain Joncaire, George could not help but have a grudging respect for the man's persistence and abilities. He remained affable and helpful while simultaneously doing his duty by attempting to gain favor with the Indians.

As George walked through the door of the small trading post, Joncaire stood. "Time to wish you *au revoir*, Major?"

George smiled wistfully and inclined his head.

Suddenly Joncaire strode across the room and grabbed George by the shoulders, quickly kissing him on each cheek. "I wish you a long and happy life, my friend, or a quick and honorable death."

Flustered, George could only respond, "And you, too," as Joncaire glided out of the cabin. As George exited, a smirking Christopher Gist was on the porch, leaning against the wall not far from the open cabin door. As he began to deliver one of his patented folksy witticisms, George cut him off: "Please, Mr. Gist, no comments. I have just been kissed by a damn Frenchman. Don't add to a poor soldier's suffering."

Gist chuckled. "How could I, Major? You stole my line." Then Gist's features darkened. "I am afraid we both could use a laugh. Mr. Van Braam and I have some unhappy news."

"What is it?" a now serious George asked.

"The Frenchies and Indians were watching our horses . . ." Gist shook his head and spit in disgust. "The poxed bastards let the poor things freeze and starve! We'll get what we can out of them, but the horses are a sorry mess, Major."

Van Braam approached, hearing Gist's complaint. "Ja. 'Tis correct."

"Well, gentlemen, I see no reason for further delay. The horses are not going to get any stronger sitting in this rat hole. Besides, the sooner we get away, the happier I will be. Load 'em up, Mr. Gist."

"Yes, Major."

Chapter 22

December 25, 1753 - Ohio Wilderness

Unfortunately Gist's assessment of the horses was correct. In short order, the horses became less able to travel each day. After a cold, wet, and uncomfortable Christmas, George came to a decision and assembled the group. "Gentlemen, the message I carry from the French must be returned to Williamsburg with the greatest dispatch so that our country may protect itself against the coming French onslaught. Therefore I have determined the most appropriate course is to place all our baggage and remaining horses in the charge of Mr. Van Braam, who will guide the party back to Virginia along the safest, albeit somewhat slower, route. In the meantime, Mr. Gist and I will load our packs and proceed by foot overland in earnest. We are in a race against time, gentlemen; I wish us all Godspeed."

After George's announcement, Gist pulled him aside. "Major, please do not take this as insolence or questioning your authority, but an overland trek is *very* difficult. You are an extraordinary horseman and obviously a very strong man, but I can tell you from personal experience, traveling by foot, even in Indian walking dress, will be profoundly challenging."

George felt a flush of anger. *If this old man can do the walk, so can I.*

"I do not believe we have any real choice, Mr. Gist. I am hopeful I will be able to keep up with *you,*" George said with sarcasm he immediately regretted.

Recognizing the argument was over, the old woodsman simply shrugged and began to pull together supplies, efficiently loading both their backpacks.

George abandoned his uniforms to the baggage train and wore only his warmest clothing and match coat, along with a backpack carrying his papers, personal ammunition, and the most basic necessities. Relaxed, but always alert, Gist seemed at ease as he perceived everything around him as they moved through the forest.

As they entered the small village of Murderingtown, an Indian approached them, making friendly gestures. Once the parties were next to each other, the Indian indicated through hand signals that he knew a shortcut to the Allegheny River and would like to travel with them.

Gist gestured for him to lead the way and whispered to George, "Something's not right, Major. This savage is up to no good. I feel like I've seen him before—maybe with Captain Joncaire. I think the safest thing is to keep him in front of us."

"I don't recognize him . . . but as you suggest, let's keep an eye on him," George gasped as he strained to keep pace. He was already so fatigued from their trek that he lacked the situational awareness possessed by the more experienced—and fitter—Gist.

After a few minutes, the Indian stopped and indicated that he was willing to carry George's pack for him. Gist looked skeptical, but an exhausted George, without any consideration, handed over the pack. However, when the Indian reached for the rifle on George's shoulder, George's veil of fatigue dropped away, and he forcefully refused. The Indian became indignant, and Gist stepped forward and unceremoniously shoved the Indian in front of them, forcing him to begin walking again.

Gist growled to George as they began moving again, "Stay on your guard, Major. This is not right. I think we are heading in the wrong direction. It feels like we are heading to the northeast."

After the trio had traveled together for about an hour, the warrior suddenly turned and attempted to fire his gun at Gist. In an apparent misfire, the gun went off before it was raised to its target.

"Are you shot?" George shouted to Gist.

But before the echo had ceased, Gist was already in a full run, tackling the Indian and smashing him into a large white oak tree as the

Indian struggled to reload his gun. The Indian was caught off guard by the speed and ferocity of Gist's charge. In one smooth motion, Gist held the man to the ground, unslung his own musket, cocked the hammer, and prepared to deliver the coup de grâce.

"No! Stop!" George barked.

"Major, for God's sake, this red devil tried to shoot us!"

If we kill this Indian, a war party will follow and stop at nothing to track and kill us. George held up his hand to stop Gist as he assessed the situation. *If we hold him, humiliate him, and release him, the Indians are less likely to follow us because we will have taken his honor, not his life.* Aloud, George said, "No! Killing him will only bring a war party down upon us."

As if the logic of the conclusion had suddenly dawned on Gist, he checked his anger and reluctantly uncocked his gun. "Very well, Major." Then, without warning, Gist punched the Indian hard in the face. "That's for shooting at us, you vile little toad."

George nodded in approval as Gist climbed off their stunned Indian prisoner. The men then waited and rested, forcing the Indian to make a fire while they considered their next step.

"As you will not have him killed, we must get him away. Then we must travel all night," Gist said with a rare hint of continued irritation. He went over to the Indian, feigned forgiveness for the man's actions, and asked if his settlement was nearby. Gist explained to the Indian that they were in need of supplies and support. The Indian, previously convinced that he was about to be executed, readily agreed to help.

Satisfied, and with a nod from George, Gist said through words and signs, "You go now. We are much fatigued and will wait here for you to return in the morning with meat."

The Indian happily departed with his life, promising a swift return with provisions.

Gist silently followed him for a distance to make sure he was leaving as promised. The two Virginians immediately picked up their packs and, at about nine o'clock, proceeded in the opposite direction to separate themselves from their assailant and his fellow warriors.

Mile after mile, the pair pressed on in a silent march through an unforgiving wind, each man lost in his own thoughts. As the excitement of the encounter with the Indian gave way to the boredom of a long trek, George's mind inevitably slid toward Sally.

In my imagination, we have countless daily conversations, yet I know, in truth, she never gives me a second thought. I desperately want to push her from my consciousness, but she resists with a strength and intentionality that seems to come from outside my troubled mind. She dominates all other considerations when I have time to think. I pray to ponder something else, someone else, anything else! But then I see her in my mind's eye, and I find myself, once again, speaking with someone who barely knows I exist.

George and Gist traveled through the night and most of the following day before they reached the fifty-yard-wide Allegheny River. They had walked more than sixty miles since they left Joncaire at the Venango Trading Post. Near total exhaustion, resting his hands on his knees, George was initially rendered speechless by despair as he contemplated the prospect of crossing the ice-choked waterway.

After a few moments without any discernible solution to their problem coming to mind, he turned and said, "I welcome your thoughts, Mr. Gist. It's too cold to swim, and following the river only takes us farther from home."

"First, Major, we take a little break. The Indians may be on our trail, I don't know, but I'm damn sure we need to rest for an hour or so, and to make a small fire. But we cannot sleep. Neither of us will get going again if we succumb to sleep in this cold. We need to build a raft. I suggest you start a little fire. With your permission, I will use our hatchet to get to work on downing some trees for a raft." Gist then unhooked his canteen from his belt and took a lengthy drink.

George's canteen was running low. He raised his hand. "May I have a sip of water?"

As George took the canteen, Gist said with a crooked grin, "I should warn you, Major: to my great surprise, a holy transfiguration occurred during our travels."

Too exhausted to understand his words, George ignored him and took a drink, only to find the canteen filled with French wine. George almost spit out the wine, laughing as he suddenly understood the joke. Gist had apparently "liberated" some fine French wine from Joncaire as a parting act of defiance.

Grinning and handing back the canteen, George said, "You are a man of many miracles, Mr. Gist."

"The good Lord helps those who help themselves, Major." Picking up the hatchet, Gist declared, "I'll go start on the raft, and I'll leave the fire in your hands."

As Gist stomped off into the woods, George began taking out their meager rations. With numb and clumsy fingers, and with much effort, he managed to start a fire.

As the fire grew, he felt its warmth spread through him. George could hear chopping coming from the woods, but he was too exhausted to get up and help.

What a truly remarkable man. He is decades older than me, yet I am spent. Where does he get his energy?

Suddenly, with a flood of guilt, George thought, *Get up! This is your command, and you're not going to let this old man best you. He's got to be tired too, and by God, you'd better get to work if you are both going to make it through.*

Forcing himself to his feet, he shouted, "Gist, where are you?"

A response quickly came a few hundred yards away: "This way, Major. I found a good stand of pines."

As George came over a rise, he was amazed to see the sweat-covered Gist had already felled a half dozen decent-sized trees with his small hatchet and was in the process of removing the protruding limbs. "Pines are straight, easy to strip, and float well for short trips," he said. "But it's always a nasty bit of work with the needles and sap."

With a sudden burst of energy caused by his embarrassment for having taken a break, George strode forward. "Well done, Mr. Gist. You need a rest too. Go back to the fire. I have some provisions set out. Take a couple of minutes and come back when you are ready."

"Upon my word, Major, I am fine—"

"I must insist. We both need to be strong. A few minutes of repose will do you good. Besides, someone needs to tend the fire."

Gist nodded, picked up his cloak, gun, and pack, and headed back toward the fire. George then finished stripping the trees Gist had felled and cut down two more before he heard Gist returning.

"Well, someone's been a busy beaver," Gist joked as he surveyed George's handiwork.

"Thank you. Give me a hand dragging these back to the river, if you please."

Despite having been up all night escaping from their Indian assailant, the men worked the remainder of the day building their log raft by strapping the logs together with ropes and strips of bark. They cut long poles to assist them in pushing it across the river. George had never built a raft like this before, certainly not with the limited resources they had. Nevertheless, he marveled at both Gist's practical approach and the quality craft they had constructed.

The sky was darkening as the men pulled the heavy raft to the water's edge. They were able to easily push off into the turbulent and forbidding river and soon made good progress as they headed into the channel. About halfway across the rough and swirling river, George saw a large piece of ice that was about to smash into their raft.

"Look out!" he called to Gist.

With all his strength, George drove his pole into the river bottom to try to redirect the raft to avoid the impact. As he did so, he realized his pole was stuck in the mud.

"I can't get the pole out!" he yelled. Even pulling with all his might, he could not avoid the oncoming ice, which smashed into the raft, throwing him into the fast-moving river.

The ice-cold water felt like a million small needles stabbing every part of his body. As he broke the surface, coughing water and gasping in surprise, he saw the raft beginning to drift away. Bewildered, but not initially panicked because he knew how to swim, he suddenly realized his heavy clothing and the ice chunks were weighing him down.

Desperately, George shouted and began thrashing toward Gist, who sat astride the remainder of the broken raft. The first inklings of fear began to pull at George's mind. He suppressed the feeling when he saw that the impact of the ice chunk had partially broken apart the raft, leaving one of the larger logs floating about halfway between himself and Gist. George managed to throw his body onto the nearby log for buoyancy.

"Major, grab a hold!" Gist shouted.

George turned to see Gist fully extending his body while using the only remaining pole to reach out for George. Violently kicking while straddling his log, George reached for Gist and managed to grab the very tip of the pole. Using all their strength, the men were again reunited. Gist's huge hand dragged George by his waterlogged match coat onto the broken raft. Somehow, with only a single pole, Gist pushed them to an island in the middle of the river.

After shivering uncontrollably on the remainder of the raft, George was now completely numb and sheeted in ice as Gist pulled him by the scruff of the neck onto the island. George tried to assist, but his feet and hands were useless.

"You're not shivering anymore, Major. That's a bad sign. We need to get you out of those clothes and start a fire, or you're going to get frostbite or worse."

Gist's knees and hands had been plunged multiple times in the freezing water, yet he persisted in building a roaring fire and partially stripping George. The fire began to warm them as the exertions of the day began to take their toll.

George lay on his side, looking at the roaring fire Gist had built. As the fire wheezed with the release of the logs' sap, and sparks coughed upward into the frozen black velvet sky, he heard the mournful and ghostly howl of a nearby wolf. Too cold and exhausted to consider yet another threat, he drifted to sleep.

When they woke the next morning, they were both covered in frost, but their clothes were largely dry. George seemed no worse for wear, although he was bruised from hitting the ice in the river. In contrast, while Gist had not fallen into the river, his fingers and toes were frozen, no doubt from saving George. Despite their mishap, they had survived and managed to retain their packs, guns, and, crucially, the dispatch to Dinwiddie in a watertight pouch. They looked across the Allegheny and saw that during the cold night, the river had frozen solid and they were able to traverse it without difficulty.

When they reached the far bank, George turned to Gist. "I must thank you. Without your actions in the river and building the fire, no doubt I would have died. I am in your debt."

Clearly uncomfortable with the compliment and George's formality, Gist shrugged. "Not at all, Major. You would have done the same thing for me. It was bad luck that we got hit and good luck that I was able to provide some assistance. At this point, we still have a long way to go—thus your gratitude may be premature. We may yet freeze to death or get killed by Indians; if so, you'll have thanked me for nothing."

"Point well taken. If the cold kills us or we get scalped, I withdraw my thanks, and you will owe me an apology for making me endure last night when I could have simply drowned in the river," George said with a grin.

With his unconquerable humor, Gist responded, "We shouldn't start counting our chickens before they are hatched, eh? It sounds to me I'm damned either way, Major. Although, I don't know about you, but the burning fires of hell sound pretty inviting about now."

With every muscle aching, and suffering from exposure, the men slogged on the next day through the heavy snow and cold. The sun was high in a brilliantly blue sky, yet it provided no warmth. Instead the light reflected uselessly off the snow-covered landscape, its brightness hurting George's eyes, which already watered under the sharp, driving wind. There was no choice but to plod on. Even Gist's normal good humor was replaced by a shivering determination to push through the wall of cold.

As a boy from the Tidewater, George had never felt this deep, hard, and biting cold. On those infrequent days of a deep freeze as a child, all stayed inside by the fire or bundled up to frolic in the rare snow. This was profoundly different. Everything was ice and frozen death. The snow that had represented joy in his boyhood was now an obstacle slowing progress and sapping what energy he still had. Meanwhile, his fingers and toes ached as needles of cold penetrated his meager gloves and mittens.

Gist said with forced confidence, "Pain is a good sign. When they stop hurtin', we'll be in a world of trouble."

The forest, which George so loved, was always full of life and sound. Now all he could hear was the howl of the wind moving through the bare trees, his own struggling breath, and the crunch of his feet on the frozen earth. Like a medieval knight, he looked at this white crystalline world through a narrow slit. His "helmet" was made by his tricorn hat and scarves wrapped around his head, but it did little to protect him from the biting wind. Despite the weight, he wore every piece of clothing he carried with him, yet still the harsh, frigid air cut through the layers like a knife, not only taking his warmth, but also turning his muscles to ice and draining his strength.

Will I ever be warm again? The cold is inside my bones, George thought as he followed the deep furrows cut in the snow by the indomitable Christopher Gist. *Don't think, just walk. As Gist said, if we stop, we die. The cabin owned by a settler, Tom Fraser, cannot be too far ahead. It was a dozen miles from the river where we started this morning. It seems we have walked twice that far already. I hope Gist knows where he is going, because I am too cold to think.*

Then a muffled shout came from in front of him. George looked up to see Gist pointing at a cabin in the distance. George could just make out a whiff of smoke coming from the chimney.

There was no consideration of Indians or the occupants of Fraser's cabin. The most primitive part of George's mind took over, and both he and Gist broke into a stumbling run. As they burst through the cabin door without bothering to knock, they immediately felt heat and overwhelming relief.

On January 16, 1754, seventy-seven days after his adventure began—a journey of more than a thousand miles on horse, canoe, and foot through the worst of winter weather—George once again stood outside the governor's office awaiting entry.

Was it only two and a half months ago that I requested this task? It feels like a lifetime. George stopped, inhaled deeply, and took a relaxing breath before knocking on the governor's door.

"Come in, Major Washington. Please, do be seated," the governor said with such unbridled concern that it took George aback.

"You are very kind, Governor, but I am fine and no worse for my ordeal. I am pleased to have the honor of presenting to you the response of the French commandant." George reached into his worn leather pouch and handed over the letter given to him by Commandant Le Gardeur.

With the practiced motion of a lifetime of handling paperwork, the governor broke the seal with a knife and flicked open the letter. "As I expected, it is in French," he said. "I could muddle through it, but I should get it properly translated." Dinwiddie signaled to his secretary to come into the office and take the document. From behind his desk, he then pointed to a chair facing him with an open hand. "Now, I must insist, Major. We both shall sit, and you shall tell me what you know. Were you told the contents of the letter?"

"Only in generalities, Governor. I have been told the French refuse to leave the Ohio."

"And your impressions of the French, their forces, and the Indians?"

George was prepared for this question and answered, "They have a substantial force and a series of forts. They have developed some Indian allies and are committed to establishing French forts down the Ohio to the Mississippi all the way to the Louisiana. I am happy to report that I established some good contacts with the Senecas, and the Half King in particular. Nevertheless, I believe the French are resolved to fight and are preparing to do so."

"And the Ohio Country, they intend to keep it?" Dinwiddie asked with growing intensity.

"Absolutely," George said, leaning forward in his chair. "They are fortifying the area as we speak. They take the position that they are the first occupiers of the lands."

"I knew it!" the governor exclaimed as he pounded his desk. "Those lands are ours, Major. We will not allow them to take them from us . . . or the Crown."

Taking the land from "us" indeed, George thought.

He was well aware that Dinwiddie had assumed Lawrence's position as director of the Ohio Company, and that he was one of the largest shareholders in the land development enterprise.

"There are other gentlemen with whom I must discuss these matters," the governor said. "I would like you to draft a complete report of all your experiences; leave nothing out. Can you provide a manuscript in the next day or so?"

What! He wants a written report? I have never done anything like that— my lack of education . . . George paused, "I . . . believe so, Governor." Twisting as if he was trapped in his chair, he stuttered, "However, I am not an experienced writer, and I am afraid you may find my text wanting."

With a wave of his hand, Dinwiddie rose to his feet and quickly replied, "Do the best you can, Major. I want as much detail as possible."

George bowed at his dismissal and went straight to his room to consult his diary and begin drafting his report. Later, despite his protestations about the seven-thousand-word report's "imperfections," Dinwiddie was enthralled and ordered the journal sent to a printer. George's story became an overnight sensation and was reprinted in newspapers throughout the Colonies. The House of Burgesses awarded George fifty pounds to "testify to our Approbation of his Proceedings in his Journey to the Ohio."

PART III
Necessity's Colonel

Your high unconquered heart makes you forget
You are a man. You rush on your destruction . . .

—JOSEPH ADDISON, *CATO: A TRAGEDY*, ACT II, SCENE II

Chapter 23

April 8, 1754 - Belvoir

George sat, once again, ensconced in the library at Belvoir with the Colonel. Trying his best to appear serene and at ease, inside, George was afire with impatience and excitement. Governor Dinwiddie concluded that Virginia must mobilize quickly to meet the French threat. Publication of George's journal had made him a bit of a celebrity. He hoped to turn it into a leadership role in the coming campaign; his brother, Jack, had even suggested he apply to lead Virginia's defense.

While decorum barred George from publicly—or evenly privately—admitting that he reveled in his newfound notoriety, he was in fact thoroughly enjoying the experience. Men and women who, because of his relatively low social position, had barely given him the time of day before now stopped him on the street to greet him and ask his opinion on weighty matters. Wherever he went, everyone seemed to be watching him with approval.

As Colonel Fairfax put down his snifter of brandy and stared into the fire, George waited patiently. The Colonel was well aware of George's aspirations; indeed, he had encouraged them. At the same time, he also had his finger on the pulse of Williamsburg politics.

Breaking the silence, the Colonel said, "I know you want to command this expedition." He held up a single finger to stifle George's protest. "It is me, my dear boy—I know you well. I do not accuse you of excessive ambition but merely state the obvious. You are gifted with intelligence and leadership ability. You want to put it to the test, but you need to move at the right time and place. While I share the governor's belief in the need to defend the Ohio Country, there is no consensus in the House of Burgesses. This may result in underfunding or make the senior officer in the expedition a highly politically charged figure. This would be even more volatile if you were so designated, given our families' involvement in the Ohio Company."

What? So I am to do nothing?

As if sensing George's growing unease, the Colonel continued. "Fear not. I do not advise you to remain behind, but I propose you seek the role of second in command."

Second in command?

"There are several advantages that flow from such a position. First, you avoid the 'political' role inherent in supreme command. Second—and this is not a criticism—rather it is an obvious truth—you are still in need of training. Being second in command provides you that opportunity. Third, and most important, if the expedition fails because of lack of support or otherwise, that failure will not rest on your shoulders. Conversely, if it succeeds, you can claim quite rightly that you played a crucial role in victory."

Fighting the desire to stand and unable to disguise his enthusiasm, George inquired, "So what do you advise next, Colonel?"

"A letter to the Military Committee of the House of Burgesses indicating that while you desire service, the command of the whole forces is neither what you look for nor expect. I know this will be hard for you to swallow, but you should openly indicate that overall command is too great given your youth and inexperience. This honest and forthright confession will put you in good stead and make you the logical choice for the post of second in command."

As the Colonel predicted, and with Austin's assistance, George was promoted to Lieutenant Colonel and second in command of the Virginia Regiment. His superior, Colonel Joshua Fry, was an Oxford-educated instructor of mathematics at the College of William and Mary. He was overweight and in his midfifties.

When he learned his pay in his new position, George was outraged. The governor had promised fifteen shillings per day; instead, he was receiving only twelve shillings and six pence. When he threatened to quit, Colonel Fairfax counseled him to be patient, indicating that he would intercede with Dinwiddie on George's behalf. In truth, George was never serious about leaving; he was thrilled to be leading the coming campaign.

George was summoned to the governor's mansion to discuss the current tactical situation brought about by increasingly aggressive incursions by the French and Indians. As he entered Dinwiddie's office, George had to stifle a small chuckle at the man's absurd appearance. It was a hot spring day, and Dinwiddie was perspiring profusely through his shirt, which, while tight along the belly, was loose in the shoulders and had extensive ruffles on the front. With his scalp covered in sweat, his wig had become askew as he hunched over a map. The half-dressed and bespectacled governor looked up as George walked in. Dinwiddie's tiny eyes and pear-shaped body reminded George of a clown he had seen performing in Williamsburg. Struggling to maintain his composure, he bowed deeply to the governor.

"Come in, come in, Colonel Washington," Dinwiddie said. "At last—I've been waiting to speak with you. Colonel Fry is en route, but I did not want to waste any time. I want you out to meet the French at our earliest opportunity." Pointing at the large map in front of them, "We know from intelligence reports that the French have deployed a thousand-man force at the fork of the Allegheny and Monongahela Rivers to construct Fort Duquesne. Some of our scouts even estimate as many as six thousand French troops are now in the Ohio Country."

Even though George was only twenty-two and a newly minted lieutenant colonel, he realized the obvious: *Even if the entire Virginia Regiment is deployed and given reinforcements, we will still be outnumbered three to one.* Rather than voicing his concerns, George simply nodded knowingly and said, "Yes, sir." He understood the logical approach was to retreat into Virginia, consolidate a defensive position, and await significant reinforcements.

The governor continued. "I know some would counsel us to withdraw in the face of the enemy. However, we have to recognize the impact of such an action on our ability to recruit Indian allies. As you know, the Half King has been pleading with us to assist him. If we show weakness, the Senecas may either choose neutrality or, in the worst case, fight alongside the French." Abruptly he began looking around the room. "Where did I put your orders?" He trundled over to a nearby paper-strewn side table, pawed through the stacks of documents, and handed George carefully written orders containing the governor's wax seal. "I want you to act on the defensive, but at the same time, if given the opportunity, you need to be ready to attack and destroy the enemy."

George could not hide his excitement at the possibility of entering the field and engaging the French. Snapping to attention, he responded forcefully, "I understand, Governor. I will carefully review your orders, but I look forward to moving out with my men as soon as possible."

"Your efforts will deter the French and support our Indian allies," Dinwiddie said with an air of finality, as if his pronouncement alone would make the statement a reality.

Even though he sensed the interview was over, George felt the need to follow up. "Er, about our supplies, Governor? We are still in the need of reinforcements, and my men are ill equipped."

With a dismissive wave, Dinwiddie snapped, "I believe you already have about 120 men." He seemed to imply this was a huge force capable of meeting the oncoming French. George knew this was absurd, but he hid any reaction.

"You can certainly get that force moving," the governor continued. "I've ordered Colonel Fry to follow with more men, as well as an additional captain, who will also be bringing up men and supplies. By the time you reach the frontier, you should have more than an adequate force and supplies to deter any French exploratory party. In particular, I am providing you with many small arms and ten small four-pounder cannons. You will send me regular reports of your progress, and I will continue to send you supplies and additional men. Good day, Colonel, and good luck."

Washington bowed and left the room.

The next day, George headed west toward the Ohio with his new recruits. A couple of days out, he found Christopher Gist waiting for him with a dictated letter from the Half King. Worn and filthy from a long hard ride, Gist approached George with the grim determination of a man intent on completing his duty before collapsing into exhausted sleep.

"Christopher, you look as tired as we did when we arrived at Fraser's cabin," George said. Since Gist had saved his life, he had fallen into the habit of calling Gist by his first name when they were in private conversation.

"I hope I don't look that bad," Gist said as his drawn features cracked into a crooked smile. "The Half King asked me to come and see you or the governor to relay his message. Having found you, I can happily avoid Williamsburg and head back home. The Half King's mighty hot and bothered about our delay in deploying our troops. He expects the French any day and warns us that they are actively building forts. He wants us to get off our backsides and get out to help him."

George thought to himself, *The governor's main goal in having me go out was to improve relations with the Indians and make sure they don't back away from their commitments. I have to get moving as soon as possible.*

"Thank you, Christopher," he replied. "Go get yourself some food and sleep. Suffice, we are moving out and will do so with greater alacrity now that we have your report."

Gist nodded in acknowledgment and sighed. "Thank you, sir. Sleep sounds mighty good."

In response to Gist's report and the Half King's entreaties, George's small force—now grown to 159 men with the addition of Captain Adam Stephen's troops—continued west toward Wills Creek, still another 40 miles into the wilderness and 160 miles from Fort Duquesne, which the French were constructing at the confluence of two great rivers that formed the mighty Ohio. Almost immediately, the challenges of moving men and material in the spring began to plague the small force. The road quickly became a sea of mud, swamping men, cannons, and beast. The soldiers were forced to thrust logs under reluctant wheels to keep them moving.

George constantly looked to the sky with unease. Every dark cloud heralded the coming of more mud, which seemed to worsen as they traveled—always present, pulling, dragging, slowing, and tiring his inexperienced men. George cajoled his troops and whipped the beasts of burden to keep his column moving as ordered. George had planned to drill his untrained men as they moved, but the horrible conditions made this virtually impossible.

As George progressed, he received another message from the Half King asking George to "have good courage . . . and come as soon as possible . . . if you do not come to our assistance now, we are entirely undone, and I think we shall never meet together again. I speak with a heart full of grief." After hearing that several English forts had been taken by the French, and given the Half King's repeated pleas for help, George deemed it prudent to call a council of war to discuss his next move. After consulting with his officers, most of whom were older, George ordered his troops to continue to move forward to the shores of the Red Stone Creek near the Monongahela. George wrote to Governor Sharpe, who was in overall command of colonial forces, that the colonies would "rouse from the lethargy that we have fallen into, and the heroic spirit of every freeborn Englishman to assert the rights and privileges of our king . . . and risk from the invasions of a usurping enemy, our majesty's property, his dignity, and lands."

A week later, tired after a long day with his troops, George examined the stack of papers before him as he sat in his tent. At the top of the pile was a letter from Governor Dinwiddie informing him that Captain MacKay, who commanded a company of South Carolina British regulars, would be joining him. Dinwiddie entreated George to cooperate with MacKay, knowing the issue of MacKay's royal commission would irritate George.

Must we always be second-class citizens? pondered George as he read Dinwiddie's letter. *Commissioned royal officers are accorded with superior rank, regardless of a colonial officer's standing.*

George held an officer's commission from Virginia. It allowed him to command Virginia's troops, but he had little authority as it related to other colonies and even less so when it came to royal troops. Officers with royal commissions had unquestioned authority, even to the point of outranking colonial officers with vastly superior rank.

To make matters worse, British redcoats are also paid more than our colonial counterparts. I have written Governor Dinwiddie that my men are "slaving dangerously." If my men received more than trifling pay, this would solve the regiment's problems recruiting noncommissioned officers, George thought.

As if to confirm his worse fears, on May 17, George's officers provided him with a signed petition to present to the governor demanding higher pay and threatening to resign en masse. In truth, George did not disagree with their complaints. Indeed, he wrote to friends at home, "I really do not see why the lives of His Majesty's subjects in Virginia should be of less value than of those in other parts of his American dominions; especially when it is well known that we must undergo double of their hardship."

Governor Dinwiddie responded immediately and did not hide his displeasure with his young commander. He agreed there was a shortage of sergeants and corporals but advised George that their concern about pay should have been considered "before engaging in the service."

Dinwiddie's letters regarding men and supplies were more encouraging. George was instructed to wait for reinforcements and supplies being brought up by Colonel Fry. George and his men cut a roadway from Wills Creek through the Appalachian Mountains, cresting Laurel Hill on May 24 and allowing them to gaze down on a large depression and field known as the Great Meadows. With some satisfaction, George knew that in less than a month, he and his three companies of men had built the first road into the Ohio Country.

Chapter 24

May 27, 1754 – Great Meadows

George believed a large French force was approaching and began to entrench his troops in the Great Meadows. The bowl-shaped field was carpeted with marsh grass about three-quarters of a mile in diameter. Under the searing spring sun, with insects rising with each shovel cut into the wet, warm earth, George and his troops began digging in.

George stood with his hands behind his back, surveying the low land meadow before him. Lieutenant Mercer approached, hesitating a bit at the prospect of interrupting George. "A good Monday morning to you, sir."

George turned to the Lieutenant and declared, "This is a charming field for an encounter. When the French arrive, imagine our lads lined up facing down the enemy across this open plain."

While only a year younger than George, Mercer looked up to him, and he hung on his commander's every word. With his many familial and social connections, George viewed Mercer as one of the men he could rely on as they faced the unknown. Mercer nodded his head in acknowledgment. As he did so, a large figure straddling an obviously tired horse came into view, and a familiar voice carried across the clearing: "Major Washington! Are you a sight for sore eyes!"

Slightly piqued that his new title hadn't been used, George's irritation evaporated when he saw Christopher Gist dismount his horse and take large strides toward him.

"A pleasure to see you, Mr. Gist. You look better than the last time I saw you. Are you well?"

"Truth be told, no, Major."

Lieutenant Mercer, who was standing behind George, interjected, "Actually it's lieutenant colonel now, Mr. Gist."

George shook his head dismissively and indicated for Gist to continue.

"Beggin' your pardon, *Colonel*," Gist said with an uncharacteristic edge in his voice. "Fifty Frenchies invaded my home. They threatened to kill my cattle and destroy my property. If it wasn't for some friendly Indians who talked them out of it, I think they would have burned my home to the ground and then done heaven knows what to my family. I had to play all nice with them, but as soon as the bastards left, I circled around and headed straight here, hoping I'd run into you."

George involuntarily removed his hands from behind his back and squeezed the top of the sword at his hip. "So are these Frenchmen heading toward us? Are they hostile?"

"That was no goddamned reconnaissance or surveying party, Colonel. They are up to no good," Gist growled.

George could feel the eyes of his men on him as he listened to Gist. *Their threats and the potential destruction of Gist's property are exactly the sort of hostile acts Dinwiddie authorized me to repulse!*

Trying to control his excitement, George said with forced formality, "Thank you, Mr. Gist. I would be grateful if you could return to Governor Dinwiddie with all dispatch and report to him our current situation. Inform him that I intend to follow up on your report and move to meet this growing threat."

Gist bobbed his head in acknowledgment and then, under his breath, whispered to George before he walked back to his horse, "Get the bastards, Colonel."

George dispatched a captain and a company of men to investigate Gist's report. Shortly after the men left, an Indian messenger named Silverheels arrived, indicating the Half King had discovered a French camp about six miles northwest of the Great Meadows. Silverheels explained that they had discovered the location having followed the footprints of two Frenchmen. He further explained that the Half King said he was on his way to join George's men and inferred that the French were planning an attack.

George decided to divide his small force. Turning to Lieutenant

Mercer, George explained, "With Silverheels's assistance, I am going to lead these thirty-three men, along with Captain Stephen, to find this French and Indian war party. You will remain and continue to improve our fortifications and watch our wagons and ammunition. This should allow us to move unencumbered toward the Indians while still permitting us to protect and entrench ourselves here."

Captain Adam Stephen was George's second in command and a decade his senior. Stephen was a Scottish-born physician who had served in the Royal Navy and had connections with George through the Fairfax family. George had met Stephen before but was not yet sure he could command such an accomplished older man.

George, Captain Stephen, their men, and Silverheels set off in a heavy rain on an inconceivably dark night. Several times, the party lost the trail and its bearings in an attempt to find the Half King and meet the advancing French force.

Chapter 25

May 28, 1754 - Jumonville Glen

As the sun rose, George and his waterlogged troops finally stumbled into the Seneca camp, where he met the Half King and about a dozen warriors. They quickly agreed to find and strike at the French. George made the decision to attack, even though England and France were not at war, the French had not yet attacked anyone, and Dinwiddie had specifically ordered him to act on the defensive. George's blood was up, and more importantly, he could not back down in front of his Indian allies. With this in mind, George ordered his men to move toward the French position.

George and his men picketed their horses near the main trail, a significant distance from the glen where the French were encamped. They were pleased to discover the French had posted no sentries around their camp.

The morning dew still clung to the ferns and brush as they moved through the forest. It was cool, but the wet leaves hinted at the coming steamy day. George drew on his hunting experience as they passed through the woods. *The fox is cornered. We must go in for the kill before he goes to ground,* he thought.

As George and his men crept to within a hundred yards of the French camp, George stopped to pull out his telescope. The Half King, Captain Stephen, and an interpreter silently slid up to either side of him. George whispered to the Half King, "Your scouts did well. The large stone slab protects one whole side of the camp and prevents a French escape. As we agreed, I will take half the men and cover the right flank." Turning to Captain Stephen, he continued, "You will take the other half of our soldiers and take the left." Then, turning back to the chief, "Your warriors will cover our rear to prevent a French retreat." As the translation was given to the Half King, he and Stephen both nodded.

George whispered as he continued to look through his telescope, "The French appear to be making breakfast, and there are a few small fires. Their guns are placed under overhangs in the large stone wall, to protect them from the rain. I see some pole-and-bark wigwams, which is where I suspect they managed to stay out of the storm the last night." George's brow rose as he looked at the men. "Any questions?"

Both the Half King and Stephen indicated they were ready.

"Wait for my signal to fire," George ordered.

At seven o'clock, using the undergrowth as cover, the British and Indians crawled forward on hands and knees and slowly approached the unsuspecting French. When they got within fifty feet of the outer perimeter of the camp, a shout went up when a French soldier saw someone from George's approaching party. The Frenchman reached for a gun, and without orders, firing erupted on both sides. In response to the bedlam, George bellowed for his men to attack and advance on the French.

A lifetime of hunting and familiarity with firearms did not prepare George for the cacophony of three dozen guns going off at the same time. The glen instantly filled with smoke and the acrid smell of black powder. The birds, which had become quiet when the soldiers pushed through the undergrowth, burst up and scattered as Washington's troops opened fire.

Despite the shouted warning from one of their soldiers, the French were taken completely by surprise. George and his men used trees and rocks to conceal themselves as they continued to pour fire on the French, who weakly returned fire, managing to kill one of the Virginians. Ten of the French died instantly when George and his men pressed the attack, and the French began to give ground. Some tried to break and run, but most remained under their officer's close direction as they realized Indians had encircled the encampment from the rear.

At the French commander's order, all began to raise their hands in the air. George's heart was pounding so hard, and his blood was up to such a great extent, that he did not project the poise essential to maintaining control of his men. He yelled at the top of his lungs for the firing to cease when it was clear the French were surrendering. The entire engagement lasted no more than fifteen minutes.

George was directed to the French detachment's leader, a Captain Jumonville who was placed up against a tree, suffering from an oozing chest wound. The French commander tried to explain through Van Braam that the French came in peace and were attempting to deliver a diplomatic message to the English. A document was handed to George who, in turn, gave it to Van Braam to translate.

The Half King suddenly exclaimed in French: "*Tu n'es pas encore mort, mon pére,*" meaning "Thou art not yet dead, my father." Then, in one fluid motion, he swung his hatchet and cracked open Jumonville's skull, pulled out his warm brains, and squeezed them through his fingers like a sponge. The chief raised the blood and gore up to his fellow Indians, shaking his fist and screaming. The warriors yelped and brayed in response, unsheathed their knives and tomahawks, then pounced on the dead and injured French soldiers. The Half King's men went on a rampage, scalping many of the wounded and even decapitating one man and impaling his head on a pike.

George stood agape in abject horror. His paralysis gave the Indians further leave to follow the Half King's lead. Never in his twenty-two years had he seen anything to prepare him for the Half King's stark brutality. As George regained some self-control, he and his troops managed to protect some of the remaining French soldiers from the Indians' wrath.

To make matters worse, when George examined papers given to him, it became apparent Jumonville was indeed carrying a diplomatic message. It appeared he had not been leading a war party, but rather on a mission like the one George led to Fort Le Boeuf a year earlier.

Later that night, after he returned to the Great Meadows with his captives, George had an opportunity to assess the situation. He fell into his habit of pacing with his hands behind his back as he stared at the ground. One of his brothers described this as "George walking like a chicken with his head cut off." George stopped, shuffled a few random steps, and turned in circles as he concentrated. As he replayed the day's events, his unease grew with each passing moment.

Never, in my wildest dreams, did I imagine the Half King would attack the helpless Jumonville. The battle was exhilarating, but my loss of control of the Indians . . . He involuntarily shuddered as he remembered the howling chief holding Jumonville's brains, blood dripping down his outstretched arms.

If the Colonel and the governor find out that we attacked a diplomatic mission and I failed to prevent an Indian massacre, I will be dismissed from the army and ostracized.

A sudden burning sensation suffused his body as a flood of panic pumped through him. The terror of a caged animal threatened to overwhelm his reason and began to cloud his mind.

I will be relegated to Ferry Farm! An outcast. A subject of ridicule. Forced to live with my mother, who will never allow me to forget my mistakes.

George stopped shuffling and involuntarily raised his hands to cover his face, succumbing to the absolute despair and certainty of youth.

What in God's name do I do? If Lawrence was alive, I would talk to him—but I cannot speak to anyone about this. Explaining this to the Colonel would permanently stunt our relationship.

A picture of his mother then popped into his mind.

I know that confessing a mistake does not necessarily lead to redemption.

After the death of his kind, gentle, and soft-spoken father, George learned repeatedly under this mother's thumb that truthfulness and honesty do not always lead to relief and forgiveness. More often than not, contrition was met with recriminations. Indeed, confession was usually rewarded with abuse and a disproportionate punishment. With this is in his mind, George concluded, *No, I will not spend the rest of my days at Ferry Farm . . . The fact is, that but for the Half King's actions, it was a very successful engagement. I will emphasize this to my family and friends.*

George resumed his unconscious shuffling as a plan formed in his mind.

I will write letters describing my "victory." I will argue that Jumonville and his men were spies.

With the growing intensity of someone convincing himself of an argument he wanted to believe, George resolved, *They were definitely up to no good. Diplomatic mission indeed! Who travels with three score of men, hides in a glen, and harasses good people like the Gists? No! This was a war party traveling with some pretext of diplomacy. The Half King's actions were his own. He is an ally, but I did not command him.*

Now convinced, George thought, *I have nothing to be ashamed of. After all, we did defeat and capture the French.* Nodding unconsciously, he concluded, *My first engagement will not be my last.*

Taking his strategy to heart, George wrote a letter to his brother Jack a few days later, saying, "I fortunately escaped without a wound, tho' the right wing where I stood was exposed to and received all the enemy's fire and was the part where the man was killed and the rest wounded. I can with truth assure you, I heard the bullets whistle and believe me there is something charming in the sound."

Dinwiddie accepted George's version of events, emphasizing in his reports to London that the Indians were the culprits for any violence against the French. "This little skirmish was by the Half King and their Indians, we were as auxiliaries to them, as my orders to commander of our forces [were] to be on the defensive."

George was still profoundly anxious. In an attempt to bolster his position, he wrote the governor, saying the French were really "Spies of the worst sort" who "ought to be hanged." Moreover, any assertion that the French were on an "Embassy" was a "mere pretense." George insisted they "never designed to have come to us but in a hostile manner." He cautioned the governor not to be duped by stories spun by prisoners he was sending back to Williamsburg.

George's writing campaign yielded positive results. Not only did his comments reach the newspapers on both sides of the Atlantic, but the master of his Masonic lodge wrote public congratulations: "Your victory over the French ... gave me and your other friends such satisfaction as is only felt by those who have hearts full of mutual affections and friendship. . . . I hope this is only a prelude to your future conquests." Governor Dinwiddie even awarded George a medal, a store of rum, and a letter of congratulations.

The crisis of the Jumonville skirmish averted, George found himself imagining when he would next see Sally to discuss the battle. *When I see her again, she will hang on my every word. Her huge and beautiful eyes will be locked on just me.*

George then thought with disgust, *I am a fool. All she knows are my awkward letters. She never thinks of me, while all I do is imagine conversations that will never happen.*

Chapter 26

June 2, 1754 – Fort Necessity

Far from Williamsburg, facing a now bloodied enemy, George considered his situation. *I need to start constructing defensive works. At least one French soldier escaped, and I have no doubt a larger French force will be coming. We are going to name our works "Fort Necessity," to reflect that we are being forced, by necessity, to be on the defensive.*

The primary focus of my efforts is construction of the road, not this new fort. If the French do appear, the open ground in front of the Fort is where our men will be able to line up for battle. This is a stout temporary bulwark against the French, but it cannot provide a meaningful long-term defense against a superior force.

As he watched his men at work, Lieutenant Mercer appeared at his side and said, "Colonel, we've cleared brush and trees about sixty yards out from the center of that depression in the middle of the meadow. I've got men digging holes where we can put the vertical slabs of lumber in the circular stockade you specified. Given the size of the trees, I think it will stick up about seven feet. Our diameter is going to be about fifty feet, with about 190 feet circumference. On the southwest side of the circle, I'm leaving a three-and-a-half-foot-wide entrance to permit access to the ammunition and supply hut. Around the outside of the stockade, a series of small and shallow trenches are being dug."

His eyes still on his men, George announced to Mercer, "When this fort is completed, we will be able to withstand the attack of five hundred men."

As the weeks went by, food and supplies began to dwindle, and George's troops and their Indian allies suffered. On June 6, Christopher

Gist returned with news that a pack train with fifty thousand pounds of supplies would arrive shortly.

Three days later, under the command of Major George Muse, 181 reinforcements arrived, along with supplies and nine two-pounder swivel guns with mounts. George was thrilled with the additional influx of needed supplies and hailed him warmly. "Major Muse, you, your men, and supplies are quite welcome."

Dismounting from his horse, Muse walked over to George with a look that did not reciprocate George's friendly greeting. Instead, he solemnly bowed and said, "I am the bearer of heavy news and responsibility, Colonel." He handed George an envelope with the governor's seal. In Dinwiddie's handwriting, George read that Colonel Fry, his commander, was dead in a freak fall from his horse. A medal was included from the governor, reaffirming George's authority and Dinwiddie's confidence. As a result of Fry's death, George, at age twenty-two, was now a full colonel, Muse a lieutenant colonel, and Stephen a major.

George responded to the news with a mixture of exhilaration and trepidation. He never really knew Colonel Fry and had only met him on two occasions. Nevertheless, he immediately ordered a ceremony be held in Fry's honor and requested that Major Stephen make a few appropriate remarks. As he listened to Stephen's invocation, the gravity of the situation began to strike home. *I am now in the situation the Colonel wanted me to avoid—I am in command, with all its political, tactical, and administrative responsibilities . . . I am in command! I have now exceeded Lawrence's rank—albeit without a royal commission—and am about to lead men in the field.*

After the ceremony, George ordered the men to drill. His trusted junior officers were providing direction to his ragtag soldiers, who were bumbling through the gyrations of formation and handling their muskets. With the confidence of youth, any fear felt by George was quickly overcome by the thrill of the moment.

George's enjoyment of being in absolute command lasted only one week. On June 14, Captain James MacKay, with a royal commission, arrived leading one hundred South Carolina redcoats to provide further reinforcements. The son of a military officer, MacKay had been soldiering since George was five years old. Because MacKay had a royal commission, he was not subject to George's authority. While neither officer was willing to take orders from the other, both struggled to maintain a polite, if strained cordiality. MacKay, to his credit, avoided further problems by setting up a separate camp well outside the fort. MacKay refused to have his soldiers do roadwork, and George declined to inspect MacKay's troops. While open hostilities between the two never occurred, their relations were extremely tense. Unfortunately matters were not helped when MacKay quickly voiced his opinion that the fort, as constructed, was a death trap.

MacKay be damned, Washington grumbled to himself a couple of days after MacKay's arrival at the fort. *I am going to take three hundred of my four hundred men out of the fort to resume road clearing. MacKay might not like the fort, but he can man it in my absence. This road is crucial to putting our forces within striking distance of Fort Duquesne while keeping us close enough to allow a safe retreat or to obtain reinforcements in the face of a French attack.*

With his work crew and soldiers in tow, George once again headed west to continue road construction. They stopped at Gist's home to meet with a group of local Indian leaders who were demanding information concerning the English strategy for defending in the Ohio Country. During three days of discussions with the Indian sachems, George's diplomatic skills proved disastrous: he not only failed to secure their assistance, but was also aggressive and condescending. He told the chiefs the sole purpose for the English actions was to "maintain your Rights" and protect the Indians from the French. The Indians found these arguments unpersuasive. Indeed, the Half King complained that George was a "good-natured man, but had not experience," and had unfairly "commanded the Indians as his slaves." George knew, but did not want to acknowledge, that the Indians' complaints were caused by a recognition that a well-supplied French force was approaching while their British allies were starving. At the same time, George found the meetings frustrating and wrote a letter saying the Indians were "treacherous Devils, who had been sent by the French as Spies."

While George's unproductive negotiations were occurring, his men suffered under almost unceasing rain, beset by bugs and awash in mud as they struggled to build the road to the west from the Great Meadows. When they began to run out of supplies, George called a council of war with his officers on June 28. Underfed and worked to exhaustion, George and his officers resolved to return to Fort Necessity. Unfortunately, in the meantime, the road they had built had transformed itself into such a muddy morass that it pulled, dragged, and slowed their twelve-mile march. George and his officers even gave up their horses to carry the meager supplies back to the fort.

When he arrived at the Great Meadows, George saw the remaining Indians collecting their belongings and preparing to leave. The Half King pulled him aside. "Brother Conotocarius, my people leave not out of fear or lack of love for the English, but because there is not enough food. Also, when the French war party arrives, this . . ."

The interpreter hesitated to complete the Half King's statement, already cowed by George's obvious irritation.

"Well, get on with it! What did he say?" George snapped.

The translator responded, "These are no fortifications at all; this is merely a little thing upon the meadow." The Half King then pointed to the fort, held his arms wide, gesturing at the surrounding forest, and drew his hands together around his neck as George waited for the translation.

"These woods will be full of French and Indian warriors who will rain death down upon you and anyone trapped here," the Half King said. "A strong warrior with a bow or an able Frenchman with a musket will be able to strike any man outside your stockade, and those within have no ability to defend themselves. Trapped, you will wait for death. I am your brother, and my fate is tied to the English, but I will not have my people stay and die with you for no reason. It is with a heavy heart that I take my leave."

Vermin! The heathens eat my food and now slip away when we need them most! Damn, damn, damn!

George stared at the implacable Indian, recognizing that he would not change the old fox's mind. He thus resolved to be gracious, even in the face of the Indian's treachery.

"I do not want you or your people to go, Great Chief. Supplies will be here soon, and I expect additional soldiers to meet the French. Your strength will be added to ours, to protect your lands from the French. This fort is stout. However, we will fight the French on this field, not from behind its walls."

Not surprisingly, the Half King shook his head, refusing the offer.

"Very well, brother, we wish you well and hope you will reconsider and join us after we defeat the French and not leave us again as you do today, but go in peace," George said with warmth he did not feel.

As the Half King walked away, George thought, *Slither away, you red snake! I've learned a valuable lesson this day. While the red men can be useful, you can never trust the lying devils.* With that, George turned to his fort and the rapid preparations of his men.

George received word that eight hundred French and four hundred Indians were on the march toward the fort, so he recalled the last of his road builders. By July 1, all the troops were either at Fort Necessity or scrambling to reach the compound, anticipating an assault. In their wake, a trail of litter and supplies stretched from Gist's home all the way to Fort Necessity. The last of George's troops arrived hungry and exhausted at the fort, completely abandoned by their Indian allies.

The jumble of British regulars and poorly clad Virginia militia huddled in an inadequate number of tents as it began to rain on the night of July 2. When roll call was called the next morning, of the four hundred men present in the fort, more than a hundred were not fit for duty.

George's depleted and exhausted men were put to work outside the walls of the fort, extending and deepening the nearby trenches and felling additional trees to strengthen the stockade. Recognizing that he had no reconnaissance screen with the loss of his Indian allies, George sent Major Stephen out with pickets to monitor a possible French approach.

Too excited to sleep, and overtired from a hard march to the fort, George walked about his hungry and overwrought men, trying to exude confidence yet knowing he was young and not truly battle tested. Nevertheless, he gave words of encouragement and double-checked the preparations for the oncoming French attack.

Chapter 27

July 3, 1754 - Fort Necessity

George's men were finishing an inadequate breakfast as a gray dawn broke. A shot suddenly broke the silence, and a soldier collapsed, wounded, outside the fort.

This is it!

"Colonel Muse, get your men in the trenches," George ordered. "Captain MacKay, I understand you will do likewise."

Both men acknowledged the instructions and began to deploy outside the fort. It had rained the day before, and the trenches were already muddy and in some places contained standing water.

The initial shot was a false alarm and likely came from a French scout. Major Stephen's pickets reported that the French and Indians were still several miles off. Meanwhile, the rain that had started as a mist grew into a heavy downpour, permeating not only the men's belongings, but dampening their spirits as well. Everything was fouled with mud: animals, food, equipment, and, most of all, the men themselves.

At about eleven o'clock in the morning, the French arrived in force, and their first volleys were fired at the fort. These shots came from more than six hundred yards away and had no impact on George's men.

As the shots began to come in earnest, George felt a sudden desire to relieve himself but knew it was not the time, as all his men were watching him. *You hear stories of men wetting themselves in the battle; God I pray it doesn't happen to me.*

As one of his soldiers crumpled in front of him, George forgot his bodily concerns. He turned to MacKay. "Captain, please order your men into columns and deploy them for action in the field while we await for the French to do likewise." George pointed to the large open area in front of the fort that gave the Great Meadows its name.

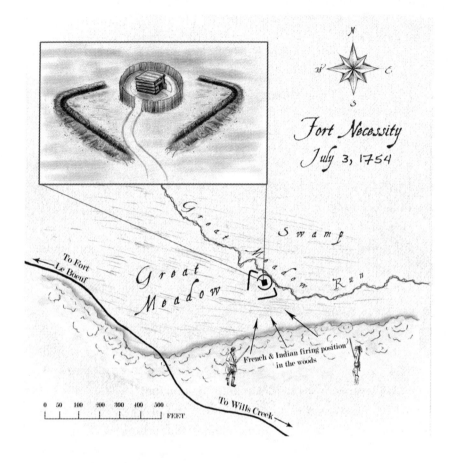

"And if the French don't come out and instead shoot at my men from behind trees? What then, Colonel?" MacKay said with barely hidden contempt.

Fighting the desire to cover the ten feet that separated them and throttle MacKay, George replied with a distinct edge in his voice, "Then we will test your men's bravery as they withdraw into the fortifications in an orderly fashion."

With the precision expected from well-drilled redcoats, MacKay's regulars marched double-step out into the field and lined up. The sergeants barked at the men to smartly dress their lines and await the French. A "traditional" European battle would entail soldiers lining up to face each other, standing approximately 100 to 150 feet apart in parallel lines. With three ranks, the front-most line would direct a volley against the enemy, then step through the two lines of men behind them, while the front line—previously the second line—stepped forward and unleashed its barrage. The reason for this three-stage system was because of the cumbersome and time-consuming loading process with flintlock muskets. Using three ranks, a well-trained English company could maintain virtually continuous fire on an enemy.

Unfortunately the French and Indians were unwilling to give up their tactical advantage of the wooded high ground to meet MacKay's soldiers on the open field. The French and Indians were led by an enraged Louis Coulon de Villiers, sieur de Jumonville, brother of the slain Captain Jumonville, whose unburied body, along with those of his scalped men, had been discovered in the glen by the French as they approached Fort Necessity. Coulon deployed his *troupes de la marine* throughout the woods, adopting Indian tactics. Once in place, the French began to snipe at MacKay's troops from sixty yards away. When MacKay attempted to direct mass fire toward the source of the French shots, the futility became immediately clear, and he ordered an impressive and unhurried retreat.

As the French moved to surround the fort, a crossfire of bullets and arrows began to inundate the trapped English from behind every little stump and bush. The French and Indian fire initially focused on the British horse and cattle to eliminate foodstuffs and beasts of burden to be used in retreat. The brays and screams of the dying horses and cattle only increased the anxiety of the soldiers trapped in the fort. When the slaughter was complete, the dead and dying animals reminded George of reefs protruding from a sea of mud.

After approximately an hour of steady triangulated fire from the hills, a great cry went out from a group of Indians who advanced, screaming and yelling. George's men in the trenches laid heavy fire into the charging braves. The English were able to bring their small swivel guns to bear, repelling the Indians' frontal charges with canister, which turned the small cannon into large shotguns spraying hundreds of small balls with each blast. As the guns erupted, a gray cloud of billowing smoke was split by an internal lance of flame, killing dozens of Indians. In the face of the withering fire, the English were given a rare opportunity to cheer as the Indians were forced to withdraw.

Several other attempts to rush the fort met with a similar fate. The French and Indians then returned to sniping from the surrounding hills. MacKay's soldiers remained at their posts in the trenches, despite inadequate cover and appalling casualties.

Throughout the entire engagement, the rain, always present, at one point was so intense that George could not see the surrounding hills. Turning to Gist, George shouted as a river of water emptied from the points of his tricorn hat, "Dear God, Christopher, they could walk right up to the fort right now and we would hardly know it!"

"Or they would drown in the attempt, Colonel," Gist agreed.

When the rain eased up somewhat, the French and Indians were able to renew their arrow and musketry fire. The enemy appeared from behind cover only long enough to fire and then return to safety. George's troops, who were stuck at the bottom of a basin without the protection of the surrounding trees, increasingly were forced to contend with unusable powder and guns incapable of returning fire. One sound sickeningly rose to George's ear above the din: the sound of flint striking metal. The click gave muted testimony to wet powder. The noise was almost always followed by profanity, in response to the absence of the expected shot. Men hid behind the stockade and in the trenches, fingers white, tightly gripping their useless muskets. Meanwhile, shots from the surrounding woods gouged chunks of flesh from George's trapped men with increasing lethality.

The "charming" sound George had enjoyed at the glen, and described to his brother Jack, was now a constant and ominous reminder of sudden death. The quick and distinctive "fftht" sound followed George as he made his way around Fort Necessity. Even with the heavy rain, the sound of lead splitting the air dogged his progress and acted as a constant reminder of the folly of this indefensible fort. To make matters worse, George's most effective weapon, the swivel cannon, had fallen silent; being poorly mounted and exposed to enemy fire, their crews were forced to abandon the guns in place. George was never able to properly deploy his larger four-pound cannons, and thus they played little role in the engagement.

While not as effective as gunfire, arrows were also a constant menace. Like bunches of porcupine needles, they stuck from every surface, reminding each man of their complete vulnerability. In the rain, the arrows were poorly aimed but came silently, announcing their arrival with the tap of their entry into wood, or screams as they drove into human and animal targets.

Captain MacKay and his British regulars occupied the outer line of defenses in the trenches. The troops in the trench surrounding the stockade were so engulfed by the mud that many lost their shoes and boots as they attempted to evade the devastating French fire. George's plan was to hold the Virginia militia in reserve in the event of a direct French assault.

The large puddles of water surrounding the fort now carried a sickening red hue reflecting the submerged dead and wounded. Everywhere George looked, he saw familiar men dead and dying; even his own slave manservant had been killed by a ball to the head early in the engagement. George knew his troops were paying for his lack of military education with their blood.

George and his men became uncomfortably aware of a terrifying developing pattern: the cough of a French rifle would be followed by the distinctive whiz of a passing ball. More often than not, the men were then forced to endure the unforgettable sound of the smack of lead meeting flesh. The crouching men would pause, anticipating a groan, or worse yet, the sickening sound of a dead man hitting the wet ground.

Despite the danger, George continued to move from man to man, indifferent to the whistling lead following his every movement. As the balls skimmed by, he was more afraid of letting his men down or demonstrating some dishonorable cowardice than he was of the prospect of meeting a sudden and violent end. George knew his example mattered because every man felt the fear and panic of a drowning animal. They were floundering in muck and blood with no ability to either attack or retreat. He needed to show confidence to keep them in the fight.

As he approached the trenches, he heard the thwack of a ball striking home. George's gaze moved from the soldier's vacant eyes to the stain slowly spreading across the man's tunic. Just as quickly, in the heavy rain, the stain disappeared, leaving only a telltale hole on the man's shirt and an accusatory, empty stare.

Another man dies under my command. Shaking it off, he thought, *Keep moving.*

As he worked his way back toward the entrance to the stockade, Lieutenant Mercer approached and said, "Colonel, the men have gotten into the rum. Half of them are drunk. I've placed a guard on what's left."

Feeling his anger rising, George shouted, "Any man that touches rum again will be shot summarily on my order!"

"I am sorry to say this, Colonel, but I found Colonel Muse hiding in the stockade. He left his men out in the trenches, and many of them followed him into the stockade. He said he was in the stockade 'inspecting.'"

"Goddamn it! If you won't say the word *coward*, well I will, by God! Is he drinking the rum?"

"No, sir. It's under guard, as I said," Mercer responded with obvious discomfort as he glanced back toward the blockhouse in the middle of the fort.

"Fine, leave the bastard in there. If we survive this day, I will see him hanged. Don't share this matter with the other men; it will only lessen their spirit." Visibly attempting to calm himself, George straightened, facing Mercer. "Get what men you can back into the trenches." Then, after taking another calming breath, he added, "Thank you, Lieutenant, go back to your men."

Grateful for the escape, Mercer was off in a flash, and George began to work his way around the fort. Meanwhile, the French guns continued to cough death into his miserable troops. The rending of man and beast was all the more hideous as the fresh corpses looked upward with unblinking eyes that were struck by raindrops.

George saw Captain MacKay encouraging his men and directing fire.

The monsoon-like rain added to the din as George approached. MacKay turned and shouted, "Well, Washington, we are in a damn pickle now!"

Even in the chaos that surrounded him, George couldn't help but notice the captain's failure to address him by his rank. *I'll worry about that slight if I live. I need suggestions, even from this poxed bastard*, thought George. "Do you have any ideas, Captain?" he asked. "Is there something we should be doing that we are not?" It galled him to have to ask the question, but George could leave no stone unturned.

"It's too bloody late now. This worthless fort will likely be the death of us all. All we can do is stay with our men, hope they don't panic, and that we all die well." MacKay replied, and he turned back to his soldiers without waiting for George's response.

George knew MacKay blamed him for the fort's construction and placement. *There is nothing I can do about it now. He is right: we must hold out as best we can.*

The fort's small force was caught in a watery hell. Thunder cracked like field guns, with lightning slicing down to meet the great volleys of rain that drenched the men and their ammunition. By the end of the afternoon, one-third of George's men were dead or dying, trapped in a giant spinning mincer of bone and flesh turned by unrelenting foes.

George moved encouraging the cringing men. As George witnessed Boyd's violent death, the unseen sun began touching the horizon. Suddenly the firing lessened, and the word *parley* was repeated down the line. A booming voice from the woods could be heard shouting, "*Voulez-vous parler*?" George's childhood French was good enough to translate the question: they wanted to talk.

George gave orders to Major Stephen as he realized that Van Braam was at his side. Van Braam explained that the French were sending an officer to negotiate.

I can't let them see the condition of the men and our troops!

Spinning on Van Braam, George barked, "Captain Van Braam, please respond that we will be sending you to the French commander to discuss parley. Obviously we do not want them to know the condition of our troops and the fort. Do you understand?"

"*Ja*, Colonel. I vill finden what the French vant. I say nothing vith-out approval," Van Braam replied, but he did not start walking toward the French.

"Good. Well, don't dawdle, man, go!" George said as he gave Van Braam a shove to get him moving. The gangly Dutchman lost his balance on the wet ground as a result of George's unexpected push. It was only the strong hand of MacKay reaching out that saved Van Braam from collapsing in the mud. With an unhappy glance over his shoulder and a nod to MacKay in thanks, Van Braam moved off toward the French.

Meanwhile, George's officers surrounded him. "Well, what do we know of the French intent?" MacKay asked the group generally, rather than properly directing his inquiry to George as the commanding officer.

"I know as much as you do," George said tersely before anyone else could respond. "The French are offering parley, and I have sent Mr. Van Braam to find out the terms."

"Oh, thank God," Lieutenant Mercer declared without thinking.

George did not hide his irritation and addressed Mercer and the other junior officers. "Gentlemen, we should use this lull as an opportunity to attend to the wounded, appropriately redeploy the men, and feed them with whatever rations are available. Keep them out of the rum—I have already told Lieutenant Mercer that I will shoot any man who touches the rum without my permission. We need to make clear to the French that we are prepared to continue the fight. Dismissed." George stood, lips closed in a grim straight line.

The junior officers hesitated for a second, then returned to their men as ordered. Captain MacKay's feet remained firmly planted. "You understand, Washington, that you have virtually no latitude here. The men are starving, we have vast numbers of injured and dead, and our ammunition is wet. This fort, in its present state, is utterly indefensible."

George faced MacKay squarely and took a full step toward MacKay so George's superior height would permit him to tower over the shorter man. In a low firm voice, George answered, "Captain, I am in command of this fort. You can rest assured that I will do what honor and duty require."

MacKay did not respond, but merely shook his head with undisguised contempt and held his ground. George pivoted toward the spot where Van Braam had entered the French lines and stood with his head held high and his hands behind his back, willing his taut muscles to unlock and trying to look absolutely calm while his heart pounded so hard that it felt as if it would burst out of his chest.

We are men standing on death's threshold and being handed an opportunity to turn and walk away, yet I need to remain calm. If I jump too quickly, the French will sense weakness and resume the attack, or my men will panic and run.

As he finished this thought, George looked up to see Van Braam returning from the tree line. Both George and MacKay had waited in stony silence for Van Braam's approach.

Looking at both men, apparently uncertain whom to address, Van Braam spoke hesitantly. "De Commandant Coulon ist villing to protect us von the Indians. We may march away, leaving our arms."

Without waiting for input from the other officers, George said, "Tell him that is unacceptable. We will not abandon this fort."

Van Braam paused as if awaiting further direction or input from MacKay.

George snapped, "Damn it, man, get on with you! Give Monsieur Coulon my answer."

As Van Braam approached the French lines, MacKay stared at George in disbelief. Without saying a word, MacKay walked to the group of young officers standing a few feet away. The men began glancing over their shoulders at George as MacKay clearly recounted George's interchange with Van Braam.

George stood alone waiting for Van Braam's return. As he did, he looked around; rent and torn bodies littered the trenches and areas surrounding his beleaguered fort. His peripheral vision picked up Van Braam's return to the lines. As he arrived, George's officers surrounded him simultaneously, waiting to hear the latest news from the French.

"De commandant's compliments, Colonel. He says his bruder, Monsieur Jumonville, vas recently killed by the English. He said his only goal here ist to avenge his bruder's death. He says no reason to fight more. He says return home in peace. The French vill protect us von the Indians, and that we may take all belonging, except artillery and munitions. We vill be permitted to keep our flags unt leave mit arms and drums. Two officers must be left behind as hostages to guarantee the terms."

"These are generous terms indeed. Colonel, how can we not accept?" MacKay said to George, and the group nodded in agreement.

Oh, now I am "Colonel," thought George. He's right, though. I believe I have met the requirements of honor, and my position is incredibly weak. As he looked at the officers surrounding him, he acknowledged to himself, *these men may not follow my commands if I push any harder.*

"Captain Van Braam, please return to the French commander and obtain articles that we may review with your assistance."

As the French drafted the surrender documents, George walked into the circular stockade enclosing the small blockhouse in its center. Drunk and injured men were strewn about, moaning or unconscious. All were mud covered and soaked to the bone, yet many still begged for water. On the back side of the blockhouse farthest from the entrance, the intrepid and blood-covered Dr. Craik tended to the wounded and dying. Severed limbs, along with the dead, were piled helter-skelter against the wall, presenting the most concrete evidence of George's failure. Fighting his desire to turn and stride away from this horrid place, George girded himself and approached Dr. Craik.

"Is there anything you need, Doctor?"

"Only the rain to stop, but I suspect that is beyond your considerable skills, Colonel. No, we'll manage. My request, in the main, is kindly bring this unhappy engagement to a conclusion." Then, looking up from his patient, he said offhandedly, "Of course, if you are withdrawing, I will need to remain with the injured."

George began to protest, but Craik raised a bloody hand. "It is a question of duty, Colonel. Yours is to leave this place, mine is to remain. I am hopeful the French will treat me well."

What courage. This is my fault, yet he gives no recriminations.

George nodded in acknowledgment.

Craik turned back to his patient and instructed his assistant, "Come and hold this chap down."

As George walked away, he heard the sickening, grinding sound of a saw on bone as Craik swiftly and expertly removed yet another unlucky soldier's limb.

Van Braam reappeared late in the evening with two copies of the articles of capitulation. The articles were written on wet and blotted paper in tightly compressed French script that was extremely difficult to read by sputtering candlelight. George and MacKay asked the exhausted Van Braam to read the entire document to them in English. Van Braam stumbled and stuttered throughout his translation. George objected to the French demand he give up all arms and ammunition; if the troops were left without powder and ball, they might be set upon by the marauding Indians. Van Braam crossed out these terms on both copies. He and another officer volunteered to act as hostages. Upon completion, George turned to MacKay, who nodded his assent. Then, in a subtle indication of his subordinate status, MacKay signed the document followed by George.

As Van Braam stomped back through the mud to the French lines, George noticed the rain had finally stopped. He knew he had until dawn to pull his men together, bury their dead, and prepare to transport the wounded. With the truce completed, the starving men killed the already wounded animals, cutting their flesh and roasting the remains over open fires, knowing their next meal could be many days off.

As the red sun rose on July 4, the puddles that filled the trenches looked like pools of mercury that had proven just as lethal to his men. The steady breeze chased out the smell of blood and smoke, but the odor of the rotting dead would soon permeate the fort.

The French troops stood between the Indians and the English while George's officers picked up provisions and munitions and ordered the completion of the grim task of burying the English dead. Private baggage, including George's best uniform, had to be left behind. The wounded, many of whom were too weak to move, were left under the care of Dr. Craik and eleven other volunteers who remained until the wounded and the baggage could be retrieved. George ordered the cannon and swivel guns spiked as he pulled out of the fort.

Despite promises by the French of protection, the Indians and some French soldiers began plundering the garrison's baggage before George's troops had left the fort. The volatile Major Stephen, whose rank insignia had been obliterated by blood and mud, stepped forward as a French soldier began to examine his portmanteau. Indifferent to the danger the French posed, Stephen threw the man out of the way as the French soldier opened his chest and began to pull out one of his uniforms. Other angry Frenchmen rushed forward, and George was forced to pull Stephen away to avoid a bloodbath as his men endured taunts from the victorious French.

George and his troops left behind a dismal scene of destruction. Above the blood- and arrow-covered, mud-soaked little fort gleamed the newly raised and pristine blue-and-white battle flag of the *troupes de la marine*, proclaiming both the French preeminence and George's defeat.

As George's troops moved forward through heavy forest, the sun looked down from a cloudless sky broken only by the canopy of giant oaks that absorbed some of the blistering heat. George knew as their march progressed that the trees could only protect them for so long before the shade would give way to oppressive humidity and the blazing afternoon sun.

His humiliated, exhausted, and dirty men made camp two days out of Fort Necessity. George began to seriously contemplate his situation, reverting to his characteristic wandering stroll. He swam against the waves of panic that washed over him as he considered his failure.

I cannot allow this engagement to be seen as a defeat. Trying to convince himself, George thought, *We were able to leave with honor. The failure was the result of insufficient supplies and ill-trained soldiers. I must convince Dinwiddie and the Colonel that if I had been adequately supported, this would never have occurred.* Nodding to himself, he formulated his plan. *In the face of an overwhelming force, we did well to survive. I need to send letters and reports as soon as possible. I need to get ahead of the discussion back in Williamsburg.*

To make matters worse, George realized, in their haste to depart, his men had marched out of Fort Necessity without the colors of the Virginia militia or his diary. These appalling oversights were not easily explained away. Worse yet, George learned the surrender documents included an admission he had "assassinated" Jumonville.

As he contemplated this horrifying situation, Captain MacKay approached. "Excuse me, Colonel, do you have a minute?"

So it's "Colonel" again? He must want something. Oh, well, let's hear what the son of a bitch has to say.

George gestured for MacKay to speak.

With surprising intensity, MacKay said, "The ruddy bastard Van Braam. We shouldn't have trusted the Dutchman when we signed that agreement." He leaned against a nearby tree. "I assume you've heard that the preamble to the surrender we signed indicates that we admit that Jumonville was assassinated in your raid. Our gooses will be truly cooked if this gets out without proper explanation. Not one officer under your command would have signed that document if we knew the word 'assassination' was included. I know we have not always seen eye to eye, but I would suggest to you that my experience in the army may provide us both some utility in dealing with the present unhappy circumstances."

George motioned for MacKay to continue.

"There is a saying in the army: 'shit flows down.'" MacKay spoke without a hint of humor. "There is a defeat here, even if we try to portray it otherwise. It will need to be excused and explained. Conveniently, our subordinate, Mr. Van Braam, is unavailable. The fact that we signed this document without understanding this term—which, by the way, is absolutely the truth—is also our best defense. To the maximum extent possible, we must blame this unfortunate admission on his treachery while characterizing the surrender as a strategic retreat." George nodded in agreement as MacKay stepped away from the tree and lowered his voice. "There is also the matter of Lieutenant Colonel Muse."

George winced in disgust at the name. MacKay said, "I see we have the same view of the man. He is a coward who left his men to hide in the stockade. For what it is worth, we both saw each other through a hail of bullets and arrows, and we did our duty. Muse deserves no consideration, and we should, without compunction, throw him to the wolves."

With a sudden wave of relief, George realized MacKay would be his ally and that his signature on the surrender documents bound them together.

Thank the Almighty. Listen to the man; he has far more experience in military politics than you.

George released a deep breath and answered, "I am grateful for your thoughts. I have already begun writing letters in the manner you suggest concerning a 'strategic retreat,' but your points on Van Braam and Muse are excellent. The fact remains that neither of us understood the implications of the document we were signing concerning the late Captain Jumonville—who, by the way, I fervently believe, was a spy. Certainly we should emphasize that Van Braam betrayed us both when he failed to properly translate the document or inform us of its meaning. As to Lieutenant Colonel Muse, I couldn't agree with you more. I know we have had our differences, but let me be clear that I was similarly as impressed by your courage in battle as I was disgusted by Muse."

"Quite right on all fronts. We exited the fort facing overwhelming forces with our soldiers at arms, our heads held high, our drums beating, and our colors flying. The fact that a foreigner misled us is not our fault, nor is it our fault that one of our senior officers behaved with cowardice, contributing to our need to strategically withdraw," MacKay said as he touched his tricorn hat. "Let it flow downhill, Colonel. We will present a unified front, potentially turning this sow's ear into a silk purse."

George smiled for the first time in days. "If you will excuse me, Captain, I have letters to write."

"As do I, Colonel. Good evening."

As he returned to his tent and correspondence, George thought, *I will not give up. There is still hope. With MacKay's and others' help, I will portray this engagement positively. I have not come this far to throw it all away and suffer the ignominy of defeat and humiliation. MacKay is right. I did not know about the admission concerning Jumonville. I would never have signed the document had I known, and I'll be damned if I will be blamed for something that is untrue.*

George's letter writing campaign emphasized that, "The interpreter was a Dutchman, little acquainted with the English tongue." George also questioned Van Braam's integrity, implying that he had deliberately skewed the translations to George's disadvantage for "whatever his motives." George consistently emphasized that any admission of guilt in the articles of capitulation "were owing to a bad interpreter and contrary to the translation made to us when we signed."

Later, George and MacKay met in Wetherburn's Tavern in Williamsburg to discuss the joint report they were required to submit to Governor Dinwiddie describing the debacle at Fort Necessity. Sitting at a table in the back of the tavern so no one could hear them, George and MacKay were surrounded by smoke and the smell of stale ale as they discussed their report in detail.

"We really have no idea how many Frenchman we killed," George lamented.

"Exactly!" MacKay said with a devious smile. "Nobody knows except the bloody French, and I don't expect anything they say will be taken seriously by our superiors. Again, we must turn this defeat, as much as possible, into a strategic victory. Given the number of rounds we expended and the cannon shots fired, I do not think it is unreasonable for us to claim three hundred French and Indians were killed. This number should prove especially helpful in the face of our thirty dead, seventy wounded, and nineteen missing men out of a total force of four hundred."

George nodded, but he leaned back in his chair to think.

MacKay hunched over the table, almost knocking over his ale, his volume rising as he continued, "Listen, George, I understand how the army works. This is also a matter of politics. My God, man, we arrived here and were lauded as heroes. Virginia and the Crown could use heroes right now. Have we not been warmly welcomed?"

"What about Dinwiddie? His reception was less than enthusiastic," George replied. He pursed his lips at the memory.

MacKay gave a dismissive roll of the eyes. "Dinwiddie sent us on a fool's errand. We were underequipped and understaffed to meet the French threat. More important, I understand that your Colonel Fairfax is supportive."

"Indeed, immediately after the battle, he wrote a wonderful note, reminding me that Lord Marlborough had demonstrated the utility of an able strategic retreat," George conceded, looking at his ale and not MacKay.

"There you go!" MacKay said as he pounded the table, rattling their mugs. "We have the assistance of Fairfax, his allies, and other reasonable men who recognize our valiant efforts in the face of an overwhelming enemy."

George's large gray eyes narrowed as he weighed his options. He felt a desire to get up and pace, but he knew he had to remain seated and decide. After a full minute passed, he finally inclined his head in agreement, allowing his chair to rock forward. Adopting a more positive note, he offered, "I am told that Speaker Robinson will move the King's council to award us three hundred pistoles and hail our bravery in defense of our country."

"George, we have done all we can," MacKay said, poking his finger at the report. "There will be politicians like Dinwiddie who will try to undercut us, but we must make the best of this difficult situation. If we present a unified front, seek the assistance of our friends, and remain resolute, I believe we will both come through this all the better."

Acknowledging the advice and experience of MacKay—his senior in both service and military politics—George agreed, and the men completed their report.

With very little prodding, Major Adam Stephen wrote a stirring account in the Virginia and Maryland newspapers defending George for bravely standing against a superior adversary. Nevertheless, criticisms arose in New York and London that George had acted too rashly and was "too ambitious of acquiring honor."

George met Colonel Fairfax in Williamsburg to discuss the aftermath of the campaign. As usual, the Colonel spoke first and set the agenda for their discussion. "This is a matter of good news and bad news, my dear boy. At least publically, Governor Dinwiddie is expressing gratitude for your service, but behind the scenes, he is insinuating that the . . ." The Colonel paused as if searching for the right word. "The 'events' at Fort Necessity were caused by—excuse my frankness—a want of proper command."

"But sir—"

Interrupting George before he could protest further, the Colonel continued. "Rest assured that this is not my view or many other good men's, as you well know. Nevertheless, you still remain in command of the regiment, which is certainly the good news."

A disheartened George sighed. "What is left of the regiment is barely worth mentioning. The governor is completely oblivious to the logistical and recruitment challenges that need to be overcome. He demands I reconstitute the regiment in preparation for an assault on Fort Duquesne. Meanwhile desertions increase, caused in no small part by Williamsburg's failure to provide pay and supplies."

"On that front, I believe you are right, George. The House of Burgesses has refused to spend any more money on the western campaigns. The governor has put you between a rock and a hard place. Rest assured, whatever happens, there are gentlemen who recognize your efforts. Take heart."

Shoulders sagging under the weight of disappointment, George intoned, "As always, Colonel, I am grateful for your advice, but on this occasion, I fear the fates have not been kind to me."

With an understanding smile, the Colonel answered gently, "Patience, my boy. Life is long, and we must see how this plays out."

George could only cast his eyes downward as he sought to control his obvious frustration.

The Colonel continued. "Patience . . ." Then, chuckling, the Colonel said, "Patience is not in your nature, my young friend. I understand your feelings but hope you will trust me."

"Always, sir," George said as he bowed and took his leave.

In this situation, George's pessimism was prophetic. Maryland's Governor Horatio Sharpe was the overall commander in chief of British forces. Sharpe was an unfortunate selection for George on two fronts: first, he had already criticized George's performance at Fort Necessity, and second, he was a fellow Scot and friend of Governor Dinwiddie. As part of the reorganization under Sharpe, and with the encouragement of Governor Dinwiddie, the Virginia Regiment was broken into separate companies with no officer holding a rank above captain. This not only decreased the autonomy of George's regiment, but it had the desired effect of forcing George to either face a humiliating demotion or resign.

In a letter to Sharpe's aide-de-camp, George angrily wrote that "the disparity between the present offer of a Company, and my former Rank" is "too great" to provide me with "any real satisfaction or enjoyment in a Corps. . . . [I]f you think me capable of holding a Commission that has neither rank or emolument annexed to it; you must entertain a very contemptible opinion of my weakness, and believe me to be more empty than the Commission itself. . . . Sir, as you truly may, of my reluctance to quit the Service . . . [as] my inclinations are strongly bent to arms."

Because Sharpe's position was not subject to change or negotiation, and, indeed, had been engineered by Governor Dinwiddie, George tendered his resignation and returned home.

Chapter 28

December 18, 1754 - Mount Vernon

Five months after the defeat at Fort Necessity, as the door on George's military career appeared to be closing, a new opportunity was opening on the home front. At age twenty-two, the prospect of returning to Ferry Farm filled him with dread. While he did everything duty and honor required of him to assist his mother, it was never enough and only added to his unhappiness.

Ann Washington had remarried while George was gone and had left Mount Vernon empty. Ann and Lawrence's last remaining child, Sarah, died on December 10, sealing Ann's resolve to permanently part with the plantation. George decided to incur the substantial expense of renting the manor house, along with eighteen slaves, a gristmill, outbuildings, and 2,298 acres. He agreed to pay Ann fifteen thousand pounds of tobacco every Christmas or an equivalent in cash rent.

In mid-December, George and his brother Jack trundled up the hill to Mount Vernon with George's meager belongings. Jack was George's closest and most trusted companion. His lean and affable brother was George's sounding board and confidant, especially since Lawrence's death. However, the younger Jack could never replace Lawrence's role of advisor and mentor.

George also tried to shake off his mother's disapproval that he left Ferry Farm for Mount Vernon. He considered how he and his brother Jack had entirely different strategies for coping with the challenge of living under their mother's thumb. While George pushed and often fought against Mary's domination, the lanky Jack maintained a bemused air of indifference, defusing tension—while out of his mother's earshot—with a well-placed joke or smirk.

Perhaps my mother is right to criticize my decision to rent Mount Vernon. What do I honestly know about running a plantation of this size? The only other great undertaking of my life—my attempt to obtain martial glory—was a catastrophic failure.

George's unease was exacerbated by the memories that filled his newly occupied home. He wanted to remember the young and vibrant Lawrence, but the ghostly, blue-lipped image of Lawrence as he lay dying dominated George's mind as he wandered through the empty house, adding to his gloom.

As the new year began, George's confidence in running Mount Vernon grew and his anxieties about leaving his mother decreased. While uncertain about his future, he found himself drawn into Virginia's social scene by invitations to parties at the homes of well-heeled planters. He remained unhappy about his military performance and longed to rejoin the fight, yet his actions against the French made him a minor celebrity, a source of interest, and often the center of attention. Because he was tall, graceful, and an accomplished dancer, young women naturally flocked to him, and George thoroughly enjoyed their company. However, his frequent trips to Belvoir to play cards and spend time with the witty and elegant Sally Fairfax quashed any interest in seeking a mate.

PART IV
Monongahela

Heavens! with what strength, what steadiness of mind,
He triumphs in the midst of all his sufferings!
How does he rise against a load of woes,
And thank the gods that throw the weight upon him!

—JOSEPH ADDISON, CATO: A TRAGEDY, ACT I, SCENE IV

Chapter 29

January 31, 1755 – Mount Vernon

Over a month after his resignation and move to Mount Vernon, in response to some prodding from older half-brother Austin, George invited Austin and Jack to spend Friday night at Mount Vernon, to be followed by a rare winter foxhunt with Colonel Fairfax. As the three brothers sat down, the candles and firelight cast a warm glow after a satisfying meal.

Austin broke the comfortable silence: "I assume you have both read the article in the *Gazette*? London has sent General Braddock to lead a new offensive to take Fort Duquesne, which the French have constructed at the confluence of two great rivers in the Ohio. What say you, George? Are you going to contact the general or his staff?"

George shifted uneasily in his chair. "I certainly would like to reenter the fray, but . . . as you know, I've had little success dealing with aristocratic generals and political governors."

Austin's response came so quickly, he almost seemed to anticipate George's concern. "I am told this latest general is *not* a politician. Unlike Governors Dinwiddie and Sharpe, Braddock is a military man through and through. His father was a major general. I suspect, with the assistance of Colonel Fairfax, introductions could be made. Braddock certainly will be in need of officers experienced in the backcountry."

George wouldn't meet Austin's gaze. After a pause, he said, "That would be a hopeful change of pace. However, now I must attend to Mount Vernon. I have only recently reopened the plantation; to abandon it for military service seems the height of folly. Who could I find to run Mount Vernon in my absence? What about planting my first spring crop? I must confess, as you can undoubtedly see, my home is still in a state of the utmost confusion."

A smiling Austin pointed an open hand at Jack, who up to this point had been listening and enjoying his wine in silence. With a look of shock, Jack sputtered, "What?"

Austin gently chuckled. "Dear brothers, I solicited George to organize this outing with ulterior motives. Jack, it is evident to me that George needs our assistance. I will help our brother in Williamsburg, and he needs your help here."

"But . . . But . . . what about Ferry Farm? What about Mother?" Jack asked as he set down his wine and leaned forward in his chair.

"Your mother has sufficient wherewithal at Ferry Farm, but George has no managerial support here. I will provide what assistance I can, but you are a bachelor, and you need to begin to strike out on your own. Managing Mount Vernon will be an excellent experience for you and allow you to escape . . . er . . . allow you to begin to live your life outside Ferry Farm," Austin responded with his usual diplomacy.

Shaking his head, George came to Jack's defense. "This is all premature. We don't even know if Colonel Fairfax thinks this is a good idea, and I am far from securing any position with General Braddock." Turning to Jack with an open expression, George emphasized, "Jack, rest assured, I do not wish to cause you pain or inconvenience, or to suffer Mother's wrath."

His intelligent eyes twinkling in the firelight, Austin interjected, "This was Colonel Fairfax's idea, George. We have all endured your doldrums long enough. Jack had no inclination of my intent, but it is time for you to stop skulking about. Did you not come to my home soliciting my blessing to pick up Lawrence's mantle?"

A taciturn George nodded in acknowledgment and remained mute as he stared into the hearth, unwilling to meet Austin's stare. Silence once again filled the room, interrupted only by the crack of the fire.

Finally, in a rare moment, Austin's veil of affability slid aside, revealing the steel beneath as he spoke with growing intensity. "You'll forgive me, George, but I will have none of your cock-and-bull excuses. Get off your backside and get on with it! Talk to the Colonel. He and I will provide whatever assistance we can in Williamsburg and with the general.

A side benefit of you returning to the army is this new opportunity for our brother Jack."

The clarity of Austin's logic, along with his rare show of emotion, had the intended effect. The recognition that there was a plan to resecure a commission, as well as a new opportunity for Jack, all clicked into place in George's mind. *Austin is right. I have been unhappy. The Colonel and Austin will support me, and Jack can come here.*

Raising his glass as he allowed himself to settle back into his comfortable chair, George said, "I defer to the wisdom of my older brother. I will follow up with the Colonel tomorrow and, if appropriate, contact General Braddock's staff."

A still reeling Jack raised his glass with such uncertainty that the contents almost sloshed over the rim and onto the floor. "Well, I'm glad someone knows what the devil's going on. I came here for supper, drinks, and a hunt, and now the two of you are deciding my destiny."

"Welcome to the club, dear brother." George toasted and emptied his glass.

As Austin predicted, the Fairfax family procured George's introduction to General Braddock, and George began corresponding with Braddock's aide-de-camp. However, George was disappointed to learn that Braddock only had authority to offer George a royal captain's commission in the British military, far beneath his Virginia colonelcy.

Braddock and his aide-de-camp, Robert Orme, earnestly wanted George's expertise in the Ohio country, and thought of a clever alternative:

March 2, 1755 Williamsburg, Virginia

Sir:

The General having been informd that you exprest some desire to make the Campaigne, but that you have declind it upon some disagreeableness that you thought might arise from the Regulation of Command, has orderd me to acquaint you that he would be very glad of your Company in his Family, by which all inconveniences of that kind will be obviated.

I shall think myself very happy to form an acquaintance with a person so universally esteem'd, and shall use every oppertunity of assuring you how much I am Sir Your most Obedt Servant.

Robt Orme, aide de camp.

George realized this was an intriguing solution to his problem with rank. Adding George to the general's military "family" would allow him to enjoy the privileges of a colonelcy without the need to obtain a formal royal commission. George responded on March 15:

I was not favoured with your agreeable Letter (of the 2d) till Yesterday; acquainting me with a notice of his Excellency [General Braddock] is pleased to honour me with, by kindly desireing my Company in his Family. Its true, Sir I have, ever since I declind a command in this Service, expresd an Inclination to [serve] the Ensuing Campaigne as a Volunteer; and this believe me, Sir, is not a little encresed since its likely to be conducted by a Gentlemen of the Generals great, good character:

But, besides this, and this laudable desire I may have to serve (with my poor abilitys) my King & Country. . . . Sir, I wish for nothing more earnestly, than to attain a small degree of knowledge of the Military Art.

I shall do myself the pleasure of waiting upon his Excellency so soon as I hear of his arrival . . . begging you'll be kind enough to assure [him] that I shall always remain a grateful Sense of the favour he was kindly pleasd to offer me.

After some intervening correspondence in which George indicated some delay in joining the army because of the logistics of caring for his mother and Mount Vernon, Orme responded:

Dear Sir

I communicated your desires to the General who expresses the greatest satisfaction in having you of our Party and Orders me to give his Compliments and to assure you his Wishes are to make it agreeable to yourself and consistent with your Affairs and therefore desires you will so settle your business at home and to join him at Wills Creek if more convenient to you and whenever you find it necessary to return he begs you will look upon yourself as entire Master, and judge what is proper to be done.

Meanwhile, at Colonel Fairfax's urging, George wrote letters to key members of the House of Burgesses to make sure all were aware that he was proceeding without pay and was focused solely on serving his country.

I am now prepareing for, and shall in a few days sett off, to serve in the ensueing Campaigne. . . . If I can gain any credit . . . it must be from serving my Country, with a free voluntary will; for I can very truely say that I have no expectation of reward but hope of meriting the love of my Country.

To Speaker of the House of Burgesses Robinson, George wrote:

The sole motive wch envites me to the Field, is, the laudable desire of servg my Country; and not for gratification of any lucrative ends; this, I flatter myself, will manifestly appear by my going a Volunteer, without expectation of reward, or prospect of attaining any Command.

In addition to drafting correspondence, George frantically prepared to leave Mount Vernon in Jack's care. George had planted oats in March and was preparing for the April planting of spring wheat, vegetables, and the all-important tobacco. To assist Jack and ensure the plantation would be run in accordance with his wishes, George spent time riding through the fields and outbuildings, generating detailed instructions and providing Jack with insights on his slaves and employees. He stayed up late into the night sending personal correspondence to various family and friends, as well as carefully packing his belongings for the trip. Despite the hectic pace, he was energized by the prospect of escaping the boredom of the past few months.

George waited for Jack with some frustration. Jack had returned to Ferry Farm to collect his belongings and was uncharacteristically late returning, delaying both George's departure and the start of Jack's new role as Mount Vernon's manager. He was relieved to see a carriage trailed by tethered and packed horses, but his heart fell when he saw the visage of his mother seated across from his brother. Jack turned his head so as to not be seen by his mother, gave a shrug, and mouthed the word "Sorry" as George reached for the carriage door.

Desperately trying to control his irritation at his mother's unexpected arrival, George said with measured politeness, "Mother, this is indeed a surprise. As Jack no doubt told you, I must leave for the army in a matter of hours."

Her strong hand reached out and grabbed George's arm as she exited the carriage. While not dressed in working clothes, neither was she dressed in a fine gown. She wore a practical, if tattered, floral dress, out of style and conservative. Her hair was somewhat disheveled, devoid of any ribbons and ornamentation, and her face revealed not even a hint of cosmetics. As she stepped down, George's eyes met those of his tall, thin, and very strong mother; despite his accomplishments, he still looked down, unable to hold her unflinching gaze.

"Well, don't just stand there. Invite me inside and have someone get my bags."

"Yes, Mother," George replied.

Jack, who clearly desired to avoid the coming confrontation, immediately piped in, "I will attend to them, Mother. I will see them to a room and join you both shortly."

Jack, you coward!

As his mother strode past him toward the home's modest entrance, George scurried to catch up and open the door for her.

"Lawrence," Mary Washington said, making a face as if she had just bitten a sour lemon, "never chose to invite me to Epsewasson, even though he only owned it because of my husband's kindness. Since you have occupied it, you have not bothered to invite me either."

Epsewasson was the name of Mount Vernon at the time Augustine Washington had purchased the property. George knew she was refusing to call the plantation "Mount Vernon" as a slight to Lawrence and to irritate George. As she talked, she walked through the home and looked into the rooms, not waiting for George to direct her or provide a tour of his new home. Opening doors and closets, she said, "Now you're going off to war again. Not only are you failing to care for me, but you are taking Jack from Ferry Farm, leaving me even more vulnerable and without the support of my eldest sons."

George felt his face turn purple with anger but still found himself tongue-tied. His mother possessed the singularly unique ability to cause George's mind to go blank and leave him unprepared for her verbal onslaughts.

With George in tow, she finally stopped, spun, and inquired, "Well, are you going to offer your mother a chair and refreshment, or will you force me to serve myself in your home?"

Attempting to regain his composure, he knew he must temporarily set aside his earnest desire to leave immediately for the army. Patiently, George held out a hand and directed his mother toward the parlor. "I apologize, Mother. I did not anticipate your arrival, so refreshments are not immediately available. I will, of course, instruct they be prepared. If you would be kind enough to follow me, we may sit."

As the pair entered the parlor, Jack came in behind them from the central hall with some of his mother's belongings. He attempted to tiptoe silently, but his burden caused the wood floor to creak and prevented his sneaking by unnoticed.

"Jack, get someone else to put those in my room. I want you to come in here so we may discuss matters with George."

The brothers exchanged a look that revealed a lifetime of understanding in dealing with their mother. As the trio sat down, their mother seized the initiative once again. "I have been patient, George. You left me at Ferry Farm for your last little adventure, and you were badly defeated. Once again, you have not only failed to return to help me, but you are now taking Jack away from me as well. I am a widow in need of the support of her children. You ignore my needs and impose yourself on your brother. We are not a wealthy family like your friends the Fairfaxes. I do the best I can, but I rely on my children. I instructed your brother to bring me here so that I may express to you my clear disappointment and to give you an opportunity to avoid this error that is injuring your family. If you think about this, the matter should be settled, and you should stop gallivanting off, grow up, and fulfill your real obligations."

Jack stared down at his feet.

George fought against a rising tide of rage threatening to overcome his control. His mother caused all around her to cower as she made pronouncements that, while infuriating, often contained some grain of truth. Nevertheless, her acidic and critical tone only strengthened George's resolve to leave.

Finally, after taking a deep breath, George began speaking with forced calmness. "Mother, as you know, Jack and I have arranged for our siblings and servants to be available to assist you at Ferry Farm. Jack will make regular visits, and in any event, we do not anticipate my service to take long.

"*Mount Vernon,*" George said with some emphasis, as his mother had chosen to refer to it by its old name, "has only recently been reopened and is in need of significant repair and management. Jack's skills are needed here. In contrast, with your wise ministrations and management, Ferry Farm does not require the same level of attentiveness and need only be adequately staffed. Indeed, as we well know, you are as good a manager as any two men in the Tidewater."

While shaking her head from side to side, her eyes never left George as she snapped, "Don't try to flatter me. The fact remains you are leaving your mother again to go play soldier, and this time you are taking your younger brother away from me."

George felt as if he was standing on a brittle sheet of thin ice separating him from a deep sea of anger. With every push and jibe by his mother, he could feel another crack bringing him closer to breaking through to the rage beneath the surface. Choosing his words carefully to prevent shattering his control, he spoke with excessive slowness: "I do not 'play' soldier, Mother. I am a colonel in the Virginia Regiment, and I have been requested by the supreme commander of all forces in the colonies to serve on his staff."

"George, can you not hear yourself? You ignore the Good Book: 'Pride goeth before destruction, and an haughty spirit before a fall.'"

George visibly shuddered under the attack but ignored her statement and continued. "Having Jack run Mount Vernon provides him with an excellent position to enhance his management skills while exposing him, to a greater degree, to the Fairfaxes and other of the best families of the Tidewater. This will create opportunities for him that do not exist in Fredericksburg or at Ferry Farm."

His mother stared blankly back at him, clearly unimpressed.

This was an old argument George had engaged in with his mother on many occasions. She looked with derision on George's—and Lawrence's—successful efforts to become members of Virginia's elite society. Thus George decided to forgo mentioning that Austin and Colonel Fairfax encouraged his plan; he knew this fact would not help in his discussions with his mother.

With growing confidence, George said with more firmness than he actually felt, "I am sorry that you are disappointed, Mother, but the matter is settled. I must serve Virginia as I believe I have served you. I have made extensive efforts to ensure there is significant support at Ferry Farm, and Jack has done likewise. I apologize that I did not invite you to Mount Vernon earlier; however, as you can see, we are still in the process of opening the home and making some renovations. I had hoped to have you out for a visit after my military service, when the home was in a more presentable condition. If you will excuse me, I will see to your room and our refreshments. Unfortunately I will be leaving later this afternoon for the campaign, but you are, needless to say, welcome to stay as long as you like."

"You will do nothing of the kind!" Mary Washington proclaimed as she stomped the floor, her eyes flaring with the rage all her children and servants knew too well. "You will not leave your mother after I have made the long carriage ride to your home for the first time. You will do me the courtesy of providing me with a room for the night and breaking the fast with me tomorrow. I would like you to show me the properties before you leave; that is, if you care at all for courtesies to your mother."

Damn it! Now I will be late meeting General Braddock. I'm trapped and she knows it. She demands this delay, but by God, I will leave first thing in the morning.

George nodded his head in resignation and replied softly, "Of course, Mother. I will see that we prepare the best supper we can under the circumstances, and I look forward to breakfasting with you before I leave."

George dreaded the coming supper and breakfast, during which his mother would, no doubt, renew her attacks and attempts to prevent him from leaving. He also knew Jack would sit as silently as possible, attempting to melt into the furniture. George girded himself to remain resolute.

As George rode away from Mount Vernon the next day with his servant John Alton, he harbored no resentment toward his brother Jack. To some extent, George felt like a coward, leaving his fine brother to their mother's wrath. While there was a kernel of truth in what she'd said about George's abandonment of her at Ferry Farm and his insistence that Jack assist him, he also knew—as Lawrence had so often counseled him—he needed to separate himself, and eventually Jack, from his mother's clutches. Her comments about "playing soldier" and her utter dismissal of his public status and success continued to grate on him as he distanced himself from Mount Vernon.

I must be resolved to the fact that no matter what I do or what success I may achieve, it will never be enough for her. The only thing that will make her happy, which I can never accept, is living with her at Ferry Farm. That I will never do. I must live with her disappointment if that is the price to pay to avoid living with her.

As the miles rolled by, the tension and frustration that he always experienced after being with his mother began to ease, and his excitement about joining the army and the prospect of serving in General Braddock's family continued to grow.

Chapter 30

April 30, 1755 – Outside Winchester

After a lengthy and difficult trip attempting to locate the army and Braddock's encampment, George was thrilled to finally be directed to the aide-de-camp, Robert Orme. The man before George was the epitome of a British officer: dashing, handsome, slender, yet strong, with dark eyes. George dismounted his horse and approached the striking young captain.

"Do I have the honor of addressing Captain Robert Orme?" George asked formally, removing his hat and bowing deeply.

Sitting under a large tree in front of an elegant collapsible camp desk covered with paperwork, Orme's already attractive appearance was magnified by a warm smile as he got to his feet. "Colonel Washington, I presume? I have heard impressive things about you, but I had no idea you were also a mountain of a man."

George was used to comments about his size and always found the best approach was to ignore them and focus on the matter at hand. Thus he responded politely, "I am at your service, Captain Orme, and am pleased to make your acquaintance."

"You are in luck to have found us. We have been on the move of late. The general is in his tent, and I am sure he will be glad to meet you, if you are so inclined." Orme gestured toward the general's tent. Behind his friendly eyes was an intelligence and intensity that resonated even after he looked away.

George met Braddock bedecked in his best colonel's uniform. Over his red britches and vest, George wore a blue coat with red lapels with gold stitching and brass buttons. His head was framed by a white high-collared shirt, with an inscribed gorget about his neck and a blue tricorn hat edged in gold held smartly under his left arm.

In contrast to George's splendor, the general was a squat, gray-haired, chubby man of sixty. Even in an imposing uniform, Braddock still managed to look disheveled. He was seated in a comfortable chair behind a beautiful, portable desk, located in the center of an impressive tent filled with the rich smell of cheroot smoke.

George had been warned of the general's foul mouth and abrasive manner, so he was pleased by the greeting he received as he entered and bowed during Captain Orme's introduction. Bounding from his chair, Braddock stood and to George's surprise, stuck out his hand. "You are quite welcome to my family, Colonel Washington."

George, somewhat confused, took the proffered hand.

"Americans shake hands, correct?" Braddock said. "I'm trying to acclimate to my bloody surroundings. One of your tasks will be to help me." As Braddock spoke, he continued to vigorously and comically shake George's hand.

Do I tell him the truth? He needs to know, but I need to be careful.

"You are correct, General. Increasingly Americans shake hands, especially in the northern colonies. In this part of the country, handshakes are used to confirm an agreement. However, we still rarely shake hands in greeting in the Tidewater of Virginia, and it is not common among colonial officers. Nevertheless, I am sure everyone will be grateful for your sensitivity and understanding."

George saw Orme nodding with approval over the general's shoulder.

Braddock let go of George's hand and exclaimed, "Goddammit! Trying to figure out you colonials is worse than the French or Indians! Every little colony has its own traditions! As you say, a man can hardly fart in New England without someone wanting to shake your hand. Then, of course, there are your savages, whose differences are utterly incomprehensible. It will be your task to make sure I know the differences and offend no one." With a wink and a laugh, Braddock turned to Captain Orme. "Or at least offend as few of the buggers as possible, eh, Robert?"

"Indeed, General, I believe Colonel Washington will be very helpful."

"Well, as you were, Colonel. Welcome. I leave you in Robert's capable hands." With that, Braddock looked down at his papers, indicating the introduction was over.

"Thank you, General," replied George with an unseen bow before exiting the tent.

Once they were out of earshot, George turned to Orme. "I hope I did not offend the general by providing him with some direction on the convention of handshaking in America?"

Orme laughed. "No, Colonel, I think you did quite well. Our general is in a most affable mood. Believe me, if he is unhappy with you, you will know it. He is a good man and an experienced general, but he does not suffer fools. I am afraid he has not had much success with either the Indians or colonials thus far."

Before arriving, George had learned that General Edward Braddock had two infantry divisions, a train of artillery, and seven hundred provincials. This was the largest professional army ever assembled in North America, totaling some 3,400 British and colonial soldiers, plus as many Indians as could be added to their ranks. Meanwhile a British fleet remained offshore to intercept any French reinforcements. Two British regiments, the Forty-Fourth and Forty-Eighth Foot, were commanded by Colonels Peter Halkett and Thomas Dunbar respectively.

George understood that Braddock was given the extraordinary title of "Generalissimo of All His Majesty's Troops in America," with command over both the British and colonial troops. Braddock was a perplexing choice to lead the American forces against the French. While he had been a successful commander of the British stronghold at Gibraltar, he had otherwise rarely served abroad, and he'd never had an active combat command. Fully versed in British military traditions and procedures, he had demonstrated neither the lust for glory nor the experience in battle one would expect for such an important and challenging command.

In response to Britain's buildup, Louis XV dispatched six thousand French regulars to reinforce his existing troops. Their goal was not to merely engage the enemy as necessary but to establish settlements and, build forts to act as a bulwark against any British advance. The ultimate French goal, as George had learned during his trip to Fort Le Boeuf, was to establish "New France," stretching from Quebec to the Gulf of Mexico via a chain of rivers and forts.

"You have been kind enough to assist me in joining the general's family," George said, "and you have the benefit of knowing, I suspect, a bit about me. I would be interested to learn more about you, Captain Orme."

"First of all, if you will permit me, when not in the presence of other soldiers or officers, we in the general's family address each other by our first names. As you have already observed, the general will also freely use our given names—although, needless to say, he is always 'General.' Thus please call me Robert."

Smiling and nodding, George said, "Good, and it is George, if you please."

"Well, *George*, I come from a military family in London. I am twenty-nine and recently of the Coldstream Guards. Along with Roger Morris, whom you will meet shortly, we three will make up the general's aides-de-camp. Young Robert Shirley is the general's secretary.

"I did not know the general prior to our deployment, but he has been an understanding and pleasant superior, although he does, as you have seen, tend toward a more 'colorful' use of language and is somewhat excitable. Nevertheless, I have yet to see him unleash that anger on those with whom he directly supervises.

"I became more fully acquainted with the general and Mr. Morris on our horrible voyage on the *Norwich*. It was one of those challenging winter transits that tends to either drive men apart or bring them together. The general brought out the best in us, and we became quite close by the time we arrived at Hampton Roads in late February."

George shuddered at the recollection of his two, comparatively brief winter voyages to Barbados.

"Unfortunately, we received a rude awakening upon our arrival. When we were being briefed in London, we had been told that reaching the French forts would be fairly easy and that they were readily accessible by water."

George gawked in surprise.

"Indeed! We were shown maps and were actually told that we could traverse most of this country and reach the forts by water."

George shook his head in disbelief as a now broadly smiling Orme elaborated. "We were met by Sir John St. Clair. You shall meet him. Suffice he is an 'interesting' gentleman—a baronet of Scotland and a former major in the Twenty-Second Foot. In many ways, he is even more direct than our general. St. Clair and your Governor Dinwiddie provided an extensive and more realistic assessment of the daunting topographical challenges misapprehended by our superiors in England. St. Clair explained to us that there were no good roads to Fort Duquesne, and the distances between Forts Cumberland and Duquesne were covered by untamed wilderness. I should confess to you, we also became acquainted with the dismal support provided by the colonials. We immediately realized that this would be a more arduous campaign than ever conceived in London."

"If I may ask," George interjected, "both you and the general have now made comments of disappointment concerning your interactions with the colonials. Did that involve the Virginians?"

Until that point, Orme and Washington had been walking at a comfortable pace from the General's tent toward the army's main camp. At George's question, Orme stopped to face George and paused, obviously uncomfortable. Choosing his words carefully, Orme replied, "Well, I want to emphasize that you are now part of the general's family; we will all rely on your discretion."

"Absolutely."

After nodding his head several times, as if he was engaged in his own internal debate, Orme answered, "Governor Dinwiddie and the general have not seen eye to eye. While I know Governor Dinwiddie is an enthusiastic supporter of this campaign, the supplies and troops we have received from Virginia have been wanting. If it provides you any solace, Virginia is not alone in failing to provide assistance to this army. Sir John St. Clair was particularly disgusted with the support, or the lack thereof, from the wealthy Pennsylvania Quakers, who ignored our desperate need for horses and wagons. We face many challenges in transporting our artillery: four brass twelve-pounders, six six-pounders, four eight-inch howitzers, and fifteen mortars. This artillery is still far less than we will face at Fort Duquesne. The general also managed to secure another four naval twelve-pounders to augment our artillery train.

"The general believes artillery will be crucial in our upcoming battle. Modern artillery has never been deployed effectively against the Indians, and the general contends it will be decisive. To assist in the overland travel, we also obtained thirty seamen to handle ropes, block, and tackle, as well as assist in constructing necessary floats to get the artillery across the rivers and streams.

"With the exception of yourself, the general has not shown a very high opinion of the colonial officer corps. I should note that his contempt is not driven by rank. I am afraid he organized a meeting with five colonial governors at Carlyle House in Virginia in April. Suffice our General and the politicians locked horns."

Aware of the meeting, George quickly ran through the five relevant colonial governors: *Sharpe, of Maryland; Shirley, of Massachusetts; DeLancey, of New York; Morris, of Pennsylvania; and Dinwiddie, of Virginia.*

"At those meetings," Orme continued, "the general vented his frustration concerning the lack of support received in troops and supplies. The response of the colonial governors was to emphasize that they were answerable to their local assemblies, who were resistant to providing further financial and logistical support."

"I believe shortly after these meetings, you and I began the pleasant correspondence that brought us together?" George interjected.

"Just so," Orme agreed. "Ultimately we had no choice but to break our large supply train into two separate columns. One column traveled through Virginia and the other through Maryland, with us meeting together in Frederick. It was only the timely intervention of a very impressive gentleman, a Master Benjamin Franklin—who managed, through some miracle of persuasion, to secure for us a large number of carts and the remarkable Conestoga wagons—that permitted our column to get moving at all. I must tell you, Mr. Franklin is a truly remarkable gentleman. I know he singlehandedly and completely changed the general's feelings about the colony of Pennsylvania. With Mr. Franklin's assistance, we have, albeit haltingly, begun our inexorable move toward Fort Duquesne."

"I do not mean to trouble you with too many questions," George said as he looked at Orme to discern any sense of irritation.

A smiling Orme replied, "Not at all. How else are you to know the lay of the land? I have been with these men for many months, and you need to catch up. Proceed."

"Please tell me about the Forty-Fourth and Forty-Eighth Foot."

As they walked down from the general's hill-top tent, there were two easily distinguishable camps spread out on the field below them, with tents spread out in even rows. Small campfires filled the open spaces, with men cooking or making coffee. Smoke rose from a hundred fires to meet the low clouds heralding the rain. Even from a distance, George could discern the overwhelming scent of the army. The sounds and smells were familiar to George, yet this presented a more orderly visage than he had experienced in Virginia.

Pointing to the left, Orme said, "There you can see the men of the Forty-Fourth. Obviously both wear redcoats and breeches with white splatter-dashes and carry the Brown Bess musket with bayonet. However, the Forty-Fourth's coats are faced with yellow silk, and the Forty-Eighth's coats are decorated with gold braid. The more elite grenadiers wear miter caps. Oh, and of course the sergeants carry halberds." Orme pointed at an enormous sergeant polishing a large axe head at the end of a lengthy pole. "We rarely get to use them in battle anymore, but they are still quite imposing. We also have about seven hundred colonials in blue and about fifty women who follow as wives, cooks, and camp followers. I should warn you that when it comes to the men, the general is a very strict disciplinarian. He puts up with no breach of order and will not hesitate to punish the men—or the women, for that matter—for desertion or drunkenness."

"I must confess, Robert, the discipline, polish, and organization is a sight to behold. I have not seen regiments like this before. It is deeply impressive."

Orme leaned close and whispered, "As I said, I come from the Coldstream Guards, who are a battle-tested bunch. I do not want to prejudice you, but these men have been pulled from garrison duty in Ireland. They are not the cream of His Majesty's army, but they are well appointed and trained, and should be able to handle a few savages and some wayward French." He turned and pointed the way, saying, "Come. We must find Roger and a billet for you and your servant."

Later that night, as George settled in, he took a moment to write a brief letter to mollify his mother, emphasizing his honest feeling: "I am very happy in the General's Family, as I am treated with complaisant freedom which is quite agreeable; so that I and have no reason to doubt the satisfaction I proposed in making the campaign."

Chapter 31

May 14, 1755 - Fort Cumberland

Upon reaching the newly constructed Fort Cumberland at Wills Creek, Braddock's first official act was to confirm George as an aide-de-camp. In a letter to Jack, George noted, "I have now a good oppertunity, and shall not neglect it, of forming an acquaintance [with General Braddock] which may be serviceable hereafter, if I can find it worth while pushing my fortune in the Military way." George was especially pleased that his unique status meant that he was "freed from all commands but his [Braddock's], and give Order's to all, which must be implicitly obey'd."

Braddock did not live up to his gruff reputation, particularly when it came to interacting with George. To Braddock's slight amusement, George would trail the general on inspection—a half a horse length behind as propriety demanded—and they would carry on a running conversation, during which George often dutifully took down notes while astride his horse.

"It is discipline, Colonel," Braddock proclaimed, "discipline and drill that drive this and every successful army in the field. The first step in discipline is making sure the men know your expectations. That is why, when we arrived at Fort Cumberland, I had the articles of war read to the entire army. We have suffered desertions and drunkenness. In this regard, I acknowledge that the redcoats have not fared much better than their colonial counterparts. The solution is a fairly administered court-martial followed by swift and unwavering corporal punishment. Floggings, my dear Colonel, are a great method of keeping the men on the straight and narrow."

George knew Braddock was not entirely correct in terms of equitable treatment. Leniency, if present at all, seemed to carry a decidedly

British bias. Rather than challenging the general's assertions, George changed the subject. "Discipline is obviously of paramount importance, General, but what of tactics? Are not tactics driven by the topography and the nature of the conflict we face?"

Bobbing his head with a knowing smile, Braddock boomed as he cantered toward the next group of men, "The lay of the land is certainly relevant. However, fundamentally, victory here will turn on superior men, their training, and their weapons. It is the Brown Bess that drives our tactics. Drill, my young friend, is how we make sure our troops can employ this weapon in its most effective manner. It is not a weapon for cowardly snipers; instead, it is the instrument of a cohesive team, acting as one."

George was already very familiar with the Brown Bess. The British infantry was armed with flintlock smooth-bore muskets with detachable bayonets. The addition of the bayonet permitted the elimination of pikemen. British tactics still emphasized a linear approach to battle, to permit concentrated and continuous fire. The reason for this intricate dance of fire and movement was the cumbersome reloading process of the Brown Bess musket. After firing the weapon, the soldier was required to draw the musket's hammer halfway back, withdraw a paper cartridge from the pouch at his side, bite off the top of the cartridge, shake the powder into the priming pan of the musket, shut the pan, and position the musket barrel up to receive the paper cartridge as wadding into the muzzle along with the balance of the powder down the barrel. The soldier then removed a ball from his pouch and inserted the ball down the barrel, withdrawing an iron ramrod from its holder attached to the gun and inserting the rod down the barrel to tamp the ball and powder. The soldier then returned the ramrod to its holder, fully cocked the weapon, aimed, and fired. A well-trained soldier could repeat this evolution several times per minute. The success or failure of a military campaign was presumed to turn on the ability to bring massed fire on a specified target. Given their inaccuracy, the ideal range for these muskets was no more than fifty yards. However, the impact of a ball that struck home was devastating on enemy troops.

Careful not to be viewed as arguing with the general, George said tentatively, "I certainly understand the rationale behind such tactics in the open fields of Europe. But, General, in my limited experience, the enemy may be disinclined to accept battle with concentrated troops where massed fire may prove effective."

George made this comment with some reservation, as he knew it raised the prospect of a discussion of his defeat at Fort Necessity. Nevertheless, he earnestly wanted to know how the general hoped to overcome the tactical conundrum they faced.

"Now we turn to the topography, Colonel. I have received reports and studied Fort Duquesne. It is *we* who will be surrounding the fort on this engagement."

George winced at the recognition that Braddock was aware of the circumstances of his defeat while trapped inside Fort Necessity.

"There are three reasons drill is crucial here and why we will prevail," Braddock intoned, raising his index finger and forcefully pointing upward as if calling on the Almighty to affirm his unquestionable wisdom. "Large fields surround the fort. If the French choose to come out and engage us in a traditional battle, we will be trained and ready to avail them to our advantage."

Another finger went up to meet the first, still raised high. "Second, we bring with us a substantial artillery train. Artillery, my dear Colonel, is the modern weapon that will prove decisive in this battle. Neither the French nor their savages have faced the full might of the British army. Modern artillery will reduce the fort to rubble in short order, then canister will make quick work of the enemy. I have no doubt that my trained gun crews and their formidable weapons will cause the Indians to turn upon their heels at the first sign of these mighty weapons of war."

George considered this strategy and had to concede that even his small swivel guns, casting a comparatively small amount of canister shot, had been effective against charging Indians. *Perhaps if properly employed, it could indeed prove as decisive as the general argues,* George thought.

Theatrically raising his third finger, Braddock stopped his horse and turned in his saddle to George. "Have you ever seen the proper storm-ing of a fort when the walls have been breached?"

George shook his head in response.

"It is a magnificent thing . . . a magnificent thing indeed." Braddock nodded with satisfaction. "Highly trained troops approaching and lay-ing waste with concentrated fire, then, having cowed the enemy, their bayonets fixed, a massive charge to the wall."

Braddock's horse took a couple of nervous steps forward as the General became more emphatic. "Training, drill, and discipline. That is how we will defeat the enemy and reduce Fort Duquesne. This is the largest concentration of British troops in North America. We have no need to skulk about the bush and fight like cowardly savages. The power and the might of His Majesty's armies are what will be decisive here."

George knew General Braddock's assertions were based on "the-ory" rather than actual combat experience. He had likely never led a siege of a fort or seen the events he described. George decided to remain tactfully silent.

As Braddock finished his pronouncement, their attention was drawn to a group of colonial troops in drill, performing badly and being abused and ridiculed by British soldiers and officers alike. George found this treatment distasteful, yet the slovenly appearance of the provincial soldiers made him hesitant to intervene on their behalf.

While busy learning and traveling with the army, George also heeded Austin's advice to keep his options open. Thus George took time to ask Jack to ask whether Will Fairfax was going to be running for the House of Burgesses. If Will chose not to run, George was considering seeking a seat. George emphasized to his brother that he should affect an "air of indifference." When Jack learned the seat would be retained by the politically connected Will Fairfax, George wisely stood aside.

After a month, George was becoming increasingly comfortable in the general's "family," yet he also sensed the tension within the campaign's leadership. George had been naturally drawn to Robert Orme. Orme warmly welcomed George into the military family and provided him with valuable insight. By age and temperament, Orme was a natural friend.

One evening, after all the other men had either left or gone to bed, George and Orme sat before a well-tended fire that cast a friendly glow and softened their surroundings as the young men enjoyed a drink after a long day. "Can you explain the division I believe I see among the officers?" George asked quietly. "I observe hostility from Colonel Halkett. Am I right?"

After a long pause, Orme nodded. "It is regrettable. I am afraid the split exists. Messrs. Burton, Morris, and I are often at odds with Messrs. Halkett, Dunbar, and St. Clair. These older men take a pessimistic view on virtually every topic. In my opinion, they are not supportive of the general or this campaign. Our differing military views have, regrettably, digressed into these gentlemen making personal attacks against me and wrongfully accusing me of attempting to curry favor from the general to their disadvantage."

George set down his drink. "Why, that is absurd. I have watched the general repeatedly in councils of war, and he takes advice from everyone. To think the general would ignore Halkett and Dunbar, who are colonels, over you—with all due respect—is ridiculous."

Orme offered a half smile. "I take no offense. Your sentiments are in line with my own. I often do not agree with Colonels Halkett and Dunbar, and I will admit to you that I do not find them affable gentlemen like yourself. Nevertheless, I have never acted in an ungentlemanly manner toward them or any others."

"Suffice, while it is my earnest desire not to 'take sides,' I believe you are being unfairly accused," George responded with more enthusiasm than he intended, further emphasizing his inclination to support Orme.

Orme took a large swig of ale and chuckled. "Well, George, let's all hope we can live to enjoy better times and improved drink. It appears I must survive the French, Halkett, Dunbar, and this miserable beer."

Grateful for the change of topic, George continued the jest. "I beg you, my friend, do not judge America by the swill you are enduring on this campaign. Hopefully, when this is over, you will be able to accept my invitation to visit Mount Vernon and Belvoir and experience the hospitality of the Old Dominion."

"To tell you the truth, George, what I most look forward to is not escaping this miserable beer but the clouds of mosquitoes and black flies that infest this swamp-covered land."

At that moment, George's servant Alton appeared and coughed discretely. George turned toward him and signaled for him to speak. "Colonel, I apologize for interrupting, but I've prepared your billet. Is there anything else?"

"No, Alton. That's all. Good night."

"Good night, sir." Bowing respectfully to Orme, Alton said, "Captain."

As the men listened to Alton's retreating footsteps, Orme turned to George. "May I ask a somewhat odd personal question? I will not be offended if you demur."

"Of course," George said, followed by a drink from his mug.

"I understand you and your family own slaves, and this is an integral part of plantation life?"

George shrugged in agreement, but thought, *They always want to talk about slavery.*

"And the slaves act not only as labor in the fields, but also as personal servants in the house?" Orme asked timidly.

George lifted his shoulders again, trying to hide his growing exasperation.

"And yet you choose to hire a white man as a servant—Alton. Aren't there slaves that could serve this function more economically? Again, I don't mean to offend."

Well . . . I didn't see that question coming.

"No, you are not offending by any means," George said as he set down his beer. "It is true that slaves can be manservants; indeed, I had such a servant until he was killed in battle. To be honest, I was frustrated, because when he was killed, Virginia would not reimburse me for the loss of my property. Having a white servant does not expose me to that same financial risk in battle, and, truth be told, having a hired white servant is easier and less stressful."

Orme looked perplexed, so George continued. "One of the greatest challenges of plantation life is managing 'our people'—which is what we prefer to call them—so they actually put in a good day's work. They are incredibly adept at not working. It is a constant battle to procure appropriate productivity. We always have punishments and rewards to create incentives, but this is often trying.

"My day-to-day relationship with my manservant should not be a test of wills. A slave manservant, in my experience, is not thinking of ways to improve my life. Additionally, I cannot always count on his discretion or judgment. In contrast, Alton is loyal and hardworking. It is an expense from which I derive value, and it saves me from the trials and tribulations of a slave manservant. My view may change, but for now I am quite content."

"Some might choose to engage in a discussion of the relative merits of free versus slave labor at this time," Orme said with a gentle smile, "but not I."

George responded evenly, "I concede that slavery is a flawed system, but my experience shows the problems we face. The differences in productivity and intellectual capacity between the races, as I have demonstrated with my manservants, only proves my point that it would be the height of irresponsibility to cast these poor wretches outside our protection."

"It does sound like managing your slaves is a bit like organizing and directing the troops."

George's mug sloshed as he set it down. "Indeed, I intend to apply many organizational procedures I have learned on this campaign at Mount Vernon." George sensed that Orme had more to say but decided to do otherwise.

"I am grateful for your insight, my friend," Orme said. "Something to ponder as I retire. I bid you pleasant dreams."

George stood and bowed. "And you, Robert."

As George readied for bed, he reflected on his recent experiences in the army, as well as his conversations with Orme. *Robert is a good man, and I am fortunate to have found a friend in the army. He seems more curious than judgmental about our people.* George then turned to the earlier conversation about the officers. *This split among the officers is disastrous. They do not talk to each other except to make attacks, either directly or through surrogates. It is bad enough to have to deal with conniving politicians, but to have this division within one's own ranks is unacceptable. Other than better supplies, higher pay, and finer uniforms, they do not appear to be better men. They all seem to be caught in a web of backstabbing politics.* George recalled MacKay's advice to blame others; while expedient, it was still distasteful and something he hoped not to repeat.

A few nights later, George sat alone in the General's musty command tent. Suffering the oppressive heat of closed flaps to keep out the mosquitoes was balanced against the prospect of a cooling breeze.

Choosing heat over bugs, a sweating George surveyed Braddock's correspondence to London. George's duties included addressing and sealing each letter and, where appropriate, having a copy made for the army's files. He held a letter he wanted to either confront the General about or tear up, but he knew he could do neither. Perspiration dripped off the end of his long nose and landed on the page Braddock had written: "The greatest part of Virginians, very indifferent men, this country affording no better; it has cost infinite pains and labor to bring them to any sort of regularity and discipline: their officers. Very little better." Nevertheless, Braddock still expressed confidence that "I flatter myself to be able to drive the French from the Ohio, and to open a communication with the rest of His Majesty's forces in the other provinces."

Disheartened by the behavior of his fellow officers and the General, and longing for home and contact with Sally, George had written her a series of increasingly pathetic and imploring letters, to the point where Sally admonished him to cease all correspondence.

Sitting alone listening to the snoring of men in nearby tents, he allowed himself to drift back to the library at Belvoir and pull from the shelves a remembered sonnet describing his situation:

Weary with toil, I haste me to bed,
The dear repose for limbs with travel tir'd;
But then begins a journey in my head
To work my mind, when body's work's expir'd:
For then my thoughts—from far where I abide—
Intend a zealous pilgrimage to thee,
And keep my drooping eyelids open wide,
Looking on darkness which the blind do see:
Save that my soul's imaginary sight
Presents thy shadow to my sightless view,
Which, like a jewel hung in ghastly night,
Makes black night beauteous and her old face new.
Lo! thus, by day my limbs, by night my mind,
For thee, and for myself, no quiet find.

I am driven to mindless distraction remembering her shining eyes, invit-
ing lips that reveal a smile that both lights and shatters my world! I know . . .
I should not write. Then, as if the pen had a mind of its own, George once again ignored his reason:

Fort Cumberland, MD   7 June 1755

To Mrs. Fairfax,
Dear Madam

I took [your] Gentle rebuke and a polite manner of forbidding my corrisponding with you; and concede this opinion is not illy founded when I reflect that I have hitherto founded imprac-ticable to engage one moment of your attention. . . . If on the contrary these are fearfull apprehensions only, how easy is it to remove my suspicions, enliven my Spirits, and make me happier than the Day is long, by honouring me with a corrispondance which you did once partly promise.

Despite his entreaties for her to write, Sally did not respond. George understood his attentions had gone too far, which only increased his misery.

Over the next month, the army faced a daunting 116-mile trek from Fort Cumberland to Fort Duquesne, requiring the construction of a new road while facing seven mountain ranges and countless rivers and streams, and carrying with it baggage and a heavily laden artillery train. The cumbersome cavalcade had to cut through hardwood forests framed by mountains in every direction. As the column began to retrace the path previously taken by George and his troops toward Great Meadows, Braddock frequently conferred with George.

"By Jove, George, this land is impenetrable and endless!" Braddock roared. "We are moving at less than two miles a day. My young friend, you might die of old age before we reach Fort Duquesne."

"I fear you are correct, General," George replied carefully. "As I have said, I was able to move my troops far more efficiently because we lacked the enormous baggage and artillery train that now slows us down. I believe a smaller, fitter, and less-burdened force could move at triple the speed."

The next day, Braddock convened a council of war in response to George's suggestion to split the force. After a lengthy conversation, in which Colonel Dunbar and other service commanders fought the idea, the general concluded, "It is settled. We will establish a 'flying column' of our best troops to make a sprint to Fort Duquesne and lead an assault. Sir John St. Clair's four hundred road builders and two companies of Virginia Rangers, along with Indian scouts, will act as the vanguard. We will bring two senior grenadier companies and the finest men from both regiments, as well as, the sailors to assist using block and tackle to move cannon, with the light horse acting as a screen. Colonel Dunbar will be responsible for the remaining troops, baggage train, and the remaining artillery. I will travel with the flying column, along with my aides-de-camp. It is my goal that Colonel Dunbar's column never lag more than one day behind our flying column, so that we may provide mutual support. Gentlemen, are there any further questions?"

All looked to Dunbar, who, downcast, shook his head in the negative.

"Very well," Braddock said, slapping his legs as he stood to conclude the meeting, "You have your orders. The flying column will move out in the morning. We need to establish a proper line of march. Messrs. Orme and Washington, will you be good enough to coordinate the orders?"

"Yes, sir," Orme and Washington responded in unison.

Yes! Finally! We will get on the move—and the general is implementing my idea! In only over forty-five days with the army, I have won General Braddock's confidence and helped make a fundamental change in strategy.

Over the next two days, George's joy was replaced with dismay. *What is the matter with these men? Instead of pushing ahead with vigor, they insist on leveling every bump in the road and erecting a bridge over every damned brook and stream! A "flying" column indeed! It is faster than Dunbar's baggage train, but the difference is so marginal as to be meaningless.*

George's displeasure turned to actual pain as he was struck with the "bloody flux," violent fevers, and headaches. He initially insisted on proceeding with the column and keeping up. However, George eventually became so ill with dysentery and hemorrhoids that he was forced to ride in a cart. Finally, on their arrival at Bear Camp—not far from the Great Meadows—on June 23, George became so sick that General Braddock issued written orders forcing George, over his objections, to remain behind to recuperate.

George lay sick and weary in a hot and leaking tent with Robert Orme at his side. "Fear not, dear fellow, the general has promised not to take the fort without you. You regain your strength. In a couple of days, you can take advantage of a cleared road and a fast horse to catch up with us. It will be difficult, but I am sure we will continue to trudge along, even without your grumbling and prodding," he joked as he surveyed his prone friend.

A miserable and humorless George murmured, "Thank you, Robert. Please keep your promise and send me notes with updates on how you are faring. You know how much I wanted to be a part of this progress."

"I will give you every sordid detail of *your* flying column," Orme said, patting George's shoulder as he stood.

With a wave, Orme was out the door. George glared disconsolately at the roof of his tent as he heard Orme putting his heels to his horse and galloping off.

So many men have died of the flux. My brother's company was virtually wiped out in South America by disease, and he never fully recovered. I might be another victim . . . or face an early death like my forefathers.

With this unhappy thought, disappointment and frustration were overcome by fatigue, and George succumbed to a restless sleep.

His despair was increased the next day when his manservant, John Alton, also fell ill. Like George, Alton was struck down with the bloody flux and was unable to attend to George during his sickness. But George was kept abreast of the column's progress:

Col. Geo. Washington   Youghiogheny River Camp
                                                    June 28, 1755

We proceed at march at our same deliberate pace. However, encounters with the local savages have become more frequent and disagreeable. For example, as we approached the ruins of the fort at the Great Meadow, one of the men of the 44th was shot and killed from an unseen enemy, presumed to be an Indian. Two days later, we dispatched four men to collect stray horses, and their bodies were found mutilated and scalped.

While we continue a pace, Colonel Dunbar's rear guard continues to be left farther behind.

I beg you, my friend, hold your constitution dear. While there is certainly evidence of hostile Indians, we receive reports the French are reeling and not likely present a serious threat at the fort. Do not sacrifice your health to join us. The general sends his warmest regards and compliments, as do all your other friends.

For my part, I remain your hm'ble & obdt Srvt.
Captain R. Orme.

On July 3, after the generous use of Dr. James's Powder, provided to him by General Braddock, a still weak George climbed into a covered wagon—leaving his ill servant behind—and began the process of rejoining the column. At the same time, Braddock decided to halt the flying line column to give them a chance to rest and for Dunbar's supplies to catch up.

Moving forward, George received another update from Orme:

The old man [St. Clair] wants the column to wait at the very threshold of our enemy's unattended fort for the arrival of Dunbar's baggage train. Needless to say, I spoke for reason and strongly urged us to take only a brief repose before making the final assault. I am pleased to inform you that the general, after due consideration, accepted my recommendation. I look forward to your approach to proceed in earnest.

As he got closer to the head of the column, George continued to receive steady reports. On July 5, Major Adam Stephen and one hundred Virginias met Braddock's flying column with one hundred oxen carrying flour. Resupplied, the column broke camp on July 6 less than twenty miles from Fort Duquesne.

Christopher Gist, having narrowly escaped capture very near the fort, reported to Orme that while the local Indians remained aggressive, the French troops were nonexistent, and the Indians were not presenting a serious threat. An enthusiastic Orme concluded in a letter to

George, "I left Ireland six months ago, and now we are about to strike the enemy's poorly manned fort. I do not expect a lengthy or glorious battle, so do not risk your health to join us, my dear friend."

Ignoring Orme's admonitions, George continued to push to join the column, enduring the violent swing of the wagon as its springs groaned under the strain. The constant shouts of the driver, the rattle of reigns, and the squeak of breaks only added to George's fatigue and discomfort on the mountain roads. Whenever he looked ahead, he longed to see the haze in the sky caused by an army on the march. Finally, on the evening of July 8, George rejoined the general at the camp on the east bank of the Monongahela. Fort Duquesne stood only eight miles to the northwest, and Dunbar's troops were still some thirty-six miles to the east of the flying column.

After hearty embraces from Captains Orme and Morris, George was led into the presence of a smiling General Braddock. George looked around at the friendly faces who were leading Braddock's attacking force. In addition to aides-de-camp, there was Secretary Robert Shirley, Sir John St. Clair, Lieutenant Colonel Ralph Burton, Lieutenant Colonel Thomas Gage, Colonel Peter Halkett, and young Lieutenant Horatio Gates. George had come to know most of these men, and he was deeply gratified by their warm reception. The general and his senior officers stood listening to a report suggesting the best route for the final approach to the fort. The scouts explained to the officers that the column was approaching an area called "the Narrows," which contained an extremely rough passage dominated by thick woodland and a narrow creek. This presented the tactically challenging position of being flanked on one side by the Monongahela River and on the other by high ground. To avoid this trap, Braddock followed the advice of his scouts to cross the Monongahela straightaway, then march north to a point where the column could recross the river and proceed to the fort.

As the meeting concluded, Braddock faced the men. "We will be vulnerable as we cross and recross the river tomorrow. Lieutenant Colonel Gage's vanguard will be deployed early, along with St. Clair's road builders. I want to know if an Indian scratches his pus-covered buttocks anywhere within a mile of this army or its crossing. It sounds as if the French and Indians are reeling, but I'll be goddamned if we get ambushed crossing the river twice in one day. Colonel Gage, you will move out at two o'clock tomorrow morning with two companies of grenadiers."

"We'll be ready, General," Gage responded, then hesitated, clearly considering whether to speak further.

"Well, out with it, man," Braddock snapped. "This is no time to keep your peace."

"If I may, I would feel more comfortable bringing with us two six-pounder cannons and some additional men to provide support. I also recommend we maintain and expand flanking parties. We should have men a hundred to two hundred yards on either side of the column with our typical deployment of a sergeant and a dozen or so privates. With ten of these units, our line of march should be fully covered and keep the Indians well at bay."

Braddock exhaled, relieved this was all that concerned Gage. "Very well. Proceed as you propose." Turning to the group, the half-joking Braddock declared, "Let's all be clear, gentlemen: I expect to be enjoying my supper at noon after our column has made its second crossing. Don't make your general go hungry."

The officers surrounding him nodded, and Braddock concluded the meeting. "One last push, gentlemen. Dismissed."

Chapter 32

July 9, 1755 – The Battle of the Monongahela

George slept harder and more peacefully than he had in weeks. However, around two o'clock in the morning, he awoke to the clang of limbered cannon and caissons as Gage's vanguard moved out of camp. Knowing a full day awaited him, George attempted, with only moderate success, to return to sleep.

At breakfast, the general's family received notice that Gage's troops had secured the first river crossing unopposed and were moving toward the second crossing two miles farther upstream. George, for the first time in two weeks, mounted his horse, sitting gingerly on a pillow to further cushion the saddle. He was still weak but pleased to be back with the army on a stunningly beautiful day. Washington, Orme, and Morris commenced the alternating duty of riding next to the general and moving up and down the column relaying orders.

As the main body of the column followed the path cut by Gage and St. Clair, a cheer went up as word was received that Gage was ready to make the second crossing. However, as Gage's men marched through three hundred yards of knee-deep water, they were met by a vertical bank about twenty feet high, precluding the army from a smooth second river crossing. Reports indicated that Gage and St. Clair's men were cutting into the bank and building a ramp to permit the remainder of the army to ascend to the shore.

With the vanguard constructing a ramp for the main column, Braddock stopped his troops and directed they be reorganized into a formal line of march. The main column reached the second crossing at about eleven o'clock. The steep opposite bank was widened to accommodate the howitzers and twelve-pounder cannon. At about noon, Braddock ordered the Forty-Fourth Regiment to cross and then deploy to the right on the opposite bank, with the Forty-Eighth Regiment to cross with pickets and deploy left.

Braddock and his aides-de-camp stood on a small hill surveying the main body of British troops as they were about to recross the river and make their way up the expertly engineered cutout. It was a brilliant day, with the summer sun sparkling on the gentle stream. The crossing was an awe-inspiring demonstration of British organization, ingenuity, and discipline. The men were marched across the river in formation, with forty regimental drums and fifes playing "The Grenadier's March." The anthem resonated through the river valley, sending the message to any nearby hostile Indians of the full might and power of this unstoppable Britannic force. The soldiers proceeded at close-shouldered arms upright, with their bayonets fixed and reflecting in the sun. The oversized King's Colour—a Union Jack with king's insignia—led the column.

Braddock, atop his charger, turned to George. "Never, Colonel Washington, in the history of North America, has His Majesty's army displayed the precision that we are now witnessing."

"Indeed, General, I have never seen finer. Simply glorious!" George exclaimed with unfeigned enthusiasm.

At that moment, George noted Christopher Gist approaching and signaling.

"General, with your permission?" George asked.

Braddock rolled a hand in assent.

George trotted his horse down to meet his former subordinate; he was genuinely glad to see Gist's weathered and friendly face.

"Christopher, what a pleasure to see you. I thought you were up front with our Indian guides."

"I was, Colonel. I am going back to the wagons to get more trinkets and gifts to satiate our friends and hopefully win some new allies." Then, under his breath, "As you may know, it has been a bit challenging, as the general hasn't exactly overwhelmed the Indians with his charm."

George knew Gist had been appointed as the head guide for Braddock's campaign in May but was constantly frustrated by Braddock's failure to follow advice and by the General's inability to maintain relationships with the Indians, thus depriving the column of crucial scouts necessary to act as a screening force as the army progressed through the wilderness.

"I know, Christopher, I have heard as much." Looking down the river, George decided to change the subject, so as not to undermine his excellent mood. "It is a damn sight more beautiful day than the last time you and I were in this neck of the woods, wouldn't you say?"

"Indeed, Colonel. In fact, Fraser's cabin is just up ahead." Gist pointed beyond the spot where troops were already moving up the bank.

"I don't know about you, but on the cold day we stumbled into that cabin, I thought it was more beautiful than any fine mansion in Philadelphia."

Gist's good humor evaporated. "The Frogs burned it, Colonel."

George's smile disappeared. "How do you know it was the French?"

A wave of darkness spread over Gist's face. "The Indians don't usually burn structures unless they have to. They understand the importance of a port in any storm—as you and I experienced. They are comfortable, mind you, burning a man alive, or cutting his skull wide open, but they'll only burn down a perfectly good building if they are making a point or it harms an enemy. In contrast, the goddamned French will burn two sticks that are found leaning together. As you know, the bastards burned down my plantation after the battle at Fort Necessity."

George winced as Gist spoke, for he knew it was his defeat at Fort Necessity that led directly to the destruction of this good man's home. While Gist's family had escaped with some belongings, George's failure had contributed to the further deterioration of Gist's limited financial resources.

Trying to lighten the conversation, George said with an awkward chuckle, "Well, they should get used to fire, because where they are heading, they can look forward to an eternity of it."

"Damn straight, Colonel." Gist quipped, shaking off his uncharacteristic bad humor. "I'd be grateful if you'd tell the general that my few scouts have not seen any indication of a French presence. If they were going to hit us, I thought it would be at this crossing."

George was relieved that Gist had moved on from the loss of his plantation, and he replied, "That was our consensus at a council of war last night. It appears the French are in retreat, and we should be in camp tonight for an assault tomorrow. I will inform the general of the conclusion of your scouts, and please give my regards to Major Stephen if you are back in the rear guard."

"I will be glad to do so, Colonel." Then, with a crooked grin, "What did that French bugger Joncaire say to you? 'I wish you a long life or a quick death'?"

George nodded, wondering where Joncaire was now. "A happy life or a quick and honorable death."

"Well, I wish you the same, Colonel." He clicked his horse a few steps ahead and said over his shoulder with a devious smile, "I'll forgo the kiss."

"Don't make me pull out my sword." George said with a laugh. "Keep your distance. It was bad enough having the Frenchman kiss me. I shudder at the prospect of your fetid breath."

"You are safe from me, Colonel. A fine day to you, sir!" Gist said as he once again started his horse toward the rear.

"And to you, Christopher," an ebullient George shouted as he turned to ride back to Braddock. "I will share your report with the general."

I should not be so familiar with Gist. Lord knows I am not as relaxed with the junior officers or men—but somehow he is different. He is always discreet; he has never made a joke in front of others. He is a remarkable fellow who manages to be both humorous while remaining deferential. Ah . . . the hell with it. I like the man and enjoy our repartee. At least with him, as a civilian, I can partially let down my guard.

George followed Braddock and his other aides across the river and forwarded Gist's optimistic report. Everyone visibly relaxed, and Braddock turned to Orme and said, "My compliments to Colonel Gage. As the enemy has not attacked us as we crossed the river, I see no reason for Colonel Gage's van to be so far ahead of the main body. As I understand it, we are now only a half dozen miles from the fort."

As the line began to move ahead, Gage's troop of grenadiers, along with St. Clair's road builders, covered a stretch of approximately 150 yards, followed by some support wagons. Approximately a hundred yards farther back were twenty-nine light horse, followed by sailors and pioneers to pull the light artillery, and approximately another hundred yards farther back was the main body, including General Braddock and his aides. Behind the main body of troops was a long train of wagons and support, followed by Halkett's rear guard, which included Major Stephen with one hundred Virginia provincials wearing blue coats with red facings and blue breeches. In all, the flying column was stretched out for almost a mile.

Having crossed the river, they moved through a dense forest with intermittent grass clearings and stone outcroppings nestled within rolling hills. Three well-concealed ravines, four or five feet deep and eight to ten feet wide, were hidden by undergrowth with a large hill on the column's right. The dappled sunlight moved under the gentle breeze, casting a white light and highlighting myriad shades of green, giving added life to the peaceful forest. As the lines moved forward, the men's attitudes matched the beauty of their surroundings.

At about 2:30 p.m., George, still at Braddock's side, was surprised to hear the unmistakable pops of muskets, followed a couple minutes later by the crash of mass directed fire. The column shuddered to a halt, and Braddock immediately ordered messengers ahead to determine what was happening. Within a couple of minutes, he received confused reports from young officers indicating that the vanguard had run into French and Indian troops, with volleys erupting directly in front of Gage's men and resulting in an indeterminate number of casualties.

As updates continued to stream in, Braddock remained composed and, apparently completely at ease on his horse, made no effort to move forward. George pulled his mount next to the general and volunteered, "Sir, if you would like, I would be pleased to go to Colonel Gage and the van and provide you with a more complete report of conditions."

Confidently surveying the troops, Braddock spoke without looking at George. "As you were, Colonel. I am receiving regular reports. Our

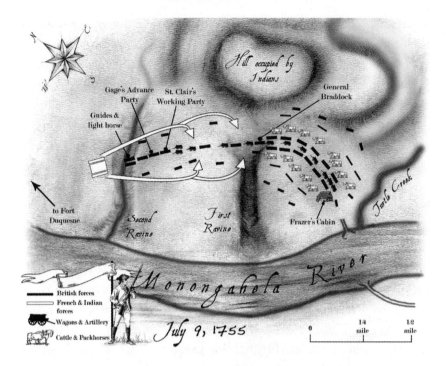

calmness inspires the men. I can't have you gallivanting off in a huff. My aides-de-camp must be at my side if the battle becomes hot. I am confident this is an exploratory force of French and Indians charged with preventing us from simply walking up and taking the fort without a shot."

"Yes, sir."

As he said it, George's temper flared: *It is more than that! And we are sitting in the middle of the road like pigs awaiting slaughter.* George added, with more urgency than he intended, "Our preliminary reports say in excess of three hundred French and Indians, General."

"Never believe the initial reports, Colonel; they are almost always wrong." Then, Braddock muttered to himself, "Where are the goddamned cannons? Gage, what the hell are you waiting for?"

George liked Thomas Gage and desperately wanted to find out what was going on and, if possible, join the fight. Then, in apparent response to the general's whispered plea, came the twin boom of Gage's six-pounder cannon. A cheer went up from the British lines.

Slapping the top of his leg with obvious pleasure, the general exclaimed, "There you go, Colonel; that will put the fear of God into the savages!" Turning to Orme, Braddock ordered with calm military precision, "Please instruct Lieutenant Colonel Burton forward to reinforce the vanguard."

Word came that Gage's troops had executed classic formations: kneeling, firing, reloading, and firing in ranks in turn. This mass firing, along with the use of the cannons, was apparently met with some initial success. However, there were also indications that Indians were moving down either side of the column and enveloping the British's unprotected flanks, limiting the British's ability to bring their superior firepower to bear.

The war whoops and battle screams of the Indians began in the surrounding woods, terrifying the British soldiers. The instant the fighting began, the unarmed road builders under St. Clair began moving to the rear. When the Indians increased their battle yells, a controlled retreat by the unarmed men turned into a full sprint, unnerving the regular soldiers who remained as road builders ran past them to the rear.

George was next to Braddock when a disturbing report arrived that Gage had apparently ordered his grenadiers to fix their bayonets and form a line of battle to rush the hill on the British right flank. The grenadiers followed the first order but then, in terror and confusion, refused to move forward as the Indians appeared to materialize from all sides.

Within fifteen minutes of the first shots, the French and Indians had moved along both sides of the British line and had taken control of the hill on the British right that Gage had neglected to secure. The concentrated British formations were ideal targets for French and Indian snipers shooting from cover. Now directed fire began to rain in from all sides, especially from the hill overlooking the right side of the British line.

Around him, George could see the main body of soldiers were nervous and fidgeting. Glimpses of running Indians could be seen in the woods. It was increasingly apparent that the French and Indians were using the trees and terrain as cover to fire on the British. Periodically a

French rifle would ring out, a nearby British soldier would scream, and a volley of British guns would blindly return fire at the hidden source of the shot.

A wounded St. Clair, shot in the shoulder and chest, was pulled on a gurney before Braddock. Delirious, St. Clair bizarrely shouted at Braddock in Italian. Braddock, without breaking stride, responded in the same language.

Amazed, George turned to Orme, who explained, "St. Clair laments that we are all going to die and should retreat. The general told him—rather directly—to shut his mouth."

George then heard St. Clair switch to English and gasp, "For God's sake, the rising on our right." Then he collapsed onto his gurney, unconscious.

George noticed for the first time what St. Clair was talking about. "He raises a good point, Robert!" George shouted above the battle's din. He pointed to the hill. "I believe the general should move our men there."

A frustrated Orme replied, "The general believes in firepower, not maneuver."

As if responding to Orme's comment, nearby artillery began to fire, but the gunners failed to find any target and mainly contributed smoke and noise to the confusion with no adverse effect on the enemy.

Meanwhile, Gage's vanguard retreated as its ranks were decimated by enemy fire. Gage's men, along with St. Clair's already fleeing road builders, smashed like waves into the main body of soldiers that, under Lieutenant Colonel Burton, were moving forward. The soldiers met each other at the base of the hill now held by the French and Indians, just as St. Clair had feared. The telescoping line was now a morass of men moving forward and backward, with units mixed in terrified confusion. Almost the entirety of Braddock's whole army was now squeezed into an area less than 250 yards in length and about a hundred feet wide, while the rear guard was still about a half mile behind. French and Indians fired volleys of arrows and ball with virtually no chance of missing. Not only did the Indians have the advantage of cover, but they also shot with rifles that had greater range and accuracy than the British smooth-bore Brown Bess muskets.

Braddock became incensed at the disorder. He slapped men with the side of his sword, bellowing, "Get back to your standards, men! There is no retreat here. Move to your officers and return fire!"

George recognized the need to move men into the woods and engage the enemy while also presenting a less inviting target. Turning to the general, George yelled, "General, we must not crowd the men! Please, General! Let me lead some men out into the bush!"

A blazing Braddock spat back, "As you were, Colonel! We need to organize our men to attack and mass fire against these heathen bastards." George acknowledged the order and turned back to the men to hide his disgust.

About forty-five minutes into the battle, George began to see the noose tighten as the French and Indian movement along either side of the British line had created an elongated half moon of French and Indians surrounding Braddock's troops. The hair-raising shouts of the Indians, coupled with steadily increasing fire, left the British feeling trapped and defenseless.

As George approached Orme, a bullet grazed George's side and hit Orme squarely in the thigh, staggering his horse. Amazingly, Orme stayed in the saddle, and, without missing a beat, he reached into his bag and pulled out a sash, tightly winding it around his injury.

"Robert, you are wounded!" George pleaded. "You should move to the rear."

"There is no rear, my friend, and I can't leave you and the general. It appears the bullet went straight through. Unfortunately it also seems to have wounded my horse. I'll stay with him as long as I can."

With George, Morris, and the wounded Orme at his side, Braddock was moving up the line toward the front of the column. They continued perhaps another twenty yards when suddenly Braddock's horse collapsed from a shot to the head. Braddock deftly jumped from the saddle, and without any apparent concern for his own safety, he turned to Orme and said, "Down you go, sir. You are wounded, and I need your horse."

"My horse has been injured, General, but he still seems to ride well," said Orme as he hopped down and helped the general mount.

"It's just a nick below the saddle," Braddock said. "Your leg and the saddle were kind enough to absorb most of the energy, Captain. You will remain here with these troops and provide direction."

George dismounted and helped Orme to a nearby tree. "Do make an effort to stay out of trouble, Robert," George said with forced levity.

Grinning despite the pain, Orme retorted, "Don't worry about me, you blasted fool. You are the largest target out here. I'd say keep your head down, but there is nowhere to hide that enormous body."

The men's conversation was suddenly cut short by the bark of General Braddock, "Goddamn it, Washington! You are with me, sir!"

George and Braddock trotted along the line. Periodically George would see flicks of Braddock's uniform spray in the air as French and Indian soldiers directed overwhelming fire on the high-sitting general.

After almost an hour of battle, men all along the line continued to drop from sniping fire and Indian arrows. Nevertheless the British remained tightly packed, falling back on training that was designed to provide mass fire in the open fields of lowland Europe.

What had started as a crystal-clear day now appeared like a foggy morning, with white powder smoke from cannon, musket, and rifle obscuring targets. Shots of canister, essentially giant shotguns, were being directed into any identified concentrations of French and Indians with minimal effect, hitting more trees and leaves than enemies. A dry dust filled the air, mixing with insects and heat to create the perfect cocktail of misery for all as canteens ran dry.

George knew the men were petrified at the prospect of being captured. They had all seen the Indians' handiwork on the mutilated bodies of unlucky British soldiers separated from the column. It was this fear, more than anything else, that kept them together.

Everything about this engagement—the sights, sounds, and smell—was different for George. When his men had endured the onslaught at Fort Necessity, the incessant rain and stifling humidity had deadened the sounds and smells of battle. In contrast, today the dust-filled air carried sound with horrifying clarity. The acrid smell of gunpowder stung everyone's eyes, and the men's faces were covered in powder from biting cartridges to refill and fire their muskets. At Fort Necessity, the Indians' arrows were both silent and largely inaccurate. Here, George would periodically hear the twang of a bow, closely followed by the scream of the arrow hitting home. Even the perspective was different. He sat high on a horse here, whereas at Necessity, he slogged in the mud. Finally, most importantly, George did not face the burden of ultimate command in this battle. He relayed orders and observed the mêlée, but he was not the man fundamentally responsible. This detachment gave him the perspective he recognized he was missing at Fort Necessity.

While the British soldiers were a crowded, paralyzed mass of mindless confusion, the Virginians instinctively took charge and began moving out into the trees and fighting "bush style," effectively pushing back the French and Indians. Moving in small groups, the men used the undergrowth, trees, and rocks for cover as they deftly approached the French and Indian position.

One group of 170 Virginians attempted to deploy into the woods. However, British officers mistook the blue-clad Virginians for French Canadians and directed mass fire, wiping out the officers and all but five of the Virginia soldiers, despite their screams that "We are English!"

Any soldiers taking the initiative and moving forward to engage were also almost immediately cut down by friendly fire. While clouds of smoke obscured vision, the misdirected fire was caused more by raw terror and a lack of leadership. George saw a Virginia soldier aggressively move forward to engage the enemy. Suddenly, the man's skull exploded like a melon hit with a hammer. George knew it was equally likely the bullet came from a friend as from a foe.

The narrow road and fire coming from all directions made traditional maneuvering virtually impossible. Still, Braddock, with George at his side, rode up and down the lines, haranguing his men to form platoons. But Braddock was unable to organize movement into any particular direction. Meanwhile, men had to avoid being run over by periodic riderless horses racing to the rear—another reminder of the dwindling number of officers.

The battle raged into its second horrendous hour, and the British line continued to absorb appalling losses. Faced with an untenable situation, the English took cold comfort in the rote actions of practiced drill: biting a powder cartridge, ignoring the foul taste of the saltpeter, priming the pan, pouring the balance down the barrel, ramming the ball and wad down the barrel, and firing. Even the sting to the face of powder igniting in the pan and the slam of the butt into a soldier's shoulder provided an illusion that "something" was being done. These soldiers could maintain this rate of fire at three to five times per minute, faster than any trained army in the world. The practiced actions had always meant victory. Reassuring as it might be, the rote motions had little effect on a hidden and protected enemy that mercilessly fired from cover on the huddled British.

The sound of passing bullet and ball became so omnipresent that George began to almost forget the air was filled with death. He was reminded of his true situation when, as the general paused to berate soldiers, Washington and Braddock were both simultaneously thrown from their horses. George, whose horse died instantly, was aware enough to jump off his saddle so as not to be pinned, but he hit the ground hard. The general's horse whinnied and buckled, yet Braddock was able to dismount as the animal began to collapse. Again without missing a beat, the general pulled his pistol and shot the horse in the head, immediately calling for a new animal to be brought up. George's horse was likewise replaced.

As George and the general moved along the line with their new mounts, they stopped under a large low-hanging tree to give orders to the surrounding troops.

What is going on? George thought as he noticed bits of leaves and bark falling down around the general wherever he went. With a terrifying realization, George understood that enemy fire was literally tearing the leaves from the trees in Braddock's wake in an attempt to shoot him. He watched in awe as the general offhandedly wiped the debris from his face, apparently indifferent or unaware of its cause.

George marveled. *The man is utterly fearless.*

The constant threat of death began to take its toll on George. His horse shied as he involuntarily squeezed the animal as the ramifications of being next to Braddock hit home. At Fort Necessity, the burden of command and the mud-filled chaos around him largely eliminated all consideration for his own safety. Here, as the minutes and hours dragged by, the carnage that followed them could not be ignored. The recognition that his instant demise was often inches or seconds away caused terror to bubble up, threatening to reveal itself as the panic that George saw in so many other men's eyes. It was only the sight of other steadfast officers and the humiliation of succumbing to such emotions that allowed him to keep his fear in check.

Before George could dwell further on his fate, he saw a horrifying sight and galloped forward to meet the man approaching him. A blood-encrusted Christopher Gist rode up in the middle of the chaos.

"Are you injured, Christopher?" George shouted.

Yelling over the screams and gunfire surrounding them, Gist grimly replied, "No, Colonel, but Colonel Halkett is dead!. There was a savage lying on the ground. I saw he was about to shoot the colonel, but I couldn't get there in time. I was . . . too slow. I . . . I should have gotten him. The bastard . . . he shot the colonel at close range and blew half his head off. Then the red devil dropped his gun and begged me for mercy. I showed him more than he deserved, because I gave him a quick death by putting my barrel against his head and pulling the trigger, then . . ." Overcome by emotion, he paused. After composing himself, he continued. "then, the colonel's son, James, was running to his father's side, and a sniper got 'im. He died on top of his father."

Frozen by Gist's report, all George could say was, "Dear God."

Shaking off the thought, George grabbed Gist by the shoulder and looked him directly in the eye to get his full attention. "What is the condition of the Virginians in rear guard and the wagons?"

"The wagoneers . . . those cowards! They all unhitched their horses from the wagons and galloped away at the first shot. I suspect they are halfway to Williamsburg by now. I can't say I'm surprised; I saw them lash that young Daniel Morgan for striking a British sergeant. The cowards are all in full flight and have left us all!"

"And the condition of my Virginians?" George asked again, fearing the worst.

"Your boys are unbroken, Colonel," Gist shouted. "It's the lobster-backs and the wagoneers that are running."

Despite horror all around him, George nodded with relief and said, "With Colonel Halkett down, Major Stephen will need your help. I'll pass on your report to the general."

Gist acknowledged the order and said, "Not the day we expected, eh, Colonel?" He turned and spurred his horse, galloping to the rear without waiting for a response.

Two and a half hours into the battle, gun smoke filled everyone's nostrils, and the moans of the dying men were only drowned out by the crack of gunshot and the subsequent thud as French and Indian bullets struck home. The sounds of screaming horses and the cries of attacking Indians swelled through the woods and added to the general pandemonium. The column endured the withering fire, yet failed to rally or make any effective counterattack. The remainder of the rear guard was approximately half a mile behind the compressed main army, but neither group could break the enemy cordon. While the terrified men did not engage in a headlong retreat, neither would they advance, despite the general's screams and accusations of cowardice.

Belatedly recognizing the need to act, Braddock signaled to one of his senior officers. "Colonel Burton, we need to dislodge the enemy from that high ground on the right." Standing in his stirrups to see who was nearby, Braddock ordered, "You need officers—Captain Morris will go with you! Take what's left of the Forty-Eighth and some grenadiers—you should still have about 150 men. Get to the top of the hill. With that ground, we should be able to push the French back!"

Burton commanded the troops to fix bayonets, and his men began to obey. George's fellow aide-de-camp, Roger Morris, stepped out in front of his troops and raised his sword. With his back to George as he advanced on the enemy, George saw Morris's head violently spin as a halo of blood and flesh filled the air and he crumpled to the ground. In an instant, George was off his horse and at Morris's side. The man's nose was largely blown off, and while conscious, he was stunned and in agony. A sergeant and several soldiers from the column also rushed forward to provide assistance.

George leaned over Morris and said with more confidence than he felt, "You'll be fine, Roger."

Wiping blood from his eyes, Morris looked and quipped, "Of course I will, and with this scratch on my face, I'll still be better looking than you, George." Then, to George's utter amazement, Morris smiled, showing his brilliant, blood-covered teeth under his mangled nose.

With a sudden wave of emotion, George thought, *How can there be men like this?*

Before George could respond, a mounted Braddock trotted up next to him and asked, "Is he alive?"

George looked up at the looming general. "Yes, sir."

"Then kindly get on your horse, Colonel. The men will tend to Captain Morris, and I need you at my side." Looking down at Morris, Braddock said, "Be strong, Roger."

George looked back at Morris, who nodded for him to go. He got back on his horse and joined Braddock.

Undaunted, Burton stepped around Morris and raised his sword to lead the bayonet charge up the hill. As he moved in front of the line and reached the base of the small hill, Burton suddenly staggered and collapsed from an arrow in the hip. Seconds later, his replacement, Lieutenant Horatio Gates also crumbled, shot in the chest. The elaborate British officer uniforms were a magnet, attracting French and Indian balls and arrows. Without leadership, the bayonet charge stalled. Every time the British redcoats attempted to move forward, they dropped like leaves in autumn under the withering French and Indian fire.

George knew their situation was dire. He received reports that fifteen of eighteen officers under Gage's command were either dead or wounded. Twenty-five of the twenty-nine Virginian light horse were also wounded or killed. Through it all, George marveled at Braddock's bravery and indifference to the death following them. Indeed, when the skull of the general's secretary, Robert Shirley, was cleaved in half by a French bullet only a few feet away from Braddock, the general merely shook his head and said, "Damn," then continued to encourage his soldiers to fight and take ammunition from the dead and wounded. Like the general, George did not have time to grieve the bright and kind young man who slid to the ground like a rag doll, a fountain of blood spraying the side of his nervous horse, who stomped the gore covered ground.

Despite the continuing decimation of his troops, Braddock repeatedly denied George's requests that he and the remainder of the colonial troops fight in the "bush style." Exasperated, and recognizing defeat was at hand if the troops did not move forward and take the hill, George rode up to Braddock and pleaded again over the fire, "General! If we don't take that hill on the right, we're finished. I don't believe many enemy troops are out there, and they must be low on ammunition. I beg you, let me lead what men we have and take the hill, but my way—with the men dispersed!"

As if the issue had only just occurred to him after three hours of battle, Braddock snapped his fingers and turned to George, nodding vigorously. "Yes! Get your men together, Colonel, and take the blasted hill!"

As Braddock turned to maneuver his horse and shout orders to support George's advance, a bullet passed under the general's arm and into his lung. He fell hard from his horse, conscious but suffering. George leaped from his mount to the general's side. He gingerly raised the general's arm to see that the bullet had driven the shirt and coat into the gash that was now welling up with dark, bubbling blood. George tore a part of the general's uniform and used it as a makeshift bandage to press on the wound and staunch the bleeding. With the help of another officer and Braddock's servant, Bishop, the general was placed under a large tree. As fate would have it, Braddock fell near the already wounded Orme, who, despite his injuries, continued to direct British fire and provide leadership.

George looked on as his brave friend, although badly wounded in the thigh, scurried over to attend to the general. George and Orme removed Braddock's red officer sash and used it to lift him onto an abandoned, two-wheeled, covered tumbrel cart. As they set him in the cart, Braddock reached for one of his pistols with surprising swiftness and began to cock the gun with the clear intent of shooting himself.

"No, General!" George shouted and swiftly pulled the gun from the general's hand and handed it to Orme.

"Washington, give me my gun back!"

"We cannot, General," George said.

"Let me die like an old Roman!"

Orme nodded in agreement with George's refusal.

"I am sorry, General," George replied.

Leaving Braddock in Orme and others' hands, George remounted his horse and attempted to reassert control over the men around him. As he did so, his horse violently whinnied, and its legs gave out. Realizing his second horse of the day had been shot, George managed to jump from the animal before it hit the ground. Picking up his hat, he noticed for the first time that it was serrated by multiple bullet holes. As he looked about him, to his surprise, Thomas Bishop, the personal servant of General Braddock, was running forward, leading by the reigns the horse the general had just been riding.

"Here you go, Colonel," Bishop said. "It looks like the general won't be usin' this one anymore."

In one smooth motion, George was back onto a horse, but in the intervening minute, everything had changed. It was now about five o'clock, and while George had already seen evidence of fear as the British soldiers absorbed French and Indian fire, the word of General Braddock's wounding spread like an avalanche—growing, unstoppable, and violent. The troops' deep and visceral terror of being left at the mercy of the Indians overcame the bravery and leadership of the British officer corps' ability to maintain control. These wide-eyed men, who previously had been willing to stay and fight, suddenly in small groups and then in whole companies, with or without their weapons in hand, began a headlong sprint down the line, ignoring all pleas and threats to remain.

Sensing the end, the Indians swarmed down from the hills with tomahawks and knives to scalp the dead and injured. Any semblance of order gave way as the Indians, yelping and screaming like ravenous hellhounds, drove the remaining British and American soldiers into headlong retreat.

The only saving grace for the British and colonials was that the French and Indians began to plunder rum found in the column, which allowed many of the retreating colonials and British to escape. George, exhausted and severely dehydrated, led a group of largely colonial soldiers as he pulled back. Whenever a group of Indians approached them, he wheeled and directed his men to fire en masse to retard the Indian advance along the trail behind them. Following this pattern, the group slowly, but inexorably, headed toward the river in the rear. Each time he stopped to direct fire, George was only faintly aware of the hum and throb of bullets directed at him. Indeed, his complete exhaustion—emotional and physical—left him beyond all such existential consideration. His only goal was to establish an orderly retreat to give as many men as possible a chance to reach the river, where he hoped a defensive perimeter could be established.

With orders given and the men moving, George became increasingly aware of his own discomfort. Waves of adrenaline had pushed him through the hours of battle, but now he felt the onset of the extreme postbattle fatigue that plagues all men after mortal combat. George, normally erect in his saddle, slumped and hunched forward as his strength failed him. Every muscle in his body quivered, and all his energy seemed to dissipate with each forward step of his horse.

George's mind began to wander as they left the battle behind and he and his men retreated. *Everything is covered in blood. The earth itself is saturated from the many wounded men who transformed the churned soil from a rich black to a repulsive reddish brown. The men themselves are a sticky mess, covered with their own blood, the blood of men they help to drag along or the spray of their comrades as we endured the punishing French and Indian fire. The gore covering the men is the perfect medium to attract dirt, leaves, twigs, and other filth. It's as if the earth itself is already consuming these men.* George looked at his blood-covered hands. *Macbeth had it right: no time or washing will remove this blood from my hands. Whose blood is this? Orme's, Morris's, the general's . . . ?*

"Colonel! What do we do now?"

George jolted back to the present. He looked down at a frightened soldier, whose face was filthy and blackened from a day of loading and firing his musket, sweat cutting white lines down his darkened skin.

"Keep moving, lads!" George shouted. "Help the injured! There will be a defensive line at the next crossing!"

Dear God, I pray so.

The men immediately around him took heart and maintained some semblance of order, reloading their guns after firing at any approaching enemies while others assisted the stragglers and injured.

As George and his men tumbled down the slope that was cut into the banks of the Monongahela, the flotsam of an army in retreat was everywhere. Uniforms, weapons, and ammunition covered the ground, mingled with the bodies of soldiers whose hideous and contorted faces were frozen in the last moments of painful death. Whenever possible, George tried to have his men drag those still alive with them, so the wounded could avoid the tortures of Indian knives.

As they finally reached the last river crossing, George was relieved to find troops set up to provide sniping positions to cover a retreat. Although both were wounded, Colonels Burton and Gage posted sentries, with the remainder of Gage's grenadiers holding a line at the river. As George and his cadre of men worked their way across the river, George looked back and realized that he was certainly the last officer, and one of the last men, to reach the safety of the east side of the river.

Once across the defensive line, the remaining officers held a brief conference. Perhaps a hundred men would hold at the river while others would move forward to assist those wounded who made it within sight of their perimeter. Over the next two hours, George saw to the needs of General Braddock and the other injured officers while organizing the remaining soldiers into viable companies, with noncommissioned officers and junior officers in command. Ironically, the grenadiers, who were in the van of the army at the beginning of the day, had retreated through the main army and were the most cohesive unit remaining to act as a rear guard and protect the retreat.

The officers surrounded General Braddock's litter and discussed the possibility of assembling a counterattack or establishing a new defensive line. All agreed their position was untenable and that an orderly retreat would be required.

General Braddock turned to George and spoke in a weak and cracking voice. "Colonel Washington, I need you to find Colonel Dunbar and instruct him to move his column forward with dispatch."

Speaking gently and patiently, George replied, "General, if I may, I know many men have retreated ahead of us. They will, no doubt, reach Colonel Dunbar shortly."

"Exactly," Braddock rasped as he reached out and grabbed George's arm, "and they will say, as cowards always do, that we were obliterated. Dunbar will believe I am Publius Quinctilius Varus."

Perhaps sensing George's confusion, Braddock continued. "Varus was the commander of the three lost Roman legions in the Teutoburg Forest. Dunbar is a student of history . . . that is what he will think. We are the lost legions . . . God help us, it is not far from the truth. We were surrounded by barbarian hordes in a hellish forest."

Braddock then stared off into space, either returning to the past few hours or imagining that ancient Prussian wilderness. He suddenly snapped back to the present and tightened his grasp on George's arm. "Colonel Dunbar will not seize the initiative. That is why I left him in the rear. No, Colonel. You are my only unwounded senior officer. Dunbar will listen to you. I need you to ride hard, get to him, and tell him to come and meet us. I fear if you do not, he may stop moving forward or—heaven help us—turn on his heels and retreat . . . believing us captured or worse." Then, almost to himself, Braddock muttered, "I am not Varus! My legacy will not be the loss of this army!" Gaining strength and determination, Braddock locked eyes with George and said through gritted teeth, "I am keenly aware of the hardship I am imposing on you. I know you have been unwell and done much today, but fate has placed us in your strong hands, my young friend." With that, Braddock's strength gave way, and his hand merely rested on George.

What an extraordinary man. He is dying and he knows it, yet he is aware of my discomfort. I cannot say no.

"I will get to Colonel Dunbar as soon as I can and give him your orders, General," George said with a strong voice, to be heard not only by the General, but the other officers around him as well.

"Thank you, Colonel, and God be with you and all of us." With that, Braddock collapsed back onto his makeshift bed, his hand sliding off George's arm as its owner no longer had the will to direct its movements.

A wrung-out George trudged over to a horse held by Braddock's dependable and omnipresent servant. "You keep bringing me horses, Bishop," George said without mirth.

"You saved the general. Only the intervention of the heavenly Father could have kept you alive during the battle. Now the general says you are off to save us all. I have looked for a horse strong enough to get you to Colonel Dunbar. This was the best horse I could find. We put some food and water in him, and there is some for you in the packs. I believe you will make it, Colonel—God rides with you."

George nodded his thanks, and with Bishop's help, he painfully remounted the horse. A wave of deep aching and soreness passed over him as he rode away from the general.

Bishop says God rides with me. I hope he does. All I know is that if I get off my horse, I'll never get back on.

Leaning forward and patting his horse on the neck, George said, "It's you and me, old boy. We both must do our duty or die in the attempt." He pushed back his heels, encouraging his horse into a trot. The hemorrhoids that had afflicted him before the battle were now like burning stones. His legs were covered in sweat from exertion and blood as the hemorrhoids gave way.

The long day gave way to an ominous dusk followed by a dark and terrible night. Through a lightless haze, the macabre groans of the wounded surrounded him. The experience was made all the worse because George was forced to ignore pleas for help, as he needed to press on to Colonel Dunbar. While completely exhausted, George already knew as long as he lived, he would never forget this hellish night. An impenetrable forest surrounded the retreating troops, who feared a sudden howl of Indians and renewed attacks from the flanks. If there was any good news for George as he trudged on, it was that he knew it would be easy to find Dunbar, as the detritus of a broken army marked the trail.

Every time his horse's head would sag toward the ground, George would give him a gentle touch with the spurs, bringing him to a cantor to allow the steed to regain his strength and wind. As time went on, all George could do was use spurs and reins to keep the animal walking in a straight line.

George had seen a reproduction of Botticelli's rendition of the hell described in Dante's *Inferno*. When the red sun finally rose, it painted the already blood-covered men crimson, reminding him of that horrific scene. Overwrought, George desperately fought to stay awake and remain in the saddle as his thoughts slid into the uncontrolled place between consciousness and sleep.

All take their repose, but I prod on through this nightmare. Everywhere I look, cowards sleep, curled up in ones or twos along the side of the road. The French and Indians, I'm sure, are asleep with the self-satisfaction of sweet victory. The courageous men around General Braddock are asleep, and the bravest men of all . . . are at eternal rest. George shook his head violently, both to stay awake and to interrupt the memories of the day's violent deaths. *I must be the only man who fought today that remains awake, yet I stumble on. "Stumble" indeed . . . This worthy horse can barely lift his hooves over rocks and twice has been down on a knee. At least he still sweats and breathes heavily. When the breathing becomes shallow and the sweat stops, I'll know the end is near.*

George's back, knees, and shoulders felt twisted and cramped with the pain that worsened with every unsteady step of his mount, which staggered from side to side with each hacking breath.

Chapter 33

July 10, 1755 – Dunbar's Camp

George knew his horse was on his last legs as the miserable pair crawled into Dunbar's camp, which was more than forty miles from the battlefield and just seven miles northwest of the Great Meadows. It was late in the morning, but there was no exaltation or sense of triumph as he approached Dunbar's tent. George dismounted with the assistance of a sturdy sergeant and paused in front of his horse to give it a final, grateful stroke on its long nose, which was met with a nuzzle in return.

Ignoring questions, he rasped, "Where is Colonel Dunbar?"

Apparently in response to the commotion caused by George's arrival, Dunbar exited his tent and surveyed George with his hands on his hips. The contrast between the two men could not have been more striking. The fifty-five-year-old Dunbar was immaculate, erect, and well rested; the twenty-three-year-old George's tattered uniform was covered with blood and dirt. George was the picture of stooped exhaustion. His normally energized gray eyes were sunken, bloodshot orbs dully staring out at the approaching Colonel Dunbar.

"Washington? Why are you not with General Braddock?"

George could not hide his irritation at the haughty and supercilious Dunbar and his air of condescension. A sudden flow of adrenaline filled George's system at the implication of cowardice. George straightened to his full height, pulled down on his matted uniform, and glared squarely at Colonel Dunbar.

"General Braddock sends his compliments. I am the last able-bodied officer who fought throughout and in the center of the entire engagement. The general sent me to instruct you to move your troops forward with all dispatch to meet the general's retreating column. He feared the retreating rabble from the army would provide you with misinformation, causing you to improperly retreat."

Given your comment about me, I see no need now to soften the general's orders.

Dunbar blanched slightly at the assertion that he would retreat, but responded coolly, "I had no intention of retreating, Colonel. We have fortified our position here and have been organizing the men as they reenter the camp. We will, of course, send troops and supplies forward to meet General Braddock and his column." Turning to the officers watching the interchange, Dunbar said with authority, "Gentlemen, you heard the colonel. Please organize a detachment of men and wagons to move forward immediately to meet General Braddock. Make sure they are well armed and supplied."

There. I did my duty. I pray Dunbar does his duty too and helps the general and my other friends . . .

Unconsciously, George returned to an uncharacteristic slouch as a day of battle and more than three dozen hard miles of riding over the last twelve hours took its toll.

Apparently for the first time, Dunbar noticed George's fatigue. "Colonel, how long has it been since you have slept? Or eaten, for that matter?"

A surprising kindness in Dunbar's eyes and his caring tone lowered what was left of George's depleted guard. Grimacing, George shook his head. "Honestly, Colonel, I do not know. I have eaten some in my saddle, and as to sleep . . . days. Someone had to get here, and the general chose me. I thank the Almighty that my horse did not give way."

Gesturing to his tent, Dunbar said, "Please, Colonel, I beg you, sit down." Then, impatiently turning to a nearby servant, he ordered, "Get Colonel Washington some food and drink immediately. I also want a bed prepared for him so he may rest as soon as I am done talking with him and he has eaten." Turning to George again, he said, "Colonel, you said you were able bodied, but are you injured? Do you require any medical treatment?"

"No, Colonel. I thank you. I just need some sleep and a bit of food. But most of all, I am quite parched."

Walking to a small camp table that held a bottle of wine and a glass, Dunbar poured a full measure and handed it to George. "I apologize, Colonel, but as you may well know, the waters in this area are all stagnant. Thus I am afraid my poor wine will have to do." As George took the glass, Dunbar continued, "As we wait for the food, I must trouble you a bit further and get a more complete story of the engagement and our current tactical situation. You and the general were quite right. I have been receiving very dire reports of the battle from men who, as I suspected and now know, retreated without orders. I am certainly relieved to hear the general is alive and the column remains intact. What can you tell me about the battle?"

Over the next hour, George drank, ate, and responded to questions from Dunbar. Describing the events of the prior day, George explained his understanding of the current condition of the army, including Braddock's grievous wound.

After walking George to a nearby tent for a well-deserved sleep, Dunbar stopped him for one final question. "Do you think the French are coming for a final attack?"

"I believe we greatly outnumbered the force attacking us, but in the face of our defeat, an emboldened French and Indian force may take advantage of our disarray and weakness. As the saying goes, we must prepare for the worst and hope for the best."

"Just so. I will bring my troops to maximum readiness in anticipation of a potential attack by the French until we receive orders to the contrary from the general when he arrives," Dunbar said with a sharp nod of his head.

"I believe the general will be well pleased. Thank you, Colonel, for your hospitality . . . and now for a good bed," George said as he pushed the tent flap aside. Without changing or removing his clothing, he collapsed onto a bed and slept for more than twenty-four hours straight.

George awoke the afternoon of July 11, when General Braddock arrived with the remainder of the wounded officer corps. An informal council of war was held in a newly erected tent for the severely wounded Braddock. George looked around a tent awash with pain and misery. Braddock was shot in the lung, Orme through the leg, Morris in the face, Burton in the hip, Gage in the belly and above the eyebrow, and Gates in the chest. The only able-bodied senior officers present were George and Dunbar. All feared the prospect of further French and Indian pursuit, and this was the focus of the discussion, along with the status of the wounded and supplies.

The meeting concluded with a halting speech from General Braddock: "We are burdened with terrible numbers of wounded men and excessive supplies, in particular cannon and ammunition. Over four hundred and fifty men are dead, but more importantly, we must move over five hundred injured by wagons and carts that are now filled with ammunition. Our priority must be getting the wounded men to the rear and saving the army. This wagon train was intended for an offensive campaign, but destiny has decided otherwise. I will not worsen our situation by unnecessarily risking the men to protect provisions and supplies. At the same time, we cannot allow supplies to fall into the enemy's hands and make our bad situation worse."

Pausing to summon his strength, Braddock continued in a weakening voice. "Colonel." Looking at Dunbar, "You will keep two six-pounder cannons with the rear guard with adequate ammunition. The remaining ammunition will be buried. I want all artillery projectiles, muskets, and tools that are not absolutely necessary destroyed so they may not provide benefit to the enemy. We need to free up wagons to load wounded troops. I want an emphasis on adequate foodstuffs. Obviously those soldiers able to fight will need their weapons and sufficient ammunition." With a resigned sigh, he concluded, "This is no longer a campaign of conquest."

Normally at this point, Braddock would stand and slap his leg, concluding the meeting. Instead he leaned back on his cot and closed his eyes.

Captain Orme, sensing everyone's unease, said decisively, "We have our orders, gentlemen."

With that, the bedraggled and wounded officer corps exited the tent. George was sickened to watch the destruction of supplies and ammunition that had been transported at such tremendous effort and cost. He agreed with the need to empty wagons and carts to accommodate the wounded, and he understood the supplies could not be left for the French and Indians, but it pained him to assist in ordering the elimination of supplies so crucial to the defense of the Ohio and, ultimately, Virginia. George witnessed the destruction and burial of more than fifteen hundred artillery projectiles and shells, cannonballs, muskets, bullets, axes, and tools, and approximately fifty thousand pounds of gunpowder was poured into a stream. Horses were dying at such a fast rate that soldiers were forced to burn a hundred wagons rather than allow them to fall into enemy hands.

George considered the butcher's bill paid by Braddock's army: two-thirds of the troops (977 of 1,459 men) had been killed or wounded, and of the eighty-six commissioned officers, sixty-three had been killed or wounded. George's Virginians had also suffered greatly. The three participating companies had virtually been destroyed, with half of their officers killed outright.

While the army around him was falling apart, George ate heartily, gratefully avoiding the return of the bloody flux. He slept hard and without dreams, giving him a significant chance to recharge. With Colonel Dunbar present and General Braddock nominally reasserting control, George felt the pressure of the battle and the retreat slowing lifting from his shoulders. However, everyone remained concerned about the prospect of a renewed engagement if the column did not get moving. As a result, early on the morning of the July 12, the officers and men continued in a tight line of march, retracing the road they had cut through the wilderness.

The next day, they reached the Great Meadows. Meanwhile, Braddock continued to deteriorate, issuing fewer and fewer orders. Calling George to his side, surrounded by the dozing aides-de-camp Morris and Orme, he gestured for George to come close and said in a weak whisper, "Colonel, your courage in battle and your steadfastness following it likely saved what's left of my army. While these brave men did much," he said, gesturing toward Orme and Morris, "I believe that if I had followed your advice earlier, the battle may have gone differently. I beg you, please take this sash that you placed me in, along with this leopard-skin pad for your saddle, which I hope will give you some comfort. Also, I give you these pistols, which I pray will provide you greater utility than they have for me of late."

"I will hold these for you, General, until we reach safer country and you have recovered," George murmured.

"My dear Colonel, I am not going with you. I am on my way to the undiscovered country." Braddock then turned to his faithful servant Bishop, who was standing in the corner. "Come closer, Thomas."

Bishop quickly moved to the general's side.

Turning to George again, Braddock continued. "Colonel Washington, I commend Thomas Bishop to you. He is a free man . . . but I offer his services to you. He has faithfully served me, and I believe his skills are suited to this New World. You may rely on his loyalty, if he can count on your protection."

A tearful Bishop nodded in acknowledgment, as did George.

"Good, good. Now . . . to sleep, perchance to dream . . ." And with a wince, Braddock whispered, "Aye, there's the rub" and closed his eyes.

Later that evening, Orme informed George that Braddock had turned to him and said in a clear voice, "We shall better know how to deal with them another time" and died peacefully in his sleep at about nine o'clock.

The remaining officers and men who could still walk buried Braddock in a crude wooden coffin. George officiated at the brief ceremony in the middle of the road, where they interred the general not far from the Great Meadows. The road was chosen to prevent the Indians from desecrating the grave and scalping Braddock. George ordered the troops to pass directly over the grave to obliterate its existence and protect the general's final resting place.

After burying Braddock, George walked through the army. He summoned all his self-control to refrain from venting his anger.

Cowards! The behavior of the wagoneers was reprehensible, but they are not soldiers. The vaunted redcoats, the men who abused and ridiculed my Virginians, don't deserve to carry their chamber pots! Attempting to calm down, George reminded himself, *Berating the men at this point would be counterproductive. In any event, it is neither my place nor duty.*

Instead George unleashed his rage in letters to family and friends, the first of which he sent to his mother:

Fort Cumberland, MD   18 July 1755

Honour'd Madm

As I doubt not but you have heard of our defeat, and perhaps have had it represented in the worst light (if possible) then it deserves; I have taken this earliest oppertunity to give you some acct of the Engagement.

We were attackd by a body of French and Indns whose number (I am certain) did not exceed 300 Men; our's consisted of abt 1,300 well armd Troops; chiefly of the English Soldiers, who were struck with such a panick, that they behaved with more cowardice than it is possible to conceive; The Officers behav'd Gallantly in order to encourage their Men, for which they suffered greatly. . . . The Virginia Troops shewd a good deal of Bravery, & were near all killd; for I believe out of 3 Companys that were there, their is scarce 30 Men left alive. . . . In short the dastardly behaviour of those they call regular's, exposd all other's that were inclind to do their duty to almost certain death; and at last, in dispight of all the efforts of the Officer's to the Contrary, they broke, and run as Sheep pursued by dogs; and it was impossible to rally them. The Genl was wounded; of wch he died 3 Days after; Sir Peter Halket was killd in the Field: where died many other brave Officer's; I luckily escapd witht a wound, tho' I had four Bullets through my Coat, and two Horses shot under me; Captns Orme & Morris two of the Genls Aides de Camp, were wounded early in the Engagemt which renderd the

duty hard upon me, as I was the only person then left to dis-
tribute the Genls Orders, which I was scarcely able to do, as I
was not half rcoverd from a violent illness. . . . I am still in weak
and Feeble condn which enduces me to halt here 2 or 3 Days
in hopes of recovg a little Strength, to enable me to proceed
homewards. . . . Please give my love [to] . . . Fds that enquire
after me. I am Hond Madm Yr most Dutiful son.

G.W-n

Simultaneously, George wrote to Dinwiddie:

The Virginians behavd like Men, and died like Soldier's; . . . The
dastardly behaviour of the English Soldier's exposd all those
who were inclin'd to do their duty to almost certain Death; and
at length, in despight of every effort to the contrary, broke & run
as Sheep before the Hounds, leavg the Artillery, Ammunition
[and] Provision. . . . [T]he poor remains of the Virginia Troops;
who now are, & will be too small to guard our Frontiers.

George also reported in correspondence of Braddock's bravery in
battle. At the same time, he sought to avoid the general's mistake of failing to hide his weaknesses, including his volatile temper: "Braddock's
good and bad qualities were intimately blended. He was brave, even to a
fault, and in regular service would have done honor to his profession—
His attachments were warm—his enmities were strong—and having
no disguise about him, both appeared in full force. He was generous and
disinterested—but plain and blunt in his manner, even to rudeness."
A letter to his brother summed up George's feelings and his amazement at being alive:

Dear Jack:

As I have heard since my arrivl at this place, a circumstantial
acct of my death and dying Speech, I take this early oppertunity

of contradicting both, and of assuring you that I [am still in the land] of the livg by the miraculous care of Providence, that protected me beyond all human expectation; . . . I had 4 Bullets through my Coat, and two Horses shot under and yet escaped unhurt. . . . Pray give my Compts to all my Fds. I am Dr Jack Yr most Affecte Brothr.

As George headed back to Mount Vernon from the defeat, he was utterly depressed and disenchanted. *I have often heard of the "smell of victory." I certainly will never forget the "stink of defeat." The summer's dry heat presented the perfect medium, mixing the smell of powder, vomit, defecation, blood, and sweat of both man and beast as the living and dead lost control over their bodies. Over this stench, there was another sickening smell worse than putrefaction. It is the smell of defeat—an odor that overrides all and fuels the men's panic. I wish it, but I suspect I shall never forget the odor of that day.*

I am cursed! Yet again I have led a doomed army into the field only to be defeated at the hands of the French and Indians. My hope of obtaining a royal commission died with General Braddock. My weight is down at least a stone, and I have neglected my farm. Perhaps my mother was right.

Chapter 34

July 26, 1755 – Mount Vernon

To his astonishment, when George arrived home, he was not the subject of derision for yet another failure, but a hero acclaimed for his unquestioned bravery and composure when the battle turned into a rout. His spirits soared as he reveled in the public accolades and relaxed in the familiar surroundings of Mount Vernon. Letters of congratulations poured in, lauding his courage. Newspapers, friends, and colleagues alike described him as the "hero of the Monongahela." Indeed, noted minister Samuel Davies preached a sermon hailing George's patriotic spirit: "I may point out to the public that heroic youth Colonel Washington, who I cannot but hope providence has hitherto preserved in so signal a manner for some important service to his country." An even more meaningful comment was made by Dr. James Craik, who was present with George at both Fort Necessity and during the Battle of the Monongahela: "I expected every moment to see him fall. His duty and station exposed him to every danger. Nothing but the superintending care of providence could have saved him from the fate all around him."

This military disaster was exactly what George needed to demonstrate that his prior failure was not entirely attributable to his own incompetence. If the sixty-year-old, experienced General Braddock could be defeated by the French, it was no stain on George's reputation to have suffered a similar fate at Fort Necessity.

In an extraordinary gesture, Colonel Fairfax sent a letter announcing he would be coming to visit Mount Vernon the next day. Sally also wrote a coquettish note:

Dear Sir:

After thanking Heaven for your safe return I must accuse you of great unkindness in refusing us the pleasure of seeing you this night I do assure you nothing but our being satisfied that our company would be dissagreable should prevent us from trying if our Legs would not carry us to Mount Virnon this Night, but if you will not come to us to morrow Morning very early, we shall be at Mount Virnon.

S. Fairfax, A Spearing, E. Dent.

George faced the prospect of not only a visit from the Colonel, but also a bevy of other visitors later in the day. While the letter was signed by three women, it was clearly in Sally's hand. George was both elated and irritated by her reversal in attitude. Only a couple of short months earlier, when he was at his lowest, she had barred him from writing. Now, when he was being lauded, she was clamoring to see him. He felt his irritation give way as he pondered the prospect of being in her presence. He sent a note inviting the Fairfaxes to join him at Mount Vernon for an evening meal and celebration of their happy reunion. Despite his fatigue from his long journey, George, with Jack's assistance, readied his home for visitors.

Chapter 35

July 27, 1755 - Mount Vernon

The next morning, Jack politely insisted that it would be more appropriate for George to meet Colonel Fairfax in private while Jack readied the home and directed the preparation of supper. While reluctant to exclude Jack from meeting the Colonel, George gratefully accepted his offer.

George met Colonel Fairfax outside the front door as the Colonel climbed down from his carriage and somewhat unsteadily placed his foot on the small step that unfolded from beneath the door. George knew the years were catching up with the old gentleman, thus making this trek to Mount Vernon all the more meaningful.

The Colonel, who had always been a fit and vigorous man, looked transformed since the last time George had seen him. His normally full cheeks were now hollow, and his skin hung loosely about his neck. In what seemed a blink of an eye, the strong man in his prime had become a frail old man.

The Colonel's face brightened with undisguised affection as he beheld George for the first time since his return to Virginia from the battle. "My dear boy! You look hale and hearty," the Colonel said as he shooed away a footman trying to assist him. For a moment, George thought the Colonel was going to embrace him. Instead he clasped him hard on the shoulder and said, "Welcome home, you have made us all very proud!"

Since the battle, George had received many compliments on his bravery under fire, and he had always accepted the praise diffidently. Even so, somehow the genuineness of the Colonel's words left him momentarily dumbstruck. A knot filled his throat, and all he could do was nod and say, "Thank you, Colonel."

Without letting go of George's shoulder, and looking him directly in the eye, the Colonel continued, "I know Lawrence and your father would have been tremendously proud in all you have accomplished."

George felt a sudden and unexpected wave of emotion. He fought desperately for control, tears forming as he swallowed hard. The Colonel, sensing George's unease, quipped with a gentle smile, "Are we going to stand here all day like a couple of women, or are you going to offer a parched old man a drink?"

Grateful for the distraction, George croaked, "Yes, by all means . . . I beg your pardon, Colonel. Drinks await us in the parlor."

Once the men settled in, and George recomposed himself, the Colonel spoke, obviously intent on having a substantive discussion. "I am told that the governor has, not surprisingly, had a change of heart and wishes you to pick up Virginia's mantle of leadership," he declared.

George knew Colonel Fairfax shared his disdain for Governor Dinwiddie, although the Colonel was better at hiding it than George. The governor had not hesitated to abandon his support for George following Fort Necessity and then so effectively undermined George's command that he was forced to resign. Now, in the face of George's demonstrated bravery, he once again claimed to be George's champion.

"Have no fear, George, we all know the bloom is off the rose when it comes to our relationship with the governor. He is a political animal with no sense of loyalty, and he is certainly no Virginia gentleman. Thus whatever command you secure, it must no longer be subject to his Machiavellian vagaries."

George had already considered this issue, but he had learned from past experience that when dealing with a man like the Colonel, it was better to seek his thoughts and advice before offering his own opinions. "Given the current position and our understanding of the governor, what do you suggest, Colonel?" George inquired.

"First of all, you should be unequivocally in charge of all Virginia forces. I have spoken with friends in the House of Burgesses, and this should present no problem. However, you must not be seen as making that demand. I can speak with my fellow Burgesses and others so that you are put in a position to accept the offer. An officer and gentleman should not be seen as seeking this sort of appointment, but rather accepting it in response to the call of the people."

"You are right as usual, Colonel. My own experience has been that to seek appointments often conveys the wrong message and puts one in a position of weakness. Do you think it is possible that we may do so without my direct involvement?"

"Absolutely, consider it done. Do you have any thoughts about other conditions, beyond being the commander of the Virginia Regiment?" the Colonel asked.

Ever since George had begun to understand the implications of his newfound celebrity following the battle, he had pondered the possibility of a new command. In particular, he had considered the changes he would make based on what he had learned at Fort Necessity and from observing General Braddock.

"You will forgive me if I am presumptuous, but I have developed a number of thoughts and conclusions, and I would be grateful for your insight."

As the Colonel sipped his drink, he rolled his hand for George to proceed.

"First and foremost, I believe our new Virginia force must be subject to strict military discipline. Our troops must be fully trained and subject to tight control. To that end, if I am in command, I will require the ability, following proper court-martial, to discipline and even execute troops to maintain order. Second, we will need adequate supplies: quality muskets, ammunition, uniforms, and food. I learned that an army ill supplied—as was the case for much of my experience leading up to Fort Necessity—leads to great challenges in discipline and readiness."

The Colonel put down his drink and looked at George with growing intensity.

"Third, if we are going to build an effective fighting force, we must look like one. We need to create standardized uniforms that Virginia's soldiers can wear with pride. Fourth, these must be professional soldiers with long-term commitments to serve. I have no respect for militia; they are the bane of the military, and we spend far more time disciplining them, seeking out deserters, and punishing drunkenness than they are worth. Indeed, my own experience at Fort Necessity was, in no small part, caused by poorly trained militia troops. Fifth, we need to make sure our troops are adequately paid. As you know, our rate of compensation is far below our British counterparts, and, indeed, is far less than levels paid by other colonies. Lastly, I will need the ability to select my own officers to support me. I will not have men under my command who are disloyal to me or answerable to politicos like Dinwiddie. Those are my initial views, but I welcome your guidance as always."

An expressionless Colonel Fairfax steepled his fingers, clearly considering George's words. The Colonel was perhaps the only person left in the world whose approval George truly wanted. The growing silence increased George's discomfort.

That is by far the longest speech I have ever given in the Colonel's presence. Does he think me conceited? Or worse yet, a young fool? George fought the desire to fidget in his chair or stand and pace.

After what seemed like minutes, the Colonel's face suddenly broke and beamed with approval. "Yes, my boy. Very well. You have thought this through, and those are all excellent ideas. The ability to discipline troops and select your command are obviously two issues that will need to be handled carefully. I do not believe supplies and uniforms should pose a particular problem, but I know that if we have a protracted conflict, supplying the troops is always difficult. Given our current situation, I do not believe insisting on well-appointed soldiers in unreasonable. I will need to speak to some friends. We will talk again about authority, discipline, and your officers. Have you thought of whom you want to serve beneath you?"

Again, George had extensively pondered this issue, and he quickly responded, "George Mercer would be an excellent aide-de-camp. Obviously Major Stephen would also be invaluable, perhaps as a lieutenant colonel and my second in command. An issue to consider is whether their names should be disclosed as part of this discussion. My concern is that if the names are submitted now, then, effectively, the governor will be approving these officers in advance. Again, in observing General Braddock's command, the greatest problems were because officers were selected without the general's input and were not universally loyal to him. I want to avoid that problem by having the power to make the selection."

Have I pushed too far?

"I know the Mercer family," the Colonel said, "and obviously Stephen's brother is a foreman of our estates—I expect he will be a loyal supporter. Given the current political climate, I do not believe the governor or his allies will be a problem." Then, raising his glass with a smile, the Colonel pronounced, "What we lack in prescience we will make up in persistence, aye?"

"Indeed, Colonel," George said with the dawning recognition that he had Colonel Fairfax's complete and unqualified support.

Having resolved the thorny political issues, the Colonel's countenance changed from that of a mentor to one George had repeatedly seen since returning: the look of a man curious to hear the story of the battle. With an uncharacteristic hesitancy, the Colonel said, "I, of course, have read the accounts and heard from some others regarding the battle. However, could I impose upon you to tell me what *actually* occurred? But, before you do so, let me caution you that I have known you too long. I will not suffer any excessive modesty on your part. You may save that for the ladies this evening." Looking directly at George, he continued, "Tell an old man the *true* story of your adventure."

The Colonel is right. Decorum requires that I not brag about my actions—that is always left to others—and that I minimize discussions of myself while noting the bravery of my fellow officers and Virginia soldiers. Nevertheless this man, above all others, deserves the unvarnished truth.

"Colonel, I recognize that it is only through your kindness and largess, more than any other, that I have received any recognition at all. Thus, as is always the case, I will assent to your instructions with the caveat that, if I do so, you will not think me ill mannered, vain, or bold in my frankness."

Impatient but still smiling, the Colonel responded, "Blast it, my boy, isn't that what I just said? Pray, tell an old man your tale!"

Following Jumonville's death and the defeat at Fort Necessity,

George had been forced to carefully consider his words with *everyone*, including the Colonel. Now he had nothing to hide. The account that followed was a detailed, truthful, and unvarnished discussion of the battle. After almost an hour of continuous speaking, with several interruptions and questions from the Colonel, George finally concluded his soliloquy.

Having heard the story of so much death and destruction, a now more serious Colonel asked, "One final question, George: I've heard a rumor that during the battle, after he was shot, General Braddock said, 'My dear Blues give them fire; you fight like men and will die like soldiers,' and that he said he could not bear the sight of a redcoat because of their cowardice, but when he saw your Virginia Blues, he said he 'hoped to live to reward them.' Is that true?"

George had heard the rumor before. "I did not hear those precise words, but it is certainly possible he could have said that outside my presence. We were at times apart. However, the sentiment is correct. He was extremely complimentary of the Blues and greatly disheartened by the performance of the British regulars—as we all were."

Nodding in understanding, Colonel Fairfax said, "It sounds as though Virginia has a right to be proud of both you and our Blues."

"Many a brave Virginian was left on that field, Colonel. I hesitate to have myself compared to them."

Waving a dismissive hand, the Colonel responded, "Nonsense. The will of the Almighty brought you back to us and will demand more from you. Your bravery—and theirs—should be acknowledged. What did you learn of tactics in the battle, George?"

"Perhaps that was my greatest revelation, Colonel. General Braddock, for all his many strengths, was excessively tied to the traditional style of fighting that dominates the lowlands of Europe. There is no place for such fighting in the wilderness. The French and the Indians' use of unconventional bush-style fighting—this is the *only* way a war can be conducted in this environment. While General Braddock was tremendously brave, he failed to grasp the situation and adapt to the tactical reality; that is, the need for bush fighting.

"On several occasions, I implored him to follow the lead of the

Virginia Blues and disperse his men fully on the flanks to engage the Indians and the French on a level playing field, if you will. He not only refused my request, but his decision caused—highly confidentially—some fratricide of our own Virginia troops. Rest assured that if I am in command, I will not be wed to the doctrine of military manuals written by men in England who have never seen our great forests."

"Anything else?" the Colonel asked.

"Yes . . . and this may relate to your earlier comments about the quality of our Virginia Blues versus the redcoats . . ." George hesitated.

"Out with it boy! Let's have it all. This is between you and me."

"The British are neither better soldiers nor better men. Indeed, as you have heard, the soldiers of the Old Dominion fought far better than the lobster-backs. We lost not only because of tactics, but also because of men. While they may want us to believe otherwise, I contend we colonials are in many ways superior. We are more able to change and adapt than the inflexible commissioned aristocracy or the British soldiers, who fight like mindless drones." George leaned forward in his chair, speaking with growing intensity, "It is my view that the undisciplined militia and the mindless obedience of the redcoats are opposite sides of the same coin, either of which can purchase failure. A good commander must be flexible to the tactical reality, maximizing his men's strengths and minimizing their weakness."

"Good," the Colonel said as he put down his drink. "This is good, George. Old men and generals are sometimes slow to adapt to change. That was Braddock's mistake, and it is sometimes mine. As you age, try to remember this lesson and remain the flexible man you are today."

"I will try, Colonel."

The Colonel suddenly looked tired but pleased. "I could use a brief respite while we await the arrival of my family."

George poorly hid his concern for the surrogate father seated before him. He offered a hand as the Colonel rose from his chair.

"Fear not, I am just tired. Age, as you will come to see, slowly strips away all vanity."

George smiled uncomfortably and directed the Colonel to a

bedroom to rest. He then walked out to speak with Bishop, who had not only agreed to remain as his manservant, but was also the chef for the evening. His other servant, John Alton, had not fully recovered from the bloody flux that had afflicted both him and George before the battle.

As George left the kitchen, he felt an odd mixture of pride and melancholy. Pride because he knew he had done well and was receiving adulation from the man he most respected. Melancholy, because his father and, more significantly, Lawrence, did not live to see this day. Meanwhile, his mother remained not only indifferent to his success, but also irritated by his absence.

Staring blankly out onto the Potomac, George thought, *What is wrong with me? I have spent my entire life trying to reach this position. Why do I feel ill at ease?* Unconsciously mimicking Braddock, he slapped his leg to shake off the emotion. *Stop it! Focus on action. As Lawrence said, carpe diem.*

Several hours later, George heard the rattle of carriage and horse approaching. He and Jack went to the front door to see two well-appointed carriages gliding toward his front door. Friendly waves were exchanged as the brothers met the party. His eyes immediately went to the elegant barouche, suspended on springs and drawn by two beautiful white horses, its collapsible roof open to the air and its small exit door embossed with the Fairfax family crest. However impressive the carriage, his gaze was inexorably drawn to Sally in a lovely bluebird egg–colored dress that shined in the July afternoon. George saw several of Sally's sisters, along with their husbands, but there was no sign of Will.

As the carriages came to a stop, George realized the Colonel had joined him and was standing at his elbow. The Colonel called out, "Sally, where is Will?"

As Sally alighted from the carriage, taking George's proffered hand, she said, "Will has been feeling unwell and sends his apologies, along with a fine bottle of Douro Valley port with his compliments."

George knew the port wine had been obtained at great expense because the war had largely stopped its shipment.

Will did not want to come and celebrate my success. I am sure he is brooding at home.

Before George could think any further, Sally grabbed his arm, pulling him close and leading him toward the house, saying, "It has been so long since I have been to Mount Vernon. Come, Colonel Washington, you must show us what changes and improvements you have made."

As George led Sally and the others into his home, he was suddenly keenly aware of the press of her dress brushing against his arm. He tried to ignore the goose bumps spreading across his skin.

The guests were seated in the parlor while George and Jack scurried about, directing servants to ensure everyone was comfortable and had a drink in hand. In the past, George had always made an effort *not* to stare at Sally. She'd always seemed oblivious to his attentions—except for that magical weekend when they had performed *Cato*. Today was different. No matter where he went, she seemed to be looking at him. George was nervous that others might notice, but everyone appeared to be looking at him with the same fixation.

As George, along with Jack and his new wife, Hannah, led the guests to the dining room, George prepared to leave the house to go to the kitchen to make sure the meal was proceeding as planned. When he returned, he ran into Sally in the central hall. He bowed, and to his surprise, she stopped and grabbed his hand. Her long, elegant fingers covered the top of George's large hand.

He looked into her large and glossy eyes reflecting in the candlelight. "George, I am so happy you are home safe," she said in a breathy voice. She literally radiated heat. Whether from drink or the warm room, she looked flushed and positively stunning. He suddenly felt as if he was standing on a sloping hill with gravity pushing him toward her. In response, he involuntary stepped backward toward the small door under the stairway, away from the entry to the dining room . . . and she moved with him. Speechless, he stood there blushing, uncomfortable with the way she had earnestly used his first name and continued to hold his hand. While it felt wonderful, he was terrified someone would come around the corner and see their tête-à-tête.

Trying to compose himself, George said, "Thank you, Mrs. Fairfax. I am grateful to be home and in the company of family again."

She's not letting go of my hand. She is not letting go of my hand! Dear God, she is so beautiful.

George stared, hypnotized, and felt himself being drawn toward her and into her unblinking, sultry gaze. He began to tilt his head toward her upturned face. At that moment, laughter down the hall broke their mutual trance, and she released his hand. Neither said a word, whether to avoid being overheard or as a result of an inability (or fear) to express feelings. George nodded politely and returned to the party while Sally continued down the hall.

As she passed out of sight, George stopped and felt the need to collect himself. With his heart pounding, George thought, *What in the hell was that? This can go no further. But, oh by heavens . . .*

George's revelry was again interrupted by the shout of Jack: "George! The food will be fine! Get in here! The Colonel and I have a question for you!"

George returned to the group. The meal and evening were a smashing success. Later, as George assisted the ladies into their carriages, he felt a mixture of guilt and exhilaration as he helped Sally into her seat. The woman he adored clearly shared some of his feelings. While neither of them could do anything about it, the affirmation was satisfying as he turned back to what was increasingly becoming *his* home.

George's newfound success and celebrity was capped when he received a letter from his uncle Joseph Ball, his mother's brother. Ball had counseled against allowing George to join the British navy at fourteen. With a sense of pride, George read Ball's letter of congratulations for his bravery at Monongahela: "It is a Sensible Pleasure to me to hear that you have behaved yourself with such a Martial Spirit in all your Engagements with the French Nigh Ohio. Go on as you have begun; and God prosper you." While his mother was loath to ever compliment him, this cherished acknowledgment of his success from his mother's family vindicated George's resolve that he had chosen the correct path for his future.

PART V

Virginia Blues

Remember what our father oft has told us:
The ways of heaven are dark and intricate,
Puzzled in mazes, and perplexed with errors:
Our understanding traces 'em in vain,
Lost and bewildered in the fruitless search;
Nor sees with how much art the windings run,
Nor where the regular confusion ends.

—JOSEPH ADDISON, CATO: A TRAGEDY, ACT I, SCENE I

Chapter 36

August 14, 1755 – Winchester

In August, relying on the Colonel's advice, George conditionally offered his services to the House of Burgesses through his brother Austin: "I can nevertheless assure you, and other's . . . that I am so little dispirited at what has happened that I am always ready and always willing, to offer my country any services that I am capable of; but never upon the terms I have done, having suffered much in my private fortune, besides impairing one of the best constitutions." Put simply, George wanted another command but would only do so if it met the conditions he discussed with the Colonel.

On August 14, the governor and House of Burgesses acceded to all of George's requests, and Governor Dinwiddie appointed George as commander in chief of all Virginia forces, with the rank of full colonel. He set up headquarters in one of the most lavish homes in Winchester, Virginia. Located more than seventy-five rugged miles northwest of Mount Vernon, it was the largest Virginian town within striking distance of the Ohio Country and the French.

Despite this "success," George knew he faced a tremendous challenge. With only a few hundred men, he was ordered to protect a frontier almost 350 miles long. Not only did George have to recruit men, but he also had to establish supply lines and set up all the logistical requirements of command while exercising authority over dozens of officers, most of whom were older and more experienced than he was. George continued his military studies, purchasing Humphrey Bland's *Treatise of Military Discipline* to further improve his management skills and emulate the organization, if not the tactics, of General Braddock.

One of George's biggest challenges was to find the loyal and capable officer corps he envisioned for his new regiment. As he had discussed with the Colonel, he was able to draw on a few men from the last campaign, foremost Adam Stephen, who was promoted to lieutenant colonel to command Fort Cumberland. George Mercer was promoted to captain and aide-de-camp.

As summer gave way to fall, George sat pressing his palms into his tired eyes to avoid looking at the mountain of letters of recommendation and requests for appointments from friends, colleagues, and even distant acquaintances covering his desk. One individual whom George earnestly wanted in his officer corps was Christopher Gist. Gist had not only saved his life, but George completely trusted his loyalty, judgment, and discretion. Following Braddock's defeat, Gist tirelessly roamed the countryside, providing George with crucial intelligence on French and Indian movements and informally recruiting officers and soldiers for George's undermanned command. Despite George's official unfettered authority to designate his officers, he met resistance from those who felt officers must come from the Virginia gentry—something Gist decidedly was not. As a compromise, George made Gist a captain of a company of scouts, thus satisfying his debt of honor to Gist while addressing Virginia's political reality.

George heard a knock on the frame of the open door and removed his hands from his eyes. Silhouetted by the brilliant October sun, the visage of the bearlike Christopher Gist filled the doorway.

"Beggin' your pardon, Colonel, do you have a minute?"

With a knowing glance at his commander, Mercer got up from behind his desk and said, "If you will excuse me, Colonel?" He then left the room.

Gist proceeded in a lower tone, so not to be heard outside the open door. "A little bird told me some folks in Williamsburg were less than enthused at the prospect of a grizzled old scout being a captain in your fine regiment, and that some pigheaded colonel made this happen anyway, not being the easiest man to refuse—or so I've heard."

"Well, *Captain* Gist, first, if you are observing that there are chimney corner politicians who have never been in battle or understand true soldierly loyalty, then I agree. Such people have mistakenly attempted to influence the composition of this regiment at their peril. Second, you are no longer a civilian, and if you are making comments about this mysterious 'colonel,' be careful, or he'll have you up on charges. I am personally shocked and appalled that some idiot had the bad judgment to make a scoundrel like yourself a captain." With a broad, closed-mouth smile, George stood and walked around the desk to grasp Gist's hand, sealing Gist's appointment with a handshake. "That being said, congratulations. This is far overdue, Captain Gist."

Overcome with emotion, Gist choked out, "I . . . am at a loss for words."

"By heavens, if I'd known it would shut you up, I'd have seen you a captain long ago!" George roared and slapped Gist's broad back.

Both men grinned as George returned to his seat and pointed for Gist to sit as well. The chair groaned under Gist's enormous bulk as he pulled out a handkerchief to wipe his eyes and blow his nose.

George's smile evaporated as he turned to the serious business of the regiment. "I am afraid you will not be able to rest on your laurels. You will have the rank and profit of a captain but will suffer greater fatigue than most for the title's honor. I need you to get out on my behalf and improve relations with these blasted Indians. Everyone is in retreat, and we need both good intelligence as well as strong warriors to defend our frontier."

"I know, Colonel. I've already got my boys out on it, and we're meeting with any Indian who will listen. I feel like we are pushin' water uphill right now, but there is no choice about it. We will keep winning them over one at a time."

"If it was easy, we wouldn't be here. Please keep me apprised, and be safe, Captain. Dismissed."

"Thank you, Colonel, and you, too."

With that, Gist was out the door, followed by the sound of hard-pounding hooves that quickly disappeared into the distance.

Despite his duties with the regiment, George was encouraged by his friends to run for the Frederick County representative to the House of Burgesses in the fall of 1755. He did not reside in Frederick, but he was a large property owner in Bullskin Creek. He was known to the electorate for not only his growing wealth, but also his bravery at the Monongahela. Unfortunately, George made no effort to campaign and failed to expend the necessary resources—usually involving purchasing large amounts of alcohol for voters—to secure an election. As a result, he lost handily.

In a surly mood, and still smarting from the defeat, George learned that yet another mere captain with a royal commission was challenging his authority. A red-faced Stephen entered in an unmistakably foul mood. While only of average height, with curly hair and a gentle face, Stephen's demeanor easily overwhelmed any perceptions of meekness.

"It looks as if you have had a hard ride down from Cumberland, Adam. What do you have to report?" George asked.

Stephen responded formally, "First of all, Colonel, I am very sorry to hear about the results of the vote for the House of Burgesses. I am sure you would have won unanimously if your friends had begun campaigning earlier and done a better job energizing the electorate. I feel myself, and others, let you down by allowing you to have your name placed on the ballot prematurely."

George waved his hand. "Think nothing of it, Adam. I am not a politician, and the results only confirm this fact. I am a soldier, and we have enough duties before us."

In truth, George was devastated by the loss, but acknowledging the fact to others was not only unmanly, but also counterproductive in both his command of the regiment and any future try for the House of Burgesses. *If I ever decide to run again, next time I will do it properly.*

"Very well, Colonel, but again, my sincerest apologies," Stephen said with genuine feeling.

"Thank you." Then, wishing to change the subject, George asked, "What do you have to report?"

"The usual problems of supply, staffing, and desertion. I have put together a written report for your consideration." Stephen reached over the desk to hand George a sealed envelope and then retreated a couple of steps to stand a respectful distance from his seated commander. "Obviously we need to continue to press for supplies." Then, with a sudden loss of control, Stephen became more urgent. "Matters have come to a head with this blasted Captain Dagworthy. The bloody shopkeeper refuses to cooperate in any way, and he has even countermanded orders to my own men! If I might speak freely . . . ?"

George knew that when Lieutenant Colonel Stephen assumed command of Fort Cumberland, he was met by Captain John Dagworthy and his thirty-man Maryland company. Dagworthy lacked any battle experience, and his prior profession was that of a shopkeeper in New Jersey. His only claim of authority was based on a 1746 royal commission.

Nodding approval, George gestured for Stephen to close the door and then said with a wry smile, "As if I could get you to speak otherwise, Adam . . ."

Stephen ignored the joke and instead roared, "Damn his eyes! Simply because a man has a royal commission, what gives him authority? The mere idea that a man like Dagworthy could presume to overrule someone like you, or me for that matter, is outrageous! This is far worse than our problems with Captain MacKay. At least he was an experienced officer and behaved like a gentleman. Dagworthy has completely frustrated my ability to run the fort appropriately!"

"Short of shooting him, what do you suggest?" George asked, Stephen's passion lightening George's mood.

Indifferent to George's attempt at levity, Stephen fought unsuccessfully to control his temper: "Obviously, if possible, I would like to see at least you and, if possible, me receive royal colonelcies from Governor Shirley. I would also like to abandon that damn rat hole—Fort Cumberland in Maryland—and build a new proper fort here in Virginia."

"I will write Governor Dinwiddie and make those suggestions." George tried hard to fight a grin as he added, "Albeit without some of your colorful language."

Stephen sat stone faced, still refusing to smile.

Becoming more serious, George replied, "While the governor and I have not always seen eye to eye, I am comfortable that he will support us on this issue. Although Dinwiddie does not have the authority to provide us with the required commissions, I believe he will be supportive with the powers that be. In the meantime, as much as possible, try to separate yourself and your men from Dagworthy. I will press both Governor Dinwiddie, and, if possible, Governor Shirley, to resolve these issues positively. I suggest you go get cleaned up, and I would be honored if you would join me for dinner."

Stephen seemed to relax slightly as he accepted George's invitation. George picked up his pen to express his frustration with Dagworthy and the perennial problem of British-claimed seniority.

Little could be done about Dagworthy in the short term; however, George could follow up on one of his goals of improving the appearance of his troops. George wanted his "Virginia Blues" to have a distinctive uniform. This was to be an elite fighting force, and he wanted uniforms that reflected this esprit de corps. Consistent with George's long fixation on his own carefully maintained appearance, he described in detail how he wanted his Blues to appear:

Every Officer of the Virginia Regiment is, as soon as possible, to provide himself with uniform Dress, which is to be of fine Broad Cloth: The Coat Blue, faced and cuffed with Scarlet, and Trimmed with Silver: The Waistcoat Scarlet, with a plain Silver Lace, if to be had—the Breeches to be Blue, and every one to provide himself with a silver-laced Hat, of a Fashionable size.

George's goal was that the Virginia Regiment would be "first in arms, of any troops on the Continent, in the present war."

Meanwhile, the problems with Captain Dagworthy persisted, and George's officers threatened to resign en masse unless the issue was resolved definitively. Finally, George received permission from Governor Dinwiddie to travel to Boston to meet with Massachusetts Governor Shirley, commander in chief of all forces in North America, to address the issue of conflicting authority once and for all. As he left on February 1, he wrote a letter to Lieutenant Colonel Stephen assuring him that "You may depend upon it, I shall leave no stone unturned for this salutary end."

Chapter 37

February 27, 1756 - Boston

E xhilarated by his trip up the eastern seaboard, George arrived in snow-covered Boston. The newspapers hailed him as the "Hon. Colonel Washington, a gentleman who has deservedly a high reputation of military skill, integrity, and valor, though success has not always attended his undertakings." He celebrated his twenty-fourth birthday with fine parties, enjoyable gambling, and spectacular shopping in the cosmopolitan city.

At the top of Milk Street, Governor Shirley occupied Province House, a fine three-story brick mansion capped by a cupola. George hoped the enthusiastic reception of the city's inhabitants would carry over to its governor. Thus, bounding into the Governor's office on the heels of Shirley's secretary, George felt confident he would prevail in his quest for a royal colonelcy. The instant he saw Shirley's haunted look, his enthusiasm evaporated in the face of a father's grief. The tall, stooped man with an enormous nose stared at him with a profound melancholy. George was aware the governor had lost both of his sons in war in the colonies. His second son, John, had died of fever in Oswego, and his eldest son, Robert, was slain at the Battle of the Monongahela.

Since my first battle, I have seen grieving wives, mothers, daughters, sisters, brothers, sons, but fathers . . . fathers are always the hardest. The women and children wail and cry. While horrible, and not something I'll ever forget, I give them a warm hug and a gentle lie about bravery and a quick death, and they seem consoled.

The fathers . . . dear God. Their stoic looks. Sometimes accusing. Sometimes just displaying a bottomless sadness. Always seeking an explanation that I can never provide. I supposed because Shirley was the commander in chief, he would be different; that I might be spared from this unhappiest of duties. Of course, that was foolish. He is still a man who has lost not one son, but both in this horrid war.

Shirley gestured to a well-upholstered chair in front of his large mahogany desk. "Please be seated, Colonel. I appreciate you taking the time to come and visit us in Boston. I am honored that a man of your courage and distinction is sitting here before me."

As George looked behind the governor's intelligent eyes, he saw the fatigue of countless sleepless nights, the familiar pleading look, the loss of legacy and immortality, and the weight of years knowing your dreams cannot continue through your sons.

"Governor Shirley, first I want to express my sincere condolences for the loss of your sons Robert and John. I did not know John, but Robert was an extraordinary young man. All in the general's family liked and respected him. I enjoyed many earnest and meaningful conversations with him on the march."

I will refrain from mentioning that we often discussed our mutual disillusionment with the infighting among Braddock's officers.

"Thank you, Colonel. Robert spoke well of you in the letters he sent us before . . ." The large eyes closed for a second to revisit the most incomprehensible of truths. "Before the battle. We also received your kind note after his death regarding Robert. It was greatly appreciated. It was appropriately discrete for the sake of his mother."

After another pregnant pause to collect his thoughts, he continued, "As a soldier, I must ask: were you were with him when he died?"

George nodded.

"I hesitate to impose, but I want to know . . . I need to know . . . how did he die?"

George knew this question was coming and was ready with an honest and straight-forward answer. "He died well. I was near him. We were in the heaviest fighting. He never flinched or wavered. He, along with other officers, showed incomparable bravery that to this day leaves me at a loss for words."

"And his death?"

George tried to hide the shiver that passed through him as he was reminded of young Shirley's violent and gruesome demise.

"It was truly instant. I know many say this to ease a family's pain, but I give you my word as an officer and a gentleman. I was . . ." George, at this point, for the first time looked directly into Shirley's bloodshot and pained gaze. "I was there. He endured no pain and avoided both the savage's and surgeon's blade. I know that is little consolation, but he did not suffer. He was a good man, and I miss him. I can only imagine your loss. Please know you have my deepest sympathy."

"And his body?"

George's mind momentarily slipped to imagine his scalped and unburied friends left to the pointed teeth of foxes, raccoons, and other woodland scavengers feeding on the corpses' cold flesh.

Now, my dear Governor, the whitest of lies . . .

"In the course of the battle, some men were buried on the spot"— *Never happened*—"and the French, I understand, also buried many of our dead"—*Untrue.* "I confess that I did not see Robert interred, but I believe given the early timing of his death"—*The timing of his death is irrelevant*—"he was likely buried."

Forgive me, Governor, for those untruths. I have no doubt your son's lovely hair and scalp are now a trophy of some savage's lodge. As to his body . . . God only knows.

"Yes . . . thank you, Colonel, you are very kind. Obviously this loss weighs heavily on me, and your words mean much, coming from a man who was there."

The veil of agony partially lifted as he tried to cast off the renewed memory of his lost son and change the subject: "Let me start by saying that I have read all the correspondence relating to this matter from Governor Dinwiddie and others. I sympathize with your situation. I do not know this Dagworthy, but you are a brave and accomplished young man who should not be shouldering these challenges. Your Governor Dinwiddie suggests that I merely issue a brevet royal colonelcy to solve this command issue. I know this seems to be the best solution at first blush."

George tried to remain impassive, but he took an involuntary, heavy intake of breach. Shirley seemed ready to grant his colonelcy.

"However, my tenure as commander in chief is limited," continued Shirley. "If I issue the brevet promotion, it will expire with my term, and it would not convert into a regular commission." The strained expression lessened as he focused on George, "No, I believe the better solution here is to examine the authority of this uncooperative captain. His commission, while originally royal in origin, also comes with a commission from the governor of Maryland, and thus he is junior to other similarly situated provincial officers—such as you, Colonel Washington. I will issue an order that you are the senior provincial officer at the fort, and that your authority shall be paramount and not subject to question. A ruling of this type is *not* subject to expiration upon the end of my tenure. Thus your command will remain unchallenged from Captain Dagworthy or other similarly situated inferior provincial officers."

Goddamn it! I didn't come all the way to Boston to control a fort. I came for a colonelcy and a royal commission. Quietly, George took in a deep breath.

Calm down. You have a victory of sorts, and you will do yourself a disservice by arguing with this man. He is an important person with whom you have developed a rapport, and you need to be gracious.

"I appreciate your careful consideration of this matter, Governor Shirley. Rest assured, I am grateful for your support, and I am hopeful such problems will be avoided in the future," George said with far more enthusiasm than he felt.

Here we go . . . I need to at least argue for a change in London to avoid this problem in the future.

Edging forward in his chair, George continued. "I believe the solution to this ongoing problem, which I have seen in the past in my admittedly short career, is for a formal ruling from London that recognizes the ability of senior colonial officers to command inferior royal officers," George said.

The always politic Shirley responded, "You raise an important issue, Colonel, which I, too, hope will be definitively addressed in London. I know you have a long trip ahead of you. I will have my secretary prepare an order consistent with our discussion. I am hopeful you will remain for the evening and enjoy some games of chance with my staff."

Standing at the obvious conclusion of the meeting, George bowed. "Of course, Governor. I am grateful for your hospitality and insight, and again, my deepest sympathy."

Shirley nodded politely, and George bowed again and left.

George's despondence worsened as his prior success playing cards earlier in his trip was wiped out by the "sharks" circling the governor's gaming table.

Chapter 38

April 7, 1756 - Winchester

George returned to his Virginia Regiment two weeks after meeting Governor Shirley. During his eight months in command, he had been absent almost half the time. After so much neglect, George began to focus on the important work of directing all aspects of the regiment. He had seen General Braddock's administration, but now the true challenges of running the regiment were almost overwhelming: suppliers had to be obtained, men had to be disciplined, promotions to be awarded, paperwork—endless correspondence and reports—had to be completed, funds had to be accounted for, and, most of all, he had to keep his bored men prepared to defend against an attack that might or might not come.

The military situation in April 1756 was dire. A third of George's force had been lost to the Indians in bush fighting. Colonial and British troops, along with average citizens, were in full retreat in response to the marauding French. In a letter to Dinwiddie, George observed, "Not an hour, nay, scarcely a minute passes, that does not produce fresh alarms and melancholy accounts."

Much of the Shenandoah Valley was in the hands of the enemy. Many settlements had been destroyed by raiding Indians, and inhabitants had been forced to retire into larger cities and towns to avoid the spreading war. George's only alternative was to recommend resettlement of frontier inhabitants into secure forts until a more cohesive strategy was implemented. In an impassioned letter to Governor Dinwiddie, George described the suffering of the people:

> Your Honor may see to what unhappy straits the distressed Inhabitants as well as I, am reduced. I am too little acquainted,

Sir, with pathetic language, to attempt a description of the peoples distresses; though I have a generous soul, sensible of wrongs, and swelling for redress—But what can I do? If bleeding, dying! would glut their insatiate revenge—I would be a willing offering to Savage Fury: and die by inches, to save a people! I see their situation, know their danger, and participate their Sufferings; without having it in my power to give them relief, than uncertain promises.

The supplicating tears of the women; and moving petitions from men, melt me into such deadly sorrow, that I solemnly declare, if I know my own mind—I could offer myself a willing Sacrifice to the butchering Enemy, provided that would contribute to the peoples ease.

George also assured the governor that, "I have done every Thing in my Power, to quiet the Minds of the Inhabitants, by detaching all the Men that I have any Command over, to the Places, which are most exposed."

At the same time, George marveled at the stamina and fighting abilities of the Indians, noting that their "cunning and craft are not to be equaled." They "prowl about like Wolves; and like them, do their mischief by Stealth." George concluded that a large, well-equipped bush-fighting force was needed to take the battle to the Indians. Crucial to George's strategy was the recruitment of Indian allies, noting "Indians are only match for Indians; and without these, we shall ever fight upon unequal Terms."

During a visit to Williamsburg, George was summoned to meet with Governor Dinwiddie. Gone were the warm greetings and affable conversation. Even Dinwiddie's secretary was stone faced as he opened the Governor's door, lest he be viewed as showing kindness to the Governor's nemesis.

Dinwiddie momentarily unweighted in his chair in an indifferent effort to acknowledge George's entry. The Governor paused, cocked his head to the side, and, after a long moment, decided to loosely flick his hand, directing George to a chair. The men stared at each other, only the sound of the Governor's clock breaking the silence, but not the tension.

Finally, George chose to speak: "Governor, I appreciate the opportunity to meet with you. With better equipment and supplies, we could concentrate our forces and attack the French and the Indians in their strongholds. We need to seize the initiative instead of constantly acting on the defensive."

As if suddenly shocked into life, the Governor became animated and violently shook his head in disagreement, his jowls continuing their gyrations long after his head stopped moving. "No, no, no, Colonel! In a vacuum, your strategy might make sense, but abandoning the people while your forces gallivant off to try to find the Indians will make a bad situation far worse. We need a series of forts dispersed along the Virginia border and manned by your troops to protect the civilian population."

George willed himself to remain calm and control his frustration with this pompous politician, who was utterly unaware of the realty facing him and his men. With strained politeness, George responded, "Respectfully, Governor, manning such a string of forts would require an inconceivable number of men, along with stores of provisions, arms, ammunition, wagons, and horses in a degree beyond what can be possibly reasonably allocated."

Dinwiddie sniffed. "Be that as it may, I at least present a strategy that the populace and the House of Burgesses may find palatable. There is no appetite in Williamsburg for an offensive war. We live in a world of the politically and financially possible. Your naive strategy is both politically and logistically *impossible*." The governor then paused to emphasize he was issuing a command: "You will deploy your men as you are ordered, and I will endeavor to provide you with the materials, supplies, and men you request."

George felt his cheeks redden. Recognizing that further discussion was hopeless, he made a minimal and perfunctory bow in acknowledgment and took his leave. However, before departing Williamsburg, he began a letter-writing campaign demanding adequate logistical support for the forts. George's frustration was so extreme that he wrote the Colonel and suggested that perhaps he should resign rather than follow a strategy he knew to be in error. Once again, Colonel Fairfax provided needed encouragement and prevented George from resigning, concluding, "Your endeavors in the service and defense of your country must redound to your honor."

As the year progressed, the tactical situation did not improve. Undermanned, underequipped, and underpaid, George's troops fought an endless war of attrition with a skilled enemy that engaged his troops at the times and places of their choosing and always to the disadvantage of George's men.

In October 1756, George was on a reconnaissance mission visiting a post situated near the origin of the Roanoke River, known as Fort Vass. Moving in a line on a narrow country road, George and twelve of his men were beginning to let their guard down as they neared the fort. Suddenly screams of attacking Indians surrounded the column, followed by a wave of arrows from all directions, and the explosion of musketry followed by telltale puffs of white smoke. One of the scouts in front of George collapsed forward, an arrow in his throat and a spray of blood, backlit by the sun, covering the dying man as he fell to the ground.

While this small force was surrounded, much as Braddock's men had been at Monongahela, their reactions were entirely different. Years of hard fighting had taught George's men how to react when under attack. Without orders, the men immediately broke left and right to either side of the trail and began to engage the enemy. Many, however, had not taken the precaution of wrapping their flintlock muskets and rifles with waxed cloth to protect them from the rain they had traveled through earlier in the day. The clicks of flint on metal gave testament to wet powder, revealing the soldiers' lack of diligence.

As George uncovered his pistol, he looked up to see a face-painted Indian screaming and running at him with a tomahawk over his head. George raised his gun, aimed at the man's chest, and pulled the trigger.

The click of the flintlock was followed by the satisfying sound of the igniting pan, flash, and report as the Indian fell to the ground. Pulling his sword, George moved ahead, yelling at his men to return fire, reload their muskets, and move out to engage the Indians. At the familiar sound of musket balls whistling by his head, George forced his horse forward into the surrounding woods and dismounted in time to see one of his sergeants use a bayonet to impale a rushing Indian, who showed surprise before the wave of death washed across his face. The skirmish lasted no more than ten minutes, but two of George's men were dead and three were injured. The battle was a tactical draw, but it reinforced in George's mind the waste of these piecemeal engagements.

Unable to control his anger, George wrote Speaker Robinson, and other prominent Virginians, lamenting the governor's strategy and suggesting that Fort Cumberland be abandoned in favor of establishing a major fort at Winchester. George asserted that Winchester's location on the frontier, as well as its access to supply lines, made it a more logical repository of military power.

Governor Dinwiddie responded to George's complaints with a critical article in the *Virginia Sentinel*. When George received word of the article, he sought advice from Austin on how to proceed. Austin assured him that "I am certain your character does not in the least suffer here, for I do assure you as far as I can inform myself (and I have taken great pains) you are in great esteem as ever with the gentlemen here and especially in the house of Burgesses." Relying on Austin's sound counsel, George chose not to respond, learning in the process a valuable lesson about avoiding being dragged into public political conflicts.

Chapter 39

March 14, 1757 - Philadelphia

D espite his many other duties and challenges over the preceding
eleven months, George continued to be obsessed with obtaining a
royal commission. Both George and Colonel Fairfax shared a hope that
the arrival of the Earl of Loudoun, Governor Shirley's replacement as
the North American commander in chief, would create a new opportunity for George and a new strategy for the war. Without the courtesy of
obtaining Dinwiddie's consent, George wrote an extremely lengthy and
obsequious letter to Lord Loudoun. The letter laid out George's belief
that a direct attack on Fort Duquesne would be the best approach to
end the war, and, while not mentioning Dinwiddie or others by name,
he criticized his inadequate support.

When he received a lackluster response from Loudoun's aide,
George sought Dinwiddie's permission to leave the army and travel to
Philadelphia to meet with the British commander. Ignoring Dinwiddie's clear and justified admonition that George had been absent from
his post too frequently, George remained undaunted. Ultimately Dinwiddie reluctantly succumbed to the George's repeated pleas: "You
seem so earnest to go I now give You Leave."

Colonel Fairfax agreed to send letters of introduction and recommendation to assist George in securing a meeting with the busy commander
in chief. Despite their differences, Dinwiddie wrote a letter to Loudoun
calling George a "person much beloved here and has gone through many
hardships and service, and I really think he has great merit." However,
Dinwiddie also used back channels to reach out to Loudoun as a fellow
Scot, to thoroughly acquaint the earl with Dinwiddie's view on the strategic situation and to emphasize George's misbehavior.

After a weeklong horse ride to Philadelphia, George was forced to spend two more weeks in Loudon's waiting room before he was allowed to see the commander. When a haughty young lieutenant finally ushered George into Loudoun's presence, George was made to feel as if he was meeting the king himself. The handsome and vital fifty-one-year-old Loudoun exuded the confidence of a man used to both command and unquestioning deference to his superior station and judgment. Unfortunately for George, Loudoun was already convinced the colonials were neither good soldiers nor effective allies in winning the war.

Loudoun's unfriendly eyes surveyed George as he sniffed and made a face as if he had just smelled something bad. The General raised his hand for silence and shifted his gaze to the ceiling as if it was more interesting than the mere Colonel standing at attention before him. With a voice that reminded George of a wagon wheel in need of grease, Loudoun intoned, "Colonel, I am displeased you are not at your post. I will be dispatching one-quarter of Virginia's forces to South Carolina, and the remainder will be divided among the six Virginia outposts. You shall return to Fort Cumberland, where you will be met by a larger force of Maryland troops. You will redeploy your men consistent with my instructions and cease writing me." Finally looking George in the eye with the same sour face, Loudoun added, "Doing your duty, Colonel, is what I expect from you and all good officers. Thank you for taking the time to visit me and good day."

With that, Loudoun turned on his heels and began to examine a large map behind his desk with his aide-de-camp.

In stunned silence, George stared at the general's back.

What? That's it? I waited weeks for this? A fifteen-second dressing-down! No mention of my strategy for attacking Fort Duquesne, no mention of a royal commission?

Before George could respond, the lieutenant who had showed him into the room was at his elbow and silently pointing to the door, indicating the interview was over. George had not been permitted to say a word. In shock, George shuffled out of the room.

Embarrassment turned to anger as George began the long ride back to his troops. *Despite everything I have done! People call me the "Hero of* the Monongahela," but this man treats me like a cowardly backcountry private. If he had only seen the behavior of his vaunted British regulars at the Monongahela... Goddamn it! Why must my advancement be subject to men of such character? Very well, I will return to the cold and barren frontiers. I will do my duty and hope other opportunities may present themselves. I only take solace in the fact that the Crown is constantly replacing these highborn prigs. Perhaps one of them will recognize ability and take my advice to end this blasted war.

George returned to his regiment and was met by the usual bevy of problems. Nevertheless, he redoubled his efforts to build and train the best and most elite fighting force in the Colonies. While a fierce disciplinarian, his loyal officer corps and experienced troops fought well against the French and Indians on the frontier on a daily basis. Despite the frustrations and disappointments imposed on him by Williamsburg and the upper echelon of the British army, the performance of his men gave George a growing sense of pride.

Chapter 40

June 14, 1757 - Winchester

As the years wore on, George felt the weight of the war like a deep ache in his bones. Each field report placed on his desk filled him with dread for the death it foretold. The politician-engineered stalemate was a constant source of frustration that he could only vent about with his trusted adjutant, Colonel Adam Stephen.

Madeira in hand, the men met on the front porch of George's comfortable Winchester home and headquarters. George pushed back in his chair while Stephen leaned on a nearby railing, focusing on the pipe clenched between his teeth. In the afterglow of a warm Virginia day, the men attempted to catch a bit of breeze to provide relief from the sultry night.

Staring into the setting sun, George spoke pushing against fatigue. "Desertion is killing us, Adam. Twenty of twenty-nine new recruits waited for their first pay and then vanished. Their behavior is repugnant, but I am at a loss as too how we can keep them from leaving their posts. I convince the Burgesses to draft fifteen hundred men, and only two hundred and sixty-four are added, and those with inadequate supplies."

Stephen set down his clay pipe. Turning from the purple and red sky, he replied with his characteristic gusto, despite the sedate environment. "The men are rakehells, but we can hardly blame them. The pay is pathetic, and the conditions are harsh. Every bloody man in this army knows that even the paltry pay is often much delayed. We need a regular, steady, and sufficient supply of funds to keep and retain troops."

Staring at the sunset, George took a hefty drink and said, "It's not just the desertion. This blasted drunkenness . . . I'm simply at wits' end. I am court-martialing men almost every day, imposing lashings, but to no avail. Meanwhile the twits in Williamsburg continue to give me hell when the troops run amok. In fact, here's the latest missive from Dinwiddie." George then opened a letter, reading:

> I hope the Affairs of the Regimt are not in so bad a Condition as represented here. The Assembly were greatly inflamed being told that the greatest Immoralities & Drunkenness have been much countenanced, and proper Discipline neglected; I am willing to think better of our Officers, & therefore suspend my Judgement till I hear from You.

Stephen shook his head in disgust. "God damn the politicians." Tapping his pipe out against the porch railing, "They don't give us what we need, then they complain that we are not performing. At the end of the day, it's their own ruddy fault. It's really a matter of resources. Men misbehave when they are underpaid and underequipped. Nevertheless, Colonel, I still believe we have built the best regiment in the Colonies and that they could go toe-to-toe with anything the British have landed on these shores, and that's with no help from the armchair generals and politicians in Williamsburg."

George nodded in agreement looking Stephen in the eye. "I have written another letter to Governor Dinwiddie, in the most forceful terms, indicating our need for additional funds and further authority to punish deserters and malcontents. While I have no desire to lash or hang men, I see we have little choice. Indeed, Colonel Fairfax has said we must proceed with a firm hand, especially with the militia."

His anger giving way to a more supportive tone, Stephen replied, "You did not create the situation. The shortages originate in Williamsburg. I see we have little choice but to mete out some serious punishment, including executions to prevent further violations."

"Thank you, Adam. We will proceed as best we can with the limited resources we have been given and attempt to catch deserting scoundrels and malcontents. It is also my view that leniency, so far from producing its desired effects, rather emboldens them to these villainous undertakings," George said with a note of finality.

"As you say, Colonel," Stephen said with a nod.

Finishing his Madeira and setting down his glass, George stood. The men exchanged pleasantries and separated for the evening.

Chapter 41

September 3, 1757 - Belvoir

C olonel Fairfax's health deteriorated throughout the summer of 1757. On a warm Saturday evening, George received notice that the Colonel had died peacefully at Belvoir.

Although he was not surprised, George still found himself deeply upset by the Colonel's passing. Before Lawrence died, the Colonel had always been a kind but unapproachable gentleman and relation. After Lawrence's death, the Colonel frequently reached out to George, inviting him to Belvoir to hunt and to use the library. As the years progressed, he became George's most trusted mentor. He assisted George in virtually every stage of his military career, providing guidance and, indispensible behind-the-scenes political assistance to facilitate his ascent.

I am never going to hear him say again, "Pray, my boy, sit and tell me what's on your mind."

With a growing sense of loss, George realized something he had not previously noticed. *He always called me "My boy."*

As another wave of emotion overcame George, he understood—as never before—that while Will was the Colonel's biological "son," it was he, George Washington, whom the Colonel had loved and supported with the kindness and generosity normally reserved between father and son. The heavy, inconsolable grief hung like a weight on his soul, and it felt as if nothing, not even time, would lift his spirit.

I hope he knew how much I admired and loved him. I was so honored to have been treated as a part of his family. With that thought, George gave in to his grief for the first time since Lawrence's death.

George penned his letters of condolences to the Fairfax family and could not help but appreciate the irony that no letter of condolence would be coming to him, even though he likely felt the loss more than the Colonel's own son, Will.

After the death of George's own father, there had been Lawrence, and after the passing of Lawrence, there had been the Colonel. Now, for the first time in his life at age twenty-six, George realized he was truly on his own. He had Jack's friendship, Austin's support, and other friends with whom he could talk, but he realized he faced a future without a mentor or benefactor.

George knew he would hear the voices of the Colonel and Lawrence guiding him—Lawrence telling him to "seize the day," and the Colonel saying, "My boy, think through the implications of your actions." The afterglow of their wisdom could assist him, but he would have to find his own path. He would need to be—more than ever—his own man. This thought was not only depressing, but terrifying.

Chapter 42

October 5, 1757 - Winchester

Following the Colonel's death, George's health and spirits began to deteriorate. Through the fall of 1757, George's disputes with Governor Dinwiddie escalated without the moderating effect of the Colonel. In fact, while George was mourning the Colonel's passing, Dinwiddie became more openly hostile. The governor demanded more information about the performance of George and his officers. Eventually Dinwiddie flatly told George that he was unmannerly and an ingrate, despite all that Dinwiddie had done for him.

George shot back a letter to Dinwiddie, stating, "No man that ever was employed in a public capacity has endeavored to discharge the trust reposed in him with greater honesty." He specifically demanded that Dinwiddie identify the basis for his charge of ingratitude and that Dinwiddie never again "stigmatize me behind my back." Following Austin's advice, George chose not to publicly reveal the dispute. He continued to receive wide political support, despite the governor's accusations.

Governor Dinwiddie's health also continued to fail through the summer and into the fall of 1757. In one of his final letters to George, informing him he would be leaving his post as governor, Dinwiddie concluded, "My conduct to you from the beginning was always friendly, but you know I had good reason to suspect you of ingratitude. . . . I wish my successor may show you as much friendship as I've done."

George responded, "I do not know what I ever gave your honor cause to suspect me of ingratitude, a crime I detest, and would most carefully avoid. If an open, disinterested behavior, carries offense, I may have offended: Because I have all along laid it down as a maxim, to represent facts, freely and impartially; but no more to others than I have to you, Sir." As their correspondence sadly reflected, their relationship was irretrievably marred and coming to a bitter end.

PART VI
Transformation

He pines, he sickens, he despairs, he dies:
His passions and his virtues lie confused,
And mixt together in so wild a tumult,
That the whole man is quite disfigured in him.
Heavens! would one think 'twere possible for love
To make such ravage in a noble soul!

—JOSEPH ADDISON, *CATO: A TRAGEDY*, ACT III, SCENE II

Chapter 43

October 20, 1757 - Winchester

After much prodding from his officers, George reluctantly visited the regimental physician, James Craik. The doctor was appalled as he completed his examination. "Dear God, Colonel, you have neglected your health in the extreme. You need a rest."

Because Craik was a neighbor who had served with him at both Fort Necessity and the Battle of the Monongahela, George considered him not only his physician, but also his close friend. "The governor . . . he has been critical of my command and my absence from it," George said weakly.

"Well, you're going to be absent permanently if you don't take my advice. By heavens, George, you can barely stand! Now you have not only the bloody flux, but a severe cough as well. This long-standing disorder has corrupted the whole mass of your blood. I hesitate to say this, but the nature of the cough reminds me of your brother Lawrence."

A cold chill shuddered through George. While he had faced death, the prospect of enduring an end like Lawrence's frightened him to the core. Halfheartedly, George responded, "I do not have the governor's leave to return home."

"Blast it, man! I will send a letter to the governor, and you should do likewise, but in the meantime, get in a carriage and go to Mount Vernon! You must seriously rest and recuperate, or you will die. It is that simple." Then, in a gentler voice, Craik said, "Make a choice, my friend: go home and convalesce, or die at your post. I see no middle ground."

George shrugged in reluctant agreement. "Very well, I will make arrangements with my subordinates to command while I am gone."

"Do what you need to, but get in that carriage today if possible, or there may be no tomorrow."

As George climbed into his carriage, exhausted and with some fear that he would not survive the ride home, he thought, *This is not sustainable. I continuously suffer from disorders of the bowels, and my breathing is increasingly labored. I believe the curse of Washington men is upon me. I have explained to the governor—not that he understands the hardships of the military service—that I hesitate to leave my post. If I do not recover shortly, I shall not at all. At least the war has reached a stalemate, without any decisive action by either party, so my absence shall not impact the outcome.*

Prostrate in his carriage, George arrived at Mount Vernon exhausted and delirious. Over the next couple of weeks, the world was a mix of jumbled memories of the strong hands of his slaves and his servant Thomas Bishop tending to his needs, and the gentle and loving hands of Jack's wife, Hannah, feeding him. Fatigue weighed on George like a blanket of stones, trapping him in his room. His only lucid moments were filled with despair and resignation that he would join his forebears in an early grave.

By mid-November, George's strength slowly began to return, and he attempted to stitch together patches of memory that had been shredded by fever and frequent bleedings. Feeling slightly better, he took the opportunity to write Sally:

Dear Madam   Mount Vernon, 15th Novr 1757

I have lingerd under an Indispostion . . . and finding no relief above, on the contrary, that I daily grew worse.

I find myself under a necessity of applying to you . . . for such materials to make Jellys as you think I may not just at this time have. for I cant get Hartshorn Shavings any where. I must also beg the favour of you to lend me a Pound, or a smaller quantity if you can't spare that, of Hyson Tea. I am quite out & cannot get a supply any where in these parts. please also lend me a bottle or two of Mountain, or Canary Wine.

Pray make my Compliments acceptable to the Young Ladies of Your Family, and believe me to be your Dr Madam Yr Most Obedt Servt.

Go: Washington

As George hoped, his plea for medicines and jellies quickly brought a visit from Sally. Although her presence raised his spirits, his health showed only marginal improvement. As November gave way to December, George barely managed to leave his room to celebrate Christmas with the Fairfaxes and his family.

Jack was often gone tending to the various farms, and Hannah frequently returned to their Shenandoah property. Sally's husband Will Fairfax had gone to England for the winter, seeking a legal appointment and attending to issues arising out of his father's passing. Thus George finally had time to sit and speak with Sally alone. They enjoyed hours together, talking and playing games of cards and chess; to George's chagrin, Sally usually won at both.

Sally's apparent amorous feelings after his success at Monongahela showed no signs of abating. Shortly before Christmas, Sally arrived with a stack of Shakespeare's poetry and plays. George could not help but notice she had selected the most romantic of Shakespeare's works. In particular, she suggested they read *Romeo and Juliet*. They agreed to split the play in half, with Sally reading all the Capulets' parts while George read the parts of the Montagues. This meant George was forced to read female roles with a falsetto high voice, and Sally to feign the low voices of the Capulet men. Both laughed with delight as they read. However, as they transitioned to the romantic scenes between Romeo and Juliet, George knew they were playing with fire. When the moments became too intense, Sally would coquettishly pull back. George resented that Sally treated his feelings merely as something for her amusement.

As one particular afternoon gave way to dusk, a ruby-red glow filled the room, casting shadows that highlighted Sally's long eyelashes as she looked down to read. Then, when she looked up, it was as if a supernova had exploded in her large eyes, reflecting the waning sun.

He found himself disappearing into those magnificent eyes as he read Romeo's description of Juliet: "Oh, she doth teach the torches to burn bright. It seems she hangs upon the cheek of night . . . As a rich jewel."

She is precious and radiant both inside and out. Yet Will casts her aside for pennies in London. By heavens . . . I am truly lost. I covet my neighbor's wife. With all my heart, I wish I did not want her. My judgment and passion battle, yet either way, I lose. The thought of her returning to Will and this coming to an end . . .

"George, are you all right?" Sally asked.

Startled back to reality, George realized he had been staring. "I . . . I apologize. My mind wandered. I beg your pardon."

Sally's clear white skin blushed as if reading his thoughts. "It is late. I believe you are fatigued. I have imposed upon you too long, Colonel Washington. My goal was to assist your recovery, not hinder it. I must take my leave."

George struggled to his feet as she stood. She moved closer and put a hand on his shoulder, keeping him in his seat. "Please, George, do not get up."

The pressure of her fingers flowed through him like a wave, causing his strong legs to buckle under her gentle touch. George could feel his own face turning scarlet.

No, I don't want her to leave. She . . . must come back.

The anguish of knowing this period of perfectly balanced joy would be shattered when the world outside Mount Vernon finally reasserted itself forced George to violate his own maxim of not quoting literature. Grinning sheepishly, he said, "'Good night, good night! Parting is such sweet sorrow.'"

Sally clapped with delight. "Why, George, then 'I shall say good night till it be morrow.' Although, I hope we do not suffer the same fate as the Bard's star-crossed lovers. If you behave and take your rest now, I promise to return."

Did she call us "star-crossed lovers"?

Again, as much from joy as habit, George tried to bound to his feet. Once more, Sally reached out; this time, she said patiently, "Tomorrow."

Her sweet breath crossed George's beaming face.

Tomorrow . . .

Unfortunately the next day brought a new round of dysentery and high fever, preventing George from seeing Sally. As December gave way to the new year, George suffered a relapse, no doubt assisted by another round of prodigiously administered bleeding.

In mid-February, Hannah sat at George's bedside. While improving, George was still exhausted and slow to rise in the morning. Nevertheless, he smiled at the sight of Jack's lovely and gentle wife.

"George, I hesitate to distress you, but I need to return to our home in the Shenandoah. The plantation has been neglected, and I should stop by and see your mother on the way home. Rest assured, Jack will stay here and minister to your needs, and Overseer Knight will keep Mount Vernon in order."

George felt a pang of guilt at having kept Hannah and Jack from their home. After Overseer Knight arrived at Mount Vernon in 1757, Hannah and Jack moved to their new home. However, Jack continued to manage Mount Vernon, Ferry Farm, and George's Bullskin property, as well as his own plantation. George's long illness had imposed a great burden on the young couple.

Nodding in understanding, George weakly replied, "I understand, Hannah. I apologize that my infirmity has separated you from your home. Please extend my mother and siblings my compliments and apologies that I cannot be there to attend to their needs."

"I will," Hannah said as she stood to leave. "I promise to be back soon."

While George knew he would miss her gentle hands and kind words, he shook his head, "No . . . no. You have done enough. You must tend to your home."

George looked up and saw Jack, who had been leaning against the door frame observing the interchange. With a forced grin, Jack said, "Well, old boy, we're bachelors again. My lovely bride gets to go visit our mother. I think we know who got the better duty." Then, with a full smirk spreading across his friendly face, he continued, "On the other hand, you can be a bloody pain."

Hannah slapped Jack's arm as she exited the room with mocking disapproval. "You are a profane and evil man, Jack Washington."

"It is only through the intersession of a fine woman like you, Hannah, that I have any hope of avoiding God's just punishment," Jack said with an exaggerated bow.

Despite his discomfort, George could not help but laugh. "Both of you, get out of my room and let me die in peace."

"Would we all be so lucky, dear brother. I will be back to check on you in an hour or so. Sleep well."

Jack closed the door, and George heard their steps move down the hall.

The following morning, Sally returned to Mount Vernon and was directed to George's room as a slave was carrying out a basin filled with blood and covered with a towel. Jack sat on a chair in the corner and stood as Sally entered the room.

"Mrs. Fairfax, it is a pleasure to see you. I am sorry I did not greet you at the door. You just missed the doctor."

"Yes, I saw his handiwork as I came in," she said with a sour look.

A deathly pale George lay covered with a blanket. The sweet, sickening smell of blood remained in the room, and a bandage was wrapped around George's left forearm.

Looking somewhat perplexed, Jack continued softly, attempting not to disturb George. "He is recovering from an efficacious bloodletting. I was told we can expect some period of discomfort to follow as his body returns to equilibrium, now that the unhelpful humors have been removed."

As Jack spoke, George tossed in his bed and groaned softly.

"I am sure you have duties," Sally replied in a measured voice. "I would be happy to tend to him on my own, if that would be helpful."

Taken aback by Sally's cool demeanor, Jack responded, "Y-Yes. Yes . . . That would be most helpful. Thank you."

As she placed the back of her hand on George's clammy forehead, Sally muttered under her breath, "Barbarians." Addressing a slave at George's side, she instructed, "Get me a cool pail of water and some clean cloths. I will tend to him." Then, addressing Jack with a straight-mouthed smile, she said, "As George requested, I have also brought some medicines that I hope will be helpful." Turning back to the exiting slave, Sally said, "Also, bring me a pot of warm water and a large cup."

Sensing his presence was no longer desired or required, Jack took his leave saying, "Please call me if I can be of any assistance." Sally nodded in response without looking up from George.

A few minutes after Jack left the room, Thomas Bishop, George's loyal manservant, arrived and asked, "Ma'am, I can stay here and assist you if—"

Sally interrupted, "No. I have matters in hand. I will call if I need you."

Bishop continued to stand in the door.

Irritated, Sally said firmly, "You are dismissed."

Bowing, Bishop left.

Moments later, a slave returned with the requested water and cloths. Sally pulled out a vial of a powder extracted from willow bark that her family frequently used to reduce fever and pain. She gently raised George's head and poured some down his throat as he lay semiconscious.

As the afternoon progressed, George, suffering the effects of his most recent bloodletting, slid in and out of delirium. His eyes fluttered open, and he saw Sally. In a fevered, blood-reduced stupor, his mind continued to roll between Marcia—the heroine in *Cato* played by Sally—and his real love for the Sally who sat next to him. Her actual touch and smell mingled with his memories and desires.

Sally remained at George's side all afternoon, holding his hand and changing the compresses to cool his forehead, refusing multiple offers from Jack and Bishop to be relieved. At one point, as she was leaning over him, George's unseeing eyes fluttered open as he mumbled, "Oh, Marcia," and, with surprising swiftness and strength, he grabbed Sally close, hugged her, and, just as quickly, released his grip and returned to unconsciousness. Sally, with her full weight on George and cheek to cheek, could not linger in fear that someone would come to the open door. George was unaware when Sally left his room with the setting sun.

The next day, Sally arrived at Mount Vernon to see a much-improved George sitting up in bed and eating. Bishop bowed respectfully as she entered the room.

George smiled, "Sally, I am so happy to see you! I believe your ministrations explain my improved condition today."

Beaming, Sally turned to George's servant. "Bishop, I will finish feeding the colonel."

"As you wish, madam." Bishop gently inclined his head and left the room.

As Sally pulled a chair next to the bed and reached for the tray of food, George commented, "I must confess that much of the last several days have been a blur. My only clear memory is of your presence and kindness. I hope I was not too great a burden."

Did I really grab her? Did I kiss her . . . or was that part of my dream of Marcia?

Sally gently grasped George's hand. "You need not be concerned, George. I am only pleased you are returning to health." Before he could react further, Sally filled a spoon with soup and said, "Now open your mouth. It is time to eat."

With a grin, George dutifully accepted his morning meal, eating heartily. When he had finished, Sally became serious. "I have a matter I wish to discuss with you and your brother, if I am going to remain and assist in your care. When I arrived yesterday, you had been prodigiously bled, and it is my belief that this is what made you so weak and ill."

What? It is inappropriate for her to have a position or opinion on medical treatment. What could she know of such things?

"I have discussed this matter with my father, who has read the works of William Harvey. As you may know, my father went to Cambridge. Professor Harvey also studied there as well; he was a professor of anatomy and a member of the Royal College of Physicians in London. My father read the professor's lectures demonstrating that blood provides sustenance to the body and that the removal of large amounts of blood only weakens the body."

More perplexed than irritated, George responded hesitantly, "Well ... that may be the opinion of some doctor in London, but I believe you would be hard pressed to find a physician in Virginia who agrees with him."

Sitting with perfect posture with her hands folded on her lap, Sally immediately answered, "Be that as it may, I am firm on this matter and confident in my conclusion—as is my father. Frankly, I do not understand why you do not agree. You have been at war and have seen that the loss of blood will result in death. How can you then, in turn, wish to see blood removed to improve a man's health?"

George spoke patiently, as if explaining something to a young child: "As you well know, the loss of blood in battle is completely different than removing bad humors caused by disease. The two situations are utterly distinct."

Exasperated, Sally declared, "I will not sit by and watch these vampires bleed you and undermine your health. I will stay with one simple condition: As long as your health is improving, you will not be bled while under my care. If you are bled, I will reluctantly take my leave. If, on the other hand, I treat you and your condition worsens, I will, of course, immediately defer to trained physicians. However, I am confident you will become stronger."

Lord knows I don't want her to leave. I believe she is wrong, but I am likely to die anyway, and I would rather die with her at my side.

George answered formally, recognizing both Sally's earnestness, as well as the ramifications of his decision. "Very well, Sally, you have my agreement."

"May I discuss the matter with Jack?" Sally said, matching his unblinking gaze.

"Of course, but I do not expect this plan to be met with much enthusiasm," George said with a crooked smile.

As George predicted, Jack was appalled by Sally's proposal, but swayed by George's insistence, Jack reluctantly agreed, emphasizing that at the slightest sign of ill health, the physicians would be contacted immediately.

Over the next week, Sally continued to make the daily trek to Mount Vernon to minister to George. Despite the protests, she was firm, and George refrained from further bloodletting.

The physical attraction that fueled his early infatuation was still present, but now his adoration included an appreciation for the intelligence beneath the beautiful façade. As it often did, George's mind turned to *Cato* and Juba's love for Marsha:

> True, she is fair, (oh how divinely fair!)
> But still the lovely maid improves her charms
> With inward greatness, unaffected wisdom,
> And sanctity of manners.

They spent hours talking about politics, the war, and the Enlightenment. They discussed the belief that reason could bring order, reform, and improvement to civil society. George had read books and articles by John Locke in the Colonel's library, and Sally had recently borrowed her father's copy of Rousseau's *Discourse on Inequality*, which emphasized the power of reason in understanding not only the natural world, but also human interaction. Sally's superb education was a source of insecurity for George, yet she never belittled him.

It was late in the afternoon, and the house had gone silent. The servants had all completed their daily tasks and retired. George and Sally sat in a wonderful bubble of isolation, lost in conversation that freely flowed from topic to topic. Finally, Sally turned to the future. "You have mentioned Captain Orme on a number of occasions and that he has encouraged you to visit him in England. Do you plan on doing so?"

"Oh, I would dearly love to, Sally, but I am a Washington. I don't suspect I will be around long enough for that dream to come true."

Horrified, Sally retorted, "What on earth does that mean?"

"We both know that I am unlikely to recover from this illness. Even if I do, I am a Washington man. We all die young. No Washington man in memory has ever seen his fiftieth year, and most die before forty-five. My bouts of illness and my weak constitution make it obvious that this apple has not fallen far from the tree."

Sally opened her mouth to disagree, but George interrupted. "It is all right. Lawrence always admonished me to live by the adage '*carpe diem.*'"

"Is that why you have been so reckless in battle?"

"Perhaps. That certainly doesn't motivate me while in the midst of the fight. I don't remember thinking about my family's short life expectancy or even my own mortality, for that matter. I always seem to have so many things to do. Too many men are looking at me to permit the luxury of focusing on myself. The honest truth is that several days or even weeks later, when I think about how close I was to death, an inch here or there, only then do I shudder at the prospect."

Aware for the first time that he'd turned away from her and was looking out the window as he spoke, he looked back at Sally and said, "To answer your question directly, no, I suspect the realization that I have not long to live drives other decisions, but not what I do under fire."

"Well, I intend to do everything I can to make sure you survive this illness, George."

Sally reached for his hand, which they were both doing with increasing frequency. As she did so, he involuntarily leaned in, savoring the contact the way a cat does when scratched behind the ears.

"With you here, I don't plan on going anywhere soon," George said with a grin as he stared into her rich brown eyes, which twinkled like twin stars.

Sally looked down with a knowing smile. She then stood and walked to George's bookshelf and pulled down a well-used copy of *Cato*. While they had read much together, including the romantic scenes of Romeo and Juliet, George believed they had, by mutual and unspoken agreement, not mentioned or read *Cato* because both understood its potential explosive effect on them. Thus George was surprised and slightly nervous when she opened the book to the climactic scene they had acted together so many years before and began to read from the text. George reached out and closed the book, and they both continued from memory. As they recited the lines, their faces grew closer. Before either realized what was happening, they kissed. George's strong hands grasped the nape of Sally's neck and pulled her close. Not resisting, she leaned forward.

Her lips are the softest, sweetest things in the world.

Her familiar fragrance filled his mind. The softness of her skin . . .

She smells like rose petals and sandalwood, and . . . Sally.

The moment was broken by a noise outside the house. Startled back to reality, their shocked eyes met. Without saying a word, Sally stood and left the room. George heard her light, quick footsteps down the hall and the front door closing firmly. Moments later, a slave called for her carriage, and within a few minutes, the jingle of reigns and the clop of hooves faded into the distance.

What have I done? Did she kiss me or did I kiss her? I grasped her neck and pulled her close. No, I did not force myself upon her, but it was . . . a mistake.

Sally did not return the next day or the next. After two days of absence, Jack walked in and ominously closed the door. In an unusually controlled tone, he said, "Do you know why Sally has not returned?"

"No," George said flatly.

What else can I say?

"The reason I ask is that she apparently left in a huff two days ago, and appeared upset. Did you two have some disagreement?"

Oh, thank God. He thinks we had a fight. He doesn't suspect . . . "No. Certainly not," George said. "She was tired and not feeling well. I don't think it is anything serious."

That should buy some time.

Jack stared at George with a long searching look. It appeared as if he was going to say something but then changed his mind. Then, apparently coming to a decision, he spoke with a slight tenor of disappointment. "Fine, George. If there is anything you want to talk about, please let me know. I have work to do. Bishop will attend to you in the meantime."

"Thank you, Jack."

George let out a sigh of relief as Jack left the room.

Chapter 44

February 19, 1758 – Mount Vernon

Early the next morning, a downcast and visibly upset Jack appeared at George's bedside holding a letter in his hand.

"Jack, what on earth?"

"It is Hannah. She is unwell. She has high fever and the flux."

Without hesitation, George said with what strength he still retained, "Go to her, Jack. Now!"

Jack answered without looking up to meet George's eyes, "But who will care for you? I have sent a note to Mother and Betsy to see if our sister can help care for Hannah. I should remain here. I should have never even mentioned this."

Using his arm to raise himself and sit fully upright in bed, George answered, "Don't be a fool. I will survive, or I will not. Your duty is not to minister to me, but to go to your wife's side. Bishop can care for me. Alton and Knight can manage Mount Vernon. You must go!"

Nodding in reluctant agreement, Jack said as he finally met George's gaze, "Very well, but I shall be back." Then suddenly, pausing with emotion, "Or, I guess, if Hannah is not well . . ." He shook the thought from his mind. "Hannah and I will be well before the end of the month. I will also send a note to Sally and ask her to continue to visit you if she is feels up to it, and I will remind her that Knight, Alton, and Bishop are present."

For the first time the realization hit George: *If Sally visits, I could be alone in the house with her. I could dismiss Bishop as we did before. Alton and Knight never enter the house without my consent. I can order the house slaves at bay or out of the house entirely.*

He stopped his thoughts from going any further.

This is irrelevant. She is not going to come. Regardless, Jack must go to Hannah now. I will not be able to live with myself if Jack is here and something happens to my sweet and loving sister-in-law. Still . . . is it destiny? If he sends the note . . . that might bring her here.

For a second, Jack, to whom George felt a tighter bond than any other, paused. George had never expressed his secret love for Sally, yet Jack seemed to hesitate at the prospect of leaving the two of them alone. Before Jack could speak again, George barked, "Go! For God's sake, Jack, go to your wife. Send the note to Sally—Mrs. Fairfax—if you must. I will be fine. The good Lord willing, you both will be happy and healthy by the end of the month and so will I. Now do your older brother a favor, and get the hell out of my room and off my land!"

A visibly moved Jack reached over and clasped George on the shoulder in an unusually intimate gesture between the closest of brothers. He then left the room, saying, "I will see you in a fortnight."

"Stop talking for once and get on your damn horse," George replied.

As Jack ran down the hall, George shouted: "Godspeed, Jack!"

These are terrible circumstances, but dare I hope that Jack's note will bring her back to me? This must surely be the hand of Providence.

The days dragged by with no sign of Sally. Each day, George waited in exquisite agony in hope of her arrival. He woke with the expectation that Sally would arrive, and by midday, he became depressed with the knowledge that she was making the prudent decision to stay away. He recognized that seeing her would only torture them both or lead to their mutual destruction.

Chapter 45

February 23, 1758 – Mount Vernon

George woke, had breakfast, and remained in his room. He had received a brief note from Jack that Hannah was improving and that Jack would be back at Mount Vernon by the end of the month as promised. George then heard a knock at the front door. A confused-looking Sally ventured hesitantly into the empty home, as no servant met her at either her carriage or the door. George ran to the bedroom door in his nightshirt and called out, "Mrs. Fairfax, please be good enough to come in." He scurried back to his bed and covered himself.

Oh, dear God, she is here.

He could feel his heart pounding in his chest. He quickly attempted to straighten his disheveled hair and sit upright in the bed as he heard her tentatively walk down the hall.

Sally stood in the doorway, and George took a sudden involuntary breath. She wore a simple yet stunning green dress that highlighted the emerald flecks in her brown eyes.

All George could say was, "I didn't think you would come."

"I tried not to. I . . . even missed your birthday. I worried about you after I received Jack's note." She looked down at the floor, her eyelashes hiding both her eyes and intent. After a pause where George dared not breathe, she looked up and said, "It wasn't simply Jack's note. I wanted to come back."

Oh, she is my light. But . . . I don't know what to say.

Minutes passed, and George and Sally just stared in silence.

Well, say something, idiot!

"I am very glad you are here," George said softly.

"I am so sorry to hear Hannah is unwell. I sent some of my willow-bark powders to their home with a note." She finally smiled, warming and becoming more relaxed.

George felt as if she, and not the sun, heated the world, and that without her, he would be cold, barren, and bereft of life.

I need to keep her talking.

"You are very kind, and I know your thoughtfulness will be appreciated. I understand she is improving." George spoke the words carefully, fearing the wrong word would cause her to flutter away.

The door remained opened, and George remained sitting in his bed.

Please, God, let her come in.

"I noticed, coming in, that there are no servants in the house."

"Except for meals and some minimal morning attendance by Bishop, I have spent days alone in the house on the oft chance that you would come back. I have told everyone that I simply want to be left alone. I have instructed all of my people to stay out of the house."

Taking a step closer, Sally said, "George, what if it becomes known we were alone?"

She seems more concerned about people knowing we're alone than the fact that we are here alone. Please, please stay.

"Bishop will notify me if anyone else approaches. Suffice, my trust in Bishop is absolute. He is outside the home, but he is watchful and discreet. I wanted time with just you."

With that, Sally slowly turned and locked the bedroom door.

Chapter 46

March 2, 1758 – Mount Vernon

A week later, George heard the carriage arrive and Jack greet Sally at the door. Sally had left that magical afternoon they spent together with a firm warning that she would not return until Jack and Hannah were once again firmly ensconced in Mount Vernon. While his health steadily improved in her absence, his longing for Sally grew daily. The day's drizzle did not lessen George's exhilaration to see her carriage coming up the drive. He quickly donned a robe, combed his hair, and left the room to meet her.

Jack looked up to see George striding down the hall as he met Sally at the door. "The monster lives!" Jack said. "Obviously, Mrs. Fairfax, your ministrations had a positive effect."

"It was not me, Mr. Washington. I was only able to visit once a few days ago, but I am thrilled to see your brother's health is improving," Sally said with a practiced smile.

"Well, whatever the reason, we are all grateful for your kindness," Jack replied. After a look from George that conveyed a lifetime of brotherly, nonverbal communication, Jack bowed and said, "If you two will excuse me, I must make sure my instructions have been followed during my absence."

As Jack left the room, Hannah burst into the front hall and gave Sally a heartfelt hug. "Thank you so much for your note. The medicines worked wonderfully! Look at the colonel—he is on his feet! We are all improving with the coming of spring, and all because of you! Stay for supper, won't you?"

"Alas, no, Hannah, I have several duties this afternoon. I wanted to stop by and check on everyone's health," she replied, involuntarily glancing at George.

Perhaps sensing the two of them wanted to be alone, Hannah said diffidently, "Well, if you will excuse me, I, too, have duties. I will leave you in the hands of our strengthening brother."

As Hannah walked away, George gestured to the parlor and Sally followed. He used all his self-control not to sweep her into his arms and kiss her.

They sat across a table from each other. George could sense Sally's formality and a disconcerting sternness in her demeanor.

Ignoring her behavior, George blurted, "Oh, Sally, I am so glad you have come back. I was—"

"Colonel Washington, we can never speak of, or repeat, our . . . our actions. Your health is improving, and it is apparent you will recover. My *husband*," she said, placing special emphasis on the word, "will return within the month. We have been, and will always remain, friends. But that is all."

"But . . . But . . . Sally . . ."

The room seemed to darken as she convulsed with disapproval.

"Fine, Mrs. Fairfax," George petulantly responded. "But . . . what about our day? What about . . . us?"

For a moment, Sally's features softened. She addressed George as if speaking to a young child: "Dear George, there can never be an 'us.' You and I both know that. There should never have been an 'us.' Our happy moments may be cherished, or perhaps better forgotten, but they can never be spoken of or repeated." She allowed a rueful smile and sighed. "Will is not a bad man. He has never beaten or mistreated me. Indeed, he endeavors to act with kindness and courtesy, despite his tendency toward melancholia. He deserves better than this . . . from both of us."

As she spoke, George could see her resolve reasserting itself.

No! I am losing her!

He looked into her eyes and saw a coldness that he had never observed—or perhaps never noticed. A wave of fear and panic suddenly washed over him.

My world is disappearing. I . . . am lost without her. She is the light of my life, and I will be cast in darkness. This cannot be happening!

With a growing sense of urgency, George spoke louder than he knew he should, "No, Sally! No. We belong together and you know it."

With a steely determination, Sally stood and moved toward George as he remained seated. Leaning toward him and looking him in the eye with all the menace her small frame could muster, she spoke in a fierce whisper, "You will *not* destroy both of us. We both know this cannot continue. I would never see you again if I thought it would help, but that would only make things more obvious to those around us. We must both be strong. You will continue to be friends with Will in business and politics. I will do my best to be a friend to your future wife."

"What? My wife? Oh, Sally . . . 'Thou wrong'st me, if thou think'st ever was love, or ever grief, like mine.'"

Without missing a beat, Sally answered, "That is the wrong quotation from *Cato*. The proper line is 'Believe me, prince, though hard to conquer love, 'tis easy to divert and break its force: absence might cure it, or a second mistress light up another flame, and put out this.'"

"What does that mean?" George said angrily.

Her eyes blazing, Sally responded, "You know exactly what it means. We cannot have you pining after something that neither of us can have. You must find a woman with whom to spend your life. It will not be me."

In a soft voice George pleaded, "But . . . you don't love Will. You love me."

With harshness and frustration, Sally growled, "Don't be a fool! This is not some romantic play. This is the life we are given. My duty is to stay with Will. Your duty is to find a fine woman. The sooner the distraction begins, the better." Then, with more pain than anger, she continued, "I have put some thought into this: You should call upon Martha Custis. I have met her. She is a lovely woman, with two healthy young children and a large fortune. I believe she can make you happy." As Sally struggled for control, tears began to fill her large eyes.

Fighting back his own tears, George snapped, "You announce we have no future and at the same time tell me with whom I must spend my life?"

Almost to herself, Sally whispered, "No, my love, it can just never be with me." With that, she rushed out the door. Moments later, George heard her carriage in motion.

Without conscious thought, George walked in stunned silence to his room. He locked his door and lost himself in grief.

Sometime later, he heard a gentle knock on the door and Jack's voice: "George, are you well? I see Sally has left. Is everything all right? Did you two fight again? Is there something you want to tell me?"

Composing himself, George responded, "I am fine. I must have absentmindedly turned the lock." George rose from the bed and opened the door. "There is no problem with Mrs. Fairfax."

Jack was clearly startled by George's appearance. "Are you all right, George? You look terrible."

"I am overdone. I think I may need a couple more days in bed."

"Do you want me to call a physician? We have followed Mrs. Fairfax's admonition long enough. Perhaps you need a good bleeding to complete your recovery."

"No, I think I just need some more rest."

"Well, I have good news. I received a letter saying that an appointment has been confirmed with Dr. John Amson in Williamsburg. He has agreed to see you if you are able."

Chapter 47

March 18, 1758 - Williamsburg

G eorge and his servant Bishop enjoyed the warming weather a little over two weeks later as they headed towards Williamsburg after an obligatory stop at Ferry Farm to visit his mother. He arrived in the capitol despondent after enduring his mother's onslaught about his lack of attentiveness, obsessing on his expected early death, and smarting from Sally's rejection.

An exceptionally pensive George was ushered into Dr. Amson's examination room. After numerous tests, pokes, and prods, the doctor said, "Colonel Washington, you are a strong man with a good constitution. I am perplexed why you are here to see me at all."

Shocked, George stammered, "I . . . I was ill . . . like my brother. Do I not have consumption?"

"My goodness, no!" the doctor answered.

"Then I am to recover?"

"Recover? My dear sir, you clearly had an illness over the new year, but you are in the process of full recovery . . . God willing."

Struggling for clarification, George asked, "Is there any further treatment required to ensure my continued health?"

"I gather you were extensively bled at the onset of this illness?"

"Of course, but I should confess that a family friend convinced me to refrain from bleeding of late, as my condition has improved," George replied sheepishly.

"Is this man a physician?"

"No . . . he . . . is not." *Mentioning that this was Sally's idea would make me sound like a fool.*

"Well, you are indeed fortunate, Colonel Washington. The initial bleeding undoubtedly removed the bad humors and cause of your underlying illness. Bleeding is not required if the underlying cause has been eliminated. I surmise, then, that it is a coincidence that the bleeding ceased, the cause of the distemper was removed, and your health improved. You can only view yourself as fortunate that you discontinued the bleeding when you did. Obviously, if the cause of your illness had still been present, and you had ceased the bleeding, you would likely be deathly ill or dead at this point." Then, with a warm smile, the doctor said, "It appears you are a fortunate man—both on and off the battlefield."

"So no further bleeding is required?" George said, mouth agape.

"Not unless your underlying illness returns. Otherwise I believe you are in need of exercise, good food, and outdoor activity. I will give you a powder, which, if taken as instructed, should speed your recovery. I predict you will return to full health and, dare I say, be in service again to the Old Dominion."

Shaking his head in disbelief, George asked, "But, Doctor, my family, that is, the men in my family . . . they . . . we . . . we have a history of dying young. Doesn't that mean the same is likely for me?"

"Nonsense! When a man dies has nothing to do with his family but rather his own constitution. Some sons die young, and some fathers live for years. In my experience, it is more about force of will than anything else. If I am any judge, young man, you can look forward to a long life."

Standing and bowing in response, "Thank you, Doctor. I will follow your advice and hope to return to my regiment."

Responding in kind, the doctor bowed and said, "Then I am well pleased to have served you and Virginia. I bid you good day, Colonel."

Leaving the doctor's office on Peacock Hill and walking east down Scotland Street, George was in a daze.

I am not going to die. I am not going to die. Suddenly, like a lever inside him had been pulled, George felt a burst of energy and joy. *I am not going to die! I am going to live a long, long life!*

Completely oblivious to his surroundings, George walked aimlessly through the streets of Williamsburg.

I must get on with my life. I am not going to be Lawrence, my father, or my grandfather. I am not going to die young! I am going to live!

Then his exhilaration was checked: *My new life . . . It is not going to be with Sally. She does not want me. No, that's not fair: we cannot be together. I must move on with another woman. What about Martha Custis? I've met her briefly on a few occasions, so . . . perhaps . . . but that is for another day. Regardless, I will return to my regiment, do my duty, and complete my tenure.*

Feeling like Lazarus risen from the dead, for the first time in months, George ambled with the wonderment of a man reborn, recognizing the years that stretched out before him. On the long stroll, with his head down and his arms behind his back, George had time to think about what he considered the "second half" of his life.

Who I have been, and what I have been doing, has been driven by others—my parents, Lawrence, and the Colonel—or by mere happenstance. I have not had a plan of my own or made conscious decisions about who I will be. I was a surveyor at Lawrence's urging. I went to Fort Le Boeuf at the Colonel's instructions. I joined the army for adventure—and, truthfully, to escape my mother and to honor the memory of my deceased brother. Glory has been the only clear goal of my life.

At the thought of "glory," George's mind recoiled from the memory of the carnage he witnessed during his retreat from the Battle of the Monongahela. *I have had my share of "glory." The prig British generals like Loudoun don't want me—and I have to admit that I have little desire to live the bureaucratic and nasty political life of an English officer. I have wasted much time trying to secure a royal commission and join the ranks of these backbiting bastards.*

While I admire Orme and a few others, I do not believe I could ever want a military life if it involves this level of intrigue. Truth be told, I recognize that the failure of the British to grant me a royal commission is less a reflection on me than proof of their ignorance and stupidity. While these may be men of titles and education, the average Virginia gentleman has more character in the tip of his little finger.

George smiled briefly as he thought of George Hume and his admonition that he had more royal blood in his little finger than George had in his whole body.

I have accomplished much. I am in undisputed command of the Virginia Regiment, my bravery is unquestioned, and I have received wide praise. While I do not have financial success, the cruel and ungentle hand of fate has given me control of Mount Vernon. Yet I have not always met my own expectations.

His mind involuntarily flashed an image of Sally.

Sally is right. While our love may be real, it is wrong and dishonorable. I have also handled my relations with politicians poorly. This will change. When I listen to echoes of the voices of Lawrence and the Colonel, I know the man I want to be. Going forward, I swear before the Almighty, I will be that man! But the question remains: Who do I want to be? What do I want to do?

George looked up and realized that he had unconsciously walked to the stout House of Burgesses, with its three arches and tall and narrow white cupola.

Yes. This is where I belong. I will choose the life of a Virginia planter over that of a soldier. There is no better place on God's green earth.

George stopped shuffling and unclasped his hands from behind his back, then straightened.

I will no longer be controlled by others or events. I will be the master of myself. I choose to complete my service and resign. I choose to return to Mount Vernon to pick up the active life of a planter, and I will join this House.

As never before, a surge of determination passed through George. As he looked at the ornate brick building, he did so with the confidence of a more mature and experienced man, self-possessed as he had never been before. He headed back to his lodgings with a newfound resolve to not only achieve success, but to do so in a way that would make the Colonel, Lawrence, and, most important, himself proud.

Chapter 48

March 21, 1758 - Poplar Grove Plantation

Three days later, George woke with the same energy and excitement that had filled him following his appointment with Dr. Amson. The weather had turned chilly, but this did not deaden his spirits. As he and Bishop left Williamsburg and worked their way north, George realized they were across the river from Poplar Grove, the plantation of William Chamberlayne.

Enjoying the moment, he turned to Bishop, "Come along, man. We are going to take the ferry to visit a dear friend."

Shocked by George's unexpected change of plans, Bishop responded demurely, "But, Colonel, your health . . . This will delay our return to Mount Vernon, and you have been . . . unwell, sir."

"Nonsense. Mount Vernon is in good hands, and I am fit as a fiddle! Don't dawdle, Bishop. Get the horses onto the ferry, and let's cross the river!" George directed with a rare toothy smile.

Bishop, who for so long had worried about his employer, nodded in acknowledgment, and the two ferried across the Pamunkey River toward the Chamberlayne estate. Appearing unannounced was contrary to George's fixation on politeness, but his state of euphoria governed both his mood and behavior.

As George and Bishop cantered their horses up to Chamberlayne's two-story brick home, several carriages could be seen parked outside, and servants and slaves were milling about.

"More good fortune!" George exclaimed. "A party awaits!"

Although not in his military uniform, George was finely dressed as a Tidewater gentlemen. As he approached the open doorway, George could hear sounds of laughter and clinking glasses drifting from a partially ajar front window. Bishop turned to attend to the horses as George knocked on the door. His six-foot-two, 180-pound frame filled almost the entire entrance. Although he was still gaunt and pale, his erect bearing and fine attire projected the appearance everyone in Virginia knew and admired. A servant opened the door, but he was immediately supplanted by a beaming Chamberlayne.

"George? Excuse me—Colonel Washington. How wonderful to see you, my friend!"

Bowing slightly, George replied, "I hope I am not intruding, but I was nearby, and I thought I might present my compliments to—"

Interrupting, Chamberlayne exclaimed, "I am so pleased! I am gratified to see you. We had heard you were unwell."

"I was, but I am on the mend," George answered and then gave a broad closed-mouth smile.

"Then I am doubly pleased that you are here and healthy. We are having a few neighbors over. We'd be honored if you would join us."

Curious to see who had come calling, the small party of less than a dozen people had fallen silent, but all were smiling with drinks in hand when Chamberlayne turned to reveal George in the doorway.

"Friends! It is our good fortune Colonel Washington on a whim has stopped by to visit. I have begged him to stay, and I know you will encourage him to join us in our modest festivities." Then, turning to George with arms open wide, Chamberlayne added, "Please, Colonel, come in and rest from your ride. Have a drink and dine with us."

George was immediately greeted by the friendly faces of the Tidewater gentry he knew so well. All now looked on him with the adoration that had normally been reserved only for his beloved Lawrence. The glow of friendship, the aroma of excellent food, and the warmth of the room enveloped him. With his renewed vitality and good humor, George felt giddy and unusually uninhibited.

As he surveyed the room, his gaze stopped at the small, round face of Martha Custis. *Sally mentions Martha Custis and here she is . . . could this be the hand of fate?*

Eight months his senior, she was just under five feet tall, with hazel eyes and dark hair. She was round, soft, plump, and somewhat plain, but she exuded a gentle affability and kindness. As the evening wore on, George spoke with the guests who, as always, wanted to hear about the regiment and the Battle of the Monongahela. However, George found himself inexorably drawn to Martha's side. He had met her before but had never spoken with her at any length. Yet tonight, George marveled at how easily he fell into conversation with her.

George and Martha sat side by side at supper, enjoying excellent meats and wines, politely conversing with others but clearly enamored with each other. George felt an immediate connection. If not yet soul mates, they were instantly comfortable in each other's presence. Martha neither put on airs nor played the coquettish games George so loathed—and that Sally so loved. Following the meal, George and Martha sat alone in the parlor before a large fire.

"I met your brother Lawrence on a couple of occasions with my late husband. Lawrence seemed a lovely man. I see much of him in you," Martha said with such genuine feeling that George suddenly found himself overcome by unexpected emotion.

Whether it was the drink or the fact that this kind woman had reminded him that he would not suffer Lawrence's fate, George suddenly fell silent. After taking a couple of minutes to regain his composure, he said, "I am sorry. You have suffered a greater, more recent loss, and I am the one to be suddenly speechless. My apologies." Uncomfortable, George shifted to stand.

Martha reached out and grasped his arm, directing him back to his seat. "You have suffered much. Whether mine is less or more I do not know, but under no circumstances are either of our losses meaningless. You have not been well, and I know this must weigh on you."

His frown changing to a broad smile that extended to his sparkling eyes, George replied emphatically, "That is the great irony: I am truly happy. I'm happy to be with you, happy to be alive. I learned only yesterday that I will not share my brother's fate. I can and will think of my future."

"Well then, let us celebrate your future, Colonel Washington," Martha said as she subtly raised her glass.

George did likewise and decided to change the subject. With genuine interest, he asked, "Tell me about your children and your plantation. How are they faring?"

"My children are healthy and strong, but the loss of their father does cause them great unease. As to the plantation . . . while I do have help, it is not in my nature to manage so much."

The Custis Estate, known as White House and located on the Pamunkey River, was a well-kept Virginia plantation. George knew Martha had inherited two hundred slaves, along with eighteen thousand acres of land worth at least £30,000. This made Martha one of the wealthiest widows in Virginia but imposed on her the great responsibility and burden of managing such a huge undertaking.

Looking at the ceiling as if seeing the stack of problems she faced, Martha continued. "What with hiring and dismissing servants, purchasing field help, making decisions about planting, of which I know very little, and the upkeep of the buildings . . ." She turned to George. "It is indeed quite trying at times." With a resigned smile and sigh, she added, "Yet one must do one's best."

George followed with questions and suggestions regarding the running of the large estate. The evening literally flew by as their conversation moved with an easy fluidity that George had rarely experienced. George and Martha also talked about army life, the death of Martha's other children, and local politics. As the clock struck midnight, the two looked up to observe that the fire before them had been reduced to embers, and the other guests had all left quietly to avoid interrupting their tête-à-tête.

Both George and Martha simultaneously realized that a friendly conspiracy had occurred, giving them privacy and the opportunity to talk. Standing, George said uncomfortably, "I am so sorry to have kept you, Mrs. Custis. This has been a thoroughly memorable and enjoyable evening, but I have detained you too long."

"It is I who have unfairly barred your timely exit," Martha protested pleasantly. "I know you have a long ride ahead, and it is my fault that you will be forced to travel under less than pleasurable circumstances. The

Chamberlaynes have already invited me to spend the night, so I will not suffer your privations."

"The pleasure of spending the evening with you makes any challenges meaningless," George replied with a grin. While her eyes were cast downward, her own smile revealed her white and shining teeth, which were framed by blushing cheeks.

No doubt hearing the commotion as the young couple moved toward the door, Chamberlayne entered the room and said, "What is this I hear of the colonel riding home at this late hour?"

"William, I came unannounced. I certainly cannot impose on you further," George said.

"I will hear none of that, my friend. I cannot send you out on this cold night and at this late hour. I have already informed your servant to unsaddle your horses and stable them for the night. I believe he is probably already asleep. A chamber has been prepared for you. You will spend the night with us, then you can be on your way in the morning. While I know you are not used to receiving orders, I am the general of this home, and you will do as I command or face a court-martial officiated by my lovely bride."

George and Martha laughed. "I will gladly accept your hospitality to avoid such ignominy. I bow to your authority," George replied with mock formality.

The next morning, George and Martha met in the parlor to find that food had been laid out, but again the Chamberlaynes had "mysteriously" disappeared, leaving a note indicating they had duties in town and on the plantation, but they hoped to see both George and Martha again soon.

As George read the note, he thought, *They are so transparent! They want us to have a chance to get to know one another. I should make some clever quip or comment to put Martha at ease.*

George suddenly found himself tongue-tied. The uncomfortable silence lingered as they both stared at the note and the food before them.

Seizing the initiative, Martha said, "Please, Colonel, we should sit down and let us break our fast. They are such dear people, are they not?"

What a perfect thing to say. She is right: they are kind, and there is no reason to say more about it than that. She always manages to say just the right thing.

Relaxing and following her lead, George replied, "They are indeed. We are both fortunate to have such kind friends." Picking up a plate from the sideboard, George asked, "What are your plans for this day, Mrs. Custis?"

As they enjoyed their breakfast, Martha described her day and followed up with questions about George's plans to return to the regiment. At the same time, George found himself thinking about the foil between time spent with Martha and time spent with Sally.

Everything with Sally is so hard. She is always pressing, teasing, testing, and either pulling me toward her or pushing me away. It is stimulating but not easy—never relaxing. Exciting perhaps, but oh so very hard. But Martha is wonderful! Conversation flows smoothly, free from the dangerous rapids I must always navigate when speaking with Sally.

As the morning drew to a close, George reluctantly said good-bye but received an invitation to visit Martha again at her plantation in two weeks.

Martha is a fine woman and would present an excellent match for me. She is healthy, strong, and intelligent. Sally may be right.

Chapter 49

March 30, 1758 - White House

G eorge approached Martha's lovely home with genuine excitement. As he mounted the front stairs, he was met by a servant who directed him to the parlor where the radiant Martha stood smiling in a beautiful light purple dress. George immediately felt truly glad to be in her company. *She could not be more different from Sally than any woman in the world, and perhaps that is for the best,* he thought.

"Thank you so much for allowing me to come and visit, Mrs. Custis," he said, as he bowed and kissed Martha's hand. "You have a lovely home, and the tulips blooming in your front gardens are exquisite."

As Martha looked up into George's eyes, her mouth opened into a glowing smile. "The pleasure is entirely mine, Colonel. I am so pleased we could arrange this visit. My son, Jacky, and my daughter, Patsy, are excited for the opportunity to meet you. Do you mind if I introduce them before we partake of refreshments?"

George stood a bit too erect, still stiff and ill at ease while trying desperately to relax. "I would very much enjoy seeing your children at any time you wish. With my younger brothers and sisters and various cousins, I enjoy youngsters. Nothing would make me happier than to meet them."

As if by some hidden signal, a mammy entered the room with two well-dressed children. Four-year-old Jacky politely bowed and two-year-old Patsy attempted a curtsy as they were introduced and then quickly ushered from the room. George liked children, and this comfortable interaction put everyone at ease.

Once again alone, Martha said, "I am glad your health is returning. How is your regiment faring?"

Very carefully put, George thought. *She wants to know if I am going to return or stay in the military.*

"I have been honored to serve our country and am grateful for the compliments of others, but my heart yearns to return to the tranquility of Mount Vernon. I expect my service will end shortly, as we are preparing for the final campaign against Fort Duquesne. Indeed, I suspect my resignation will be coming in a matter of months—although I would be grateful if you could keep that information in your confidence."

I hope that reassures her, and I have given her a "secret" that will not hurt me if it gets out.

Martha nodded in acknowledgment, as if processing the implications of his remark. She smiled and offered him some beautifully decorated cakes, then asked, "Would you care to see White House and our grounds? You mentioned my tulips. I must confess my gardens bring me great joy."

As she talked, George gazed directly into her soft and friendly eyes, which held only a hint of sadness, whether from the death of Daniel Custis or something else he could not discern. Interested in seeing a new and prosperous plantation, George responded with unmasked enthusiasm, "Absolutely."

"I'm afraid the fields, gardens, and outbuildings are too dispersed for a leisurely stroll, but I will order a carriage brought around." Martha then nodded to a servant standing placidly at the doorway who turned and left the room. Moments later, a fully appointed carriage was heard pulling to the front of the home.

Impressive. She has planned ahead. This is not a woman to be trifled with.

As they drove about the plantation, George noticed signs of disrepair and a lack of attentiveness in management. Although Martha seemed oblivious to specific problems, she did note on several occasions her challenges in managing her many employees and slaves.

A not-too-subtle hint that she needs a man to assist her in running this substantial enterprise, George mused.

As with almost no other woman in his life, George felt completely at ease but, at the same time, interested in this unusual woman. George could not help but compare Martha to other women he knew, who were often fidgety or nervous or felt compelled to fill any silence with mindless prattle, irritating George and everyone around them. Indeed, even the self-possessed Sally Fairfax seemed uncomfortable with significant lapses in conversation. In contrast, Martha revealed a remarkable level of self-possession as she and George rode around the plantation.

Although George had only planned to remain for the evening, by the time the carriage ride was over, he had accepted an invitation to dine and to spend the night. Indeed, he was so transfixed by Mrs. Custis that he failed to inform Bishop he would be staying. It wasn't until well after the evening meal that he remembered and arranged for Bishop to stand down his horse, eat, and go to bed.

As he left the next day, George received an invitation to return soon. Aware that her servants would have a greater influence than was typical because of the absence of any other relations in the home, George made a point of extravagantly tipping her staff to create an appropriately positive impression.

She is a good match and can bring me money that I desperately need. The children are wonderful, and she appears healthy and strong. More children will come. I will make some inquiries, but I must beat other suitors to the punch. I'll ask Jack and Austin's thoughts, but barring something unknown, the sooner I ask her, the better.

George smiled as he recalled the afternoon and their surprisingly enjoyable carriage ride. But for now, it was back to the regiment.

PART VII
Forbes Campaign

Better to die ten thousand thousand deaths,
Than wound my honour.

—Joseph Addison, *Cato: A Tragedy*, Act I, Scene IV

Chapter 50

April 10, 1758 - Winchester

When George returned to his regiment after an absence of almost five months, he considered the changed military situation. *There is now a real commitment to end this war. England has sent nearly twenty thousand men to America, and all the colonies are bolstering their commitments to the war both with manpower and money. Meanwhile, the Royal Navy has pinned down the French fleet and its army in Europe. Everyone is talking about a multipronged attack: one army advancing into Canada, one coming up Lake Champlain from New York, another attacking up the St. Lawrence, and a final one attacking the Ohio. England has also finally resolved the issue of rank. I will only be junior in standing to redcoats at my own or higher rank. I will no longer be frustrated by tiresome fools with a royal captaincy. With Dinwiddie gone, I can start fresh with the new governor. I will avoid the political infighting and will* not *be dragged into the machinations of Williamsburg politics.*

On George's arrival at Winchester, he was warmly welcomed by Colonel William Byrd. The elegant and poised Byrd had risen to lead the Second Virginia Regiment and was generally liked and respected. George's former aide-de-camp, George Mercer, was now a lieutenant colonel and serving under Byrd; both men were still under George's overall command.

George immediately began jockeying to take a lead role in the upcoming campaign. The high command in England dispatched General John Forbes, a fifty-year-old Scotsman with extensive military experience, to take Fort Duquesne. George wrote his acquaintances in the British army, including his friend Colonel Thomas Gage, who was advising Forbes, asking them to "mention me to General Forbes." While he indicated to others his only motive was his "zeal for the service," his ambition was evident to all.

George was warmly received by Forbes. His regiment was initially ordered to assemble at Winchester pending further instruction. George was hopeful his relationship with Forbes's advisor Sir John St. Clair would also prove useful: "I shall think myself quite happy, if I should continue to stand well in your good opinions to the end of the campaign; for I have long since given over expecting any other reward for my endeavors in the service, than what arises from consciousness of doing my duty and from the good liking of my friends."

Chapter 51

May 9, 1758 - White House

After a couple of months with the regiment, George returned to Williamsburg at the request of Sir John St. Clair to discuss the status of the regiment and to address other matters relating to the progress of Forbes's coming campaign. While back in Williamsburg, George took the opportunity to once again visit Martha.

Their first two encounters were so pleasant, George hoped this next encounter would be even more momentous. His plan to woo Martha included a saddlebag filled with toy soldiers for Jack and a doll for Patsy.

Having just left meetings with politicians and officers in Williamsburg, George was dressed in his finest military regalia. He knew he looked his best and was feeling fitter than he had in years. As George approached Martha's White House Plantation, he was still deeply torn and barely noticed his surroundings.

This is an excellent match. She is a fine, pleasant, and attractive woman. Her wealth is what I need, and hopefully she will want me. Other men would kill to be in my position right now, but . . . Sally. A frown crossed his face. *Don't be a fool! Sally is impossible—we would be outcasts, or worse. She's made her decision and so have I. I now must resolve and be glad. Martha's children are lovely, as is she . . . damn it! I will stop vacillating. If it's to be done, let it be done well and quickly.*

With this mind-set, George bowed deeply and kissed Martha's hand when she met him at the door in a lovely spring gown. With obvious feeling, he looked into Martha's eyes and said, "You look stunning in that dress."

Before she could respond, Jacky darted from behind Martha, just out of reach of his frustrated mammy. Also coming from behind her mother was the toddler, Patsy. Her large eyes seemed only interested in the glitter of George's polished uniform buttons, whereas Jacky's eyes, as with most young boys, went straight to George's sword. Without hesitation, the boy stepped forward to reach for the sword's hilt.

Martha, grabbing his shoulder, kept Jacky from actually grabbing the weapon without permission. The precocious Jacky asked, "Welcome, Colonel Washington! May I see your sword?"

Looking down and smiling, George said gently, "That is entirely up to your mother, young Master Custis."

Martha nodded assent, and George knelt down to Jacky to show him the sword in its scabbard. Then, remembering his bag, he whispered conspiratorially, "Perhaps you would be more interested in the gifts I have brought you and your sister?"

The sword was shoved back toward George, and all eyes immediately turned to the benevolent Martha, who smiled with approval. Patsy, who toddled up behind her mother, hung on her skirt and looked curiously at this giant, kneeling man.

George pulled out a fine wooden box and handed it to Jacky. "You should have your own regiment," George said. "I had these decorated to look like the Virginia Blues."

The exquisitely made pewter soldiers were all painted in the blue and red of the Virginia Regiment. One distinctive soldier sported a gold colonel's braid. George handed it to Jacky. "This one is me," he said.

Jacky looked at the piece painted in the officer's uniform and responded with a frown, "No, it isn't! It's not taller than all the others, so it can't be you."

Martha could not help but laugh, and George joined in. Patting Jacky's head, George responded, "Clever boy."

Patsy, finally surrendering to her curiosity, moved out of her mother's reach and stared at George with wide eyes.

"Fear not, Patsy, I have something for you as well," George said. He grinned as he handed her a beautiful doll, which she quickly grasped and held with a joyful smile.

"What do you say, children?" Martha asked.

"Thank you, sir," they responded in unison. With that, both children dropped to the floor in the foyer and began playing in earnest.

Martha gestured to the parlor, and George followed. They sat down, separated by a table holding fine cakes and tea.

"You are very kind, Colonel. The gifts are perfect. You have certainly conquered my children's hearts."

Well, there is my opening—time to rush the hill. "I am pleased, but it is not simply their hearts I desire . . . madam. I am a soldier, so will you please forgive my directness? I am not one to play the games of the heart or to mince words."

George had practiced this opening earlier in the day, and hoped he struck the right tone. Moreover, it was truthful, for he needed to be direct and make his intentions clear before he returned to the regiment.

"Nor am I, Colonel. Please proceed," Martha said with an encouraging incline of her head.

With a nod of resolve, George slid off his chair and planted his left knee on the rug. His heart was pounding so loudly he could barely hear the rustle of his uniform as he reached forward and gently took Martha's proffered hand, which had been resting on her lap. As she did so, a rise in the corner of her mouth was all that she revealed as she looked down at their clasped hands. His bent leg brushing her dress, he was now eye to eye as he returned to his memorized speech: "You are lovely, pleasant, and I very much like your children. I have had some success in service of my country and hope to have more in returning to this fine land and developing Mount Vernon. I may presume too much, especially given our limited encounters, but I believe we are well suited, and I would be honored if you would consider the possibility of a union." George could feel his face flush, but he tried to control his expression as he finished.

Martha did not make him wait in an uncomfortable silence as many women would. Instead, she looked him in the eye as she said firmly, "I am not the prettiest belle in the Dominion." Martha held up her other hand to silence George's protests. "But I am healthy and not ugly. More importantly, I am blessed with wealth. The man I marry must be honorable and protect and maintain my son's estate."

She is going to decline. I don't have any money. I was a fool.

"I have made inquiries, and I share your belief that we are well matched."

Thank God!

"However, it can go no further as long as you are in active service of the king. You are brave, but I cannot risk being widowed twice in such a short period. You have indicated that your tenure is coming to an end shortly. Before any formal union can be announced, I believe your status must be resolved."

She has thought this through. She is bright and formidable. So . . . is she saying yes, on the condition that I resign?

Impulsively, George blurted out, "So is there hope of an announcement when I resign? For I would do so now, if it would make you happy."

Smiling demurely, she said, "There is hope, but I would not put our happiness ahead of Virginia. Complete your service—quickly—and come back to me. I will be here."

George moved from his knee onto the couch next to Martha. "I will come back to you soon."

"I know, George," she murmured, then they shared their first brief and gentle kiss.

George rode from White House feeling profoundly satisfied. He had, apparently, won the heart of one of the most eligible woman in Virginia. He was exhilarated by their conditional engagement.

As he headed back to the regiment, he found himself feeling that for the first time in his life, a *real* plan existed. One path represented honor, success, and future happiness. The other represented love but disgrace. Duty seemed, unequivocally, to illuminate the proper path. Confident in his future, and his coming exodus from the military, George hired a master builder to begin the substantial additions and remodeling of Mount Vernon, which would follow the careful plans he had drawn himself.

Chapter 52

July 2, 1758 - Rays Town

G eorge was further pleased to receive orders from St. Clair to move his regiment as part of a joint expedition directed at Fort Duquesne. George's troops, along with Pennsylvanians, immediately went to work repairing and expanding the road to Rays Town from Fort Cumberland, allowing St. Clair's supplies to flow into the fort that would become the army's logistics base. While supply headaches continued to dog George, his interchanges with St. Clair and the newly appointed Virginia governor, Francis Fauquier, were courteous and professional.

On July 2, George met Colonel Henry Bouquet, General Forbes's deputy commander. A Swiss-born former member of the Dutch army, Bouquet's portly round face and soft body were the antithesis of the soldierly bearing George expected. Yet beneath his soft façade, his bright eyes revealed a razor-sharp mind. In the three months since George had returned to the regiment, *everything* he had heard of both Bouquet and General Forbes gave him hope for the coming campaign.

Forbes's temporary headquarters was in a well-built, neat, whitewashed farmhouse. His office had been set up in the parlor and was now being occupied by his adjutant, Colonel Bouquet, who sat before a mound of paperwork at a desk placed in front of the large window, taking advantage of the incoming light. Bouquet's desk was perpendicular to the entry. When George came into the room, Bouquet spun on the swivel chair, politely stood, and bowed. George reciprocated. Pointing with an open hand to the only other chair in the room, Bouquet gestured for George to sit.

After discussing current dispositions and supply issues, Bouquet turned to the pressing issues of strategy for the upcoming campaign. "Allow me to be blunt, Colonel Washington. We do not wish to repeat the errors of our unfortunate predecessor, General Braddock. He insisted on conducting the campaign as if we were fighting in lowland Europe. I have already learned we are far removed from that reality. While you have been courteous and complimentary of General Braddock, it has also come to my attention that you have differing views and have developed alternative strategies for dealing with travel and engaging the enemy in this country."

If it was possible, George sat even straighter in his chair as he replied evenly, "General Braddock, in my opinion, was a great man, and I cannot and will not criticize him. However, the experience of my regiment over the last several years has taught me the importance of allowing my men to be properly attired and, in many ways, adopting Indian strategies of attack and defense. I recognize this is unbecoming, but military necessity must supersede both fashion and dogma."

Bouquet maintained eye contact with George, as he spoke, but absently rubbed his chin as he asked, "Tell me more about this 'Indian dress' and what your recommendations to the general would be on these issues."

Unable to hide his enthusiasm, George answered, "Respectfully, if I was permitted to make the decision, I would allow all the soldiers to immediately wear moccasins, leggings, breechclout, and a hunting shirt made of linen, wool, or linsey-woolsey. This would not only permit easier movements, but also likely simplify logistics."

To George's surprise, Bouquet nodded in agreement. "I will recommend to the general that it will be so. I have already discussed this matter with General Forbes, and I am confident that he will adopt your proposed dress, which will serve as the pattern for this expedition. Furthermore, we also share your thoughts concerning tactics, including the greater use of rangers and scouts. Doing so will help us avoid the fate of Braddock's forces and permit our men more flexibility to engage the enemy at close quarters without defaulting to traditional mass-fire European techniques. We will be looking to your Virginia troops to act as our vanguard as we engage the Indian and French forces in this endeavor."

George couldn't help but swell with pride and pleasure as, for the first time in his career, his strategies and tactics were being adopted. He left the meeting feeling confident that he would play a central role in the upcoming campaign. Indeed, within the week, he received written confirmation that Forbes had adopted George's recommendation on Indian dress for the entire expedition.

The camp was quiet after dark. The men were exhausted from another hard day of road building. Even the insects, which were so deafening and exuberant in spring, were subdued as the summer progressed. George sat at his desk completing paperwork, frustrated that no one was assisting him. His skin itching as his shirt soaked through with sweat, he chose to remain inside the canvas tent, avoiding the bug-filled night. In truth, he knew his discomfort was caused not simply by the heat and bugs, but also by his growing angst that no word had come regarding his second attempt to run for the House of Burgesses. Unable to leave the army because of his obligations to General Forbes, George resolved to proceed with a long-distance campaign while the army continued its march on Fort Duquesne.

This time George decided to invest money and solicit the assistance of his friends in ensuring a more vigorous campaign. Will Fairfax and his brother-in-law, John Carlyle, rode to the Shenandoah Valley to secure the support of tenant farmers with the generous use of alcohol. Indeed, George spent thirty-nine pounds on thirty-four gallons of wine, three pints of brandy, thirteen gallons of beer, eight quarts of cider, and forty gallons of rum punch. Nevertheless, the question remained whether all his hard-earned money and the efforts of his friends were for naught. George fought off a pang of guilt as he considered Will Fairfax's efforts on his behalf. Since Will's return, George had endeavored, at Sally's insistence, to maintain a "normal" relationship for the sake of propriety.

Receiving mail was always a frustratingly proposition, but especially so when letters were attempting to catch up with an army on the move. As George contemplated yet another day of anxiety, he heard the shuffle of footsteps outside his tent and the muffled laughs of men.

Suddenly, without a knock or request to enter, his tent flap burst open, and the small space was filled with his officers, who were in a boisterous mood. Standing and trying to control his anger at their uninvited entrance, George began to speak, but Lieutenant Colonel Stephen raised his hand, stifling George's protests. Following an unsteady bow, Stephen announced with his right hand held formally across his chest, "If I may, we party of Virginia gentlemen have come to deliver happy news to our leader and better."

A confused George surveyed the smiling faces of his officers, Byrd, Mercer, Stephen, and even a grinning Christopher Gist, who stood in the back of the group a head above the rest. While Gist was not a senior officer, all knew of Colonel Washington's special bond with the old scout.

With his hands on his hips, unable to control his irritation any longer, George finally barked, "What in the blazes is going on here?"

Byrd, who spoke with the melodious tones of the most genteel Virginia gentleman, responded, "The colonel is right; we are being rude to His Excellency, our commander and our leader in the House of Burgesses."

What?

Lieutenant Colonel Mercer stepped forward and handed George a letter reporting George's victory. With a shy smile, Mercer confessed, "You know there are no secrets in the mail. Congratulations, sir."

My God, I won.

Chagrined by his prior outburst and unable to meet the twinkling eyes of his men, George said, looking at his feet, "Thank you very much, gentlemen. I am grateful for your kindness, and I really don't know what to say."

"That, my dear Colonel, is why the good Lord invented liquor," Colonel Stephen quipped.

Glasses then suddenly materialized and were filled all around. Colonel Byrd faced George and raised his glass in a toast. "To the newest member of the House of Burgesses . . . I give you Colonel Washington."

All the men responded in unison: "Colonel Washington!"

George knew he should give some brief speech, but it was not in his nature. These men, more than any others, would forgive his lack of eloquence, so he simply responded by raising his glass and meeting their eyes. "To Virginia."

"To Virginia," the men roared as they finished their drinks, unconcerned they were likely waking the entire camp.

"Please, gentlemen, take a seat and let us finish Adam's fine bottle." As if by magic, chairs, bread, and cheese appeared, and the men sat around the table, enjoying their food and drink and celebrating George's victory.

Gist's long arms held out a fine box filled with cheroots. George was not a habitual smoker; however, late in the evening, he did enjoy the relaxing comfort of good tobacco.

"A taste of home, gentlemen," Gist offered.

"You mean the aroma!" Stephen said. He laughed as the men reached into the box, helping themselves with nods of approval to the old scout. Laughter and smoke filled the tent late into the night as Stephen's bottle gave way to another miraculously produced by Gist.

The honeymoon between George and Forbes ended when Forbes began considering his plan of march. While no longer under George's daily supervision, Colonel Adam Stephen remained one of his most trusted officers and a frequent visitor. With a perfunctory knock, Stephen stormed into George's cramped tent.

"The bastards! The whoring Pennsylvanians are conniving with the addle-minded Forbes to build the goddamned road through Pennsylvania!"

Over Stephen's shoulder, George saw Colonel Byrd glide in and nod in agreement. Byrd led Virginia's Second Regiment but was also under George's overall command.

George knew Forbes had two choices to advance on Fort Duquesne: He could take the road cleared by George and previously taken by Braddock—known as "Braddock's Road"—or he could order a new road built straight west. This new road would be well north of Braddock's

Road, which cut more directly through Pennsylvania and provided obvious economic advantages to that state.

George was aware this issue had been raised, but he did not seriously believe until this point that Forbes would follow the route advocated by the Pennsylvanians.

"Are you sure?" he asked.

Pointing at the ground, but never taking his eyes off Washington, Stephen declared, "As sure as I am standing here. One of my men heard Bouquet and Forbes talking, and they seem resolved to go north!"

Byrd, a member of Virginia's elite and always cognizant of the political ramifications of his actions, stepped next to Stephen. "I do not believe any of us should have illusions. This will be a disaster for Virginia and, to be frank, may reflect badly on us."

Unable to remain seated in the face of this revelation, George stood to face the two men but almost immediately began to pace in the small space behind his desk like a caged animal. Alternately looking at the ground and at his two officers, George declared, "Gentlemen, I will attempt to dissuade Colonel Bouquet and the general of the folly of this route. I also believe we should contact our friends in Williamsburg to see if they can provide some assistance in ensuring this mistake does not occur. Let me be clear: I do not view this as a political issue. It simply makes no military sense to build a new road when one already exists. We, more than virtually anyone in the army, understand the difficulty of hacking a road through virgin forest while under the watchful eye of our enemy. The army faces monstrous mountains covered with woods and rocks if we go north. Let us resolve to fight this error as we are also resolved to fight our enemy. I shall present our arguments to Colonel Bouquet as soon as possible. Thank you and good day."

The men bowed at the dismissal, and George immediately picked up his pen to write the governor, the speaker of the House of Burgesses, and other prominent Virginians.

⚜ ——— ⚜

George and Bouquet met again on July 29. The friendliness of their prior meeting had disappeared, and the tension in the room was palpable. While directing George to a chair, Bouquet's irritation was evident.

"Let me get directly to the point, Colonel Washington: The general is unhappy with indications that you have been critical of his decision to construct a northern road to Fort Duquesne. He has decided not to follow the unsuccessful path of General Braddock. You may view this from the standpoint of your colony, but General Forbes cares nothing for economic or political considerations." George opened his mouth to protest but knew it was impolite and forced himself to remain silent as Bouquet continued. "The General is instead focused primarily on the military situation. It is our assessment that the northern route involves one less major river crossing, and logistical support will flow to the army more easily from heavily populated Pennsylvania than from its sparsely populated counterpart in the south. Better logistical support and a shorter baggage train, we believe, will make the difference. Indeed, it is our assessment, and that of Colonel St. Clair, that this path will avoid the excessive logistical challenges that were one of General Braddock's many undoings."

George tried desperately to contain his frustration and anger as Bouquet explained his approach. Not only would the northern road have disastrous implications for Virginia and the Ohio Company, but George genuinely believed it was the wrong route. His darkening expression and growing desire to respond was finally acknowledged with a nod from Bouquet. George's normal slow and deliberate speaking style gave way to a emphatic torrent of words: "Sir, it is my belief this route will be a profound mistake on *military* grounds. We already have an existing road that needs only to be refurbished and widened. It will take us to the absolute gates of Fort Duquesne without any serious delay. In contrast, I speak from many years of experience as well as the hard lessons from General Braddock's campaign. The challenges of constructing a new road through dense territory should not be easily discounted. Moreover, large mountains, thick woods, and inclement weather encumber the northern route are not presented in the south. Likewise the existing road will present a firmer and better road surface than could possibly be constructed if we were to proceed afresh. I doubt the new route will be passable even for packhorses. Finally, the southern colonies are making the maximum effort to support this campaign. To proceed to the advantage of the north is a tactical and strategic error." Already leaning forward in his chair as he spoke, George unconsciously emphasized his point by driving his finger with an audible knock on the top of Bouquet's desk.

Realizing he risked offending Bouquet with his comments, George nevertheless pressed on: "I watched one general I admired fail because of major tactical blunders, and I earnestly do not wish to see another. Both you and the general have been kind to me and respected my experience in bush fighting. I would hope that you will understand that my fervent belief in following Braddock's Road is based on experience and my concerns for this army and is not driven by politics that I personally eschew."

George saw Bouquet's eyebrow rise slightly at his disclaimer of interest in politics.

No doubt he is aware of my recent election to the House of Burgesses.

For a moment, it seemed as if Bouquet would take George to task, but instead he straightened in his chair and said formally, "The general and I are grateful for your input. We know you seek only the best for this army, and it would be unfortunate if your service came to an end. Nevertheless, the general has made his decision, and you will withdraw your men from Braddock's Road and redeploy them as instructed to expand the northern route." Bouquet stood to make clear no further discussion was invited. "Thank you, Colonel. Dismissed." Without further comment, George bowed and left the room.

Outside the cabin, he clasped his hands behind his back and began to pace. *Bloody hell! Will these commissioned officers ever listen? The threat to me is clear. Fate seems to be pushing me inexorably away from the military and back to Mount Vernon. Despite my service for Braddock, I am always treated as some backwater fool. I thought Forbes and Bouquet were different, but their opinion of me is now crystal clear. They hold both Virginia and me in contempt. There is no real prospect of serving the Crown. Indeed, I face a future of continued disappointment and frustration.*

A future with Martha as a planter and Burgess presents a great oppor-tunity. While I would dearly like to simply resign and be done with this, I believe the Crown has committed sufficient resources to take Fort Duquesne. I will remain with the army through the taking of the fort, or, at the very least, through this year. If, at the end of the year, the fort is not taken, I will reassess.

My final accomplishment must be to convince General Forbes to approach by way of Braddock's Road and not across Pennsylvania. Not only would the expansion of Braddock's Road help my friends and family in our investments in the Ohio, but it would also prevent Pennsylvania from having its own road built to access this valuable land.

Chapter 53

September 12, 1758 - Fort Cumberland

Almost a month and a half had passed since George had met with Bouquet. His inability to convince Forbes to follow Braddock's Road, his strained relations with Bouquet, and his longing to return to Mount Vernon had all led to a growing despair. Meanwhile his "success" in wooing Martha was increasingly tempered by his longing for Sally.

George felt himself captured by a single moment in time. He could not escape the memory of the afternoon with Sally. As she had turned and locked the door, her siren's beauty had pulled on George then, as it did now. His reason was being destroyed by a desire he could not control. George knew men driven to their ruin by drink. Now, for the first time in his life, he understood that weakness. His longing to once again experience bliss in Sally's arms was overwhelming his judgment.

Since Will's return from England, George had maintained regular contact with him. Indeed, with great guilt and anxiety, he'd accepted Will's generous offer to assist him in the renovations of Mount Vernon. Will was clearly happy to be home and thrilled with George's pending marriage to Martha. He seemed completely oblivious to any liaison between George and Sally.

As well he should be—I am a trusted family friend, thought George as he tapped the letter he held in his hands behind his back. *It is inconceivable that Sally and I could be anything more than dear friends.*

As he stood, shuffled, and looked at the ground, he thought, *This fixation is eating me alive! When I am with Sally, I beg time to stand still. When we are apart, I pine like a fool to experience those magical moments in her presence. This must end! With this letter, I will know once and for all!*

As George stared down at the letter he had just completed, he began to reread:

Camp at Fort Cumberland   12th Septr 1758

Dear Madam,

'Tis true, I profess myself a Votary to Love—I acknowledge that a Lady is in the Case—and further I confess, that this Lady is known to you.

I know I need to be circumspect should this letter fall into the wrong hands, but I want her to know how much I love her.

Yes Madam, as well as she is to one, who is too sensible of her Charms to deny the Power, whose Influence he feels and must ever Submit to.

She needs to know the power and influence she still has over me and that I will submit to her charms, if she will allow me to.

I feel the force of her amiable beautics in the recollection of a thousand tender passages that I coud wish to obliterate, till I am bid to revive them.—but experience alas!

What we said to each other and, more importantly our "experience"—I must remind her. It must mean something to her.

sadly reminds me how Impossible this is.—and evinces an Opinion which I have long entertaind, that there is a Destiny, which has the Sovereign controul of our Actions—not to be resisted by the strongest efforts of Human Nature.

When she cast me aside, she talked about destiny and honor, but it seems to me that destiny is pulling me toward her and not away from her. We must resolve this issue once and for all.

You have drawn me my dear Madam, or rather have I drawn myself, into an honest confession of a Simple Fact—misconstrue not my meaning—'tis obvious—doubt it not, nor expose it,—the World has no business to know the object of my Love, declard in this manner to—you when I want to conceal it

I know we must conceal our love, but I still need to declare it and I need her to declare it for me too. Somehow, if I knew one way or another that she still loved me, it could make life more bearable.

—One thing, above all things in this World I wish to know, and only one person of your Acquaintance can solve me that, or guess my meaning.—but adieu to this, till happier times, if I ever shall see them.

[B]e assured that I am Dr Madam with the most unfeigned regard, Yr Most Obedient & Most Obldgd Hble Servt

Go: Washington

Sending this is a mistake. It is surrendering to my most formidable nemesis: myself. The voices of Lawrence and the Colonel, indeed my own judgment, all scream at me not to send this letter. Yet, if I am to truly be reborn and move on with Martha, I must know Sally's heart. If I do not send this, I fear I will either explode or disappear for the loss of my soul.
I am a fool ruled by my passion, but so be it. I will send it.

Chapter 54

September 16, 1758 – Fort Cumberland

F our days later, George met with Forbes face-to-face. The normally pleasant Forbes looked both ill and agitated as George entered the tent with Colonel Byrd at his side. The two Virginians stood facing the sitting Forbes, with Bouquet standing behind the general. There were no exchanges of courtesies or invitations to sit.

George's complaints within the army about its route and to his allies in Williamsburg had finally come to a head when one of George's letters fell into the hands of Forbes and Bouquet. Additionally, Adam Stephen's temper boiled over when he refused to work on the new road, resulting in his arrest and a charge of mutiny by St. Clair. Bouquet ultimately intervened and had Stephen released and the charges were dropped, but the tension remained.

The gaunt and pale Forbes sat before them looking sleep deprived, yet lit up as he began to speak. "Gentlemen. This must stop!" As he spoke, he tossed an open letter onto the desk which was immediately recognizable as filled with George's handwriting. "You have served the king honorably in the past, but your attacks on my decision to proceed with the northern route are unacceptable. I have acted based upon the best intelligence provided to me without favoring one province over another. I regret to say that Virginians are the only people I have dealt with who appear to place attachment to province above sound military reality. Your weakness appears to place your colony above the good of the army."

Both men stiffened at the rebuke, but an enraged Forbes continued on: "It is my opinion that you publically declare favor of one road over another without knowing the first thing about which route is better. I confess that I value your provincial interest, jealousies, or suspicions not one single twopence. You have brought this to a head, gentlemen. I do not want to lose you as officers under my command, but this is *my* command. I will countenance no further disagreements. If your conscience cannot allow you to follow my instructions, I will regrettably understand."

So . . . "Follow my orders, resign, or be dismissed from the army."

Without waiting for Byrd to respond, George bowed slightly and then tilted his hands, which had been hanging at his sides, to show his open palms as he spoke deferentially. "Sir. I never meant any disrespect, although I believe the best interests of the army and, as you say, of my province coincide here. The most efficacious route is Braddock's Road. I will, of course, follow your instructions if you have decided otherwise."

Forbes let out an exasperated sigh and stared at George, clearly trying to make a decision. With some understanding and less anger, he replied, "I know you are under intense political pressure from your home, but I will not allow it to influence you here. As Colonel Bouquet has already acknowledged, you have demonstrated bravery in battle, and I am greatly impressed by your theories and tactics. You can rightly take pride in your regiment. They have performed better than their other colonial counterparts, and I believe they are a superb vanguard and screening force for our troops as we move forward. However, this discussion about the road is *over*. My decision is final. I require your word that you will not engage in any further insubordinate activity."

Well, he has me cornered. I will give him my word not to complain. This is the wrong decision—but his order is clear.

"Of course, General. We are grateful for the confidence you have shown in our regiment, and we will not let you down."

Colonel Byrd bowed in agreement with George's pronouncement. "I expect you will not, gentlemen. Dismissed."

Chapter 55

September 25, 1758 - Rays Town

G eorge waited almost two weeks in anguish for a response to his entreaty to Sally. He knew it was irrational; his future with Martha was prudent and would probably be happier. When the letter from Sally finally arrived, it was mixed with a stack of other correspondence George needed to address on behalf of the regiment. It took all of his self-discipline to delay tearing open the letter until after his staff had been dismissed and he had time to privately review the correspondence. Heart pounding, and with a slight tremor in his hand, George opened the letter and read:

Dear Colo. Washington:

Thank you for your kind letter of Sept 12th. We share your deep and abiding friendship. We wish nothing more than your safe and healthy return to our connected families and the joy of seeing you successfully establish a new household at Mount Vernon.

We hope you will return to Belvoir as we may soon reprise Cato, despite the play's unhappy bent, it is instructive on its manifest demonstrations of honour and sacrifice.

Please forgive the length of this letter as we wanted to convey our finest wishes and beg you to be safe and return to visit both of us, your family, at Belvoir.

Yr dear friends and Most Obed't servants.

Mr. & Mrs. G. W. Fairfax.

George read and reread the brief and carefully written letter in Sally's hand. *This letter is from both Will and Sally, although I have no doubt that Will never saw it.*

After years of longing for Sally and enduring the storms of emotional tumult that had tortured him over the last several months, George had expected to receive her rejection with a rending agony and disappointment. He had always imagined that if their love came to an end, it would be a life-shattering moment of supreme anguish. Instead, to his surprise, it came like the inevitable setting sun, the gradual, brute realization that a hope and dream was truly and finally over. The adolescent fantasy of love prevailing over all, quite simply, was not to be.

The open wound, I suspect, will always be there, but I must cauterize it now and move on. I will send Sally one final carefully written letter of "adieu" and then my focus, as it must be, will be on Martha.

Camp at Rays Town   25th Septr 1758

Dear Madam,

Do we still misunderstand the true meaning of each others Letters? I think it must be so, thô I would feign hope the contrary as I cannot speak plainer without—but I'll say no more, and leave you to guess the rest.

She must have understood what my prior letter meant when I confessed that I am her "Votary to Love." I wish we could both be more forthright, but we cannot risk an open discussion falling into the wrong hands.

I should think my time more agreeable spent believe me, in playing a part in Cato with the Company you mention, & myself doubly happy in being the Juba to such a Marcia as you must make.

Her reference to Will, family, and Cato *in her letter is clear: duty must come first. She is resolved—it is over. But I want her to know I still cherish being Juba to her Marcia.*

Adieu dear Madam, you possibly will hear something of me, or from me before we shall meet. I must beg the favour of you to make my Compliments to Colo. Cary and the Ladies with you, & believe that I am most unalterabl Yr Most Obedt & Oblig'd

Go: Washington

Honor must triumph over love. Perhaps true love will yet come with Martha. Regardless, I must accept Sally's "adieu" and move on. Fate has separated us, and I must accept her "friendship." If I am to achieve anything in my life, it will be with Martha and not Sally at my side. I shall not write her again until long after Martha and I are wed. This chapter of my life is "most unalterably," and finally, closed.

George's fixation with Sally did not prevent him from fully participating in Forbes's campaign. Indeed, a couple of weeks after sending Sally his final letter, George submitted a "Plan of an Order of March" describing how to move the army through a wooded area, which included bush-style tactics that not only demonstrated the complete evolution in George's thinking from his earliest experiences at Fort Necessity, but also recognized the lessons learned in bloodied combat at Monongahela. Forbes and Bouquet, to their credit, accepted and endorsed George's proposed tactics and approach. With the adoption of George's plan, engagements with the French in mid-October resulted in relatively minimal losses as the army progressed toward its goal of taking Fort Duquesne.

Chapter 56

November 12, 1758 - Forbes Road Near Loyalhanna

In the month since Forbes adopted his line of march, George had continued his efforts to change the route. At the same time, he could not help but respect the skill and ability of Forbes and Bouquet in handling the complex challenges of administration for such a huge army.

On a warm fall afternoon, Colonel Bouquet approached George at the top of the hill where the Virginians were cleaning equipment and training. George watched with some amusement as the rotund Bouquet trundled up the hill. Keeping a straight face, George touched his hat in acknowledgment as the out-of-breath colonel approached.

"Colonel Washington . . . Forbes sends . . . his compliments," a gasping Bouquet sputtered, resting his hands on his knees.

"Colonel, please take a moment and catch your breath. You could have sent a runner for me. I am, as always, at your disposal," George said with a straight face, but his amusement was revealed by his bright eyes.

"That hill is bigger than it looks. I thought the exercise would do me good . . . although that remains to be seen, aye, Colonel?" a now grinning Bouquet said to George.

George inclined his head in agreement, trying to hide his growing smile lest it be misinterpreted as disrespectful.

The mirth disappeared from Bouquet's face as the topic shifted to military matters. "As you know, two hundred enemy raiders struck our supply post near Loyalhanna. The general ordered five hundred men from the Second Regiment under Lieutenant Colonel Mercer to investigate. We've heard reports of some heated contact with the enemy. The general would like you and your men to move out and provide support. If a more generalized engagement occurs, you are to take command in the field and report back to me immediately."

While George's feet remained planted, his mind was already moving, thinking about preparations to get his soldiers ready and on their way.

Sensing George's anticipation, Bouquet concluded, "Thank you, Colonel, you have your orders. I wish you good luck and good hunting."

George nodded his head in acknowledgment and turned to his men, putting the regiment into motion.

As George's men entered the woods, the last remnants of the day gave way to dusk. The clear sky was turning a brilliant azure and violet, transforming the forest into a colorless world of shadow where George's men strained to see and hear their enemy.

Soon, even this hint of light evaporated, plunging Washington's men into total darkness. Suddenly a shout and a musket pan flared, revealing a soldier's face, followed by a loud report and lance of flames as an unknown force opened fire on George's troops. An instant later, only three dozen yards away, George's men and the opposing line both erupted with sound and blinding light. Despite his desire to remain focused and in command, the spears of light and loud gunfire were mesmerizing, presenting the greatest light show George had ever witnessed. Each shot threw a curtain of gray smoke, repeated hundreds of times, contributing to the "fog of war," overwhelming his senses, and preventing him from perceiving the "real events" unfolding around him. Through the flashes, George saw a soldier next to him drop so suddenly it was like a marionette puppet whose strings had been cut. In that blink of an eye, life and vitality were just gone.

The first barrage shredded his ranks. Wounded men lay all around as George tried desperately to understand what was happening. He strained to listen, but he could only hear the moans of the wounded and the scrape of ramrods reloading muskets. Then, from across the void, he heard orders: "Aim below the flashes boys, wait and make them—" Then another volley erupted.

Was that English? Dear God, that sounded like Mercer! Lord no! Those are my men!

George turned to his captain and screamed, "Stop! Those are Mercer's men!"

The horror and revulsion at the prospect of his own men being killed at the hands of fellow Virginians overcame reason. George ran along the line, muskets going off inches from his head. He violently slapped up the extended weapons with his sword. As his men began to cease fire, George ran into the dark, smoked-filled no-man's-land between the two lines, bellowing at the top of his lungs for Mercer to cease firing. The hot breath of musket balls filled the air all around him, and the familiar whiz of the lead intensified as he approached the other regiment's line.

Finally, after what seemed like an eternity, George heard "Cease fire!" from the men firing almost directly at him, closely followed by shouts of fear and horror: "Is that Colonel Washington?"

After a few more terrifying minutes, shouts from officers on both sides stopped the firing, and the sound of musket fire gave way to the angry protests and cries of the wounded.

George strode past shocked and injured men. With his heart pumping and adrenaline almost overwhelming his reason, George screamed, "Where's Lieutenant Colonel Mercer?" His frustration peaked when he heard someone yell, "Colonel Washington! He's down here. He's been shot!"

George stormed along the lines, alternately pushing stunned men out of his way and trying to avoid the dead and dying. He heard the all-too-familiar laments of the injured calling for help, or their wives or mothers. He was relieved to see Mercer's wound was not life threatening and that he was conscious. George used all his self-control to not demand an explanation from his former aide-de-camp. He instinctually knew it would do no good to vent his anger at his wounded friend. George's only solace was the capture of two Indian prisoners and a British traitor working with the French, who might provide useful information.

Birdsong announced the dawn of an unseasonably warm and beautiful day as George left Lieutenant Colonel Mercer's bedside the morning after the firefight, yet George was oblivious to the pleasant morning.

No one will ever know what really happened in those dark woods: who fired first, who could have given a warning, George thought. *At the end of the day, I must bear the burden of the engagement. I never wanted to return to this campaign. Forbes has built this idiotic new road that will harm Virginia, and now—my own regiment has wounded itself. Damn it!*

At that instant, a young corporal timidly approached, removing his hat and holding it against his chest so tightly that it looked as if he feared George would try to take it from him. "Colonel Washington? Colonel Stephen sends his compliments. The prisoner is with the colonel. Apparently he . . . I mean the British prisoner . . . I mean the traitor . . ."

"Well, get on with it, man!" George snapped. "What does the colonel say?"

"Begging your pardon, he says the traitor is not willing to talk."

The pressure of exhaustion, humiliation, and frustration erupted in an uncontrolled burning torrent of anger.

Honorable Virginians are dead, and this traitorous pig refuses to talk! What shall I tell the forlorn fathers I must face when I return to the Old Dominion? "I am sorry, sir. We could have gotten more information to give your son's death meaning, but the bastard wouldn't talk?" By heavens, not while my heart beats!

George now completely gave way to postbattle catharsis and the anger he normally tried so hard to control. His steely gray eyes flared with white-hot rage. As he stormed toward the tent where the prisoner was being held, men scurried to get out of his way. George tore the tent flap open so violently that the entire tent shook. All turned to see the figure filling the entrance. The apparition's eyes reflected the lamplight illuminating the dark tent, giving George's already fierce expression a demonic intensity. Covered in dirt and the blood of his fellow Virginians, George took two long strides to the British traitor, pulled him from his chair, and effortlessly lifted him off the ground by the front of his shirt.

The wide-eyed man's feet dangled a foot off the ground. George's strong, adrenaline-driven grip and powerful arms held him in place. His face, contorted by fury, was inches from the stupefied prisoner. "I'll be damned if I allow a cowardly traitor to smugly refuse to answer our questions!" George snarled. "Good men—better men than you—have died this day. By God, I will run you through!"

George viciously threw the traitor to the tent's packed-dirt floor. The man bounced, rolled, and crashed into the empty chair. In one smooth motion, George pulled his sword.

The dumbstruck soldiers in the room moved as one to prevent George from following through on his threat. Shaking off his comrades, he stormed out of the tent without another word.

As George cleaned off the gore and grime of battle, he felt a growing unease about his loss of control in front of his men. His father, Lawrence, and the Colonel were true gentlemen. While possessing tempers and great strength, they never allowed anger to extend to physical violence. In fact, his mother's inability to restrain her temper and her liberal use of corporal punishment caused George to hold in low regard those who reverted to violence to vent their rage.

I must control the anger inside me. I swear I will not lose physical control again. I . . . am a better man than that.

"Colonel? Excuse me. I have some promising news."

George was startled to see Adam Stephen standing stiffly at the entrance to his tent. Stephen was obviously still ill at ease from the recent encounter with the prisoner.

"Yes, Adam?"

With forced casualness and a smile that did not extend to his eyes, Colonel Stephen reported, "It appears your . . . charade with the prisoner worked. He sang like a canary the moment you left the tent. We've learned the fort is lightly defended, and the French have largely abandoned the works. The Indians are outraged at the withdrawal, but they are pulling back as well."

He knows it was no "charade," but God bless him.

"Do you believe him?" George asked.

"We would not have. However, your 'persuasion' made it very clear to all of us that he is telling the truth. We let him know that if he lied to us in any way, he would be left to your tender mercies or shot, and he seemed to fear you more." Then, with obvious pleasure, Stephen said, "The little bastard gave us every little detail of the fort, the Indians, and the French disposition. We spent an hour with the bloody knave trying to get him to talk, and after just one minute with you, he would have told us the deepest secrets of his soul." Stephen paused, then asked, "Shall we inform the general?"

Pulling on his coat, George replied, "Indeed, Adam, let's go, but we can forgo explaining my techniques of persuasion."

"Absolutely, Colonel," Stephen said with a knowing look.

The men went straight to General Forbes's tent. "General, if we may?" George said as he stuck his head into the general's tent. They found the general with Colonel Bouquet, huddled over piles of paper that George well knew were the bane of all commanding officers.

General Forbes stood as he gestured for Washington to enter the tent. "Colonel Washington. I was so distressed to hear of the engagement last night. Your men?"

"I regret to inform you, twenty-six Virginians were wounded and fourteen were killed outright, sir," George said while looking at his feet.

Before George could go further, Forbes walked around his desk and grabbed George's arm—a very rare gesture for a man of Forbes's normal formality. "Do not punish yourself, my young friend. These things happen, especially at night. I have heard your brave actions helped lessen casualties."

Stephen broke in: "Indeed, General. Colonel Washington ran between the lines, knocking up guns."

"We are grateful you were unhurt. Do you have anything else to report?" Forbes asked as he returned to his seat.

"Yes, General," George answered. "That is the reason we came. We captured a British subject who was a traitor working for the French in the fort. He has informed us that the French and Indians have pulled back from the fort, and that it is largely undefended."

"Are you confident in this information?" Bouquet asked.

George signaled to Stephen, who replied, "Yes, Colonel. The man is available for your questioning, but suffice we are convinced he is telling the truth."

A look was exchanged between Forbes and his adjutant. Bouquet nodded as if an unspoken conversation had occurred. "Colonel Washington, please summon the senior officers for a council of war immediately," Bouquet ordered. "Alert the camp to prepare to get moving."

As an obviously sick Forbes shuffled into the tent, all his officers rose in unison. "As you were, gentlemen," Forbes said. "Please be seated." Pointing to the large map pinned on a wall board, Forbes continued, "We are close, gentlemen. Thanks to the fine intelligence received by Colonel Washington, we are in a position to make a final push to the fort, which we now understand is undefended and largely abandoned. To that end, I am going to detach a force of twenty-five hundred men to proceed toward the fort with all dispatch. A number of our troops' enlistments expire on November 30, and we will make the supreme effort to complete the campaign before this unfortunate event occurs. This force will consist of three brigades. Lieutenant Colonel Montgomery, you will select men from the Seventy-Seventh. Colonel Bouquet has already identified men under his command. Finally, Colonel Washington, you will select three companies of your Virginians to act as our vanguard." Waiving his hand casually toward George and the two other colonels as if this was an everyday occurrence, Forbes announced, "I am brevetting you three as brigadier generals."

By heavens, I am a general officer!

Either ignoring or indifferent to the impact of the promotions, Forbes continued with growing strength. "Please have no illusions, gentlemen. This will be hard work, and I will demand much. We must clear many miles of roadway each day if we are going to exploit this tactical advantage. You will need to brief your officers and men. General Bouquet will be providing written orders following this meeting. Are there any further questions?"

Snapping back to reality, George realized he still owed a duty to Virginia to make the final "push" to follow Braddock's Road instead of the route advocated by the Pennsylvanians and mindlessly adopted by Forbes and Bouquet. "If I may, General," he asked, "what route do we intend to follow to complete this final push to Fort Duquesne? As you know, there is already a route completed almost to the gates of Duquesne by General Braddock, if we are truly pressed for time . . ."

An exasperated Forbes looked at Bouquet to respond. "*General Washington*." Bouquet replied, emphasizing the new title with the implicit threat that failure to cooperate would mean its quick removal. "We have discussed this on many occasions, and we are committed to this new northern route. You have pledged to both the general and me that you will support the general's decisions. If you do not, regretfully, we may need to alter our command structure."

There it is. "Support us or we will relieve you." They hold a carrot and a stick, and it is up to me to decide. It is an easy one: insisting on a road that will not be taken and having myself relieved serves no purpose, harms me, and does not benefit Virginia.

Recognizing defeat, George quickly responded, "I do not seek to question the general's decision or renege on any commitments. I merely seek clarification."

Bouquet walked over to the map and pointed with strained patience. "I believe the map makes it crystal clear, General Washington. We are to complete the road along the route previously identified, which should, in short order, have us besieging Fort Duquesne."

Forbes stood, and in response, all the other men in the room did likewise. "You have your orders, gentlemen. We need to detach this column and begin cutting our new road."

While still upset about Forbes's refusal to follow Braddock's Road,

George was thrilled with his brevet generalcy and attacked the road construction with gusto, despite shortages of tools and supplies. George and his men made a supreme effort, cutting up to five miles a day of new road, working side by side with British regulars.

Chapter 57

November 25, 1758 - Fort Duquesne

After almost two weeks of arduous and unceasing effort, the troops were a mere ten miles from their destination when they heard an enormous explosion: the French had lit their magazine and abandoned Fort Duquesne. To everyone's surprise—and relief—there was no final climatic battle or siege; instead, the enemy melted into the forest. Ragged, underfed, and exhausted, George's men were surprised to merely walk into Fort Duquesne.

On November 25, 1758, George stood on the spot where, five years earlier, he had noted that the topography offered an excellent location for a fort. Since that time, the fort had become the main focus of the British effort in the Ohio.

George saw the fort was in shambles; some buildings still burned, with naked chimneys standing in silent testament to the fort's sudden demise at the hands of the French. George and his men, along with the other members of Forbes's army, shook hands, clasped each other on the back, and took a moment to savor their victory. A flag was raised and a ceremony briefly held. What George did not expect was the overwhelming feeling of anticlimax. For so long, achieving this fort had been not only his goal, but also the desire of the British army. Now, with the fort secured, his mind turned to Virginia, Mount Vernon, and Martha.

George's criticisms of Forbes's strategy were quickly forgotten and replaced with praise of Forbes's "great merit." George was warmly received by General Forbes and Colonel Bouquet. All exchanged effusive compliments as George was granted leave to return to Virginia. Having left a small number of soldiers behind to garrison the fort, George led his remaining officers and men back toward Winchester and home.

After visiting with Lieutenant Colonel Mercer, George entered his Winchester office and found Colonel Stephen behind his desk.

"In my chair already, Adam?" George said with a grin.

"Colonel! No, sir. Just catching up on some paperwork," Colonel Stephen replied as he stood and began to move from behind the desk.

"Relax. It is your chair now. I have come to take my leave of you and offer you my best wishes."

"Colonel, please, let me ask you one more time to reconsider. The regiment and this army need your leadership," Stephen said as he now stood directly in front of George.

"You are too kind, but the time has come. My plantation has been neglected for too long. I could not leave in the face of the enemy, but we have now reduced Fort Duquesne, and final victory is only a matter of time." Pausing with a satisfied smile, George continued. "I am gratified the officers I have brought to this regiment, and you most of all, will remain to honorably carry on in my stead." Indicating for Stephen to return to his chair, George sat likewise and took on a more wistful tone: "It seems like a lifetime ago that you and I met those French spies in the glen. We have been through so much: Fort Necessity, Monongahela, and victory last week. I leave knowing my—our—regiment is in able hands."

"Very well, Colonel. It has been an honor, sir. Godspeed and all my best." Stephen stood and bowed.

George did likewise. "I beg you to visit me at Mount Vernon as you promised."

"I will, Colonel."

As George was about to exit, he turned and asked, "Have you seen Mr. Gist?"

"No, Colonel. I believe he was out meeting with the Indians and is not in town."

George's head sagged in disappointment as he stepped outside.

Damn. I had hoped to see Gist before I left.

As he walked to where he planned to meet Bishop, he was delighted to see Gist holding his horse. Bishop was a respectful distance away, finalizing the loading of bags on a packhorse. The buckskin-clad, mud-spattered Gist had clearly ridden hard to make this rendezvous.

George bellowed as he strode forward, "I should have known you would be dillydallying about . . . up to no good."

With his characteristic mischievous twinkle in his eye, Gist retorted, "Well, Colonel, a little bird told me you were leaving us, and I couldn't let you scamper off without saying good-bye."

Laughing, George asked, "How does one find these little birds that constantly keep you apprised of all that is going on, Christopher?"

With his grin now cracking into a broad smile, Gist answered, "Well now, Colonel, this old scout needs to keep some of his secrets."

Now only a few feet apart, George could see all the signs of the ride Gist must have endured to be standing in front of him. He felt his humor give way to deep affection and sadness at the prospect of leaving behind this truly good man.

In a softer voice tinged with emotion, George said, "Old scout indeed. It's been over five years since we left for Fort Le Boeuf. So much has changed . . . I've changed." Then, with a pause of realization, "But you haven't, old friend. You have been a consistent, dependable, and constant pain . . . for which I will be eternally grateful."

With that, as had become a tradition between the men, George stuck out his hand and Gist did likewise.

George noticed for the first time the lattice of deep wrinkles that radiated from Gist's eyes were filling with tears. "I'm going to miss you, sir."

The men released each other's hands, and George mounted his horse. Looking up at George, Gist shook off his sadness and continued their running joke: "A long, happy life or a quick and honorable death, Colonel. And, again, I'll forgo the kiss."

"I am heading back to Mount Vernon, Christopher. I'll take the long, happy life. I hope you will come to visit soon."

"That I will, Colonel."

George clicked his horse into motion, and Bishop followed him out of town. As he trotted away, he came to fully appreciate the transformative experience of the last five years. *I have not only fought battles and learned organization, but more importantly, I have grown to understand men of all types throughout the colonies: hard men, laborers, farmers, gentry, tradesmen, and even the vaunted English aristocracy. Through these experiences, I now know who I am, what I want, and my path going forward.*

George immediately visited Martha on his return to Mount Vernon. Shortly thereafter, on December 20, he resigned his commission, ready to begin his new life. Their engagement, which was already a poorly kept secret, was publicly announced shortly thereafter.

On December 31, 1758, twenty-seven officers of the regiment sent a letter to George:

The happiness we have enjoy'd and the Honor we have acquir'd, together with the mutual Regard that has always subsisted between you and your Officers, have implanted so sensible an Affection in the Minds of us all, that we cannot be silent on this critical Occasions.

[W]e must be Affected with the loss of such an excellent Commander, such a sincere Friend, and so affable a Companion.

A few days later, George responded:

I must esteem an honor that will constitute the greatest happiness of my life, and afford in my latest hours the most pleasing reflections. I always thought it, and it really was, the greatest honor of my life to command Gentlemen, who made me happy in their company & easy by their conduct. Gentlemen, with uncommon sincerity & true affection for the honor you have done me—for if I have acquired any reputation, it is from you I derive it.

Newspaper reports of his successes had made George one of the most famous men in the American colonies. He, along with Benjamin Franklin, were the most well-known Americans on either side of the Atlantic. He was far more prominent than either his patrons, the Fairfaxes, or his beloved Lawrence.

Chapter 58

January 6, 1759 - White House

G eorge and Martha were married at White House. The lavish wedding was officiated by the Anglican Reverend David Mossom and attended by forty of Virginia's most elite gentry. The notable exception was George's mother, who boycotted the wedding because of a perceived slight in the invitation and her objections to its ostentatious display.

Martha wore a rich and elegant gold wedding dress trimmed with silver lace at the neck and sleeves, with an open skirt in front to show a petticoat of white silk with silver interweavings. Her dark hair was accented by pearls, and her purple satin high-heeled slippers were covered with pearl-and-silver trimming. George wore a fine new blue velvet suit, with new shoes with shiny gold buckles deliberately sending a message to everyone present that his days in the military were over.

As he hung up his sword, he believed the most exciting days of his short life were past. His new focus would be on starting a family, growing his fortune, and pursuing Virginia politics. George was the quintessential self-made man; neither a British aristocrat, nor a Virginia grandee, his self-confidence had been won through accomplishment—not through inherited position.

On his twenty-seventh birthday, as George took his seat as a member of the House of Burgesses, his friend and onetime aide-de-camp, Colonel Mercer, described George as follows:

Straight as a Indian, measuring 6 feet 2 inches in his stockings, and weighing 175 lbs when he took his seat in the House of Burgesses in 1759. His frame is padded with well developed muscles, indicating great strength. His bones and joints are large as are his hands and feet. He is wide shouldered but has not a deep or round chest; is neat waisted, but is broad across the hips, and has rather long legs and arms. His head is well shaped, though not large, but is gracefully poised on a superb neck. A large and straight rather than prominent nose; blue grey penetrating eyes which are widely separated and overhung by a heavy brow. His face is long rather than broad, with high round cheek bones, and terminates in a good firm chin. He has clear tho rather colorless pale skin which burns with the sun. A pleasing and benevolent tho a commanding countenance, dark brown hair which he wears in a cue. His mouth is large and generally firmly closed, but which from time to time discloses some defective teeth. His features are regular and placid with all the muscles of his face under perfect control, tho flexible and expressive of deep feelings when moved by emotions. In conversation, he looks you full in the face, is deliberate, deferential, and engaging. His demeanor at all times composed and dignified. His movements and gestures are graceful, his walk majestic, and he is a splendid horseman.

Surrounded by friends and colleagues, George's preeminent status was confirmed in an unanimous acclamation of the House of Burgesses: "Thanks of the House be given to George Washington, Esq; a Member of this House, late Colonel of the first Virginia Regiment, for his faithful Services to his Majesty, and this Colony, and for his brave and steady Behaviour, from the first Encroachments and Hostilities of the French and their Indians, to his Resignation, after the happy Reduction of Fort Du Quesne."

Epilogue

September 20, 1759 - Mount Vernon

After a wonderful meal with Hannah and Martha, George and Jack retired to the parlor for a nightcap.

A relaxed Jack turned to his older brother: "Do you miss it, George?"

As is the way between close friends and brothers, Jack did not need to explain he was asking about the regiment.

George smiled as he stared into the fire. "Indeed I do not. I am fixed here in Mount Vernon with an agreeable consort for life. I will enjoy my happy retirement away from a wide and bustling world." Both men raised their glasses to George's newfound contentment.

George could not know that true "retirement" was almost four decades away . . .

Author's Note

I t is often said that "men don't change"—and for most men (and women), that is probably true. However, George Washington uniquely learned from his mistakes. By the time of the Revolution and his presidency, Washington had gained control of his emotions, but that was not always so. The brash, ambitious, passionate, and angry young man described in this book was transformed by experience. Early successes and, perhaps more importantly, failures changed George Washington into America's indispensable man, who led the country to independence and secured the most enduring democracy in world history. His greatness is all the more remarkable when one understands the challenges he overcame. Success was not an accident; it was the product of experience, intelligence, and (most of all) persistence.

Washington would likely disagree with my characterization of his misbehavior after the slaughter at Jumonville and the defeat at Fort Necessity, including his willful attempt to blame others. The undisputed facts support the conclusion he engaged in these indiscretions, as well as his subsequent efforts to place a positive spin on these and other disasters.

In *George Washington & the Virginia Backcountry,* John Ferling contends that Washington made three egregious errors in his command of the Virginia Regiment, which he remedied as a revolutionary general. First, he placed personal glory above the tactical situation by making a stand at Fort Necessity against a vastly superior enemy. His desire to achieve the "esteem of mankind" supplanted better judgment and led to a humiliating defeat. While there were many failures in the Revolutionary War, George never again allowed his command to be trapped in such a vulnerable position as he was on that hot day in July 1754— although he came close in New York early in the Revolution.

Second, and perhaps more significantly, Washington avoided his previous thin-skinned and petulant behavior when it came to civil authorities. His alienation of Governor Dinwiddie and his constant political backstabbing and complaints were not repeated during the Revolution. Indeed, his persistent deference to Congress only strengthened his position and reputation during and after the Revolution.

Third, his greatest mistake in the French and Indian War was an extravagant lifestyle and absent command. He chose the most lavish house in Winchester as his residence and repeatedly left his troops to seek promotion, attend to his health, or visit Mount Vernon and Belvoir. In contrast, in more than six years in command of the Continental Army, he only returned to Mount Vernon once, and that was on his way to his victory at Yorktown.

During the French and Indian War, we see the portrait of an ambitious, strong, determined, yet self-centered and insecure young man. With this understanding and backdrop, we turn to his relationship with Sally Fairfax and the most notable and controversial part of this book. Historians widely agree that Sally was the first love of George's life and a source of early infatuation. The disagreement relates to how far their relationship progressed and whether it was ever consummated.

There is a remarkable confluence in events that puts Sally and George together in early 1758. Sally was present at Mount Vernon during George's protracted illness. The extent to which other individuals were present at Mount Vernon is unknown, and there certainly could have been opportunities during this time for Sally and George to be alone. I have invented a plausible reason for Jack and Hannah Washington to leave, and George likely could have relied on the discretion of his lifelong servant, Thomas Bishop.

George's belief in an early and impending death may have also lessened his concerns about the long-term implications of his actions. Likewise, the protracted absence of Sally's insecure husband in England certainly created an "opportunity" that the young couple may have seized. Finally, the deaths of his mentors—Lawrence Washington and

Colonel William Fairfax—may have left this remarkable *young* man adrift at this vulnerable and opportune moment.

What is indisputable is given the overwhelming social and moral constraints of that time, disclosure of any intimacy would have destroyed them. George's imploring letters and Sally's apparent firm rejection in 1758 are consistent with a more mature and experienced woman guiding them both down the separate paths that destiny required—even if their desires were otherwise.

It is possible, and indeed likely, that the man who was able to transform himself in so many significant ways would also be able to give up an errant affair with Sally in favor of a loving partnership with Martha. George's subsequent marriage to Martha was a tremendous success and his most enduring and important relationship.

Later in life, both George and Sally expressed their undiminished admiration for each other. Significantly, Sally, long after her husband's death, revealed her preference for the self-made man—in stark contrast to her late husband.

In 1798, George wrote a final letter to Sally from Mount Vernon. After winning the Revolution and serving two terms as president, Washington observed that "many important events occurred and changes in men and things have taken place" since their last correspondence, but all of the events taken together have not "been able to eradicate from my mind the recollections of those happy moments, the happiest of my life, that I have enjoyed in your company."

Like the heroes and heroines of *Cato*, the play Washington loved above all others, George and Sally fulfilled their destinies as honor required, save, perhaps, during the month of February 1758.

—STEPHEN YOCH

Acknowledgments

I am really lucky. My amazing and loving wife Andrea never blinked at the time, money, and obsession required to complete this book. She is a great writer and former sports reporter, thus I solicited her thoughts on my many drafts. Our boys patiently welcomed George into our happy family. My fantastic parents gave me the gift of an education that emphasized the joy of risk taking and life-long learning.

My friend, co-worker, and partner in this project, Deborah Murphy, typed every word of this book. Since my mid-twenties, I have battled a condition that affects the use of my arms, which among other things prevents me from typing more than a few lines at a time. Deb not only muddled through my dictation, but provided encouragement and sage advice at every stage of drafting. My gratitude for her support is endless.

Thomas Crocker, author of the wonderful book *Braddock's March* (upon which I heavily relied), took his valuable time to edit and comment on my second draft—eliminating multiple (and embarrassing) historical errors. He also encouraged and directed me with patience and understanding.

Following the advice of Stephen King in his book *On Writing*, I asked very different and extremely bright friends to review my book. Patti Meras, Susan Truman, and Steve Lieb read an early draft. Michael Aydt and Wendy Brekken gave feedback on a late draft. I was given the gift of their diverse and valuable insights. Thankfully, our friendships survived my imposition on them.

My friend Peg Roessler provided invaluable PR insight and support. Computer super genius Joel Leger was kind enough to assist with my web site, despite enormous (and exciting) changes in his busy life.

Lindsey Arthur, a scion of the Minnesota legal community and author of *The Litigators*, provided invaluable counsel as I began exploring publishing the book. Edward Norton, a family friend and noted author encouraged and educated me on the history and reality of modern publishing.

Wise Ink's expertise was evident throughout the publishing process. Laura Zats deftly led her team as we passed through editing, cover art, maps, and formatting to get me to the finish line. I am grateful for their support and skill.

Wrangler, cattleman, and lawyer Tim Hassett provided real world direction on living in a horse-centered world. Nancy VanderVort and others at my wonderful law firm kindly provided logistical and moral support.

Finally, I wish to thank family, co-workers, clients, and friends too numerous to name, who provided encouragement. Any errors in the form or substance of this book are mine, but credit and thanks goes to many.

S. YOCH

Biographical Summaries

John Alton (?–December 3, 1785): Manservant of Washington during the Braddock campaign who later acted as overseer of Mount Vernon.

John Amson: Doctor in Williamsburg who, in March 1758, told George Washington he was not dying and would fully recover.

Thomas Bishop (1705–1795): Manservant of General Braddock. At Braddock's request, was hired by Washington following the Battle of the Monongahela. Left Washington's employment briefly after the conclusion of the French and Indian War but returned to permanent employment with Washington beginning in 1761 until his death. His wife, Susanna, became the primary midwife for the enslaved population at Mount Vernon until her death in 1785.

Henry Bouquet (1719–1765): Colonel and deputy to General Forbes during the campaign against Fort Duquesne. Swiss-born former member of the Dutch army, transferred to the new royal American Regiment in 1755.

Edward Braddock (January 1695–July 13, 1755): Major general who led 1755 campaign into the Ohio Country. Killed at the Battle of the Monongahela.

Ralph Burton (?–1768): Lieutenant colonel. One of the commanders of Braddock's army who, while injured, survived the battle.

William Byrd III (1728–1777): Colonel of the Second Virginia Regiment in 1758. Succeeded Washington as colonel in command of the entire Virginia Regiment on Washington's retirement in 1759.

Wilson Cary: Father of Sarah Cary Fairfax. Owner of Ceelys on the James in Hampton Roads, Virginia. Member of the House of Burgesses.

William Chamberlayne: Friend of Washington and a neighbor of Martha Custis; hosted and facilitated their courtship in March 1758.

Gedney Clarke (1711–1764): Planter and merchant in Barbados. Host of George and Lawrence Washington in 1751. Friend and colleague of Governor Dinwiddie and Colonel William Fairfax.

Louis Coulon de Villiers (August 17, 1710–November 2, 1757): Brother of Joseph Coulon de Villiers, sieur de Jumonville. Defeated George Washington at Fort Necessity on July 3, 1754.

James Craik (1730–1814): Physician and friend of George Washington. Served under Washington at the Battle of Fort Necessity and accompanied the army during Braddock's Campaign. Attended Washington at his death.

John Dagworthy: Captain with royal commission. Disputed George Washington and Adam Stephen's authority in 1755.

John Davison: Woodsman and interpreter capable of speaking multiple Indian languages. Accompanied Washington on his 1753 journey to Fort Le Boeuf.

Robert Dinwiddie (1693–1770): Appointed lieutenant governor of Virginia in 1751. An investor and advocate of Britain's development of the Ohio Country, he was an early supporter and later adversary of Washington.

Thomas Dunbar (1700–1767): Colonel and commander of the Forty-Eighth Foot under Braddock. His reputation never recovered from his actions surrounding the retreat and destruction of supplies.

George William ("Will") Fairfax (1725–April 3, 1787): Born in the Bahamas; son of Colonel William Fairfax. Friend of George Washington and went on survey expeditions with him in 1748. Married Sarah (Sally) Fairfax in 1748. Elected to the House of Burgesses. Immigrated to England in 1773.

Sarah ("Sally") Cary Fairfax (1730–1811): Married George William Fairfax in 1748. Daughter of Colonel Wilson Cary. Immigrated to England with her husband, George William Fairfax, in 1773.

William ("the Colonel") Fairfax (1691–1757): Colonel of Virginia militia. Cousin of Lord Thomas Fairfax and appointed as his agent in Virginia in 1734. Constructed Belvoir in the 1740s. Father of Ann Fairfax (wife of Lawrence Washington) and George William Fairfax (husband of Sally Fairfax). Acted as mentor for George Washington after Lawrence's death.

Francis Fauquier (1703–1768): Succeeded Governor Dinwiddie as lieutenant governor of Virginia.

John Forbes (September 5, 1707–March 11, 1759): General in command of force that captured Fort Duquesne in 1758, effectively ending the French and Indian War.

Joshua Fry (1700–1754): Colonel of Virginia Regiment and Washington's superior. Following Washington's return from Fort Le Boeuf, Fry, an Oxford-educated mathematician who taught at William and Mary, was appointed the head of the Virginia Regiment. He died en route to Washington when he fell off his horse, breaking his neck and simultaneously elevating young Washington to the head of the Virginia Regiment.

Thomas Gage (1721–1787): Lieutenant colonel leading vanguard at the Battle of the Monongahela. In 1774, he was made governor of Massachusetts. In April 1775, he ordered British troops to seize a magazine in Concord, Massachusetts, which led to the Battles of Lexington and Concord.

Horatio Gates: (1727–1806): Lieutenant wounded during Braddock's defeat. Shot in the chest. Led American forces in the victory of the Battle of Saratoga in the Revolution. Unsuccessfully vied for leadership of the American cause.

James Genn: Surveyor with whom George Washington and George William Fairfax performed the survey of the Northern Neck in Virginia in March–April 1748.

Christopher Gist (1706–1759): Veteran frontiersman, explorer, surveyor, and Indian trader. Employed by the Ohio Company, he explored vast lands and reported to its owners. Gist was present with Washington at most major events during his early life as a young officer, including the trip to Fort Le Boeuf, the Battle of Fort Necessity, the Battle of the Monongahela, and the surrender at Fort Duquesne. Acted as a captain of scouts in Washington's regiment. Died of smallpox shortly after Washington returned to Mount Vernon in 1758.

"Half King," aka Tanacharison, aka Tanaghrisson (1700–1754): Chief of the Seneca Indians met by George Washington at outset of the French and Indian War. A loyal supporter of the British, he remained faithful even when other Indians defected to the French after Fort Necessity. He died not long after the defeat at Fort Necessity in October 1754.

Humphrey Knight (?–1758): Overseer at Mount Vernon from 1757–1758. Responsible for managing both the enslaved population and assisting in the renovations of Mount Vernon.

Sir Peter Halkett (1703–1755): Colonel and commander of the Forty-Fourth Foot under Braddock. Died along with his son James at the Battle of the Monongahela.

William Hillary (1697–1763): Physician trained in Leiden; became Lawrence's physician in Barbados.

George Hume (1698–1760): Prominent Virginia surveyor who instructed Washington. Born in Wedderburn Castle, Scotland, as the second son of the Tenth Baronett in the line. Fought against the Hanovarian King in the first Jacobite Rebellion of 1715. Banished to Virginia and became the Crown surveyor of Spotsylvania, Orange, and Frederick Counties, Virginia. His son, Captain Francis Hume, fought in the Revolution and was one of the original members of the Society of Cincinnati.

Philippe Thomas de Joncaire, sieur de Chabert (1707–1766): Captain in the French army. Son of a Seneca Indian mother and a French father. Met George Washington on his diplomatic mission to Fort Le Boeuf. Washington did not see Joncaire again after Fort Le Boeuf.

Joseph Coulon de Villiers, sieur de Jumonville (September 8, 1718–May 28, 1754): French emissary; wounded and taken prisoner on May 28, 1754, by George Washington and killed by the Half King.

John Lanahan (1699–1762): Physician who treated George Washington during his outbreak of smallpox in 1751 in Barbados.

BIOGRAPHICAL SUMMARIES

Jacques Le Gardeur, sieur de Saint-Pierre (1701–1755): Commandant of Fort Le Boeuf. Met Washington as part of the 1753 expedition.

Earl of Loudoun (John Campbell) (May 5, 1705–April 27, 1782): Met George Washington in Philadelphia in spring 1757. Rejected George's Washington's battle plan. Treated him badly and ignored his request for a commission.

James MacKay (?–1785): Captain with a royal commission. Commander of South Carolinian provincial unit that joined George Washington at Fort Necessity. Signed articles of surrender with Washington.

George Mercer (1733–1784): Served under Washington throughout the French and Indian War, including in the battles of Fort Necessity and Monongahela. Later appointed lieutenant colonel of the newly raised Second Virginia Regiment. After the war, Mercer served in the House of Burgesses with Washington. Became a Loyalist during the Revolution and remained abroad after the war.

Roger Morris (1727–1794): Captain and one of the principal officers in the Braddock Campaign. Part of Braddock's military "family" and acted as an aide-de-camp. Injured at the Battle of the Monongahela.

George Muse (1720–1790): Lieutenant colonel who joined Washington before the battle of Fort Necessity and was accused of cowardice and resigned in disgrace.

Robert Orme (1725–1790): Captain and one of the principal officers in the Braddock Campaign. Part of Braddock's military "family" and acted as an aide-de-camp. Wounded in the Battle of the Monongahela.

John Robinson (1705–1766): Speaker of the Virginia Assembly and friend of Washington during his years as the head of the Virginia Regiment.

Horatio Sharpe (1718–1790): Governor of Maryland. In 1754, given command of all British forces in North America. Critical of Washington's leadership.

Sir John St. Clair (?–1767): Sent as a preliminary scout for the Braddock expedition. Wounded at the Battle of the Monongahela. Recovered sufficiently to attain the rank of colonel and participate in the final assault on Fort Duquesne in 1758 under General Forbes.

William Shirley (1694–1771): Massachusetts governor and in charge of all British forces in America. In 1755, George Washington petitioned him for a commission and was politely denied.

Adam Stephen (1721–1791): A Scottish-born, university-trained medical doctor and Royal Navy veteran. Rose from captain to colonel of Virginia Militia. His brother worked for the Fairfax family. Wrote a glowing account defending George Washington's actions at Fort Necessity. Was wounded at the Battle of the Monongahela. Recovered to fight on the frontier, along with Washington and others, during the intervening years until the ultimate defeat of the French at Fort Duquesne in 1758. Became a brigadier general in the Continental Army during the Revolution. Military career came to an abrupt end after alleged improper conduct in the Battle of Germantown in November 1777.

Jacob Van Braam (1725–1784): Employed by Washington in 1753 as part of the expedition to Fort Le Boeuf. Became captain in the regiment and translated George Washington's surrender letter at Fort Necessity. Was blamed by Washington for incriminating language in the surrender documents. Was held as a prisoner by the French until 1760. After his release, he secured a royal commission and moved to Wales.

Ann Fairfax Washington (Lee) (1728–1761): Eldest daughter of Colonel William Fairfax. Married Lawrence Washington in July 1743. Following the death of Lawrence Washington, married into the Lee family of Virginia.

Augustine ("Gus") Washington (1694–April 12, 1743): Father of George Washington. Married to Jane Butler (mother of only two surviving sons: Lawrence and Austin); married Mary Ball (mother of six) after the death of Jane Butler. Farmer, foundry owner, justice of the peace, church warden, and sheriff.

Augustine ("Austin") Washington (1736–1787): Son of Jane Butler and Augustine Washington, along with Lawrence Washington. Half brother of George Washington.

George Washington (February 22, 1732–December 14, 1799): Eldest of Augustine and Mary Washington's six children.

Hannah Bushrod Washington: Wife of John ("Jack") Augustine Washington.

John ("Jack") Augustine Washington: Younger brother and closest friend and confidant of George. Son of Mary Ball Washington.

Lawrence Washington (1718–1752): Beloved half brother of George Washington. Eldest son of Augustine and Jane Butler Washington. Major in Virginia Militia and hero of the War of Jenkins' Ear in 1739, fought in the Caribbean and South America. In 1743, married Ann Fairfax, part of the elite Fairfax family. Bequeathed Mount Vernon to George Washington. Member of the House of Burgesses, justice of the peace, adjutant general of the Virginia Militia, and major of the Virginia Militia.

Martha Dandridge Custis Washington (June 2, 1731–May 22, 1802): Grew up in a prosperous but not genteel or wealthy home. First husband was Daniel Custis. Married George Washington in 1759.

Mary Ball Washington (1708–1789): Married Augustine Washington on March 6, 1731. George Washington was the eldest of her six children.

Bibliography

Abbot, W. W., ed. *1 The Papers of George Washington, Colonial Series—1748–August 1755.* Charlottesville, VA: University Press of Virginia, 1983.

Abbot, W. W., ed. *2 The Papers of George Washington, Colonial Series—August 1755–April 1756.* Charlottesville, VA: University Press of Virginia, 1983.

Abbot, W. W., ed. *3 The Papers of George Washington, Colonial Series—April 1756–November 1756.* Charlottesville, VA: University Press of Virginia, 1984.

Abbot, W. W., ed. *4 The Papers of George Washington, Colonial Series—November 1756–October 1757.* Charlottesville, VA: University Press of Virginia, 1984.

Abbot, W. W., ed. *5 The Papers of George Washington, Colonial Series—October 1757–September 1758.* Charlottesville, VA: University Press of Virginia, 1988.

Abbot, W. W., ed. *6 The Papers of George Washington, Colonial Series—September 1758–December 1760.* Charlottesville, VA: University Press of Virginia, 1988.

Abbot, W. W., ed. *2 The Papers of George Washington, Retirement Series—January–September 1798.* Charlottesville, VA: University Press of Virginia, 1998.

Addison, Joseph. *Cato: A Tragedy and Selected Essays.* (J. Tonson & Sons, 8th ed., 1713) Liberty Fund 2004.

Anderson, Fred. *George Washington Remembers: Reflections on the French & Indian War.* Lanham, MD: Rowman & Littlefield Publishers, Inc., 2004.

Axelrod, Alan. *Blooding at Great Meadows: Young George Washington and the Battle that Shaped the Man.* Philadelphia: Running Press, 2007.

Center for Infectious Disease Research & Policy, University of Minnesota. "Smallpox." Last updated February 24, 2014. www.cidrap.umn.edu/cidrap/content/bt/smallpox/biofacts/smallpox_clindx.html

Chadwick, Bruce. *The General & Mrs. Washington.* Naperville, IL: Sourcebooks, Inc., 2007.

Chernow, Ron. *Washington: A Life.* New York: Penguin Press, 2010.

Clary, David A. *George Washington's First War: His Early Military Adventures.* New York: Simon & Schuster, 2011.

Crocker, Thomas E. *Braddock's March: How the Man Sent to Seize a Continent Changed American History.* Yardley, PA: Westholme Publishing, 2009.

Ellis, Joseph J. *His Excellency George Washington.* New York: Vintage Books, 2004.

Ferling, John. *The Ascent of George Washington: The Hidden Political Genius of an American Icon.* New York: Bloomsbury Press, 2009.

Fleming, Thomas. "George Washington in Love: The Vivacious Sally Fairfax Stole the Young Man's Heart Long Before He Met Martha," *American Heritage Magazine*, Issue 3, Fall 2009, 59.

Flexner, James Thomas. *Washington: The Indispensible Man.* New York: Little, Brown & Company, 1969.

Freeman, Douglas Southall. *Washington* (Abridgment). New York: Simon & Schuster, 1968.

Hofstra, Warren R., ed. *George Washington & the Virginia Backcountry.* Madison, WI: Madison House, 1998.

Hume, Edgar E., "Memorial to George Hume, Esquire, Crown Surveyor of Virginia and Washington's Teacher of Surveying," *Tylers's Quarterly Historical and Genealogical Magazine*, Issues 1 and 2, July and October, 1939.

Jackson, Donald, and Dorothy Twohig, eds. *The Diaries of George Washington: Volume I, 1748–65.* Charlottesville, VA: University Press of Virginia, 1976.

Knollenberg, Bernhard. *George Washington: The Virginia Period 1732–1775.* Durham, NC: Duke University Press, 1964.

Kopperman, Paul E. *Braddock at the Monongahela.* Pittsburgh: University of Pittsburgh Press, 1977.

Lengel, Edward G. *George Washington: A Military Life.* New York: Random House, 2005.

Marshall, John. *The Life of George Washington, Volume 2.* Reprint, Citizen's Guild of Washington's Boyhood Home, Fredricksburg, Virginia, 1926.

Powell, Allan. *Christopher Gist: Frontier Scout.* Shippensburg, PA: Burd Street Press, 1992.

Randall, Willard Sterne. *George Washington: A Life.* New York: Holt Paperbacks, 1997.

Rhodehamel, John, ed. *Washington—Writings.* New York: The Library of America, 1997.

Stephenson, Mary A. "Block No. 36, Lot 212 & 217 Historical Report, Colonial Williamsburg Foundation Library Research Report Series–1620." Colonial Williamsburg Foundation Library, 1990.

Thompson, Mary A. "A Compendium of Hired and Indentured Laborers at George Washington's Mount Vernon." October 16, 2003–July 29, 2011.

Twohig, Dorothy, ed. *George Washington's Diaries—An Abridgment.* Charlottesville, VA: University of Virginia Press, 1999.

Unger, Harlow Giles. *The Unexpected George Washington—His Private Life.* Hoboken, NJ: John Wiley & Sons, 2006.

Washington, George. *George Washington's Rules of Civility and Decent Behavior in Company and Conversation*. Carlisle, MA: Applewood Books, 1988.

Wiencek, Henry. *An Imperfect God: George Washington, His Slaves and the Creation of America*. New York: Farrar, Straus and Giroux, 2003.

Wyld, Samuel. *The Practical Surveyor*. Reprint of 1725 First Edition. Woodbridge, VA: Flower–de–Luce Books, the Invisible College Press, 2001.

Yoder, Carolyn P., ed. *George Washington–The Writer: A Treasury of Letters, Diaries, and Public Documents*. Honesdale, PA: Boyds Mills Press, 2003.

Young, Jeff C. *The Fathers of American Presidents*. Jefferson, NC: McFarland & Company, 2003.

Extended Author's Notes

Prologue

George Boyd was killed at the Battle of Fort Necessity, but we do not know if he was ever promoted or the circumstances under which he died.

Chapter 1

Most biographers described Mary Washington as a demanding, strict, and unloving mother. See generally R. Chernow, *Washington: A Life* (Penguin Press 2010), 10–11; W. Randall, *George Washington: A Life* (Holt Paperbacks 1997), #8 16, 26; J. Flexner, *The Indispensible Man* (Little, Brown & Company 1969), 5; H. Unger, *The Unexpected George Washington—His Private Life* (John Wiley & Sons 2006), 11; and D. Clary, *George Washington's First War: His Early Military Adventures* (Simon & Schuster 2011), 9–10. This book expands on the position taken by these leading historians and assumes a confrontational relationship that appears supported by the limited documentary evidence.

Colonel William (the "Colonel") Fairfax was the father-in-law of Lawrence Washington, father of Ann Fairfax Washington, father of George William ("Will") Fairfax, and father-in-law of Sally Cary Fairfax. Not only was Washington related to these individuals, who played central roles in his young life, but the Colonel also acted as a crucial mentor in his early development. In order to avoid confusion with the many other individuals named "William," Colonel William Fairfax is referred to as "the Colonel," and his son, George William Fairfax, is referred to as "Will."

A number of authors have described Ann Fairfax's nickname as "Nancy." See, for example, D. Freeman, *Washington* (Abridgment) (Simon & Schuster 1968), 22; A. Axelrod, *Blooding at Great Meadows: Young George Washington and the Battle that Shaped the Man* (Running Press 2007), 39; and W. Randall, *George Washington: A Life* (Holt Paperbacks 1997), 35. While "Nancy" was a nickname for "Ann" at the time, no author provides any citations to support the use of this name, and thus I have continued to use "Ann," which is reflected in the historical record.

Chapter 2

We do not know precisely when Washington began his formal training as a surveyor. It may have predated his mother's decision to bar him from the navy, but it likely began in earnest in the summer of 1747. See W. Hofstra, *George Washington & the Virginia Backcountry* (Madison House 1998), 162. Additionally, the identity of the experienced surveyor who instructed Washington during this period has not been definitively discovered; however, some tutoring was necessary and no doubt occurred. See J. Ferling, *The Ascent of George Washington: The Hidden Political Genius of an American Icon* (Bloomsbury Press 2009), 12; and H. Unger, *The Unexpected George Washington—His Private Life* (John Wiley & Sons 2006), 16. Indeed, Professor Ferling states that "it is probable that he was tutored by some of the surveyors employed by the Fairfaxes." See J. Ferling, *The Ascent of George Washington: The Hidden Political Genius of an American Icon* (Bloomsbury Press 2009), 12. The journals of George Hume, Hume's employment as the Fairfax surveyor, and common sense all support the conclusion that Mr. Hume was Washington's instructor. See E. Hume, "Memorial to George Hume, Esquire, Crown Surveyor of Virginia and Washington's Teacher of Surveying," *Tyler's Quarterly Historical and Genealogical Magazine*, Issues 1 and 2 (July and October 1939), 9.

Chapter 3

Hume's reference to "*O mihi praeteritos referat si Jupiter annos*" is correctly translated as "If only Jupiter would restore those bygone years to me." Virgil, *The Aeneid*, Book VIII, line 560. The translation Hume gives Washington is from John Dryden's 1697 translation of *The Aeneid*. E. Hume, "Memorial to George Hume, Esquire, Crown Surveyor of Virginia and Washington's Teacher of Surveying," *Tyler's Quarterly Historical and Genealogical Magazine*, Issues 1 and 2 (July and October 1939), 76.

Chapter 4

We do not know the "nickname" or "shortened name" George Washington used in his daily interactions with George William Fairfax. However, there are indications that George William Fairfax used the name "William" in day-to-day correspondence. See, for example, W. Abbott, 5 *The Papers of George Washington, Colonial Series—October 1757–September 1758* (University Press of Virginia 1988), 372, 437. It should be noted, however, that while George William Fairfax's own letters identify him as "Wm. Fairfax," George Washington, at least once, described George William Fairfax as "George Fairfax, Esqr." See D. Twohig, *George Washington's Diaries—An Abridgment* (University of Virginia Press 1999), 2. In the face of this inconsistent historical record, and to avoid confusion with Colonel William Fairfax, I have opted to identify George William Fairfax in this book as "Will," which was a common contraction of "William" at the time.

Chapter 5

Washington's first exposure to Sally was likely at an engagement party. See generally J. Flexner, *Washington: The Indispensible Man* (Little, Brown & Company 1969), 19. Some place Washington's first meeting at a celebration following the wedding at Belvoir. See D. Freeman, *Washington* (Abridgment) (Simon & Schuster 1968), 23.

Chapter 6

This book has focused on Washington's relationship with Colonel William Fairfax, with whom Washington had a close personal relationship and who played a defining role in his young life. However, Lord Thomas Fairfax, beginning in February 1748, also developed a bond with Washington and played a crucial role in permitting the surveying of Fairfax lands and bringing political power for Washington's benefit. See generally D. Freeman, *Washington* (Abridgment) (Simon & Schuster 1968), 18; and W. Randall, *George Washington: A Life* (Holt Paperbacks 1997), 75. Nevertheless, I chose not to address Washington's relationship with Lord Fairfax.

Chapter 7

The modern diagnosis for consumption is tuberculosis.

Chapter 11

The invitation from Sally and the performance that follows are fictional, although consistent with the practice of Virginia's aristocracy performing plays themselves. Correspondence between Washington and Sally confirms they, at some point, performed *Cato* together. See generally T. Fleming, "George Washington in Love: The Vivacious Sally Fairfax Stole the Young Man's Heart Long Before He Met Martha," *American Heritage Magazine*, Issue 3 (Fall 2009).

Chapter 15

The "Ohio Country" consists of modern-day Pennsylvania, Ohio, and parts of West Virginia.

Chapter 16

The confluence of the Ohio and Monongahela Rivers is the location for Fort Duquesne and modern-day Pittsburgh, Pennsylvania.

Chapter 17

The Half King was also commonly referred to as Tanacharison. Washington initially made contact with the Oneida warrior chief Monacatoocha and Delaware chief Shingas. W. Hofstra, *George Washington & the Virginia Backcountry* (Madison House 1998), 124–126. They helped facilitate Washington's meeting with the Half King. R. Chernow, *Washington: A Life* (Penguin Press 2010), 33. The conversations between the Half King and Washington are rewritten versions of portions of Washington's journal. See D. Jackson & D. Twohig, *The Diaries of George Washington: Volume I, 1748–65* (University Press of Virginia 1976), 137–140

Chapter 20

Washington's heated exchange with the commandant is fictional. Washington was generally treated courteously by the French, however he did protest the incarceration of British citizens. See D. Twohig, *George Washington Diaries—An Abridgment* (University of Virginia Press 1999), 27.

Chapter 24

There are some inconsistencies as to the exact date Christopher Gist arrived at the Great Meadows. W. Abbot, *1 The Papers of George Washington, Colonial Series—1748–August 1755* (University Press of Virginia

1983), 104–106 (GW to Robert Dinwiddie, May 27, 1754); compare E. Lengel, *George Washington: A Military Life* (Random House 2005), 35 (May 27); and W. Randall, *George Washington: A Life* (Holt Paperbacks 1997), 92 (May 24).

Chapter 25

We do not know who fired the first shot at the glen. D. Clary, *George Washington's First War: His Early Military Adventures* (Simon & Schuster 2011), 85.

While Washington will later claim otherwise, most agree Jumonville carried a diplomatic message. D. Clary, *George Washington's First War: His Early Military Adventures* (Simon & Schuster 2011), 85; see J. Flexner, *Washington: The Indispensible Man* (Little, Brown & Company 1969), 16.

The graphic description of Jumonville's death is presented by several biographers. See R. Chernow, *Washington: A Life* (Penguin Press 2010), 42–43; E. Lengel, *George Washington: A Military Life* (Random House 2005), 37–38; J. Ellis, *His Excellency George Washington* (Vintage Books 2004), 13–14; D. Clary, *George Washington's First War: His Early Military Adventures* (Simon & Schuster 2011), 85–87; and J. Ferling, *The Ascent of George Washington: The Hidden Political Genius of an American Icon* (Bloomsbury Press 2009), 22. Not all scholars accept the version described in this book. Many simply note that Jumonville was killed in the skirmish and fail to include the gruesome details of his partial decapitation or the Half King's exclamation. See A. Axelrod, *Blooding at Great Meadows: Young George Washington and the Battle that Shaped the Man* (Running Press 2007), 182; W. Randall, *George Washington: A Life* (Holt Paperbacks 1997), 94; and J. Flexner, *The Indispensible Man* (Little, Brown & Company 1969), 16.

Chapter 26

Unfortunately, Washington did virtually everything wrong in constructing Fort Necessity. Most forts where constructed on high ground surrounded by large open fields, to offer those in the fort advantageous fields of fire. The cleared area around Fort Necessity was too small to provide the structure with any advantage.

Washington built the fort in a swale in the meadow dominated by the surrounding hills and within musket range, allowing the attackers to shoot from cover while leaving the fort exposed. Moreover, the meadow abutted a large swamp that prevented any line of retreat. See H. Unger, *The Unexpected George Washington—His Private Life* (John Wiley & Sons 2006), 23–24.

Even the shape of the fort was wrong. Most forts built at this time were triangular or squared, with carefully constructed firing locations to allow concentration of forces and supporting fire. The circular Fort Necessity contained none of these advantages. In fact, its high stockades prevented those inside from returning fire, and the two parallel trenches heading out diagonally from the fort were approximately four feet wide at the top and two feet at the bottom, and thus were too shallow to provide meaningful cover for troops. A. Axelrod, *Blooding at Great Meadows: Young George Washington and the Battle that Shaped the Man* (Running Press 2007), 193–195.

Chapter 27

Most indicate the drinking of rum started as it became dark at the end of the battle. See W. Abbot, *1 The Papers of George Washington, Colonial Series—1748–August 1755* (University Press of Virginia 1983), 164 n. 5; and R. Chernow, *Washington: A Life* (Penguin Press 2010), 47–48. Col. Muse's cowardice is well documented but somewhat enhanced here. Washington and MacKay actually chose to de-emphasize Muse's cowardice in their report. See W. Abbot, *1 The Papers of George Washington, Colonial Series—1748–August 1755* (University Press of Virginia 1983), 161–162 n. 2; and A. Axelrod, *Blooding at Great Meadows: Young*

George Washington and the Battle that Shaped the Man (Running Press 2007), 227. What is clear in the aftermath is "Washington had developed a pattern of claiming victory while passing any fault onto others: Jumonville was responsible for his own death because he was a spy, van Braam for Fort Necessity because he made a translation error." See generally D. Clary, *George Washington's First War: His Early Military Adventures* (Simon & Schuster 2011), 112.

Chapter 30

It is likely Washington first met Braddock before he reported for duty in April 1755. Freeman, *Washington* (Abridgment) (Simon & Schuster 1968), 73.

Chapter 31

There is no documentary or other support for the proposition that Washington preferred free versus enslaved servants. Indeed, during the Revolutionary War, Washington famously was served by his enslaved manservant, Billy Lee. However, the fictional discussion with Orme did reflect Washington's desire to extract productivity from enslaved peoples at Mount Vernon and his belief on the inferiority of enslaved peoples.

Washington's ability to recall Shakespeare's Sonnet 27 is consistent with both his experience and his taste. Like many gentlemen of Tidewater Virginia, Washington read and wrote romantic poetry. See W. Abbot, *1 The Papers of George Washington, Colonial Series—1748–August 1755* (University Press of Virginia 1983), 46–47. He also loved Shakespeare throughout his life. See generally R. Chernow, *Washington: A Life* (Penguin Press 2010), 677 and 729. It is not a stretch to believe he poured over Shakespeare's sonnets in the library at Belvoir and committed his favorites to memory.

Washington's June 7, 1755, letter to Sally is particularly interesting. W. Abbot, *1 The Papers of George Washington, Colonial Series—1748–August 1755* (University Press of Virginia 1983), 308–309 (GW to Sally Fairfax, June 7, 1755). He was obviously uncomfortable about this letter. Washington later edited and corrected much of his prior correspondence for spelling and grammar because of his embarrassment regarding his lack of education. However, letters to Sally were not only corrected for grammar, but, in the case of this letter, also substantially rewritten. Washington's apparent desire to recast his correspondence with Sally further reveals his uncomfortably strong feelings for her, which he desired to downplay in later life.

We know Orme communicated during Washington's convalescence. Orme's journal supports the fictional letters from Orme to Washington presented in this chapter. See generally W. Abbot, *1 The Papers of George Washington, Colonial Series—1748–August 1755* (University Press of Virginia 1983), 327–328 n. 19; and D. Clary, *George Washington's First War: His Early Military Adventures* (Simon & Schuster 2011), 142–143.

Chapter 32

I relied heavily on the excellent book by Thomas Crocker, *Braddock's March*, in describing both the build-up and the battle itself.

During the battle, Gist refers to Daniel Morgan and the lashing Morgan received from a British Sergeant. See W. Randall, *George Washington: A Life* (Holt Paperbacks 1997), 129. The punishment Morgan endured contributed to his absolute hatred of the British in the Revolution, when he led his famous "Morgan's Riflemen."

There is support for the assertion that Braddock tried to kill himself with his pistols. Most accounts have George Croghan preventing Braddock from killing himself and refusing Braddock's demand that he be permitted to "die like an old Roman." See P. Kopperman, *Braddock at the Monongahela* (University of Pittsburgh Press 1977), 87; and T. Crocker, *Braddock's March: How the Man Sent to Seize a Continent Changed American History* (Westholme Publishing 2009), 224.

While there is no indication in the record that Braddock actually referred to the defeat of Publius Quinctilius Varus in the Teutoburg Forest, the story of the three lost legions would certainly have been known to a classically educated general from a military family like Braddock's. The similarities between his loss and Varus's could not have been far from Braddock's mind.

"The estimates of the overall English losses vary. Of the total 1,466 English and Americans present, 456 were killed and 421 wounded, for a total of 877 out of 1,466." In contrast, only eleven French were killed and twenty-nine wounded. H. Unger, *The Unexpected George Washington—His Private Life* (John Wiley & Sons 2006), 27; and T. Crocker, *Braddock's March: How the Man Sent to Seize a Contingent Changed American History* (Westholme Publishing 2009), 227.

Washington rarely provided information on his early life, but he did describe the difficult night ride to a biographer in later life. While Washington did not ride totally alone as depicted in the book, it was also a night he never forgot as one of the worst of his life. See R. Chernow, *Washington: A Life* (Penguin Press 2010), 60; and F. Anderson,

Washington Remembers Reflections on the French & Indian War (Rowman & Littlefield Publishers, Inc. 2004), 20.

Chapter 35

Washington cherished this letter from Joseph Ball, which "were probably the first words of praise he had ever read from a family member." W. Randall, *George Washington: A Life* (Holt Paperbacks 1997), 145; and W. Abbot, *2 The Papers of George Washington, Colonial Series—August 1755–April 1756* (University Press of Virginia 1983) (Joseph Ball to GB, September 5, 1755).

Chapter 37

A "brevet" commission is a temporary promotion, subject to confirmation or revocation by higher authority. See W. Abbot, *2 The Papers of George Washington, Colonial Series—August 1755–April 1756* (University Press of Virginia 1983), 286 n. 5.

Chapter 38

The exact circumstances of this skirmish are unknown, but it is indicative of the low-intensity battles that plagued Washington's troops. F. Anderson, *Washington Remembers Reflections on the French & Indian War* (Rowman & Littlefield Publishers, Inc. 2004), 57 n. 62.

Chapter 39

Washington was treated badly in his interview with Lord Loudoun, but I have shortened the interview for dramatic effect.

Chapter 43

There is no evidence in the record to indicate when Jack or Hannah came and went from Mount Vernon during Washington's long convalescence. However, given Jack's duties to manage Mount Vernon, Ferry Farm, the Bullskin properties, and his own farm, it is likely he was often absent from Mount Vernon. Hannah no doubt also had to tend to her own home. W. Abbot, 5 *The Papers of George Washington, Colonial Series—October 1757–September 1758* (University Press of Virginia 1988), 253 (Jack and Hannah were developing a plantation in the Shenandoah Valley at this time). Indeed, some authors have taken the position that Washington was largely alone during his convalescence at Mount Vernon, except for care provided by his servants. See D. Clary, *George Washington's First War: His Early Military Adventures* (Simon & Schuster 2011), 235.

I have invented the story about Sally being opposed to bleeding. We do not have any indication in the record that either Sally or her father opposed bleeding, but her father did go to Cambridge, where William Harvey did oppose bloodletting. See generally,W. Randall, *George Washington: A Life* (Holt Paperbacks 1997), 52.

Chapter 44

No such note exists from Jack Washington to Sally Fairfax asking her to check on Washington. This is part of the fiction, though consistent with Jack and Hannah's multiple familial duties. Additionally, frequent illnesses were treated very seriously at the time.

Chapter 45

This conversation between Washington and Sally, and what transpired after she locked the door, is fictional. However, the timing of her visits, Bishop's loyalty, and Washington's illness are all well established. There is simply insufficient evidence for anyone to make a definitive conclusion one way or the other about what ultimately transpired between the two; they certainly never openly acknowledged anything. The majority of authors, I believe most reasonably, conclude the facts can never be known. See J. Ellis, *His Excellency George Washington* (Vintage Books 2004), 36 ("The evidence is scanty, but convincing beyond any reasonable doubt, that Washington had fallen in love with his best friend's wife several years earlier. Just when the infatuation began, and whether it ever crossed the sexual threshold, has resisted surveillance by generations of historians and biographers."); see also W. Randall, *George Washington: A Life* (Holt Paperbacks 1997), 169 ("There can be no doubt that George Washington loved Sally Fairfax, whether or not she reciprocated that love or felt she was even free to express it. Whatever passed between them during those three months when she cooked for him and nursed him, it had to stop now that [Will] Fairfax was home."). Other authors have taken the position that an affair was extremely unlikely. See R. Chernow, *Washington: A Life* (Penguin Press 2010), 83–84 ("We will never know whether their affair was consummated. . . . [I]t seems hard to believe that he ever lured Sally into outright infidelity. . . . At the same time, there is little doubt of George's passionate attachment to this woman or the lasting power she exerted on his feverish imagination."); see also D. Clary, *George Washington's First War: His Early Military Adventures* (Simon & Schuster 2011), 23. Finally, there are others who have dogmatically asserted that an affair could not have occurred. See H. Unger, *The Unexpected George Washington—His Private Life* (John Wiley & Sons 2006), 37 ("[I]t is absurd to suggest that he would jeopardize—indeed, violate—his friendship with both the Fairfaxes and with his patron, George William's father, Colonel Fairfax, by having a sexual liaison with Sally."); D. Freeman, *Washington* (Abridgment) (Simon & Schuster 1968), 120 ("[Though] George secretly regarded himself as in love with Sally Cary Fairfax, he knew that nothing more than the happiest of friendships could or would exist between him and his Neighbor's wife."). For a further discussion on the rationale for the consummation of the affair, please see the Author's Note.

Chapter 46

There was no possibility of divorce in colonial Virginia. See W. Randall, *George Washington: A Life* (Holt Paperbacks 1997), 169; and T. Fleming, "George Washington in Love: The Vivacious Sally Fairfax Stole the Young Man's Heart Long Before He Met Martha" *American Heritage Magazine*, Issue 3 (Fall 2009) ("Realistically, in 1758 Virginia, there was no way that Sally Fairfax could have left her husband and married Washington. It would have triggered an immense scandal that would have made both of them social outcasts.").

Chapter 51

There is not a consensus among historians about the exact date on which the proposal occurred. See W. Abbot, *6 The Papers of George Washington, Colonial Series –September 1758–December 1760* (University Press of Virginia 1988), 13 n. 3. Professor Chadwick places both the proposal, and its acceptance, in the first week in May. See B. Chadwick, *The General and Mrs. Washington* (Sourcebooks, Inc. 2007), 9–10. Others believe it occurred in March. See D. Clary, *George Washington's First War: His Early Military Adventures* (Simon & Schuster 2011), 236 (Washington asked for Martha's hand during the March visits); D. Freeman, *Washington* (Abridgment) (Simon & Schuster 1968), 120 ("Washington bowed low to her [Martha] on March 16, 1758."). Still others place the date in early June.

Chapter 54

Scholars vary greatly in interpreting the significance of this remarkable letter. W. Abbot, *6 The Papers of George Washington, Colonial Series— September 1758–December 1760* (University Press of Virginia 1988), 10–12 (GW to Sally Fairfax, September 12, 1758). Most agree this is not a letter about Martha Custis and instead reflects Washington's amorous feelings toward Sally. See R. Chernow, *Washington: A Life* (Penguin Press 2010), 84–85 ("So why did Washington write such a daring letter?

There is always the possibility that he was testing the waters with Sally one last time before he committed to marriage. Or perhaps, at the end, he wanted some final vindication of his powerful longings for Sally, some recognition that she, too, had been deeply touched by taboo feelings.... Whatever the true situation, Sally must have recognized and treasured the frank admission of love, for she retained the letter until she died in 1811—a period of more than fifty years"); see also J. Ellis, *His Excellency George Washington* (Vintage Books 2004), 36–38 ("Washington wrote to Sally in September 1758 while serving in the Forbes campaign.... Only someone dedicated to denying the full import of this evidence [regarding the citations to *Cato*] could reject the conclusion that Washington was passionately in love with Sally Fairfax. The titillating 'consummation' question is almost as irrelevant as it is unanswerable. The more important and less ambiguous fact is that Washington possessed a deep-seated capacity to feel powerful emotions."); see also W. Randall, *George Washington: A Life* (Holt Paperbacks 1997), 179 ("[H]is fatalistic allusion to a controlling destiny all must have made it perfectly clear that he was still in love with Sally Fairfax, even if he was resigned to marriage without excitement to Martha Custis."). Another view is that the letter is "little more than an ineptly facetious piece of banter" or "was really awkward gallantries," W. Abbot, 6 *The Papers of George Washington, Colonial Series—September 1758–December 1760* (University Press of Virginia 1988), 13 n. 3; see also D. Clary, *George Washington's First War: His Early Military Adventures* (Simon & Schuster 2011), 254 ("[The letter] had no meaning beyond the flirtation popular among gentry at the time. He was going to marry Martha, and he showed no hesitation or doubt."); H. Unger, *The Unexpected George Washington— His Private Life* (John Wiley & Sons 2006), 38 ("Again, the historians! Some cite this letter as proof of his love for Sally, but others who have been to war recognize the words of a lonely soldier on the eve of battle, homesick for friendship and the pleasures of home.").

Chapter 55

It is likely Sally would have signed letters "Colonel and Mrs. George William Fairfax" at this time. George William ("Will") Fairfax was a colonel in the Frederick County Militia, although he never saw any active military service. See W. Abbot, 2 *The Papers of George Washington, Colonial Series—August 1755–April 1756* (University Press of Virginia 1983), 107 n. 9. To avoid unnecessary confusion with Colonel William Fairfax, Will's father, I have deleted any reference to Will's status as a colonel in this book.

This letter is fiction because the response by Sally was lost. However, it is consistent with Washington's previous and subsequent correspondence. See R. Chernow, *Washington: A Life* (Penguin Press 2010), 85 ("Although Sally's response has been lost, we can surmise its contents from Washington's September 25 reply. Apparently, she either feigned ignorance of the mystery lady's identity, or pretended it was Martha. . . . That Sally refused to credit his love or openly reciprocate it suggests that she was an artful woman who had enjoyed having her vanity stroked by a handsome younger man."). Whether Washington lost or destroyed Sally's response is unknown. What is clear is that if it was found in his personal correspondence at his death, Martha may have destroyed it when she burned all the correspondence between herself and Washington. See generally R. Chernow, *Washington: A Life* (Penguin Press 2010), 814.

Washington's September 25 letter to Sally was important because it was his last letter to her before he married Martha. W. Abbot, 6 *The Papers of George Washington, Colonial Series—September 1758–December 1760* (University Press of Virginia 1988), 41–43 (GW to Sally Fairfax, September 25, 1758); see also W. Randall, *George Washington: A Life* (Holt Paperbacks 1997), 181. Significantly, in Washington's "surviving letters to Sally, Washington never before wrote 'most unalterably.' Once more he was telling her the secret that they would share for the rest of their lives. They were the lovers that destiny had tragically separated, as history had forever parted Marcia and Juba." T. Fleming, "George Washington in Love: The Vivacious Sally Fairfax Stole the

Young Man's Heart Long Before He Met Martha," *American Heritage Magazine*, Issue 3 (Fall 2009), 59.

Interestingly, Washington maintained a parallel correspondence with Will Fairfax during this time. That is, on the same date he wrote Sally Fairfax the letter apparently concluding their romantic relationship, he wrote a remarkably mundane letter to Will Fairfax providing an update on the military situation and discussing the continued renovations to Mount Vernon. See W. Abbot, *6 The Papers of George Washington, Colonial Series—September 1758–December 1760* (University Press of Virginia 1988), 38–40 (GW to George William Fairfax, September 25, 1758); see also W. Abbot, *5 The Papers of George Washington, Colonial Series—October 1757 –September 1758* (University Press of Virginia 1988), 328–329 (George William Fairfax to GW, July 25, 1758), 371–372 (George William Fairfax to GW, August 5, 1758), 436–439 (George William Fairfax to GW, September 1, 1758); and W. Abbot, *6 The Papers of George Washington, Colonial Series –September 1758– December 1760* (University Press of Virginia 1988), 19–20 (George William Fairfax to GW, September 15, 1758).

Chapter 56

Evidence supports Captain Bullitt, rather than Washington, running between the lines. R. Chernow, *Washington: A Life* (Penguin Press 2010), 90; W. Randall, *George Washington: A Life* (Holt Paperbacks 1997), 188; and J. Flexner, *Washington: The Indispensible Man* (Little, Brown Company 1969), 34; as opposed to E. Lengel, *George Washington: A Military Life* (Random House 2005), 75. In any event, it was a tremendously upsetting incident for Washington.

There is no historical evidence that Washington interrogated the witness in the manner described in this book. Nevertheless, the humiliation of this engagement, the wounding of Mercer, and the death of so many of his men weighed heavily on him. Indeed, thirty years later, this event was one of the rare instances where Washington was willing to provide biographical information to discuss what occurred. See H. Unger, *The Unexpected George Washington—His Private Life* (John Wiley & Sons 2006), 38–39; F. Anderson, *Washington Remembers Reflections on the French & Indian War* (Rowman & Littlefield Publishers, Inc. 2004), 127.

Chapter 57

Stephen did not succeed Washington despite Washington's expectation. See generally W. Abbot, *6 The Papers of George Washington, Colonial Series—September 1758–December 1760* (University Press of Virginia 1988), 173–174 (Robert Stewart to GW, December 29, 1758: discussing the resignation of Washington and appointment of Adam Stephen); 189 n.

READING GROUP GUIDE

1. Did this book change your view of George Washington? Do you admire him more or less?

2. The Extended Author's Notes indicate that most historians agree Washington lied and blamed others after the massacre at the Jumonville Glen and the loss at Fort Necessity. Did this surprise you?

3. If Washington had behaved honorably and admitted his mistakes after Jumonville and/or Fort Necessity, could he still have succeeded? How would his life path have changed?

4. We see Washington fixated on becoming a colonel in the British Army. What impact did the repeated refusals by the British have on him later in life? If he had been given that position, would he have been a revolutionary in 1775–1776?

5. Many great leaders in history lost their fathers at a young age. This book seems to indicate George was able to quickly transfer his affections to Lawrence and in turn Colonel Fairfax. How did the loss of both his father and Lawrence impact George?

6. Mary Washington's unflattering portrayal in this book is supported by historical evidence. On the balance, was George's relationship with his mother a positive or negative in his transformation?

7. As discussed in the Author's Notes, most historians agree George loved Sally. Did you "like" Sally? Did you sympathize with her?

8. Do you believe George's relationship with Sally was consummated? If it did occur, does it change your view of Washington?

9. A stream of people impacted young George's life and development. Who did you find the most interesting and why?

10. In the United States, George Washington has been treated with an almost religious reverence. Indeed, the painting in the US Capitol rotunda dome shows angels lifting him to heaven. There are a number of actions in his early life that cast an unfavorable light on his character, including his lies and a potential affair with Sally Fairfax. Is America willing to accept a more "human" view of our leading founding father?